Bevis
The Story of a Boy

by

Richard Jefferies

Double 9
BOOKS

Bevis
The Story of a Boy
by Richard Jefferies

Copyright © 2024

All Rights reserved.

ISBN: 978-93-61150-00-5

Published by

DOUBLE 9 BOOKS

2/13-B, Ansari Road
Daryaganj, New Delhi – 110002
info@double9books.com
www.double9books.com
Tel. 011-40042856

This book is under public domain

ABOUT THE AUTHOR

English author, essayist, and naturalist Richard Jefferies (1848–1887) is most known for his writings that championed rural life and the natural environment in England. His writing was profoundly affected by his time spent in the countryside after being born on November 6, 1848, close to Swindon, Wiltshire. As a journalist, Jefferies started his writing career by submitting pieces to several magazines. But the books and essays he wrote about nature were what made him famous. He had an excellent capacity for observation and a profound understanding of the nuances of the natural world. Jefferies not only wrote about nature, but also fiction. One of his works, "Bevis: The Story of a Boy" (1882), illustrates his conviction that a child's character development is greatly aided by nature. Vibrant descriptions, strong connection to the country, and meaningful observations are hallmarks of Richard Jefferies' writing style.

CONTENTS

Volume One

VOLUME ONE

Chapter One
Bevis at Work

One morning a large wooden case was brought to the farmhouse, and Bevis, impatient to see what was in it, ran for the hard chisel and the hammer, and would not consent to put off the work of undoing it for a moment. It must be done directly. The case was very broad and nearly square, but only a few inches deep, and was formed of thin boards. They placed it for him upon the floor, and, kneeling down, he tapped the chisel, driving the edge in under the lid, and so starting the nails. Twice he hit his fingers in his haste, once so hard that he dropped the hammer, but he picked it up again and went on as before, till he had loosened the lid all round.

After labouring like this, and bruising his finger, Bevis was disappointed to find that the case only contained a picture which might look very well, but was of no use to him. It was a fine engraving of "An English Merry-making in the Olden Time," and was soon hoisted up and slung to the wall. Bevis claimed the case as his perquisite, and began to meditate what he could do with it. It was dragged from the house into one of the sheds for him, and he fetched the hammer and his own special little hatchet, for his first idea was to split up the boards. Deal splits so easily, it is a pleasure to feel the fibres part, but upon consideration he thought it might do for the roof of a hut, if he could fix it on four stakes, one at each corner.

Away he went with his hatchet down to the withy-bed by the brook (where he intended to build the hut) to cut some stakes and get them ready. The brook made a sharp turn round the withy-bed, enclosing a tongue of ground which was called in the house at home the Peninsula, because of its shape and being surrounded on three sides by water. This piece of land, which was not all withy, but partly open and partly copse, was Bevis's own territory, his own peculiar property, over which he was autocrat and king.

He flew at once to attack a little fir, and struck it with the hatchet: the first blow cut through the bark and left a "blaze," but the second did not produce anything like so much effect, the third, too, rebounded, though the tree shook to its top. Bevis hit it a fourth time, not at all pleased that the fir would not cut more easily, and then, fancying he saw something floating down the stream, dropped his hatchet and went to the edge to see.

It was a large fly struggling aimlessly, and as it was carried past a spot where the bank overhung and the grasses drooped into the water, a fish rose and took it, only leaving just the least circle of wavelet. Next came a dead dry twig, which a wood-pigeon had knocked off with his strong wings as he rose out of the willow-top where his nest was. The little piece of wood stayed a while in the hollow where the brook had worn away the bank, and under which was a deep hole; there the current lingered, then it moved quicker, till, reaching a place where the channel was narrower, it began to rush and rotate, and shot past a long green flag bent down, which ceaselessly fluttered in the swift water. Bevis took out his knife and began to cut a stick to make a toy boat, and then, throwing it down, wished he had a canoe to go floating along the stream and shooting over the bay; then he looked up the brook at the old pollard willow he once tried to chop down for that purpose.

The old pollard was hollow, large enough for him to stand inside on the soft, crumbling "touchwood," and it seemed quite dead, though there were green rods on the top, yet it was so hard he could not do much with it, and wearied his arm to no purpose. Besides, since he had grown bigger he had thought it over, and considered that even if he burnt the tree down with fire, as he had half a mind to do, having read that that was the manner of the savages in wild countries, still he would have to stop up both ends with board, and he was afraid that he could not make it water-tight.

And it was only the same reason that stayed his hand from barking an oak or a beech to make a canoe of the bark, remembering that if he got the bark off in one piece the ends would be open and it would not float properly. He knew how to bark a tree quite well, having helped the woodmen when the oaks were thrown, and he could have carried the short ladder out and so cut it high enough up the trunk (while the tree stood). But the open ends puzzled him; nor could he understand nor get any one to explain to him how the wild men, if they used canoes like this, kept the water out at the end.

Once, too, he took the gouge and the largest chisel from the workshop, and the mallet with the beech-wood head, and set to work to dig out a boat from a vast trunk of elm thrown long since, and lying outside the rick-yard, whither it had been drawn under the timber-carriage. Now, the bark had fallen off this piece of timber from decay, and the surface of the wood was scored and channelled by insects which had eaten their way along it. But though these little creatures had had no difficulty, Bevis with his gouge and his chisel and his mallet could make very little impression, and though he chipped out pieces very happily for half an hour, he had only formed a small hole. So that would not do; he left it, and the first shower filled the hole he had cut with water, and how the savages dug out their canoes with flint choppers he could not think, for he could not cut off a willow twig with the sharpest splinter he could find.

Of course he knew perfectly well that boats are built of plank, but if you try to build one you do not find it so easy; the planks are not to be fitted together by just thinking you will do it. That was more difficult to him than gouging out the huge elm trunk; Bevis could hardly smooth two planks to come together tight at the edge or even to overlap, nor could he bend them up at the end, and altogether it was a very cross-grained piece of work this making a boat.

Pan: the spaniel, sat down on the hard, dry, beaten earth of the workshop, and looked at Bevis puzzling over his plane and his pencil, his footrule, and the paper on which he had sketched his model; then up at Bevis's forehead, frowning over the trouble of it; next Pan curled round and began to bite himself for fleas, pushing up his nostril and snuffling and raging over them. No. This would not do; Bevis could not wait long enough; Bevis liked the sunshine and the grass under foot. Crash fell the plank and bang went the hammer as he flung it on the bench, and away they tore out into the field, the spaniel rolling in the grass, the boy kicking up the tall dandelions, catching the yellow disk under the toe of his boot and driving it up in the air.

But though thrown aside like the hammer, still the idea slumbered in his mind, and as Bevis stood by the brook, looking across at the old willow, and wishing he had a boat, all at once he thought what a capital raft the picture packing-case would make! The case was much larger than the picture which came in it; it had not perhaps been originally intended for that engraving. It was broad and flat; it had low sides; it would not be water-tight, but perhaps he could make it—yes, it was just the very thing. He would float down the brook on it; perhaps he would cross the Longpond.

Like the wind he raced back home, up the meadow, through the garden, past the carthouse to the shed where he had left the case. He tilted it up against one of the uprights or pillars of the shed, and then stooped to see if daylight was visible anywhere between the planks. There were many streaks of light, chinks which must be caulked, where they did not fit. In the workshop there was a good heap of tow; he fetched it, and immediately began to stuff it in the openings with his pocket-knife. Some of the chinks were so wide, he filled them up with chips of wood, with the tow round the chips, so as to wedge tightly.

The pocket-knife did not answer well. He got a chisel, but that cut the tow, and was also too thick; then he thought of an old table-knife he had seen lying on the garden wall, left there by the man who had been set to weed the path with it. This did much better, but it was tedious work, very tedious work; he was obliged to leave it twice—once to have a swing, and stretch himself; the second time to get a hunch, or cog, as he called it, of bread and butter. He worked so hard he was so hungry. Round the loaf there were indentations, like a cogged wheel, such as the millwright made. He had one of these cogs of bread cut out, and well stuck over with pats of fresh butter, just made and fresh from the churn, not yet moulded and rolled into shape, a trifle salt but delicious.

Then on again, thrusting the tow in with the knife, till he had used it all, and still there were a few chinks open. He thought he would get some oakum by picking a bit of rope to pieces: there was no old rope about, so he took out his pocket-knife, and stole into the waggon-house, where, first looking round to be sure that no one was about, he slashed at the end of a cart-line. The thick rope was very hard, and it was difficult to cut it; it was twisted so tight, and the rain and the sun had toughened it besides, while the surface was case-hardened by rubbing against the straw of the loads it had bound. He haggled it off at last, but when he tried to pick it to pieces he found the larger strands unwound tolerably well, but to divide them and part the fibres was so wearisome and so difficult that he did not know how to manage it. With a nail he hacked at it, and got quite red in the face, but the tough rope was not to be torn to fragments in a minute; he flung it down, then he recollected some one would see it, so he hurled it over the hedge into the lane.

He ran indoors to see if he could find anything that would do instead, and went up into the bench-room where there was another carpenter's bench (put up for amateur work), and hastily turned over everything; then he pulled out the drawer in his mamma's room, the drawer in which she kept odds and ends, and having upset everything, and mixed her treasures, he lighted on some rag which she kept always ready to bind round the fingers that used to get cut so often. For a makeshift this, he thought, would do. He tore a long piece, left the drawer open, and ran to the shed with it. There was enough to fill the last chink he could see; so it was done. But it was a hundred and twenty yards to the brook, and though he could lift the case on one side at a time, he could not carry it.

He sat down on the stool (dragged out from the workshop) to think; why of course he would fasten a rope to it, and so haul it along! Looking for a nail in the nail-box on the bench, for the rope must be tied to something, he saw a staple which would do much better than a nail, so he bored two holes with a gimlet, and drove the staple into the raft. There was a cord in the summer-house by the swing, which he used for a lasso—he had made a running noose, and could throw it over anything or anybody who would keep still—this he fetched, and put through the staple. With the cord over his shoulder he dragged the raft by main force out of the shed, across the hard, dry ground, through the gate, and into the field. It came very hard, but it did come, and he thought he should do it.

The grass close to the rails was not long, and the load slipped rather better on it, but farther out into the field it was longer, and the edge of the case began to catch against it, and when he came to the furrows it was as much as he could manage, first to get it down into the furrow, next to lift it up a little, else it would not move, and then to pull it up the slope. By stopping a while and then hauling he moved it across three of the furrows, but now the cord quite hurt his shoulder, and had begun to fray his jacket. When he looked back he was about thirty yards from where he had started, not halfway to the gateway, through which was another meadow, where the mowing-grass was still higher.

Bevis sat down on the sward to rest, his face all hot with pulling, and almost thought he should never do it. There was a trail in the grass behind where the raft had passed like that left by a chain harrow. It wanted something to slip on; perhaps rollers would do like those they moved the great pieces of timber on to the saw-pit. As soon as he had got his breath again, Bevis went back to the shed, and searched round for some rollers. He could not find any wood ready that would do, but there was a heap of poles close by. He chose a large, round willow one, carried the stool down to it, got the end up on the stool, and worked away like a slave till he had sawn off three lengths.

These he took to the raft, put one under the front part, and arranged the other two a little way ahead. Next, having brought a stout stake from the shed, he began to lever the raft along, and was delighted at the ease with which it now moved. But this was only on the level ground and down the slope of the next furrow, so far it went very well, but there was a difficulty in getting it up the rise. As the grass grew longer, too, the rollers would not roll; and quite tired out with all this work, Bevis flung down his lever, and thought he would go indoors and sit down and play at something else.

First he stepped into the kitchen, as the door was open; it was a step down to it. The low whitewashed ceiling and the beam across it glowed red from the roasting-fire of logs split in four, and built up on the hearth; the flames rushed up the vast, broad chimney—a bundle of flames a yard high, whose tips parted from the main tongues and rose disjointed for a moment by themselves: the tiny panes of yellowish-green glass, too, in the window reflected the light. Such a fire as makes one's lips moist at the thought of the juicy meats and the subtle sweetness imparted by the wood fuel, which has a volatile fragrance of its own. Bevis thought he would get the old iron spoon, and melt some lead, and cast some bullets in the mould—he had a mould, though they would not let him have a pistol—he knew where there was a piece of lead-pipe, and a battered bit of guttering that came off the house.

Or else he would put in a nail, make it white hot, and hammer it into an arrowhead, using the wrought-iron fire-dog as an anvil. The heat was so great, especially as it was a warm May day, that before he could decide he was obliged to go out of the kitchen, and so wandered into the sitting-room. His fishing-rod stood in the corner where he had left it; he had brought it in because the second joint was splitting, and he intended (as the ferrule was lost) to bind it round and round with copper wire. But he did not feel much inclined to do that either; he had half a mind to go up in the bench-room, and take the lock of the old gun to pieces to see how it worked. Only the stock (with the lock attached) was left; the barrel was gone.

While he was thinking he walked into the parlour, and seeing the bookcase open—the door was lined within with green material—put his hand involuntarily on an old grey book. The covers were grey and worn and loose; the back part had come off; the edges were rough and difficult to turn over, because they had not been cut by machinery; the margin, too, was yellow and frayed. Bevis's fingers went direct to the rhyme he had read so often, and in an instant everything around him disappeared, room and bookcase and the garden without, and he forgot himself, for he could see the "bolde men in their deeds," he could hear the harper and the minstrel's song, the sound of trumpet and the clash of steel; how—

> "As they were drinking ale and wine
> Within Kyng Estmere's halle:
> When will ye marry a wyfe, brother,
> A wyfe to glad us all?"

How the kyng and "Adler younge" rode to the wooing, and the fight they had, fighting so courageously against crowds of enemies,—

> "That soone they have slayne the Kempery men,
> Or forst them forth to flee."

Bevis put himself so into it, that he did it all, *he* bribed the porter, *he* played the harp, and drew the sword; these were no words to him, it was a living picture in which he himself acted.

He was inclined to go up into the garret and fetch down the old cutlass that was there among the lumber, and go forth into the meadow and slash away at "gix" and parsley and burdocks, and kill them all for Kempery men, just as he out them down before when he was Saint George. As he was starting for the cutlass he recollected that the burdocks and the rest where not up high enough yet, the Paynim scoundrels had not grown tall enough in May to be slain with any pleasure, and a sense that you were valiantly swording. Still there was an old wooden bedstead up there, on which he could hoist up a sail, and sail away to any port he chose, to Spain, or Rhodes, or where the lotus-eaters lived. But his mind, so soon as he had put down the grey book, ran still on his raft, and out he raced to see it again, fresh and bright from the rest of leaving it alone a little while.

Chapter Two
The Launch

As he came near a butterfly rose from the raft, having stayed a moment to see what this could be among the dandelions and buttercups, but Bevis was too deeply occupied to notice it. The cord was of no use; the rollers were of no use; the wheelbarrow occurred to him, but he could not lift it on, besides it was too large, nor could he have moved it if it would go on. Pan was not strong enough to help him haul, even if he would submit to be harnessed, which was doubtful. The cart-horses were all out at work, nor indeed had they been in the stable would he have dared to touch them.

What he wanted to do was to launch his raft before any one saw or guessed what he was about, so that it might be a surprise to them and a triumph to him. Especially he was anxious to do it before Mark came; he might come across the fields any minute, or along the road, and Bevis wished to be afloat, so that Mark might admire his boat, and ask permission to stop on board. Mark might appear directly; it was odd he had not heard his whistle before. Full of this thought away went Bevis back to the house, to ask Polly the dairymaid to help him; but she hunted him out with the mop, being particularly busy that day with the butter, and quite deaf to all his offers and promises. As he came out he looked up the field, and remembered that John was stopping the gaps, and was at work by himself that day; perhaps he would slip away and help him.

He raced up the meadow and found the labourer, with his thick white leather gloves and billhook, putting thorn bushes in the gaps, which no one had made so much as Bevis himself.

"Come and help me," said Bevis. Now John was willing enough to leave his work and help Bevis do anything—for anything is sweeter than the work you ought to do—besides which he knew he could get Bevis to bring him out a huge mug of ale for it.

But he grinned and said nothing, and simply pointed through the hedge. Bevis looked, and there was the Bailiff with his back against the great oak, under which he once went to sleep. The Bailiff was older now, much older, and though he was so stout and big he did not do much work with his hands. He stood there, leaning his back against the oak, with his hazel staff in his hand, watching the stone-pickers, who were gathering up the bits of broken earthenware and rubbish from among the cowslips out of the way of the scythe; watching, too, the plough yonder in the arable field beyond; and with his eyes now and then on John. While those grey eyes were about, work, you may be sure, was not slack. So Bevis pouted, and picked up a stone, and threw it at the Bailiff, taking good care, however, not to hit him. The stone fell in the hedge behind the Bailiff, and made him start, as he could not think what creature it could be, for rabbits and weasels and other animals and birds move as silently as possible, and this made a sharp tap.

Bevis returned slowly down the meadow, and as he came near the house, having now given up hope of getting the raft to the brook, he caught sight of a cart-horse outside the stable. He ran and found the carter's lad, who had been sent home with the horse; the horse had been hauling small pieces of timber out of the mowing-grass with a chain, and the lad was just going to take off the harness.

"Stop," said Bevis, "stop directly, and hitch the chain on my raft."

The boy hesitated; he dared not disobey the carter, and he had been in trouble for pleasing Bevis before.

"This instant," said Bevis, stamping his foot; "I'm your master."

"No; that you beant," said the boy slowly, very particular as to facts; "your feyther be my master."

"You do it this minute," said Bevis, hot in the face, "or I'll *kill* you; but if you'll do it I'll give you—sixpence."

The boy still hesitated, but he grinned; then he looked round, then he turned the horse's head—unwilling, for the animal thought he was going to the manger—and did as Bevis told him. Behind the strong cart-horse the raft was nothing, it left a trail all across the grass right down to the brook; Bevis led the way to the drinking-place, where the ground sloped to the water. The boy once embarked in the business, worked with a will—highly delighted himself with the idea—and he and Bevis together pushed the raft into the stream.

"Now you hold the rope," said Bevis, "while I get in," and he put one foot on the raft.

Just then there came a whistle, first a long low call, then a quaver, then two short calls repeated.

"That's Mark," said Bevis, and in he hastened. "Push me off," for one edge of the raft touched the sandy shore.

"Holloa!" shouted Mark, racing down the meadow from the gateway; "stop a minute! let me!—"

"Push," said Bevis.

The boy shoved the raft off; it floated very well, but the moment it was free of the ground and Bevis's weight had to be entirely supported, the water squirted in around the edges.

"You'll be drownded," said the carter's lad.

"Pooh!" said Bevis.

"I shall jump in," said Mark, making as if he were about to leap.

"If you do I'll hit you," said Bevis, doubling his fists; "I say!—"

For the water rushed in rapidly, and was already half an inch deep. When he caulked his vessel, he stopped all the seams of the bottom, but he had overlooked the chinks round the edges, between the narrow planks that formed the gunwales or sides, and the bottom to which they were fastened.

Bevis moved towards the driest side of the raft, but directly he stepped there and depressed it with his weight the water rushed after him, and he was deeper than over in it. It came even over his boots.

"Let I get in," said the boy; "mine be water-tights."

"Pull me back," said Bevis.

Mark seized the rope, and he and the boy gave such a tug that Bevis, thrown off his balance, must have fallen into the brook had he not jumped ashore and escaped with one foot wet through to the ankle.

"Yaa—you!" they heard a rough voice growling, like a dog muttering a bark in his throat, and instantly the carter's lad felt a grip on the back of his neck. It was the Bailiff who marched him up the meadow, holding the boy by the neck with one hand and leading the cart-horse with the other. Bevis and Mark were too full of the raft even to notice that their assistant had been haled off.

First they pulled till they had got it ashore; then they tilted it up to let the water run out; then they examined the chinks where it had come in.

"Here's my handkerchief," said Mark; "put that in."

The handkerchief, a very dirty one, was torn into shreds and forced into the chinks. It was not enough, so Bevis tore up his; still there were holes. Bevis roamed up and down the grass in his excitement, gazing round for something to stop these leaks.

"I know," said he suddenly, "moss will do. Come on."

He made for a part of the meadow much overshadowed by trees, where the moss threatened to overcome the grass altogether, so well did it flourish in the coolness and moisture, for the dew never dried there even at noonday. The Bailiff had it torn up by the harrow, but it was no good, it would grow. Bevis always got moss from here to put in his tin can for the worms when he went fishing. Mark was close behind him, and together they soon had a quantity of moss. After they had filled the chinks as they thought, they tried the boat again, Bevis insisting on his right to get in first as it was his property. But it still leaked, so they drew it out once more and again caulked the seams. To make it quite tight Bevis determined to put some clay as well, to line the chinks with it like putty. So they had to go home to the garden, get the trowel out of the summer-house where Bevis kept such things, and then dig a few lumps of clay out of the mound.

There was only one place where there was any clay accessible, they knew the spot well—was there anything they did not know? Working up the lumps of clay with their hands and the water so as to soften and render it plastic, they carefully lined the chinks, and found when they launched the raft that this time it floated well and did not admit a single drop. For the third time, Bevis stepped on board, balancing himself with a pole he had brought down from the garden, for he had found before that it was difficult to stand upright on a small raft. Mark pushed him off: Bevis kept one end of the pole touching the bottom, and so managed very well. He guided the raft out of the drinking-place, which was like a little pond beside the brook, and into the stream.

There the current took it, and all he had to do was to keep it from grounding on the shallows, where the flags were rising out of the mud, or striking against the steep banks where the cowslips overhung the water. With his feet somewhat apart to stand the firmer, his brow frowning (with resolution), and the pole tight in his hands—all grimed with clay—Bevis floated slowly down the stream. The sun shone hot and bright, and he had of course left his hat on the sward where it had fallen off as he stooped to the caulking: the wind blew and lifted his hair: his feet were wet. But he never noticed the heat, nor the wind, nor his wet feet, nor his clayey hands. He had done it—he was quite lost in his raft.

Round the bend the brook floated him gently, past the willow where the wood-pigeon built (he was afraid to come near his nest while they were about), past the thick hawthorn bushes white with may-bloom, under which the blackbirds love to stay in the hottest days in the cool shadow by the water. Where there were streaks of white sand sifted by the stream from the mud, he could see the bottom: under the high bank there was a swirl as if the water wrestled with something under the surface: a water-rat, which had watched him coming from a tiny terrace, dived with a sound like a stone dropped quietly in: the stalks of flags grazed the bottom of the raft, he could hear them as it drew on: a jack struck and rushed wildly up and down till he found a way to slip by; the raft gave a heave and shot swiftly forward where there had once been a bay and was still a fall of two inches or so: a bush projected so much that he could with difficulty hold the boughs aside and prevent the thorns from scratching his face: a snag scraped the bottom of the boat and the jerk nearly overthrew him—he did not mind that, he feared lest the old stump had started a seam, but fortunately it had not done so.

Then there was a straight course, a broad and open reach, at which he shouted with delight. The wind came behind and pushed his back like a sail and the little silvery ripples ran before him, and dashed against the shore, destroying themselves and their shadows under them at the same time. The raft floated without piloting here, steadily on. Bevis lifted his pole and waved his hand in triumph.

From the gateway the carter's lad watched him; he had got away from the angry Bailiff. From the garden ha-ha, near the rhubarb patch, Polly the dairymaid watched him, gesticulating every now and then with her arms, for she had been sent to call him to dinner. Mark, wild with envy and admiration and desire to share the voyage, walked on the bank, begging to come in, for Bevis to get out or let him join him, threatening to leap aboard from the high bank where the current drifted the raft right under him, pulling off his shoes and stockings to wade in and seize the craft by main force; then, changing his mind, shouting to Bevis to mind a boulder in the brook, and pointing out the place.

The raft swept with steady, easy motion down the straight broad reach; Bevis did not need his pole, he stood without its help, all aglow with joy.

The raft came to another bend, and Bevis with his pole guided it round, and then, looking up, stamped his foot with vexation, for there was an ancient, hollow willow right in front, so bowed down that its head obstructed the fair way of the stream. He had quite hoped to get down to the Peninsula, and to circumnavigate it, and even shoot the cataract of the dam below, and go under the arch of the bridge, and away yet farther. He was not fifty yards from the Peninsula, and Mark had run there to meet him; but here was this awkward tree, and before he could make up his mind what to do, bump the raft struck the willow, then it swung slowly round and one side grounded on the bank, and he was at a standstill.

He hit the willow with his pole, but that was of no use, and called to Mark. Bevis pushed the willow with his pole, Mark pulled at a branch, and together they could shake it, but they could not move it out of the way; the stream was blocked as if a boom had been fastened across it. The voyage was over.

While they consulted, Polly came down, having failed to make them hear from the garden, and after she had shook them each by the shoulder brought them to reason. Though she would have failed in that too had not the willow been there, not for dinner or anything would Bevis have abandoned his adventure, so bent was he always on the business he had in hand.

But the willow was obstinate, they could not get past it, so reluctantly he agreed to go home. First Polly had to fetch his hat, which was two hundred yards away on the grass by the drinking-place; then Mark had to put his shoes and stockings on, and take one off again because there was a fragment of stone in it. Next, Bevis had to step into the raft again—a difficult thing to do from the tree—in order to get the cord fastened to the staple to tie it up, not that there was the least risk of the raft floating away, still these things, as you know, ought to be done quite properly.

After he had tied the cord or painter to a branch of the willow as firmly as possible, at last he consented to come. But then catching sight of the carter's lad, he had first to give him his sixpence, and also to tell him that if he dared go near the raft, even to look at it, he would be put in the brook. Besides which he had to wash his hands, and by the time Mark and he reached the table the rest had finished. The people looked at them rather blackly, but they did not mind or notice in the least, for their minds were full of projects to remove the willow, about which they whispered to each other.

Pan raced beside them after dinner to the ha-ha wall, down which they jumped one after the other into the meadow. The spaniel hesitated on the brink, not that he feared the leap, which he had so often taken, but reflection checked him. He watched them a little way as they ran for the brook, then turned and walked very slowly back to the house; for he knew that now dinner was over, if he waited till he was remembered, a plateful would come out for him.

Chapter Three
The Mississippi

They found the raft as they had left it, except that petals of the may-bloom, shaken from the hawthorn bushes by the breeze, as they came floating down the stream had lodged against the vessel like a white line on the water. Already, too, the roach, which love a broad shadow to play about its edge, had come underneath, but when they felt the shaking of the bank from the footsteps turned aside, and let the current drift them down. Bevis fetched his hatchet from the Peninsula and began to hack at the willow; Mark, not without some difficulty, got leave to climb into the raft, and sit in the centre. The chips flew, some fell on the grass, some splashed into the brook; Bevis made a broad notch just as he had seen the men do it; and though his arm was slender, the fire behind it drove the edge of the steel into the wood. The willow shook, and its branches, which touched the water, ruffled the surface.

But though the trunk was hollow it was a long way through, and when Bevis began to tire he had only cut in about three inches. Then Mark had to work, but before he had given ten strokes Bevis said it was of no use chopping, they could never do it, they must get the grub-axe. So they went back to the house, and carried the ungainly tool down to the tree.

It was too cumbrous for them, they pocked up a little turf, and just disturbed the earth, and then threw the clumsy thing on the grass. Next they thought of the great saw—the cross-cut—the men used, one at each end, to saw though timber; but that was out of their reach, purposely put up high in the workshop, so that they should not meddle with it or cut themselves with its terrible teeth.

"I know," said Mark, "we must make a fire, and burn the tree; we are savages, you know, and that is how they do it."

"How silly you are!" said Bevis. "We are *not* savages, and I shall not play at that. We have just discovered this river, and we are going down it on our raft; and if we do not reach some place to-night and build a fort, very likely the savages will shoot us. I believe I heard one shouting just now; there was something rustled, I am sure, in the forest."

He pointed at the thick double-mound hedge about a hundred yards distant.

"What river is it?" said Mark. "Is it the Amazon, or the Congo, or the Yellow River, or the Nile—"

"It is the Mississippi, of course," said Bevis, quite decided and at ease as to that point. "Can't you see that piece of weed there. My papa says that weed came from America, so I am sure it is the Mississippi, and nobody has ever floated down it before, and there's no one that can read within a thousand miles."

"Then what shall we do?"

"O, there's always something you can do. If we could only get a beaver now to nibble through it. There's always something you can do. I know," and Bevis jumped up delighted at his idea, "we can bore a hole, and blow it up with gunpowder!"

"Lot us fetch an auger," said Mark. "The gimlet is not big enough."

"Be quick," said Bevis. "Run back to the settlement, and get the auger; I will mind the raft and keep off the savages; and, I say, bring a spear and the cutlass; and—I say—"

But Mark was too far, and in too much of a hurry to hear a word. Bevis, tired of chopping, rolled over on his back on the grass, looking up at the sky. The buttercups rose high above his head, the wind blew and cooled his heated forehead, and a humble-bee hummed along: borne by the breeze from the grass there came the sweet scent of green things growing in the sunshine. Far up he saw the swallows climbing in the air; they climbed a good way almost straight up, and then suddenly came slanting down again.

While he lay there he distinctly heard the Indians rustling again in the forest. He raised himself on one arm, but could not see them; then recollecting that he must try to conceal himself, he reclined again, and thought how he should be able to repel an attack without weapons. There was the little hatchet, he could snatch up that and defend himself. Perhaps they would sink the raft? Perhaps when Mark returned they had better tow it back up stream, and draw it ashore safely at home, and then return to the work of clearing the obstruction. As he lay with his knees up among the buttercups he heard the thump, thump of Mark's feet rushing down the hill in eager haste with the auger. So he sat up, and beckoned to him to be quiet, and explained to him when he arrived that the Indians were certainly about. They must tow the raft back to the drinking-place. Bevis untied the cord with which the raft was fastened to the willow, and stepped on board.

"Don't pull too quick," he said to Mark, giving him the cord; "or perhaps I shall run aground."

"But you floated down," said Mark. "Let me get in, and you tow; it's my turn."

"Your turn?" shouted Bevis, standing up as straight as a bolt. "This is *my* raft."

"But you always have everything, and you floated down, and I have not; you have everything, and—"

"You are a great story," said Bevis, stamping so that the raft shook and the ripples rushed from under it. "I don't have everything, and you have more than half; and I gave you my engine and that box of gun-caps yesterday; and I hate you, and you are a big story."

Out he scrambled, and seizing Mark by the shoulders, thrust him towards the raft with such force that it was with difficulty Mark saved himself from falling into the brook. He clung to the willow—the bark gave way under his fingers—but as he slipped, he slung himself over the raft and dropped on it.

"Take the pole," said Bevis, still very angry, and looking black as thunder. "Take the pole, and steer so as not to run in the mud, and not to hit against the bank. Now then," and putting the cord over his shoulder, off he started.

Mark had as much as ever he could do to keep the raft from striking one side or the other.

"Please don't go so fast," he said.

Bevis went slower, and towed steadily in silence. After they had passed the hawthorn under the may-bloom, Mark said, "Bevis," but Bevis did not answer.

"Bevis," repeated Mark, "I have had enough now; stop, and you get in."

"I shall not," said Bevis. "You are a great story."

In another minute Mark spoke again:—

"Let me get out and tow you now." Bevis did not reply. "I say—I say—I say, Bevis."

No use. Bevis towed him the whole way, till the raft touched the shallow shore of the drinking-place. Then Mark got out and helped him drag the vessel well up on the ground, so that it should not float away.

"Now," said Bevis, after it was quite done. "Will you be a story any more?"

"No," said Mark, "I will not be a story again."

So they walked back side by side to the willow tree; Mark, who was really in the right, feeling in the wrong. At the tree Bevis picked up the auger, and told him to bore the hole. Mark began, but suddenly stopped.

"What's the good of boring the hole when we have not got any gunpowder," said he.

"No more we have," said Bevis. "This is very stupid, and they will not let me have any, though I have got some money, and I have a great mind to buy some and hide it. Just as if we did not know how to use powder, and as if we did not know how to shoot! Oh, I know! We will go and cut a bough of alder—there's ever so many alders by the Longpond—and burn it and make charcoal; it makes the best charcoal, you know, and they always—use it for gunpowder, and then we can get some saltpetre. Let me see—"

"The Bailiff had some saltpetre the other day," said Mark.

"So he did: it is in the dairy. Oh yes, and I know where some sulphur is. It is in the garden-house, where the tools are, in the orchard; it's what they use to smother the bees with—"

"That's on brown paper," said Mark; "that won't do."

"No it's not. You have to melt it to put it on paper, and dip the paper in. This is in a piece, it is like a short bar, and we will pound it up and mix; them all together and make capital gunpowder."

"Hurrah!" cried Mark, throwing down the auger. "Let's go and cut the alder. Come on!"

"Stop," said Bevis. "Lean on me, and walk slow. Don't you know you have caught a dreadful fever, from being in the swamps by the river, and you can hardly walk, and you are very thin and weak? Lean on my arm and hang your head."

Mark hung his head, turning his rosy cheeks down to the buttercups, and dragged his sturdy fever-stricken limbs along with an effort.

"Humph!" said a gruff voice.

"It's the Indians!" cried Bevis, startled; for they were so absorbed they had not heard the Bailiff come up behind them. They quite jumped, as if about to be scalped.

"What be you doing to that tree?" said the Bailiff.

"Find out," said Bevis. "It's not your tree: and why don't you say when you're coming?"

"I saw you from the hedge," said the Bailiff. "I was telling John where to cut the bushes from for the new harrow." That caused the rustling in the forest. "You'll never chop he down."

"That we shall, if we want to."

"No, you won't—he stops your ship."

"It isn't a ship: it's a raft."

"Well, you can't get by."

"That we can."

"I thinks you be stopped," said the Bailiff, having now looked at the tree more carefully. "He be main thick,"—with a certain sympathy for stolid, inanimate obstruction.

"I tell you, people like us are never stopped by anything," said Bevis. "We go through forests, and we float down rivers, and we shoot tigers, and move the biggest trees ever seen—don't we, Mark?"

"Yes, that we do: nothing is anything to us."

"Of course not," said Bevis. "And if we can't chop it down or blow it up, as we mean to, then we dig round it. O, Mark, I say! I forgot! Let's dig a canal round it."

"How silly we were never to think of that!" said Mark. "A canal is the very thing—from here to the creek."

He meant where the stream curved to enclose the Peninsula: the proposed canal would make the voyage shorter.

"Cut some sticks—quick!" said Bevis. "We must plug out our canal—that is what they always do first, whether it is a canal, or a railway, or a drain, or anything. And I must draw a plan. I must get my pocket-book and pencil. Come on, Mark, and get the spade while I get my pencil."

Off they ran. The Bailiff leaned on his hazel staff, one hand against the willow, and looked down into the water, as calmly as the sun itself reflected there. When he had looked awhile he shook his head and grunted: then he stumped away; and after a dozen yards or so, glanced back, grunted, and shook his head again. It could not be done. The tree was thick, the earth hard—no such thing: his sympathy, in a dull unspoken way, was with the immovable.

Mark went to work with the spade, throwing the turf he dug up into the brook; while Bevis, lying at full length on the grass, drew his plan of the canal. He drew two curving lines parallel, and half an inch apart, to represent the bend of the brook, and then two, as straight as he could manage, across, so as to shorten the distance, and avoid the obstruction. The rootlets of the grass held tight, when Mark tried to lift the spadeful he had dug, so that he could not tear them off.

He had to chop them at the side with his spade first, and then there was a root of the willow in the way; a very obstinate stout root, for which the little hatchet had to be brought to cut it. Under the softer turf the ground was very hard, as it had long been dry, so that by the time Bevis had drawn his plan and stuck in little sticks to show the course the canal was to take, Mark had only cleared about a foot square, and four or five inches deep, just at the edge of the bank, where he could thrust it into the stream.

"I have been thinking," said Bevis as he came back from the other end of the line, "I have been thinking what we are, now we are making this canal?"

"Yes," said Mark, "what are we?—they do not make canals on the Mississippi. Is this the Suez canal?"

"Oh no," said Bevis. "This is not Africa; there is no sand, and there are no camels about. Stop a minute. Put down that spade, don't dig another bit till we know what we are."

Mark put down the spade, and they both thought very hard indeed, looking straight at one another.

"I know," said Bevis, drawing a long breath. "We are digging a canal through Mount Athos, and we are Greeks."

"But was it the Greeks?" said Mark. "Are you sure—"

"Quite sure," said Bevis. "Perfectly quite sure. Besides, it doesn't matter. We can do it if they did not, don't you see?"

"So we can: and who are you then, if we are Greeks?"

"I am Alexander the Great."

"And who am I!"

"O, you—you are anybody."

"But I must be somebody," said Mark, "else it will not do."

"Well, you are: let me see—Pisistratus."

"Who was Pisistratus?"

"I don't know," said Bevis. "It doesn't matter in the least. Now dig."

Pisistratus dug till he came to another root, which Alexander the Great chopped off for him with the hatchet. Pisistratus dug again and uncovered a water-rat's hole which went down aslant to the water. They both knelt on the grass, and peered down the round tunnel: at the bottom where the water was, some of the fallen petals of the may-bloom had come in and floated there.

"This would do splendidly to put some gunpowder in and blow up, like the miners do," said Bevis. "And I believe that is the proper way to make a canal: it is how they make tunnels, I am sure."

"Greeks are not very good," said Mark. "I don't like Greeks: don't let's be Greeks any longer. The Mississippi was very much best."

"So it was," said Bevis. "The Mississippi is the nicest. I am not Alexander, and you are not Pisistratus. This is the Mississippi."

"Let us have another float down," said Mark. "Let me float down, and I will drag you all the way up this time."

"All right," said Bevis.

So they launched the raft, and Mark got in and floated down, and Bevis walked on the bank, giving him directions how to pilot the vessel, which as before was brought up by the willow leaning over the water. Just as they were preparing to tow it back again, and Bevis was climbing out on the willow to get into the raft they heard a splashing down the brook.

"What's that?" said Mark. "Is it Indians?"

"No, it's an alligator. At least, I don't know. Perhaps it's a canoe full of Indians. Give me the pole, quick; there now, take the hatchet. Look out!"

The splashing increased; then there was a "Yowp!" and Pan, the spaniel, suddenly appeared out of the flags by the osier-bed. He raced across the ground there, and jumped into the brook again, and immediately a moorcock, which he had been hunting, scuttled along the water, beating with his wings, and scrambling with his long legs hanging down, using both air and water to fly from his enemy. As he came near he saw Bevis on the willow, and rose out of the brook over the bank. Bevis hit at him with his pole, but missed; and Mark hurled the hatchet in vain. The moorcock flew straight across the meadow to another withy-bed, and then disappeared. It was only by threats that they stopped the spaniel from following.

Pan having got his plateful by patiently waiting about the doorway, after he had licked his chops, and turned up the whites of his eyes, to see if he could persuade them to give him any more, walked into the rick-yard, and choosing a favourite spot upon some warm straw—for straw becomes quite hot under sunshine—lay down and took a nap. When he awoke, having settled matters with the fleas, he strolled back to the ha-ha wall, and, seeing Bevis and Mark still busy by the brook, went down to know what they were doing. But first going to a place he well knew to lap he scented the moorcock, and gave chase.

"Come here," said Bevis; and, seizing the spaniel by the skin of his neck, he dragged him in the raft, stepped in quickly after, and held Pan while Mark hauled at the tow-line. But when Bevis had to take the pole to guide the raft from striking the bank Pan jumped out in a moment, preferring to swim rather than to ride in comfort, nor could any persuasions or threats get him on again. He barked along the shore, while Mark hauled and Bevis steered the craft.

Having beached her at the drinking-place on the shelving strand, they thought they had better go up the river a little way, and see if there were any traces of Indians; and, following the windings of the stream, they soon came to the hatch. Above the hatch the water was smooth, as it usually is where it is deep and approaching the edge, and Bevis's quick eye caught sight of a tiny ripple there near one bank, so tiny that it hardly extended across the brook, and disappeared after the third wavelet.

"Keep Pan there!" he said. "Hit him—hit him harder than that; he doesn't mind."

Mark punched the spaniel, who crouched; but, nevertheless, his body crept, as it were, towards the hatch, where Bevis was climbing over. Bevis took hold of the top rail, put his foot on the rail below, all green and slippery with weeds where the water splashed, like the rocks where the sea comes, then his other foot further along, and so got over with the deep water in front, and the roar of the fall under, and the bubbles rushing down the stream. The bank was very steep, but there was a notch to put the foot in, and a stout hawthorn stem—the thorns on which had long since been broken off for the purpose—gave him something to hold to and by which to lift himself up.

Then he walked stealthily along the bank—it overhung the dark deep water, and seemed about to slip in under him. There was a plantation of trees on that side, and on the other a hawthorn hedge, so that it was a quiet and sheltered spot. As he came to the place where he had seen the ripple, he looked closer, and in among a bunch of rushes, with the green stalks standing up all round it, he saw a moorhen's nest. It was made of rushes, twined round like a wreath, or perhaps more like a large green turban, and there were three or four young moorhens in it. The old bird had slipped away as he came near, and diving under the surface rose ten yards off under a projecting bush.

Bevis dropped on his knee to take one of the young birds, but in an instant they rolled out of the nest, with their necks thrust out in front, and fell splash in the water, where they swam across, one with a piece of shell clinging to its back, and another piece of shell was washed from it by the water. Pan was by his side in a minute; he had heard the splash, and seen the young moorhens, and with a whine, as Mark kicked him—unable to hold him any longer—he rushed across.

"They are such pretty dear little things," said Bevis, in an ecstasy of sentiment, calling to Mark. "Lie down!" banging Pan with a dead branch which he hastily snatched up. The spaniel's back sounded hollow as the wood rebounded, and broke on his ribs. "Such dear little things! I would not have them hurt for anything."

Bang again on Pan's back, who gave up the attempt, knowing from sore experience that Bevis was not to be trifled with. But by the time Mark had got there the little moorhens had hidden in the grasses beside the stream, though one swam out for a minute, and then concealed itself again.

"Don't you love them?" said Bevis. "I do. I'll *smash* you,"—to Pan, cowering at his feet.

The moorhens did not appear again, so they went back and sat on the top of the steep bank, their legs dangling over the edge above the bubbling water.

A broad cool shadow from the trees had fallen over the hatch, for the afternoon had gone on, and the sun was declining behind them over the western hills. A broad cool shadow, whose edges were far away, so that they were in the midst of it. The thrushes sang in the ashes, for they knew that the quiet evening, with the dew they love, was near. A bullfinch came to the hawthorn hedge just above the hatch, looked in and out once or twice, and then stepped inside the spray near his nest. A yellow-hammer called from the top of a tree, and another answered him across the field. Afar in the mowing-grass the crake lifted his voice, for he talks more as the sun sinks.

The swirling water went round and round under the fall, with lines of white bubbles rising, and quivering masses of yellowish foam ledged on the red rootlets under the bank and against the flags. The swirling water, ceaselessly beaten by the descending stream coming on it with a long-continued blow, returned to be driven away again. A steady roar of the fall, and a rippling sound above it of bursting bubbles and crossing wavelets of the hastening stream, notched and furrowed over stones, frowning in eager haste. The rushing and the coolness, and the song of the brook and the birds, and the sense of the sun sinking, stilled even Bevis and Mark a little while.

They sat and listened, and said nothing; the delicious brook filled their ears with music.

Next minute Bevis seized Pan by the neck and pitched him over into the bubbles. In an instant, before he came to the surface, as his weight carried him beneath, Pan was swept down the stream, and when he came up he could not swim against it, but was drifted away till he made for the flags, which grew on a shallow spot. There he easily got out, shook himself, and waited for them to come over.

"I am hungry," said Mark. "What ought we to have to eat; what is right on the Mississippi? I don't believe they have tea. There is Polly shouting for us."

"No," said Bevis thoughtfully; "I don't think they do. How stupid of her to stand there shouting and waving her handkerchief, as if we could not find our way straight across the trackless prairie. I know—we will have some honey! Don't you know? Of course the hunters find lots of wild honey in the hollow trees. We will have some honey; there's a big jar full."

So they got over the hatch, and went home, leaving their tools scattered hither and thither beside the Mississippi. They climbed up the ha-ha wall, putting the toes of their boots where the flat stones of which it was built, without mortar, were farthest apart, and so made steps while they could hold to the wiry grass-tufts on the top.

"Where's your hat?" said Polly to Bevis.

"I don't know," said Bevis. "I suppose it's in the brook. It doesn't matter."

Chapter Four
Discovery of the New Sea

Next morning Bevis went out into the meadow to try and find a plant whose leaves, or one of them, always pointed to the north, like a green compass lying on the ground. There was one in the prairies by which the hunters directed themselves across those oceans of grass without a landmark as the mariners at sea. Why should there not be one in the meadows here—in these prairies—by which to guide himself from forest to forest, from hedge to hedge, where there was no path? If there was a path it was not proper to follow it, nor ought you to know your way; you ought to find it by sign.

He had "blazed" ever so many boughs of the hedges with the hatchet, or his knife if he had not got the hatchet with him, to recognise his route through the woods. When he found a nest begun or finished, and waiting for the egg, he used to cut a "blaze"—that is, to peel off the bark—or make a notch, or cut a bough off about three yards from the place, so that he might easily return to it, though hidden with foliage. No doubt the grass had a secret of this kind, and could tell him which was the way, and which was the north and south if he searched long enough.

So the raft being an old story now, as he had had it a day, Bevis went out into the field, looking very carefully down into the grass. Just by the path there were many plantains, but their long, narrow leaves did not point in any particular direction, no two plants had their leaves parallel. The blue scabious had no leaves to speak of, nor had the red knapweed, nor the yellow rattle, nor the white moon-daisies, nor golden buttercups, nor red sorrel. There were stalks and flowers, but the plants of the mowing-grass, in which he had no business to be walking, had very little leaf. He tried to see if the flowers turned more one way than the other, or bowed their heads to the north, as men seem to do, taking that pole as their guide, but none did so. They leaned in any direction, as the wind had left them, or as the sun happened to be when they burst their green bonds and came forth to the light.

The wind came past as he looked and stroked everything the way it went, shaking white pollen from the bluish tops of the tall grasses. The wind went on and left him and the grasses to themselves. How should I knew which was the north or the south or the west from these? Bevis asked himself, without framing any words to his question. There was no knowing. Then he walked to the hedge to see if the moss grew more on one side of the elms than the other, or if the bark was thicker and rougher.

After he had looked at twenty trees he could not see much difference; those in the hedge had the moss thickest on the eastern side (he knew which was east very well himself, and wanted to see if the moss knew), and those in the lane just through it had the moss thickest on their western side, which was clearly because of the shadow. The trees were really in a double row, running north and south, and the coolest shadow was in between them, and so the moss grew there most. Nor were the boughs any longer or bigger any side more than the other, it varied as the tree was closely surrounded with other trees, for each tree repelled its neighbour. None of the trees, nor the moss, nor grasses cared anything at all about north or south.

Bevis sat down in the mowing-grass, though he knew the Bailiff would have been angry at such a hole being made in it; and when he was sitting on the ground it rose as high as his head. He could see nothing but the sky, and while he sat there looking up he saw that the clouds all drifted one way, towards his house. Presently a starling came past, also flying straight for the house, and after a while another. Next three bees went over as straight as a line, all going one after another that way. The bees went because they had gathered as much honey as they could carry, and were hastening home without looking to the right or to the left. The starlings went because they had young in their nests in a hole of the roof by the chimney, and they had found some food for their fledglings. So now he could find his way home across the pathless prairie by going the same way as the clouds, the bees, and the starlings.

But when he had reached home he recollected that he ought to know the latitude, and that there were Arabs or some other people in Africa who found out the latitude of the place they were in by gazing at the sun through a tube. Bevis considered a little, and then went to the rick-yard, where there was a large elder bush, and cut a straight branch between the knots with his knife. He peeled it, and then forced out the pith, and thus made a tube. Next he took a thin board, and scratched a circle on it with the point of the compasses, and divided it into degrees. Round the tube he bent a piece of wire, and put the ends through a gimlet-hole in the centre of the board. The ends were opened apart, so as to fasten the tube to the board, allowing it to rotate round the circle. Two gimlet-holes were bored at the top corners of the board, and string passed through so that the instrument could be attached to a tree or post.

He was tying it to one of the young walnut-trees as an upright against which to work his astrolabe, when Mark arrived, and everything had to be explained to him. After they had glanced through the tube, and decided that the raft was at least ten degrees distant, it was clearly of no use to go to it to-day, as they could not reach it under a week's travel. The best thing, Mark thought, would be to continue their expedition in some other direction.

"Let's go round the Longpond," said Bevis; "we have never been quite round it."

"So we will," said Mark. "But we shall not be back to dinner."

"As if travellers ever thought of dinner! Of course we shall take our provisions with us."

"Let's go and get our spears," said Mark.

"Let's take Pan," said Bevis.

"Where is your old compass?" said Mark.

"O, I know—and I must make a map; wait a minute. We ought to have a medicine-chest; the savages will worry us for physic: and very likely we shall have dreadful fevers."

"So we shall, of course; but perhaps there are wonderful plants to cure us, and we know them and the savages don't—there's sorrel."

"Of course, and we can nibble some hawthorn leaf."

"Or a stalk of wheat."

"Or some watercress."

"Or some nuts."

"No, certainly not; they're not ripe," said Bevis, "and unripe fruit is very dangerous in tropical countries."

"We ought to keep a diary," said Mark. "When we go to sleep who shall watch first, you or I?"

"We'll light a fire," said Bevis. "That will frighten the lions; they will glare at us, but they can't stand fire—you hit them on the head with a burning stick."

So they went in, and loaded their pockets with huge double slices of bread-and-butter done up in paper, apples, and the leg of a roast duck from the pantry. Then came the compass, an old one in a brass case; Mark broke his nails opening the case, which was tarnished, and the card at once swung round to the north, pointing to the elms across the road from the window of the sitting-room. Bevis took the bow and three arrows, made of the young wands of hazel which grow straight, and Mark was armed with a spear, a long ash rod with sharpened end, which they thrust in the kitchen fire a few minutes to harden in the proper manner.

Besides which, there was Bevis's pocket-book for the diary, and a large sheet of brown paper for the map; you see travellers have not always everything at command, but must make use of what they have. Pan raced before them up the footpath; the gate that led to the Longpond was locked, and too high to be climbed easily, but they knew a gap, and crept through on hands and knees.

"Take care there are no cobras or rattlesnakes among those dead leaves," said Mark, when they were halfway through, and quite over-arched and hidden under brambles.

"Stick your spear into them," said Bevis, who was first, and Mark, putting his spear past him, stirred up the heap of leaves.

"All right," said he. "But look at that bough—is it a bough or a snake?"

There was an oak branch in the ditch, crooked and grey with lichen, half concealed by rushes; its curving shape and singular hue gave it some resemblance to a serpent. But when he stabbed at it with his spear it did not move; and they crept through without hurt. As they stood up in the field the other side they had an anxious consultation as to what piece of water it was they were going to discover; whether it was a lake in Central Africa, or one in America.

"I'm tired of lakes," said Mark. "They have found out such a lot of lakes, and the canoes are always upset, and there is such a lot of mud. Let's have a new sea altogether."

"So we will," said Bevis. "That's capital—we will find a new sea where no one has ever been before. Look!"—for they had now advanced to where the gleam of the sunshine on the mere was visible through the hedge— "look! there it is; is it not wonderful?"

"Yes," said Mark, "write it down in the diary; here's my pencil. Be quick; put 'Found a new sea'—be quick—there, come on—let's run—hurrah!"

They dashed open the gate, and ran down to the beach. It was a rough descent over large stones, but they reached the edge in a minute, and as they came there was a splashing in several places along the shore. Something was striving to escape, alarmed at their approach. Mark fell on his knees, and put his hand where two or three stones, half in and half out of water, formed a recess, and feeling about drew out two roach, one of which slipped from his fingers; the other he held. Bevis rushed at another splashing, but he was not quick enough, for it was difficult to scramble over the stones, and the fish swam away just as he got there. Mark's fish was covered with tiny slippery specks. The roach had come up to leave their eggs under the stones. When they had looked at the fish they put it back in the water, and with a kind of shake it dived down and made off. As they watched it swim out they now saw that three or four yards from the shore there were crowds upon crowds of fish travelling to and fro, following the line of the land.

They were so many, that the water seemed thick with them, and some were quite large for roach. These had finished putting their eggs under the stones, and were now swimming up and down. Every now and then, as they silently watched the roach—for they had never before seen such countless multitudes of fish—they could hear splashings further along the stones, where those that were up in the recesses were suddenly seized with panic fear without cause, and struggled to get out, impeding each other, and jammed together in the narrow entrances. For they could not forget their cruel enemies the jacks, and dreaded lest they should be pounced upon while unable even to turn.

A black cat came down the bank some way off, and they saw her swiftly dart her paw into the water, and snatch out a fish. The scales shone silver white, and reflected the sunshine into their eyes like polished metal as the fish quivered and leaped under the claw. Then the cat quietly, and pausing over each morsel, ate the living creature. When she had finished she crept towards the water to get another.

"What a horrid thing!" said Mark. "She ate the fish alive—cruel wretch! Let's kill her."

"Kill her," said Bevis; and before he could fit an arrow to his bow Mark picked up a stone, and flung it with such a good aim and with such force that although it did not hit the cat, it struck a stone and split into fragments, which flew all about her like a shell. The cat raced up the bank, followed by a second stone, and at the top met Pan, who did not usually chase cats, having been beaten for it, but seeing in an instant that she was in disgrace, he snapped at her and drove her wild with terror up a pine-tree. They called Pan off, for it was no use his yapping at a tree, and walked along the shore, climbing over stones, but the crowds of roach were everywhere; till presently they came to a place where the stones ceased, and there was a shallow bank of sand shelving into the water and forming a point.

There the fish turned round and went back. Thousands kept coming up and returning, and while they stayed here watching, gazing into the clear water, which was still and illuminated to the bottom by the sunlight, they saw two great fish come side by side up from the depths beyond and move slowly, very slowly, just over the sand. They were two huge tench, five or six pounds a-piece, roaming idly away from the muddy holes they lie in. But they do not stay in such holes always, and once now and then you may see them like this as in a glass tank. The pair did not go far; they floated slowly rather than swam, first a few yards one way and then a few yards the other. Bevis and Mark were breathless with eagerness.

"Go and fetch my fishing-rod," whispered Bevis, unable to speak loud; he was so excited.

"No, you go," said Mark; "I'll stay and watch them."

"I shan't," said Bevis sharply, "you ought to go."

"I shan't," said Mark.

Just then the tench, having surveyed the bottom there, turned and faded away into the darker deep water.

"There," said Bevis, "if you had run quick!"

"I won't fetch everything," said Mark.

"Then you're no use," said Bevis. "Suppose I was shooting an elephant, and you did not hand me another gun quick, or another arrow; and suppose—"

"But *I* might be shooting the elephant," interrupted Mark, "and you could hand me the gun."

"Impossible," said Bevis; "I never heard anything so absurd. Of course it's the captain who always does everything; and if there was only one biscuit left, of course you would let me eat it, and lie down and die under a tree, so that I might go on and reach the settlement."

"I *hate* dying under a tree," said Mark, "and you always want everything."

Bevis said nothing, but marched on very upright and very angry, and Mark followed, putting his feet into the marks Bevis left as he strode over the yielding sand. Neither spoke a word. The shore trended in again after the point, and the indentation was full of weeds, whose broad brownish leaves floated on the surface. Pan worked about and sniffed among the willow bushes on their left, which, when the lake was full, were in the water, but now that it had shrunk under the summer heat were several yards from the edge.

Bevis, leading the way, came to a place where the strand, till then so low and shelving, suddenly became steep, where a slight rise of the ground was cut as it were through by the water, which had worn a cliff eight or ten feet above his head. The water came to the bottom of the cliff, and there did not seem any way past it except by going away from the edge into the field, and so round it. Mark at once went round, hastening as fast as he could to get in front, and he came down to the water on the other side of the cliff in half a minute, looked at Bevis, and then went on with Pan.

Bevis, with a frown on his forehead, stood looking at the cliff, having determined that he would not go round, and yet he could not get past because the water, which was dark and deep, going straight down, came to the bank, which rose from it like a wall. First he took out his pocket-knife and thought he would cut steps in the sand, and he did cut one large enough to put his toe in; but then he recollected that he should have nothing to hold to. He had half a mind to go back home and get some big nails and drive into the hard sand to catch hold of, only by that time Mark would be so far ahead he could not overtake him and would boast that he had explored the new sea first. Already he was fifty yards in front, and walking as fast as he could. How he wished he had his raft, and then that he could swim! He would have jumped into the water and swam round the cliff in a minute.

He saw Mark climbing over some railings that went down to the water to divide the fields. He looked up again at the cliff, and almost felt inclined to leave it and run round and overtake Mark. When he looked down again Mark was out of sight, hidden by hawthorn bushes and the branches of trees. Bevis was exceedingly angry, and he walked up and down and gazed round in his rage. But as he turned once more to the cliff, suddenly Pan appeared at an opening in the furze and bramble about halfway up. The bushes grew at the side, and the spaniel, finding Bevis did not follow Mark, had come back and was waiting for him. Bevis, without thinking, pushed into the furze, and immediately he saw him coming, Pan, eager to go forward again, ran along the face of the cliff about four feet from the top. He seemed to run on nothing, and Bevis was curious to see how he had got by.

The bushes becoming thicker, Bevis had at last to go on hands and knees under them, and found a hollow space, where there was a great rabbit-bury, big enough at the mouth for Pan to creep in. When he stood on the sand thrown out from it he could see how Pan had done it; there was a narrow ledge, not above four inches wide, on the face of the cliff. It was only just wide enough for a footing, and the cliff fell sheer down to the water; but Bevis, seeing that he could touch the top of the cliff, and so steady himself, never hesitated a moment.

He stepped on the ledge, right foot first, the other close behind it, and hold lightly to the grass at the edge of the field above, only lightly lest he should pull it out by the roots. Then he put his right foot forward again, and drew his left up to it, and so along, keeping the right first (he could not walk properly, the ledge being so narrow), he worked himself along. It was quite easy, though it seemed a long way down to the water, it always looks very much farther down than it does up, and as he glanced down he saw a perch rise from the depths, and it occurred to him in the moment what a capital place it would be for perch-fishing.

He could see all over that part of the lake, and noticed two moorhens feeding in the weeds on the other side, when puff! the wind came over the field, and reminded him, as he involuntarily grasped the grass tighter, that he must not stay in such a place where he might lose his balance. So he went on, and a dragonfly flew past out a little way over the water and then back to the field, but Bevis was not to be tempted to watch his antics, he kept steadily on, a foot at a time, till he reached a willow on the other side, and had a bough to hold. Then he shouted, and Pan, who was already far ahead, stopped and looked back at the well-known sound of triumph.

Running down the easy slope, Bevis quickly reached the railings and climbed over. On the other side a meadow came down to the edge, and he raced through the grass and was already halfway to the next rails when some one called "Bevis!" and there was Mark coming out from behind an oak in the field. Bevis stopped, half-pleased, half-angry.

"I waited for you," said Mark.

"I came across the cliff," said Bevis.

"I saw you," said Mark.

"But you ran away from me," said Bevis.

"But I am not running now."

"It is very wrong when we are on an expedition," said Bevis. "People must do as the captain tells them."

"I won't do it again," said Mark.

"You ought to be punished," said Bevis, "you ought to be put on half-rations. Are you quite sure you will never do it again?"

"Never."

"Well then, this once you are pardoned. Now, mind in future, as you are lieutenant, you set a good example. There's a summer snipe."

Out flew a little bird from the shore, startled as Pan came near, with a piping whistle, and, describing a semicircle, returned to the hard mud fifty yards farther on. It was a summer snipe, and when they approached, after getting over the next railings, it flew out again over the water, and making another half-circle passed back to where they had first seen it. Here the strand was hard mud, dried by the sun, and broken up into innumerable holes by the hoofs of cattle and horses which had come down to drink from the pasture, and had to go through the mud into which they sank when it was soft. Three or four yards from the edge there was a narrow strip of weeds, showing that a bank followed the line of the shore there. It was so unpleasant walking over this hard mud, that they went up into the field, which rose high, so that from the top they had a view of the lake.

Chapter Five
By the New Nile

"Do you see any canoes?" said Mark.

"No," said Bevis. "Can you? Look very carefully."

They gazed across the broad water over the gleaming ripples far away, for the light wind did not raise them by the shore, and traced the edge of the willows and the weeds.

"The savages are in hiding," said Bevis, after a pause. "Perhaps they're having a feast."

"Or gone somewhere to war."

"Are they cannibals?" said Mark. "I should not like to be gnawn."

"Very likely," said Bevis. "No one has ever been here before, so they are nearly sure to be; they always are where no one has been. This would be a good place to begin the map as we can see so far. Let's sit down."

"Let's get behind a tree, then," said Mark; "else if we stay still long perhaps we shall be seen."

So they went a little farther to an ash, and sat down by it. Bevis spread out his sheet of brown paper.

"Give me an apple," said Mark, "while you draw." Bevis did so, and then, lying on the ground at full length, began to trace out the course of the shore; Mark lay down too, and held one side of the paper that the wind might not lift it. First Bevis made a semicircle to represent the stony bay where they found the roach, then an angular point for the sandy bar, then a straight line for the shelving shore.

"There ought to be names," said Mark. "What shall we call this?" putting his finger on the bay.

"Don't splutter over the map," said Bevis; "take that apple pip off it. Of course there will be names when I have drawn the outline. Here's the cliff." He put a slight projection where the cliff jutted out a little way, then a gentle curve for the shore of the meadow, and began another trending away to the left for the place where they were.

"That's not long enough," said Mark.

"It's not finished," said Bevis. "How can I finish it when we have only got as far as this? How do I know, you stupid, how far this bay goes into the land? Perhaps there's another sea round there," pointing over the field. "Instead of saying silly things, just find out some names, now."

"What sea is it?" said Mark thoughtfully.

"I can't tell," said Bevis. "It is most extraordinary to find a new sea. And such an enormous big one. Why how many days' journey have we come already?"

"Thirty," said Mark. "Put it down in the diary, thirty days' journey. There, that's right. Now, what sea is it? Is it the Atlantic?"

"No; it's not the Atlantic, nor the Pacific, nor the South Sea; it's bigger than all those."

"It's much more difficult to find a name than a sea," said Mark.

"Much," said Bevis. They stared at each other for awhile. "I know," said Bevis.

"Well, what is it?" said Mark excitedly, raising himself on his knees to hear the name.

"I know," said Bevis. "I'll lie down and shut my eyes, and you take a piece of grass and tickle me; then I can think. I can't think unless I'm tickled."

He disposed himself very comfortably on his back with his knees up, and tilted his straw hat so as to shade that side of his face towards the sun. Mark pulled a bennet.

"Not *too* ticklish," said Bevis, "else that won't do: don't touch my lips."

"All right."

Mark held the bending bennet (the spike of the grass) bending with the weight of its tip, and drew it very gently across Bevis's forehead. Then he let it just touch his cheek, and afterwards put the tip very daintily on his eyelid. From there he let it wander like a fly over his forehead again, and close by, but not in the ear (as too ticklish), leaving little specks of pollen on the skin, and so to the neck, and next up again to the hair, and on the other cheek under the straw hat. Bevis, with his eyes shut, kept quite still under this luxurious tickling for some time, till Mark, getting tired, put the bennet delicately on his lip, when he started and rubbed his mouth.

"Now, how stupid you are, Mark; I was just thinking. Now, do it again."

Mark did it again.

"Are you thinking?" he asked presently.

"Yes," whispered Bevis. They were so silent they heard the grasshoppers singing in the grass, and the swallows twittering as they flew over, and the loud midsummer hum in the sky.

"Are you thinking?" asked Mark again. Bevis did not answer—he was asleep. Mark bent over him, and went on tickling, half dreamy himself, till he nodded, and his hat fell on Bevis, who sat up directly.

"I know."

"What is it?"

"It is not one sea," said Bevis; "it is a lot of seas. That's the Blue Sea, there," pointing to the stony bay where the water was still and blue under the sky. "That's the Yellow Sea, there," pointing to the low muddy shore where the summer snipe flew up, and where, as it was so shallow and so often disturbed by cattle, the water was thick for some yards out.

"And what is that out there!" said Mark, pointing southwards to the broader open water where the ripples were sparkling bright in the sunshine.

"That is the Golden Sea," said Bevis. "It is like butterflies flapping their wings,"—he meant the flickering wavelets.

"And this round here," where the land trended to the left, and there was a deep inlet.

"It is the Gulf," said Bevis; "Fir-Tree Gulf," as he noticed the tops of fir-trees.

"And that up at the top yonder, right away as far as you can see beyond the Golden Sea?"

"That's the Indian Ocean," said Bevis; "and that island on the left side there is Serendib."

"Where Sinbad went?"

"Yes; and that one by it is the Unknown Island, and a magician lives there in a long white robe, and he has a serpent a hundred feet long coiled up in a cave under a bramble bush, and the most wonderful things in the world."

"Let's go there," said Mark.

"So we will," said Bevis, "directly we have got a ship."

"Write the names down," said Mark. "Put them on the map before we forget them."

Bevis wrote them on the map, and then they started again upon their journey. Where the gulf began they found a slight promontory, or jutting point, defended by blocks of stone; for here the waves, when the wind blew west or south, came rolling with all their might over the long broad Golden Sea from the Indian Ocean. Pan left them while they stood here, to hunt among the thistles in an old sand-quarry behind. He started a rabbit, and chased it up the quarry, so that when they looked back they saw him high up the side, peering into the bury. Sand-martins were flying in and out of their round holes. At one place there was only a narrow strip of land between the ocean and the quarry, so that it seemed as if its billows might at any time force their way in.

They left the shore awhile, and went into the quarry, and winding in and out the beds of nettles and thistles climbed up a slope, where they sank at every step ankle deep in sand. It led to a broad platform of sand, above which the precipice rose straight to the roots of the grass above, which marked the top of the cliff with brown, and where humble-bees were buzzing along the edge, and, bending the flowers down on which they alighted, were thus suspended in space. In the cool recesses of the firs at the head of Fir-Tree Gulf a dove was cooing, and a great aspen rustled gently.

They took out their knives and pecked at the sand. It was hard, but could be pecked, and grooves cut in it. The surface was almost green from exposure to the weather, but under that white. When they looked round over the ocean they were quite alone: there was no one in sight either way, as far as they could see; nothing but the wall of sand behind, and the wide gleaming water in front.

"What a long way we are from other people," said Mark.

"Thousands of miles," said Bevis.

"Is it quite safe?"

"I don't know," doubtfully.

"Are there not strange creatures in these deserted places?"

"Sometimes," said Bevis. "Sometimes there are things with wings, which have spikes on them, and they have eyes that burn you."

Mark grasped his knife and spear, and looked into the beds of thistles and nettles, which would conceal anything underneath.

"Let's call Pan," he whispered.

Bevis shouted "Pan."

"Pan!" came back in an echo from another part of the quarry. "Pan!" shouted Bevis and Mark together. Pan did not come. They called again and whistled; but he did not come.

"Perhaps something has eaten him," said Mark.

"Very likely," said Bevis. "We ought to have a charm. Don't forget next time we come to bring a talisman, so that none of these things can touch us."

"I know," said Mark. "I know." He took his spear and drew a circle on the platform of sand. "Come inside this. There, that's it. Now stand still here. A circle is magic, you know."

"So it is," said Bevis. "Pan! Pan!"

Pan did not come.

"What's in those holes?" said Mark, pointing to some large rabbit-burrows on the right side of the quarry.

"Mummies," said Bevis. "You may be sure there are mummies there, and very likely magic writings in their hands. I wish we could get a magic writing. Then we could do anything, and we could know all the secrets."

"What secrets?"

"Why, all these things have secrets."

"All?" said Mark.

"All," said Bevis, looking round and pointing with an arrow in his hand. "All the trees, and all the stones, and all the flowers—"

"And these?" said Mark, picking up a shell.

"Yes, once; but can't you see it is dead, and the secret, of course, is gone. If we had a magic writing."

"Let's buy a book," said Mark.

"They are not books; they are rolls, and you unroll them very slowly, and see curious things, pictures that move over the paper—"

Boom!

They started. Mark lifted his spear, Bevis his bow. A deep, low, and slow sound, like thunder, toned from its many mutterings to a mighty sob, filled their ears for a moment. It might have been very distant thunder, or a cannon in the forts far away. It was one of those mysterious sounds that are heard in summer when the sky is clear and the wind soft, and the midsummer hum is loud. They listened, but it did not come again.

"What was that?" said Mark at last.

"I don't know; of course it was something magic."

"Perhaps they don't like us coming into these magic places," said Mark. "Perhaps it is to tell us to go away. No doubt Pan is eaten."

"I shall not go away," said Bevis, as the boom did not come again. "I shall fight first;" and he fitted his arrow to the string. "What's that!" and in his start he let the arrow fly down among the thistles.

It was Pan looking down upon them from the edge above, where he had been waiting ever since they first called him, and wondering why they did not see him. Bevis, chancing to glance up defiantly as he fitted his arrow to shoot the genie of the boom, had caught sight of the spaniel's face peering over the edge. Angry with Pan for making him start, Bevis picked up a stone and flung it at him, but the spaniel slipped back and escaped it.

"Fetch my arrow," said Bevis, stamping his foot.

Mark went down and got it. As he came up the sandy slope he looked back.

"There's a canoe," he said.

"So it is."

A long way off there was a black mark as it were among the glittering wavelets of the Golden Sea. They could not see it properly for the dazzling gleam.

"The cannibals have seen us," said Mark. "They can see miles. We shall be gnawn. Let's run out of sight before they come too near."

They ran down the slope into the quarry, and then across to the fir-trees. Then they stopped and watched the punt, but it did not come towards them. They had not been seen. They followed the path through the firs, and crossed the head of the gulf.

A slow stream entered the lake there, and they went down to the shore, where it opened to the larger water. Under a great willow, whose tops rose as high as the firs, and an alder or two, it was so cool and pleasant, that Mark, as he played with the water with his spear, pushing it this way and that, and raising bubbles, and a splashing as a whip sings in the air, thought he should like to dabble in it. He sat down on a root and took off his shoes and stockings, while Bevis, going a little way up the stream, flung a dead stick into it, and then walked beside it as it floated gently down. But he walked much faster than the stick floated, there was so little current.

"Mark," said he, suddenly stopping, and taking up some of the water in the hollow of his hand, "Mark!"

"Yes. What is it?"

"This is fresh water. Isn't it lucky?"

"Why?"

"Why, you silly, of course we should have died of thirst. *That's* the sea," (pointing out). "This will save our lives."

"So it will," said Mark, putting one foot into the water and then the other. Then looking back, as he stood half up his ankles, "We can call here for fresh water when we have our ship—when we go to the Unknown Island."

"So we can," said Bevis. "We must have a barrel and fill it. But I wonder what river this is," and he walked back again beside it.

Mark walked further out till it was over his ankles, and then till it was half as deep as his knee. He jumped up both feet together, and splashed as he came down, and shouted. Bevis shouted to him from the river. Next they both shouted together, and a dove flew out of the firs and went off.

"What river is this?" Bevis called presently.

"O!" cried Mark suddenly; and Bevis glancing round saw him stumble, and, in his endeavour to save himself, plunge his spear into the water as if it had been the ground, to steady himself; but the spear, though long, touched nothing up to his hand. He bent over. Bevis held his breath, thinking he must topple and fall headlong; but somehow he just saved himself, swung round, and immediately he could ran out upon the shore. Bevis rushed back.

"What was it?" he asked.

"It's a hole," said Mark, whose cheeks had turned white, and now became red, as the blood came back. "An awful deep hole—the spear won't touch the bottom."

As he waded out at first on shelving sand he laughed, and shouted, and jumped, and suddenly, as he stepped, his foot went over the edge of the deep hole; his spear, as he tried to save himself with it, touched nothing, so that it was only by good fortune that he recovered his balance. Once now and then in the autumn, when the water was very low, dried up by the long summer heats, this hole was visible and nearly empty, and the stream fell over a cataract into it, boiling and bubbling, and digging it deeper. But now, as the water had only just begun to recede, it was full, so that the stream ran slow, held back and checked by their sea.

This hollow was quite ten feet deep, sheer descent, but you could not see it, for the shore seemed to slope as shallow as possible.

Mark was much frightened, and sat down on the root to put on his shoes and stockings. Bevis took the spear, and going to the edge, and leaning over and feeling the bottom with it, he could find the hole, where the spear slipped and touched nothing, about two yards out.

"It is a horrid place," he said. "How should I have got you out? I wish we could swim."

"So do I," said Mark. "And they will never let us go out in a boat by ourselves—I mean in a ship to the Unknown Island—till we can."

"No; that they won't," said Bevis. "We must begin to swim directly. My papa will show me, and I will show you. But how should I have got you out if you had fallen? Let me see; there's a gate up there."

"It is so heavy," said Mark. "You could not drag it down, and fling it in quick enough. If we had the raft up here."

"Ah, yes. There is a pole loose there—that would have done." He pointed to some railings that crossed the stream. The rails were nailed, but there was a pole at the side, only thrust into the bushes. "I could have pulled that out and held it to you."

Mark had now got his shoes on, and they started again, looking for a bridge to cross the stream, and continue their journey round the New Sea. As they could not see any they determined to cross by the railings, which they did without much trouble, holding to the top bar, and putting their feet on the second, which was about three inches over the water. The stream ran deep and slow; it was dark, because it was in shadow, for the trees hung over from each side. Bevis, who was first, stopped in the middle and looked up it. There was a thick hedge and trees each side, and a great deal of fern on the banks. It was straight for a good way, so that they could see some distance till the boughs hid the rest.

"I should like to go up there," said Mark. "Some day, if we can get a boat under these rails, let us go up it."

"So we will," said Bevis. "It is proper to explore a river. But what river is this?"

"Is it the Congo?" said Mark.

"O! no. The Congo is not near this sea at all. Perhaps it's the Amazon."

"It can't be the Mississippi," said Mark. "That's a long way off now. I know—see it runs slow, and it's not clear, and we don't know where it comes from. It's the Nile."

"So it is," said Bevis. "It is the Nile, and some day we will go up to the source."

"What's that swimming across up there?" said Mark.

"It is too far; I can't tell. Most likely a crocodile. How fortunate you did not fall in."

When they had crossed, they whistled for Pan, who had been busy among the fern on the bank, sniffing after the rabbits which had holes there. Pan came and swam over to them in a minute. They travelled on some way and found the ground almost level and so thick with sedges and grass and rushes that they walked in a forest of green up to their waists. The water was a long way off beyond the weeds. They tried to go down to it, but the ground got very soft and their feet sank into it; it was covered with horsetails there, acres and acres of them, and after these shallow water hidden under floating weeds. Some coots were swimming about the edge of the weeds too far to fear them. So they returned to the firm ground and walked on among the sedges and rushes. There was a rough path, though not much marked, which wound about so as to get the firmest footing, but every now and then they had to jump over a wet place.

"What immense swamps," said Mark; "I wonder where ever we shall get to."

Underfoot there was a layer of the dead sedges of last year which gave beneath their weight, and the ground itself was formed of the roots of sedges and other plants. The water had not long since covered the place where they were, and the surface was still damp, for the sunshine could not dry it, having to pass through the thick growth above and the matted stalks below. A few scattered willow bushes showed how high the water had been by the fibres on the stems which had once flourished in it and were now almost dried up by the heat. A faint malarious odour rose from the earth, drawn from the rotting stalks by the hot sun. There was no shadow, and after a while they wearied of stepping through the sedges, sinking a little at every step, which much increases the labour of walking.

The monotony, too, was oppressive, nothing but sedges, flags, and rushes, sedges and horsetails, and they did not seem to get much farther after all their walking. First they were silent, labour makes us quiet; then they stopped and looked back. The perfect level caused the distance to appear more than it really was, because there was a thin invisible haze hovering over the swamp. Beyond the swamp was the gulf they had gone round, and across it the yellow sand-quarry facing them. It looked a very long way off.

Chapter Six
Central Africa

"We shall never get round," said Mark, "just see what a way we have come, and we are not half up one side of the sea yet."

"I wonder how far it is back to the quarry," said Bevis. "These sedges are so tiresome."

"We shall never get round," said Mark, "and I am getting hungry, and Pan is tired of the rushes too."

Pan, with his red tongue lolling out at one side of his mouth, looked up, showed his white tusks and wagged his tail at the mention of his name. He had ceased to quest about for some time; he had been walking just at their heels in the path they made.

"We *must* go on," said Bevis, "we *can't* go back; it is not proper. Travellers like us never go back. I wish there were no more sedges. Come on."

He marched on again. But now they had once confessed to each other that they were tired, this spurt soon died away, and they stopped again.

"It is as hot as Central Africa," said Mark, fanning himself with his hat.

"I am not sure that we are not in Central Africa," said Bevis. "There are hundreds of miles of reeds in Africa, and as we have crossed the Nile very likely that's where we are."

"It's just like it," said Mark, "I am sure it's Africa."

"Then there ought to be lions in the reeds," said Bevis, "or elephants. Keep your spear ready."

They went on again a little way.

"I want to sit down," said Mark.

"So do I," said Bevis; "in Africa, people generally rest in the middle of the day for fear of sunstrokes."

"So they do; then we ought to rest."

"We can't sit down here," said Bevis; "it is so wet, and it does not smell very nice: we might have the fever, you know, if we stopped still long."

"Let's go to the hedge," said Mark, pointing to the hedge which surrounded the shore and was a great way on their left hand. "Perhaps there is a prairie there. And I am so thirsty, and there is no water we can drink; give me an apple."

"But we must not go back," said Bevis; "I can't have that; it would never do to let the expedition fail."

"No," said Mark. "But let us sit down first."

Bevis did not quite like to leave the sedges, but he could not gainsay the heat, and he was weary, so they left the rough path and went towards the hedge, pushing through the sedges and rushes. It was some distance, and as they came nearer and the ground very gradually rose and became drier, there was a thick growth of coarse grass between the other plants, and presently a dense mass of reed-grass taller than their shoulders. This was now in bloom, and the pollen covered their sleeves as they forced a way through it. The closer they got to the hedge the thicker the grasses became, and there were now stoles of willow, and tall umbelliferous plants called "gix," which gave out an unpleasant scent as they rubbed against or pushed them down and stepped on them. It was hard work to get through, and when at last they reached the hedge they were almost done up.

Now there was a new difficulty, the hedge had grown so close and thick it was impossible to creep through it. They were obliged to follow it, searching for a gap. They could not see a yard in front, so that they could not tell how far they might have to go. The dust-like pollen flying from the shaken grasses and the flowering plants got inside their nostrils and on the roofs of their mouths and in their throats, causing an unbearable thirst and tickling. The flies, gathering in crowds, teased them, and would not be driven away. Now and then something seemed to sting their necks, and, striking the place with the flat hand, a stoatfly dropped, too bloated with blood, like a larger gnat, to attempt to escape the blow.

Pushing through the plants they stumbled into a hollow which they did not see on account of the vegetation till they stepped over the edge and fell in it. Mark struck his knee against a stone, and limped; Bevis scratched his hands and wrist with a bramble. The hollow was a little wet at the bottom, not water, but soft, sticky mud, which clung to their feet like gum; but they scrambled out of it quickly, not really hurt, but out of breath and angry. They were obliged to sit down, crushing down the grasses, to rest a minute.

"Let's go back to the path in the sedges," said Mark.

"I shan't," said Bevis savagely. He got up and went on a few steps, and then took out his knife. "Couldn't we cut a way through the bushes?" he asked. They went nearer the hedge and looked, but it had been kept thick that cattle might not stray into the marsh. The outside twigs could be cut of course, but hawthorn is hard and close-grained. With such little tools as their pocket-knives it would take hours—very likely they would break them.

"If we only had something to drink," said Mark. They had no more apples. Though it was a marsh, though they were on the shore, there was not a drop of water; if they went back to the sedges they could not get at the water, they would sink to the knees in mud first. The tall reed-grass and "gix," and other plants which so impeded their progress, were not high enough to protect them in the least from the sun. The hedge ran north and south, and at noonday gave no shadow. As they went slowly forward, Mark felt the ground first with his spear to prevent their falling into another hollow. They pulled rushes, and bit the soft white part which was cool to the tongue. But the stalks of plants and grass, each so easily bent when taken by itself, in the mass like this began to prove stronger than they were.

They had to part them with their arms first, like swimming, and then push through, and the ceaseless resistance wore out their power. Even Bevis at last agreed that it was not possible, they must go back to the path in the sedges on their right. After standing still a minute to recover themselves they turned to the right and went towards the sedges. In about twenty yards Mark, who had been sounding with his spear, touched something that splashed, he stopped and thrust again, there was no mistake, it was water. On going nearer, and feeling for the bottom with the spear, Mark found it was deep too, he could not reach the bottom. The grasses grew right to the edge, and the water itself was so covered with weeds that, had they not prodded the ground before they moved, they would have stepped over the brink into it. The New Sea, receding, had left a long winding pool in a hollow which shut them off from getting to the path in the sedges unless by returning the weary way they had come.

"This is dreadful," said Mark, when they had followed the water a little distance and were certain they could not cross. "We can't get out and we can't go back; I am so tired, I can't push through much longer."

"We must go on," said Bevis; "somehow or other we must go on." He too dreaded the idea of returning through the entangled vegetation. It was less dense on the verge of the pool than by the hedge, and by feeling their way with the spear they got on for a while. Thirsty as he was Mark could not drink from the weed-grown water; indeed he could not see the water at all for weeds and green scum, and if he pushed these aside with his spear the surface bubbled with marsh gases. Bevis too persuaded him not to drink it. Slowly they worked on, the marsh on one side, and the hedge on the other.

"Look," said Mark presently. "There's a willow; can't we climb up and see round?"

"Yes," said Bevis; and they changed their course to get to it; it was nearer the hedge. They felt the ground rise, it was two yards higher by the willow, and harder; when the sea came up the spot in fact was an islet. There were bushes on it, brambles, and elder in flower; none of these grow in water itself, but flourish on the edge. There were several tall willow-poles. Bevis put down his bow and arrows, took off his jacket (the pockets of which were stuffed full of things), took hold of a pole, and climbed up. Mark did the same with another. The poles were not large enough to bear their weight very high; they got up about six or eight feet.

"There's Sindbad's Island," said Mark, pointing to the right. Far away, beyond the sedges and the reeds, there was a broad strip of clear water, and across it the island of Serendib. "If we only had a canoe."

"Perhaps we could make one," said Bevis. "They make them sometimes of willow—and from oak, only we have nothing to cover the framework; sometimes they weave the rushes so close as to keep out water—"

"I can plait rushes," said Mark; "I can plait eight; but they would not keep out water. What's over the hedge?"

They looked that way; they could see over the thick, close hawthorn, but behind it there rose tall ash-poles, which shut out the view completely.

"It is a thick double-mound," said Bevis. "There's ash in the middle; like that in our field, you know."

In front they could see nothing but the same endless reed-grass, except that there were more bushes and willows interspersed among it, showing that there must be numerous banks. Tired of holding on to the poles, which had no boughs of size enough to rest on, they let themselves gradually slide down. As they descended Mark spied a dove's nest in one of the hawthorn bushes; tired as he was he climbed up the pole again, and looked into it from a higher level. There was an egg in it; he had half a mind to take it, but remembered that it would be awkward to carry.

"We shall never get home," he said, after he had told Bevis of the nest.

"Pooh," said Bevis. "Here's something for you to drink." He had found a great teazle plant, whose leaves formed cups round the stem. In four of these cups there was a little darkish water, which had been there since the last shower. Mark eagerly sipped from the one which had the most, though it was full of drowned gnats; it moistened his lips, but he spluttered most of it out again. It was not only unpleasant to the taste but warm.

"I hate Africa," he shouted; "I *hate* it."

"So do I," said Bevis; "but we've got to get through it somehow." He started again; Mark followed sullenly, and Pan came behind Mark. Thus the spaniel, stepping in the track they made, had the least difficulty of either. Pan's tail drooped, he was very hungry and very thirsty, and he knew it was about the time the dishes were rattling in the kitchen at home.

"Listen," said Mark presently, putting his hand on Bevis's shoulder, and stopping him.

Bevis listened. "I can't hear anything," he said, "except the midsummer hum."

The hum was loud in the air above them, almost shrill, but there was not another sound. Now Mark had called attention to it the noonday silence in that wild deserted place was strange.

"Where are all the things?" said Mark, looking round. "All the birds have gone."

Certainly they could hear none, even the brook-sparrows in the sedges by the New Sea were quiet. There was nothing in sight alive but a few swifts at an immense height above them. Neither wood-pigeon, nor dove, nor thrush called; not even a yellow-hammer.

"I know," whispered Bevis. "I know—they are afraid."

"Afraid?"

"Yes; can't you see Pan does not hunt about?"

"What is it?" asked Mark in an undertone, grasping his spear tightly. "There are no mummies here?"

"No," said Bevis. "It's the serpent, you know; he's a hundred feet long; he's come over from the Unknown Island, and he's waiting in these sedges somewhere to catch something; the birds are afraid to sing."

"Could he swallow a man?" said Mark.

"Swallow a man," with curling lip. "Swallow a buffalo easily."

"Hush! what's that?" A puff of wind rustled the grasses.

"It's the snake," said Mark, and off he tore. Bevis close behind him, Pan at his heels. In this wild panic they dashed quickly through the grasses, which just before had been so wearisome an obstacle. But the heat pulled them up in ten minutes, panting.

"Did you see him?" said Bevis.

"Just a little bit of him—I think," said Mark.

"We've left him behind."

"He'll find us by our track."

"Let's tie Pan up, and let him swallow Pan."

"Where's a rope? Have you any string? Give me your handkerchief."

They were hastily tying their handkerchiefs together, when Mark, looking round to see if the monstrous serpent was approaching, shouted,—

"There's a tree!"

There was a large hollow willow or pollard in the hedge. They rushed to it, they clasped it as shipwrecked men a beam. Mark was first, he got inside on the "touchwood," and scrambled up a little way, then he worked up, his back against one side, and his knees the other. Bevis got underneath, and "bunted" him up. Bunting is shoving with shoulder or hands. There were brambles on the top; Mark crushed through, and in a minute was firmly planted on the top.

"Give me my spear, and your bow, and your hand," he said breathlessly.

The spear and the bow were passed up: Bevis followed, taking Mark's hand just at the last. Mark put the point of his spear downwards to stab the monster. Bevis fitted an arrow to his bow. Pan looked up, but could not climb. They watched the long grasses narrowly, expecting to see them wave from side to side every instant, as the python wound his sinuous way. There was a rustling beneath, but on the other side of the hedge. Bevis looked and saw Pan, who had crept through.

"What are you going to do?" said Mark, as Bevis slung his bow on his shoulder as if it was a rifle, and began to move out on the hollow top of the tree, which as it became hollow had split, and partly arched over. Bevis did not answer: he crept cautiously out on the top which vibrated under him; then suddenly seizing a lissom bough, he slipped off and let himself down. He was inside the hedge that had so long baffled them. Mark saw in an instant, darted his spear down and followed. So soon as he touched ground, off they set running. There were no sedges here, nothing but short grasses and such herbage as grows under the perpetual shade of ash-poles, and they could run easily. The ease of motion was, in itself, a relief, after the struggle in the reed-grass. When they had raced some distance, and felt safe, they stopped.

"Why, this is a wood!" said Mark, looking round. Ash-stoles and poles surrounded them on every side.

"So it is," said Bevis. "No, it's a jungle."

They walked forward and came to an open space, round about a broad spreading oak.

"I shall sit down here," said Bevis.

But as they were about to sit down, Pan, who had woke up when he scented rabbits, suddenly disappeared in a hollow.

"What's that," said Mark. He went to see, and heard a sound of lapping.

"Water!" shouted Mark, and Bevis came to him. Deep down in a narrow channel there was the merest trickle of shallow water, but running, and clear as crystal. It came from chalk, and it was limpid. Pan could drink, but they could not. His hollow tongue lapped it up like a spoon; but it was too shallow to scoop up in the palm of the hand, and they had no tube of "gix," or reed, or oat straw, or buttercup stalk to suck through. They sprang into the channel itself, alighting on a place the water did not cover, but with the stream under their feet they could not drink. Nothing but a sparrow could have done so.

Presently Bevis stooped, and with his hands scratched away the silt which formed the bottom, a fine silt of powdered chalk, almost like quicksand, till he had made a bowl-like cavity. The stream soon filled it, but then the water was thick, being disturbed, and they had to wait till it had settled. Then they lapped too, very carefully, with the hollow palm, taking care that the water which ran through their fingers should fall below, and not above the bowl, or the weight of the drops would disturb it again. With perseverance they satisfied their thirst; then they returned to the oak, and took out their provisions; they could eat now.

"This is a jolly jungle," said Mark, with his mouth full.

"That's a banyan," said Bevis, pointing with the knuckle-end of the drum-stick he was gnawing at the oak over them. "It's about eleven thousand years old."

Then Mark took the drum-stick, and had his turn at it. When it was polished, Pan had it: he cracked it across with his teeth, just as the hyenas did in the cave days, for the animals never learnt to split bones, as the earliest men did. Pan cracked it very disconsolately: his heart was with the fleshpots.

Boom!

They starred. It was the same peculiar sound they had heard before, and seemed to come from an immense distance. A pheasant crowed as he heard it in the jungle close by them, and a second farther away.

"What can it be?" whispered Mark. "Is there anything here?"—glancing around.

"There may be some genii," said Bevis quietly. "Very likely there are some genii: they are everywhere. But I do not know what that was. Listen!"

They listened: the wood was still; so still, they could hear a moth or a chafer entangled in the leaves of the oak overhead, and trying to get out. Looking up there, the sky was blue and clear, and the sunlight fell brightly on the open space by the streamlet. There was nothing but the hum. The long, long summer days seem gradually to dispose the mind to expect something unusual. Out of such an expanse of light, when the earth is tangibly in the midst of a vast illumined space, what may not come?—perhaps something more than is common to the senses. The mind opens with the enlarging day.

It is said the sandhills of the desert under the noonday sun emit strange sounds; that the rocky valleys are vocal; the primeval forest speaks in its depths; hollow ocean sends a muttering to the becalmed vessel; and up in the mountains the bound words are set loose. Of old times the huntsmen in our own woods met the noonday spirit under the leafy canopy.

Bevis and Mark listened, but heard nothing, except the entangled chafer, the midsummer hum, and, presently, Pan snuffling, as he buried his nostrils in his hair to bite a flea. They laughed at him, for his eyes were staring, and his flexible nostrils turned up as if his face was not alive but stuffed. The boom did not come again, so they finished their dinner.

"I feel jolly lazy," said Mark. "You ought to put the things down on the map."

"So I did," said Bevis, and he got out his brown paper, and Mark held it while he worked. He drew Fir-Tree Gulf and the Nile.

"Write that there is a deep hole there," said Mark, "and awful crocodiles: that's it. Now Africa—you want a very long stroke there; write reeds and bamboos."

"No, not bamboos, papyrus," said Bevis. "Bamboos grow in India, where we are now. There's some," pointing to a tall wild parsnip, or "gix," on the verge of the streamlet.

"I'm so lazy," said Mark. "I shall go to sleep."

"No you won't," said Bevis. "I ought to go to sleep, and you ought to watch. Get your spear, and now take my bow."

Mark took the bow sullenly.

"You ought to stand up, and walk up and down."

"I can't," said Mark very short.

"Very well; then go farther away, where you can see more round you. There, sit down there."

Mark sat down at the edge of the shadow of the oak. "Don't you see you can look into the channel; if there are any savages they are sure to creep up that channel. Do you see?"

"Yes, I see," said Mark.

"And mind nothing comes behind that woodbine," pointing to a mass of woodbine which hung from some ash-poles, and stretched like a curtain across the view there. "That's a very likely place for a tiger: and keep your eye sharp on those nut-tree bushes across the brook—most likely you'll see the barrel of a matchlock pushed through there."

"I ought to have a matchlock," said Mark.

"So you did; but we had to start with what we had, and it is all the more glory to us if we *get* through. Now mind you keep awake."

"Yes," said Mark.

Bevis, having given his orders, settled himself very comfortably on the moss at the foot of the oak, tilted his hat aside to shelter him still more, and, with a spray of ash in his hand to ward off the flies, began to forget. In a minute up he started.

"Mark!"

"Yes;" still sulky.

"There's another oak—no, it's a banyan up farther; behind you."

"I know."

"Well, if you hear any rustle there, it's a python."

"Very well."

"And those dead leaves and sticks in the hole there by the stump of that old tree?"

"I see."

"There's a cobra there."

"All right."

"And if a shadow comes over suddenly."

"What's that, then?" said Mark.

"That's the roc from Sinbad's Island."

"I say, Bevis," as Bevis settled himself down again. "Bevis, don't go to sleep."

"Pooh!"

"But it's not nice."

"Rubbish."

"Bevis."

"Don't talk silly."

In a minute Bevis was fast asleep. He always slept quickly, and the heat and the exertion made him forget himself still quicker.

Chapter Seven
The Jungle

Mark was alone. He felt without going nearer that Bevis was asleep, and dared not wake him lest he should be called a coward. He moved a little way so as to have the oak more at his back, and to get a clearer view on all sides. Then he looked up at the sky, and whistled very low. Pan, who was half asleep too, got up slowly, and came to him; but finding that there was nothing to eat, and disliking to be stroked and patted on such a hot day, he went back to his old place, the barest spot he could find, mere dry ground.

Mark sat, bow and arrow ready in his hand, the arrow on the string, with the spear beside him, and his pocket-knife with the big blade open, and looked into the jungle. It was still and silent. The chafer had got loose, and there was nothing but the hum overhead. He kept the strictest watch, scarce allowing himself to blink his eyes. Now he looked steadily into the brushwood he could see some distance, his glance found a way through between the boughs, till presently, after he had searched out those crevices, he could command a circle of view.

Like so many slender webs his lines of sight thus drawn through mere chinks of foliage radiated from a central spot, and at the end of each he seemed as if he could feel if anything moved as much as he could see it. Each of these webs strained at his weary mind, and even in the shade the strong glare of the summer noon pressed heavily on his eyelids. Had anything moved, a bird or moth, or had the leaves rustled, it would have relieved him. This expectation was a continual effort. His eyes closed, he opened them, frowned and blinked; then he reclined on one arm as an easier position. His eyes closed, the shrill midsummer hum sounded low and distant, then loud, suddenly it ceased—he was asleep.

The sunburnt woodbine, the oaks dotted with coppery leaves where the second shoot appeared, the ash-poles rising from the hollow stoles, and whose pale sprays touching above formed a green surface, hazel with white nuts, stiff, ragged thistles on the stream bank, burrs with brown-tipped hooks, the hard dry ground, all silent, fixed, held in the light.

The sun slipped through the sky like a yacht under the shore where the light wind coming over a bank just fills the sails, but leaves the surface smooth. Through the smooth blue the sun slipped silently, and no white fleck of foam cloud marked his speed. But in the deep narrow channel of the streamlet there was a change—the tiny trickle of water was no longer illumined by the vertical beams, a slight slant left it to run in shadow.

Burr! came a humble-bee whose drone was now put out as he went down among the grass and leaves, now rose again as he travelled. Burr! The faintest breath of air moved without rustling the topmost leaves of the oaks. The humble-bee went on, and disappeared behind the stoles.

A little flicker of movement happened among the woodbine, not to be seen of itself, but as a something interrupting the light like a larger mote crossing the beam. The leaves of the woodbine in one place were drawn together and coated with a white web and a tiny bird came to take away the destroyer. Then mounting to a branch of ash he sang, "Sip, sip—chip, chip!"

Again the upper leaves of the oak moved and jostling together caused a slight sound. Coo! coo! there was a dove beyond the hazel bushes across the stream. The shadow was more aslant and rose up the stalks of the rushes in the channel. Over the green surface of the ash sprays above, the breeze drew and rippled it like water. A jay came into the farther oak and scolded a distant mate.

Presently Pan awoke, nabbed another flea, looked round and shook his ears, from which some of the hair was worn by continual rubbing against the bushes under which he had crept for so many years. He felt thirsty, and remembering the stream, went towards it, passing very lightly by Bevis, so closely as to almost brush his hat. The slight pad, pad of his paws on the moss and earth conveyed a sense of something moving near him to Bevis' mind. Bevis instantly sat up, so quickly, that the spaniel, half alarmed, ran some yards.

Directly Bevis sat up he saw that Mark had fallen asleep. He thought for a moment, and then took a piece of string from his pocket. Stepping quietly up to Mark he made a slip-knot in the string, lifted Mark's arm and put his hand through the loop above the wrist, then he jerked it tight. Mark scrambled up in terror—it might have been the python:—

"O! I say!"

Before he could finish, Bevis had dragged him two or three steps towards an ash-pole, when Mark, thoroughly awake, jerked his arm free, though the string hung to it.

"How dare you?" said Bevis, snatching at the string, but Mark pushed him back. "How dare you? you're a prisoner."

"I'm not," said Mark very angrily.

"Yes, you are; you were asleep."

"I don't care."

"I will tie you up."

"You shan't."

"If you sleep at your post, you have to be tied to a tree, you know you have, and be left there to starve."

"I won't."

"You must, or till the tigers have you. Do you hear? stand still!"

Bevis tried to secure him, Mark pushed him in turn.

"You're a wretch."

"I hate you!"

"I'll kill you!"

"I'll shoot you!"

Mark darted aside and took his spear; Bevis had his bow in an instant and began to draw it. Mark, knowing that Bevis would shoot his hardest, ran for the second oak. Bevis in his haste pulled hard, but let the arrow slip before he could take aim. It glanced upon a bough and shot up nearly straight into the air, gleaming as it went—a streak of light—in the sunshine. Mark stopped by the oak, and before Bevis could fetch another arrow poised his spear and threw it. The spear flew direct at the enemy, but in his haste Mark forgot to throw high enough, he hurled it point-blank, and the hardened point struck the earth and chipped up crumbling pieces of dry ground; then it slid like a serpent some way through the thin grasses.

Utterly heedless of the spear, which in his rage he never saw, Bevis picked up an arrow from the place where he had slept, fitted the notch to the string and looked for Mark, who had hidden behind the other oak. Guessing that he was there, Bevis ran towards it, when Mark shouted to him,—

"Stop! I say, it's not fair; I have nothing, and you'll be a coward."

Bevis paused, and saw the spear lying on the ground.

"Come and take your spear," he said directly; "I won't shoot." He put his bow on the ground. Mark ran out, and had his spear in a moment. Bevis stooped to lift his bow, but suddenly in his turn cried,—

"Stop! Don't throw; I want to say something."

Mark, who had poised his spear, put it down again on the grass.

"We ought not to fight now," said Bevis. "You know we are exploring, people never fight then, else the savages kill those who are left; they wait till they get home, and then fight."

"So they do," said Mark; "but I shall not be left tied to a tree."

"Very well, not this time. Now we must shake hands."

They shook hands, and Pan, seeing that there was now no danger of a chance knock from a flying stick, came forth from the bush where he had taken shelter.

"But you want everything your own way," said Mark sulkily.

"Of course I do," said Bevis, glaring at him, "I'm captain."

"But you do when you are not captain."

"You are a big story."

"I'm not."

"You are."

"I'm not."

"People are not to contradict me," said Bevis, looking very defiant indeed, and standing bolt upright. "I say I am captain."

Mark did not reply, but picked up his bat, which had fallen off. Without another word each gathered up his things, then came the question which way to go? Bevis would not consult his companion; his companion would not speak first. Bevis shut his lips very tight, pressing his teeth together; he determined to continue on and try and get round the New Sea. He was not sure, but fancied they should do so by keeping somewhat to the right. He walked to the channel of the stream, sprang across it, and pushing his way through the hazel bushes, went in that direction; Mark followed silently, holding his arm up to stop the boughs which as Bevis parted them swung back sharply.

After the hazel bushes there was fairly clear walking between the ash-poles and especially near the oak-trees, each of which had an open space about it. Bevis went as straight as he could, but had to wind in and out round the stoles and sometimes to make a curve when there was a thick bramble bush in the way. As they passed in Indian file under some larger poles, Mark suddenly left the path and began to climb one of them. Bevis stopped, and saw that there was a wood-pigeon's nest. The bird was on the nest, and though she felt the ash-pole tremble as Mark came up, hand over hand, cracking little dead twigs, though her nest shook under her, she stayed till his hand almost touched it. Then she flew up through the pale green ash sprays, and Mark saw there were two eggs, for the sticks of which the nest was made were so thinly put together that, now the bird was gone, he could see the light through, and part of the eggs lying on them.

He brought one of the eggs down in his left hand, sliding down the pole slowly not to break it. The pure white of the wood-pigeon's egg is curiously and delicately mottled like the pores of the finest human skin. The enamel of the surface, though smooth and glossy, has beneath it some water-mark of under texture like the arm of the Queen of Love, glossy white and smooth, yet not encased, but imperceptibly porous to that breath of violet sweetness which announces the goddess. The sunlight fell on the oval as Mark, without a moment's pause, took a pin from the hem of his jacket and blew the egg.

So soon as he had finished, Bevis went on again, and came to some hawthorn bushes, through which they had much trouble to push their way, receiving several stabs from the long thorns. As it was awkward with the egg in his hand, Mark dropped it.

There was a path beyond the hawthorn, very little used, if at all, and green, but still a path—a trodden line—and Bevis went along it, as it seemed to lead in the direction he wished. By the side of the path he presently found a structure of ash sticks, and stopped to look at it. At each end four sticks were driven into the ground, two and two, the tops crossing each other so as to make a small V. Longer sticks were laid in these V's, and others across at each end.

"It's a little house," said Mark, forgetting the quarrel. "Here's some of the straw on the ground; they thatch it in winter and crawl under." (It was about three feet high.)

"I don't know," said Bevis.

"I'm sure it is," said Mark. "They are little men, the savages who live here, they're pigmies, you know."

"So they are," said Bevis, quite convinced, and likewise forgetting his temper. "Of course they are, and that's why the path is so narrow. But I believe it's not a house, I mean not a house to live in. It's a place to worship at, where they have a fetich."

"I think it's a house," said Mark.

"Then where's the fireplace?" asked Bevis decidedly.

"No more there is a fireplace," said Mark thoughtfully. "It's a fetich-place."

Bevis went on again, leaving the framework behind. Across those bars the barley was thrown in autumn for the pheasants, which feed by darting up and dragging down a single ear at a time; thus by keeping the barley off the ground there is less waste. They knew this very well.

"Bevis," said Mark presently.

"Yes."

"Let's leave this path."

"Why?"

"Most likely we shall meet some savages—or perhaps a herd of wild beasts, they rush along these paths in the jungle and crush over everything—perhaps elephants."

"So they do," said Bevis, and hastily stepped out of the path into the wood again. They went under more ash-poles where the pigeons' nests were numerous; they counted five all in sight at once, and only a few yards apart, for they could not see far through the boughs. Some of the birds were sitting, others were not. Mark put up his spear and pushed one off her nest. There was a continual fluttering all round them as the pigeons came down to, or left their places. Never had they seen so many nests—they walked about under them for a long time, doing nothing but look up at them, and talk about them.

"I know," said Bevis, "I know—these savages here think the pigeons sacred, and don't kill them—that's why there are so many."

Not much looking where they were going, they came out into a space where the poles had been cut in the winter, and the stoles bore only young shoots a few feet high. There was a single waggon track, the ruts overhung with grasses and bordered with rushes, and at the end of it, where it turned, they saw a cock pheasant. They tried to go through between the stoles, but the thistles were too thick and the brambles and briars too many; they could flourish here till the ash-poles grew tall and kept away the sun. So they followed the waggon track, which led them again under the tall poles.

To avoid the savages they kept a very sharp lookout, and paused if they saw anything. There was a huge brown crooked monster lying asleep in one place, they could not determine whether an elephant or some unknown beast, till, creeping nearer from stole to bush and bush to stole, they found it to be a thrown oak, from which the bark had been stripped, and the exposed sap had dried brown in the sun. So the vast iguanodon may have looked in primeval days when he laid him down to rest in the brushwood.

"When shall we come to the New Sea again?" said Mark presently, as they were moving more slowly through a thicker growth.

"I cannot think," said Bevis. "If we get lost in this jungle, we may walk and walk and walk and never come to anything except banyan-trees, and cobras, and tigers, and savages."

"Are you sure we have been going straight?"

"How do I know?"

"Did you follow the sun?" asked Mark. "No, indeed, I did not; if you walk towards the sun you will go round and round, because the sun moves."

"I forgot. O! I know, where's the compass?"

"How stupid!" said Bevis. "Of course it was in my pocket all the time."

He took it out, and as he lifted the brazen lid the white card swung to and fro with the vibration of his hand.

"Rest your hand against a pole," said Mark. This support steadied Bevis's hand, and the card gently came to a standstill. The north, with the three feathers, pointed straight at him.

"Now, which way was the sea?" said Mark, trying to think of the direction in which they had last seen it. "It was that side," he said, holding out his right hand; he faced Bevis.

"Yes, it was," said Bevis. "It was on the right hand, now that would be east," (to Mark), "so if we go east we must be right."

He started with the compass in his hand, keeping his eye on it, but then he could not see the stoles or bushes, and walked against them, and the card swung so he could not make a course.

"What a bother it is," he said, stopping, "the card won't keep still. Let me see!" He thought a minute, and as he paused the three feathers settled again. "There's an oak," he said. "The oak is just east. Come on." He went to the oak, and then stopped again.

"I see," said Mark, watching the card till it stopped. "The elder bush is east now."

They went to the elder bush and waited: there was a great thistle east next, and afterwards a bough which had fallen. Thus they worked a bee-line, very slow but almost quite true. The ash-poles rattled now as the breeze freshened and knocked them together.

"What a lot of leaves," said Bevis presently; "I never saw such a lot."

"And they are so deep," said Mark. They had walked on dead leaves for some little while before they noticed them, being so eagerly engaged with the compass. Now they looked the ground was covered with brown beech leaves, so deep, that although their feet sunk into them, they could not feel the firm ground, but walked on a yielding substance. A thousand woodcocks might have thrown them over their heads and hidden easily had it been their time of year. The compass led them straight over the leaves, till in a minute or two they saw that they were in a narrow deep coombe. It became narrower and with steeper sides till they approached the end, when the chalk showed not white but dull as it crumbled, the flakes hanging at the roots of minute plants.

"I don't like these leaves," said Mark. "There may be a cobra, and you can't see him; you may step on him without knowing."

Hastily he and Bevis scrambled a few feet up the chalky side; the danger was so obvious they rushed to escape it before discussing. When they had got over this alarm, they found the compass still told them to go on, which they could not do without scaling the coombe. They got up a good way without much trouble, holding to hazel boughs, for the hazel grows on the steepest chalk cliffs, but then the chalk was bare of all but brambles, whose creepers came down towards them; why do bramble creepers, like water, always come down hill? Under these the chalk was all crumbled, and gave way under the foot, so that if they put one foot up higher it slipped with their weight, and returned them to the same level.

Two rabbits rushed away, and were lost beneath the brambles. Without conscious thinking they walked aslant, and so gained a few feet every ten yards, and then came to a spot where the crust of the top hung over, and from it the roots of beech-trees came curving down into the hollow space in search of earth. To one of these they clung by turns, some of the loose chalky clods fell on them, but they hauled themselves up over the projecting edge. Bevis went first, and took all the weapons from Mark; Pan went a long way round.

At the summit there was a beautiful beech-tree, with an immense round trunk rising straight up, and they sat down on the moss, which always grows at the foot of the beech, to rest after the struggle up. As they sat down they turned round facing the cliff, and both shouted at once, — "The New Sea!"

Chapter Eight
The Witch

The blue water had lost its glitter, for they were now between it and the sun, and the freshening breeze, as it swept over, darkened the surface. They were too far to see the waves, but that they were rising was evident since the water no longer reflected the sky like a mirror. The sky was cloudless, but the water seemed in shadow, rough and hard. It was full half a mile or more down to where the wood touched the shore of the New Sea and shut out their view, so that they could not tell how far it extended. Serendib and the Unknown Island were opposite, and they could see the sea all round them from the height where they sat.

"We left the sea behind us," said Mark. "The compass took us right away from it."

"We began wrong somehow," said Bevis. In fact they had walked in a long curve, so that when they thought the New Sea was on Mark's right, it was really on his left hand. "I must put down on the map that people must go west, not east, or they will never get round."

"It must be thousands of miles round," said Mark; "thousands and thousands."

"So it is," said Bevis, "and only to think nobody ever saw it before you and me."

"What a long way we can see," said Mark, pointing to where the horizon and the blue wooded plain below, beyond the sea, became hazy together. "What country is that?"

"I do not know; no one has ever been there."

"Which way is England?" asked Mark.

"How can I tell when I don't know where we are?"

The ash sprays touching each other formed a green surface beneath them, extending to the right and left—a green surface into which every now and then a wood-pigeon plunged, closing his wings as the sea-birds dive into the sea. They sat in the shadow of the great beech, and the wind, coming up over the wood, blew cool against their faces. The swallows had left the sky, to go down and glide over the rising waves below.

"Come on," said Bevis, incapable of rest unless he was dreaming. "If we keep along the top of the hill we shall know where we are going, and perhaps see a way round presently."

They followed the edge of the low cliff as nearly as they could, walking under the beeches where it was cool and shady, and the wind blow through. Twice they saw squirrels, but they were too quick, and Bevis could not get a shot with his bow.

"We ought to take home something," said Mark. "Something wonderful. There ought to be some pieces of gold about, or a butterfly as big as a plate. Can't you see something?"

"There's a dragonfly," said Bevis. "If we can't catch him, we can say we saw one made of emerald, and here's a feather."

He picked up a pheasant's feather. The dragonfly refused to be caught, he rushed up into the air nearly perpendicularly; and seeing another squirrel some way ahead, they left the dragonfly and crept from beech trunk to beech trunk towards him.

"It's a red squirrel," whispered Mark. "That's a different sort." In summer the squirrels are thought to have redder fur than in winter. Mark stopped now, and Bevis went on by himself; but the squirrel saw Pan, who had run along and came out beyond him. Bevis shot as the squirrel rushed up a tree, and his arrow struck the bark, quivered a moment, and stuck there.

"The savages will see some one has been hunting," said Mark. "They are sure to see that arrow."

In a few minutes they came to some hazel bushes, and pushing through these there was a lane under them in a hollow ten feet deep. They scrambled down and followed it, and came to a boulder-stone, on which some specks sparkled in the sunshine, so that they had no doubt it was silver ore. Round a curve of the lane they emerged on the brow of a green hill, very steep; they had left the wood behind them. The trees from here hid the New Sea, and in front, not far off, rose the Downs.

"What are those mountains?" asked Mark.

"The Himalayas, of course," said Bevis. "Let's go to them."

They went along the brow, it was delicious walking there, for the sun was now much lower, and the breeze cool, and beneath them were meadows, and a brook winding through. But suddenly they came to a deep coombe—a nullah.

"Look!" said Mark, pointing to a chimney just under them. The square top, blackened by soot, stood in the midst of apple-trees, on whose boughs the young green apples showed. The thatch of the cottage was concealed by the trees.

"A hut!" said Bevis.

"Savages!" said Mark, "I know, I'll pitch a stone down the chimney, and you get your bow ready, and shoot them as they rush out."

"Capital!" said Bevis. Mark picked up a flint, and "chucked" it—it fell very near the chimney, they heard it strike the thatch and roll down. Mark got another, and most likely, having found the range, would have dropped it into the chimney this time, when Bevis stopped him.

"It may be a witch," he said. "Don't you know what John told us? if you pitch a stone down a witch's chimney it goes off bang! and the stone shoots up into the air like a cannon-ball."

"I remember," said Mark. "But John is a dreadful story. I don't believe it."

"No, no more do I. Still we ought to be careful. Let's creep down and look first."

They got down the hillside with difficulty, it was so steep and slippery—the grass being dried by the sun. At the bottom there was a streamlet running along deep in a gully, a little pool of the clearest water to dip from, and a green sparred wicket-gate in a hawthorn hedge about the garden. Peering cautiously through the gate they saw an old woman sitting under the porch beside the open door, with a black teapot on the window-ledge close by, and a blue teacup, in which she was soaking a piece of bread, in one hand.

"It's a witch," whispered Mark. "There's a black cat by the wall-flowers—that's a certain sign."

"And two sticks with crutch-handles," said Bevis. "But just look there." He pointed to some gooseberry bushes loaded with the swelling fruit, than which there is nothing so pleasant on a warm, thirsty day. They looked at the gooseberries, and thirsted for them; then they looked at the witch.

"Let's run in and pick some, and run out quick," whispered Mark.

"You stupid; she'd turn us into anything in a minute."

"Well—shoot her first," said Mark. "Take steady aim; John says if you draw their blood they can't do anything. Don't you remember, they stuck the last one with a prong."

"Horrid cruel," said Bevis.

"So it was," said Mark; "but when you want gooseberries."

"I wish we had some moly," said Bevis; "you know, the plant Ulysses had. Mind before we start next time we must find some. Who knows what fearful magic people we might meet?"

"It was stupid not to think of it," said Mark. "Do you know, I believe she's a mummy."

"Why?"

"She hasn't moved; and I can't see her draw her breath."

"No more she does. This is a terrible place."

"Can we get away without her seeing?"

"I believe she knows we're here now, and very likely all we have been saying."

"Did she make that curious thunder we heard?"

"No; a witch isn't strong enough; it wants an enchanter to do that."

"But she knows who did it?"

"Of course she does. There, she's moved her arm; she's alive. Aren't those splendid gooseberries?"

"I'll go in," said Bevis; "you hold the gate open, so that I can run out."

"So I will; don't go very near."

Bevis fitted an arrow to the string, and went up the garden path. But as he came near, and saw how peaceful the old lady looked, he removed the arrow from the string again. She took off her spectacles as he came up; he stopped about ten yards from her.

"Mrs Old Woman, are you a witch?"

"No, I bean't a witch," said the old lady; "I wishes I was; I'd soon charm a crock o' gold."

"Then, if you are not a witch, will you let us have some gooseberries? here's sixpence."

"You med have some if you want's 'em; I shan't take yer money."

"What country is this?" said Bevis, going closer, as Mark came up beside him.

"This be Calais."

"Granny, don't you know who they be?" said a girl, coming round the corner of the cottage. She was about seventeen, and very pretty, with the bloom which comes on sweet faces at that age. Though they were but boys they were tall, and both handsome; so she had put a rose in her bosom. "They be Measter Bevis and Measter Mark. You know, as lives at Longcot."

"Aw, to be sure." The old lady got up and curtseyed. "You'll come in, won't 'ee?"

They went in and sat down on chairs on the stone floor. The girl brought them a plate of the gooseberries and a jug of spring-water. Bevis had not eaten two before he was up and looking at an old gun in the corner; the barrel was rusty, the brass guard tarnished, the ramrod gone, still it was a gun.

"Will it go off?" he said.

"Feyther used to make un," said the girl.

Next he found a big black book, and lifted up the covers, and saw a rude engraving of a plant.

"Is that a magic book?" said he.

"I dunno," she replied. "Mebbe. Granny used to read un."

It was an old herbal.

"Can't you read?" said Bevis.

The girl blushed and turned away.

"A' be a lazy wench," said the old woman. "A' can't read a mossel."

"I bean't lazy."

"You be."

Bevis, quite indifferent to that question, was peering into every nook and corner, but found nothing more.

"Let's go," said he directly.

Mark would not stir till he had finished the gooseberries.

"Tell me the way round the—the—" he was going to say sea, but recollected that they would not be able to understand how he and Mark were on an expedition, nor would he say pond—"round the water," he said.

"The Longpond?" said the girl. "You can't go round, there's the marsh— not unless you goes back to Wood Lane, and nigh handy your place."

"Which way did 'ee come?" asked the old woman.

"They come through the wood," said the girl. "I seen um; and they had the spannul."

She was stroking Pan, who loved her, as she had fed him with a bone. She knew the enormity of taking a strange dog through a wood in the breeding-season.

"How be um going to get whoam?" said the old woman.

"We're going to walk, of course," said Bevis.

"It's four miles."

"Pooh! We've come thousands. Come on, Mark; we'll get round somehow."

But the girl convinced him after a time that it was not possible, because of the marsh and the brook, and showed him too how the shadows of the elms were lengthening in the meadow outside the garden at the foot of the hill. Bevis reluctantly decided that they must abandon the expedition for that day, and return home. The girl offered to show them the way into the road. She led them by a narrow path beside the streamlet in the gully, and then along the steep side of the hill, where there were three or four more cottages, all built on the slope, steep as it was. The path in front of the doors had a kind of breastwork, that folk might not inadvertently tumble over and roll—if not quite sober—into the gully beneath. Yet there were small gardens behind, which almost stood up on end, the vegetables appearing over the roofs.

Upon the breastwork or mound they had planted a few flowers, all yellow, or yellow-tinged, marigolds, sunflowers, wall-flowers, a stray tulip, the gaudiest they knew. These specks of brightness by the dingy walls and grey thatch and whitened turf, for the chalk was but an inch under, came of instinct on that southern slope, as hot Spain flaunts a yellow flag.

Six or eight children were about. One sat crying in the midst of the path, so unconscious under the wrong he had endured as not to see them, and they had to step right over his red head. Some stared at them with unchecked rudeness; one or two curtseyed or tugged at their forelocks. The happiest of all was sitting on the breastwork (of dry earth) eating a small turnip from which he had cut the dirt and rind with a rusty table-knife. As they passed he grinned and pushed the turnip in their faces, as much as to say, "Have a bite." Two or three women looked out after they had gone by, and then some one cried, "Baa!" making a noise like a sheep, at which the girl who led them flushed up, and walked very quickly, with scorn and rage, and hatred flashing in her eye. It was a taunt. Her father was in gaol for lamb-stealing. Her name was Aholibah, and they taunted her by dwelling on the last syllable.

The path went to the top of the hill, and round under a red barn, and now they could see the village, of which these detached cottages were an outpost, scattered over the slope, and on the plain on the other side of the coombe, a quarter of a mile distant.

"There's the windmill," said the girl, pointing to the tower-like building. "You go tow-ward he. He be on the road. Then you turn to the right till you comes to the handing-post. Then you go to the left, and that'll take 'ee straight whoam."

"Thank you," said Bevis. "I know now; it's not far to Big Jack's house. Please have this sixpence," and he gave her the coin, which he had unconsciously held in his hand ever since he had taken it out to pay for the gooseberries. It was all he had; he could not keep his money.

She took it, but her eyes were on him, and not on the money; she would have liked to have kissed him. She watched them till she saw they had got into the straight road, and then went back, but not past the cottages.

They found the road very long, very long and dull, and dusty and empty, except that there was a young labourer—a huge fellow—lying across a flint heap asleep, his mouth open and the flies thick on his forehead. Bevis pulled a spray from the hedge and laid it gently across his face. Except for the sleeping labourer, the road was vacant, and every step they took they went slower and slower. There were no lions here, or monstrous pythons, or anything magic.

"We shall never get home," said Mark.

"I don't believe we ever shall," said Bevis; "I hate this road."

While they yawned and kicked at stray flints, or pelted the sparrows on the hedge, a dog-cart came swiftly up behind them. It ran swift and smooth and even balanced, the slender shafts bending slightly like the spars of a yacht.

It was drawn by a beautiful chestnut mare, too powerful by far for many, which struck out with her fore-feet as if measuring space and carrying the car of a god in the sky, throwing her feet as if there were no road but elastic air beneath them. The man was very tall and broad and sat upright—a wonderful thing in a countryman. His head was broad like himself, his eyes blue, and he had a long thick yellowy beard. The reins were strained taut like a yacht's cordage, but the mare was in the hollow of his strong hand.

They did not hear the hoofs till he was close, for they were on a flint heap, searching for the best to throw.

"It's Jack," said Mark.

Jack looked them very hard in the face, but it did not seem to dawn upon him who they were till he had gone past a hundred yards, and then he pulled up and beckoned. He said nothing but tapped the seat beside him. Bevis climbed up in front, Mark knelt on the seat behind—so as to look in the direction they were going. They drove two miles and Jack said nothing, then he spoke:—

"Where have you been?"

"To Calais."

"Bad—bad," said Jack. "Don't go there again." At the turnpike it took him three minutes to find enough to pay the toll. He had a divine mare, his harness, his cart were each perfect. Yet for all his broad shoulders he could barely muster up a groat. He pulled up presently when there were but two fields between them and the house at Longcot; he wanted to go down the lane, and they alighted to walk across the fields. After they had got down and were just turning to mount the gate, and the mare obeying the reins had likewise half turned. Jack said,—

"Hum!"

"Yes," said Mark from the top bar.

"How are they all at home?" i.e. at Mark's.

"Quito well," said Mark.

"All?" said Jack again.

"Frances bruised her arm—"

"Much?" anxiously.

"You can't see it—her skin's like a plum," said Mark; "if you just pinch it it shows."

"Hum!" and Jack was gone.

Late in the evening they tried hard to catch the donkey, that Mark might ride home. It was not far, but now the day was over he was very tired, so too was Bevis. Tired as they were, they chased the donkey up and down—six times as far as it was to Mark's house—but in vain, the moke knew them of old, and was not to be charmed or cowed. He showed them his heels, and they failed. So Mark stopped and slept with Bevis, as he had done so many times before. As they lay awake in the bedroom, looking out of the window opposite at a star, half awake and half asleep, suddenly Bevis started up on his arm.

"Let's have a war," he said.

"That would be first-rate," said Mark, "and have a great battle."

"An awful battle," said Bevis, "the biggest and most awful ever known."

"Like Waterloo?" said Mark.

"Pooh!"

"Agincourt?"

"Pooh!"

"Mal—Mal," said Mark, trying to think of Malplaquet.

"Oh! more than anything," said Bevis; "somebody will have to write a history about it."

"Shall we wear armour?"

"That would be bow and arrow time. Bows and arrows don't make any banging."

"No more they do. It wants lots of banging and smoke—else its nothing."

"No; only chopping and sticking."

"And smashing and yelling."

"No—and that's nothing."

"Only if we have rifles," said Mark thoughtfully; "you see, people don't see one another; they are so far off, and nobody stands on a bridge and keeps back all the enemy all by himself."

"And nobody has a triumph afterwards with elephants and chariots, and paints his face vermilion."

"Let's have bow and arrow time," said Mark; "it's much nicer—and you sell the prisoners for slaves and get heaps of money, and do just as you like, and plough up the cities that don't please you."

"Much nicer," said Bevis; "you very often kill all the lot and there's nothing silly. I shall be King Richard and have a battle-axe—no, let's be the Normans."

"Wouldn't King Arthur do?"

"No; he was killed, that would be stupid. I've a great mind to be Charlemagne."

"Then I shall be Roland."

"No; you must be a traitor."

"But I want to fight your side," said Mark.

"How many are there we can get to make the war?"

They consulted, and soon reckoned up fourteen or fifteen.

"It will be jolly awful," said Mark; "there will be heaps of slain."

"Let's have Troy," said Bevis.

"That's too slow," said Mark; "it lasted ten years."

"Alexander the Great—let's see; whom did he fight?"

"I don't know; people nobody ever heard of—nobody particular, Indians and Persians and all that sort."

"I know," said Bevis; "of course! I know. Of course I shall be Julius Caesar!"

"And I shall be Mark Antony."

"And we will fight Pompey."

"But who shall be Pompey?" said Mark.

"Pooh! there's Bill, and Wat, and Ted; anybody will do for Pompey."

Chapter Nine
Swimming

"Put your hands on the rail. Hold it as far off as you can. There—now let the water lift your feet up behind you."

Bevis took hold of the rail, which was on a level with the surface, and then leaning his chest forward upon the water, felt his legs and feet gradually lifted up, till he floated. At first he grasped the rail as tight as he could, but in a minute he found that he need not do so. Just to touch the rail lightly was enough, for his extended body was as buoyant as a piece of wood. It was like taking a stick and pressing it down to the bottom, and then letting it go, when it would shoot up directly. The water felt deliciously soft under him, bearing him up far more gently than the grass, on which he was so fond of lying.

"Mark!" he shouted. "Do like this. Catch hold of the rail—it's capital!"

Mark, who had been somewhat longer undressing than impatient Bevis, came in and did it, and there they both floated, much delighted. The water was between three and four feet deep. When Bevis's papa found that they could not be kept from roaming, and were bent on boating on the Longpond, which was a very different thing to the shallow brook, where they were never far from shore, and out of which they could scramble, he determined to teach Bevis and his friend to swim. Till Bevis could swim, he should never feel safe about him; and unless his companion could swim too, it was of no use, for in case of accident, one would be sure to try and save the other, and perhaps be dragged down.

They had begged very hard to be allowed to have one of the boats in order to circumnavigate the New Sea, which it was so difficult to walk round; and he promised them if they would really try and learn to swim, that they should have the boat as a reward. He took them to a place near the old quarry they had discovered, in one corner of Fir-Tree Gulf, where the bottom was of sand, and shelved gently for a long way out; a line of posts and rails running into the water, to prevent cattle straying, as they could easily do where it was shallow like this. The field there, too, was away from any road, so that they could bathe at all times. It was a sunny morning, and Bevis, eager for his lesson, had torn off his things, and dashed into the water, like Pan.

"Now try one hand," said his "governor."

"Let one hand lie on the water—put your arm out straight—and hold the rail with the other."

Bevis, rather reluctantly, did as he was told. He let go with his right hand, and stretched it out,—his left hand held him up just as easily, and his right arm seemed to float of itself on the surface. But now, as the muscles of his back and legs unconsciously relaxed, his legs drew up under him, and he bottomed with his feet and stood upright.

"Why's that?" he said. "Why did I come up like that?"

"You must keep yourself a little stiff," said the governor; "not rigid—not quite stiff—just feel your muscles then."

Bevis did it again, and floated with one hand only on the rail: he found he had also to keep his left arm quite straight and firm. Then he had to do it with only two fingers on; while Mark and the governor stood still, that no ripple might enter his mouth, which was only an inch above the surface. Next, Mark was taken in hand, and learnt the same things; and having seen Bevis do it, he had not the least difficulty. The governor left them awhile to practise by themselves, and swam across to the mouth of the Nile, on the opposite side of the gulf. When he came back he found they had got quite confident; so confident, that Bevis, thinking to surpass this simple lesson, had tried letting go with both hands, when his chin immediately went under, and he struggled up spluttering.

The governor laughed. "I thought you would do that," he said. "You only want a little—a very little support, just two fingers on the rail; but you must have some, and when you swim you have to supply it by your own motion. But you see how little is wanted."

"I see," said Bevis. "Why, we can very nearly swim now—can't we, Mark?"

"Of course we can," said Mark, kicking up his heels and making a tremendous splash.

"Now," said the governor, "come here;" and he made Bevis go on his knees in shallow water, and told him to put both hands on the bottom. He did so; and when he was on all fours, facing the shore, the water only reached just above his elbow, which was not deep enough, so he had to move backwards till it touched his chest. He had then to extend his legs behind him, till the water lifted them up, while his hands remained on the bottom. His chest rested on the water, and all his body was buoyed up in the same pleasant way as when he had hold of the rail.

By letting his arms bend or give a little, he could tell exactly how much the water would bear him up, exactly how strong it was under him. He let himself sink till his chin was in the water and it came halfway to his lower lip, while he had his head well back, and looked up at the sycamore-trees growing in the field above the quarry. Then he floated perfectly, and there seemed not the least pressure on his hands; there was a little, but so little it appeared nothing, and he could fancy himself swimming.

"Now walk along with your hands," said the governor.

Bevis did so; and putting one hand before the other, as a tumbler does standing on his head, moved with ease, his body floating, and having no weight at all. One hand would keep him, or even one finger when he put it on a stone at the bottom so that it did not sink in as it would have done into the sand; but if he extended his right arm, it had a tendency to bring his toes down to the bottom. Mark did the same thing, and there they crawled about in the shallow water on their hands only, and the rest floating, laughing at each other. They could hardly believe that it was the water did it; it kept them up just as if they were pieces of wood. The governor left them to practise this while he dressed, and then made them get out, as they had been in long enough for one morning.

"Pan does not swim like you do," said Mark, as they were walking home.

"No," said the governor, "he paddles; he runs in the water the same as he does on land."

"Why couldn't we do that?" asked Mark.

"You can, but it is not much use: you only get along so slowly. When you can swim properly, you can copy Pan in a minute."

The governor could not go with them again for two days on account of business; but full of their swimming, they looked in the old bookcase, and found a book in which there were instructions, and among other things they read that the frog was the best model. Out they ran to look for a frog; but as it was sunny there were none visible, till Mark remembered there was generally one where the ivy of the garden wall had spread over the ground in the corner.

In that cool place they found one, and Bevis picked it up. The frog was cold to the touch even in the summer day, so they put it on a cabbage-leaf and carried it to the stone trough in the yard. No sooner did it feel the water than the frog struck out and crossed the trough, first in one direction, and then in another, afterwards swimming all round close to the sides, but unable to land, as the stone was to it like a wall.

"He kicks," said Mark, leaning over the trough; "he only kicks; he doesn't use his arms."

The frog laid out well with his legs, but kept his forelegs, or arms, still, or nearly so.

"Now, what's the good of a frog?" said Bevis; "men don't swim like that."

"It's very stupid," said Mark; "he's no model at all."

"Not a bit."

The frog continued to go round the trough much more slowly.

"No use watching him."

So they went away, but before they had gone ten yards Bevis ran back.

"He can't get out," he said; and placing the cabbage-leaf under the frog, he lifted the creature out of the trough and put him on the ground. No sooner was the frog on the ground than he went under the trough in the moist shade there, for the cattle as they drank splashed a good deal over. When they told the governor, he said that what they had noticed was correct, but the frog was a good model in two things nevertheless; first in the way he kicked, and secondly in the way he leaned his chest on the water. But a man had to use his arms so as to balance his body and keep his chin and mouth from going under, besides the assistance they give as oars to go forward.

Next morning they went to the bathing-place again. Bevis had now to hold the rail as previously, but when he had got it at arm's length he was told to kick like the frog.

"Draw your knees up close together and kick, and send your feet wide apart," said the governor. Bevis did so, and the thrust of his legs sent him right up against the rail. He did this several times, and was then ordered to go on hands and knees in the shallow water, just as he had done before, and let his legs float up. When they floated he had to kick, to draw his knees up close together, and then strike his feet back wide apart. The thrust this time lifted his hands off the bottom on which they had been resting, lifted them right up, and sent him quite a foot nearer the shore. His chest was forced against the water like an inclined plane, and he was thus raised an inch or so. When the impulse ceased he sank as much, and his hands touched the bottom once more.

This pleased him greatly—it was quite half-swimming; but he found it necessary to be careful while practising it that there were no large stones on the bottom, and that he did not get in too shallow water, else he grazed his knees. In the water you scarcely feel these kind of hurts, and many a bather has been surprised upon getting out to find his knees or legs bruised, or even the skin off, from contact with stones or gravel, of which he was unaware at the time.

Mark had no difficulty in doing the same, it was even easier for him, as he had only to imitate, which is not so hard as following instructions. The second, indeed, often learns quicker than the first. They kicked themselves along in fine style.

"Keep your feet down," said the governor; "don't let them come above the surface, and don't splash. Mark, you are not drawing your knees up, you are only lifting your heels; it makes all the difference."

He then made them hold on to the rail in the deepest water they could fathom—standing himself between them and the deeper water—and after letting their legs float, ordered them to kick there, but to keep their arms straight and stiff, not to attempt to progress, only to practise the kick. The object was that they might kick deep and strong, and not get into a habit of shallow kicking, as they might while walking on their hands on the sand. All that lesson they had to do nothing but kick.

In a day or two they were all in the water again, and after a preliminary splashing, just to lot off their high spirits—otherwise they would not pay attention—serious business began.

"Now," said the governor, "you must begin to use your arms. You are half-independent of touching the bottom already—you can feel that you can float without your feet touching anything; now you must try to float altogether. You know the way I use mine."

They had seen him many times, and had imitated the motion on shore, first putting the flat hands together, thumb to thumb; the thumbs in their natural position, and not held under the palm; the tips of the thumbs crossing (as sculls cross in sculling); the fingers together, but not squeezed tight, a little interstice between them matters nothing, while if always squeezed tight it causes a strain on the wrist. The flat hands thus put together held four to six inches in front of the breast, and then shot out—not with a jerk, quick, but no savage jerk, which wastes power—and the palms at the extremity of the thrust turned partly aside, and more as they oar the water till nearly vertical.

Do not attempt a complete sweep—a complete half-circle—oar them round as far as they will go easily without an effort to the shoulders, and then bring them back. The object of not attempting a full sweep is that the hands may come back easily, and without disturbing the water in front of the chest and checking progress, as they are apt to do. They should slip back, and then the thumbs being held naturally, just as you would lay your flat hand on the table, they do not meet with resistance as they do if held under the palm. If the fingers are kept squeezed tight together when the hands are brought back to the chest, should they vary a hair's breadth from a level position they stop progress exactly like an oar held still in the water, and it is very difficult to keep them absolutely level. But if the fingers are the least degree apart, natural, if the hand inclines a trifle, the fingers involuntarily open and the water slips through, besides which, as there is no strain, the hands return level with so much greater ease. The thrust forward is so easy—it is learnt in a moment—you can imitate it the first time you see it—that the bringing back is often thought of no account. In fact, the bringing back is *the* point, and if it be not studied you will never swim well. This he had told them from time to time on shore, and they had watched him as he swam slowly by them, on purpose that they might observe the manner. But to use the arms properly on shore, when they pass through air and meet with no resistance, is very different to using them properly in the water.

Bevis had to stand facing the shore in water as deep as his chest; then to stoop a little—one foot in front of the other for ease—till his chin nearly rested on the surface, and then to strike out with his arms. He was not to attempt anything with his feet, simply to stand and try the stroke. He put his flat hands together, pushed them out, and oared them round as he had often done on land. As he oared them round they pushed him forward, so that he had to take a step on the bottom; they made him walk a step forward. This he had to repeat twenty times, the governor standing by, and having much trouble to make him return his hauds to his chest without obstructing his forward progress.

Bevis became very impatient now to swim arms and legs together; he was sure he could do it, for his arms, as they swept back, partly lifted him up and pushed him on.

"Very well," said the governor. "Go and try. Here, Mark."

He took Mark in hand, but before they had had one trial Bevis had started to swim, and immediately his head went under unexpectedly, so that he came up spluttering, and had to sit on the rail till he could get the water out of his throat. While he sat there in no good temper Mark had his lesson. The governor then went for a swim himself, being rather tired of reiterating the same instructions, leaving them to practise. On his return— he did not go far, only just far enough to recover his patience—he set them to work at another thing.

Bevis had to go on his hands on the bottom as he had done before, and let his limbs float behind. Then he was told to try striking out with the right hand, keeping the left on the sand to support himself. He did so, and as his arm swept back it pushed him forward just as an oar would a boat. The next time he did it he kicked with his legs at the same moment, and the impetus of the kick and the motion of his right arm together lifted his left hand momentarily off the bottom, and sent him along. This he did himself without being told, the idea of doing so would occur to any one in the same position.

"That's right," said the governor. "Do that again."

Bevis did it again and again, and felt now that he was three-parts swimming; he swam with his legs, and his right arm, and only just touched the bottom with his left hand. After he had repeated it six or seven times he lifted his left hand a little way, and made a quarter stroke with it too, and then jumped up and shouted that he could swim.

Mark had to have his lesson some yards away, for Bevis had so splashed the water in his excitement that it was thick with the sand he had disturbed. Bevis continued his trials, raising his left arm a little more every time till he could very nearly use both together. They were then both set to work to hold on to the rail, let their limbs float, and strike out with one arm, alternately left and right, kicking at the same moment. This was to get into the trick of kicking and striking out with the hands together. Enough had now been done for that morning.

They came up again the next day, and the governor left them this time almost to themselves to practise what they had learnt. They went on their hands on the sand, let their limbs float, and by degrees began to strike out with both hands, first lifting the left hand a few inches, then more, till presently, as they became at home in the water, they could nearly use both.

The next time they bathed the governor set Bevis a fresh task. He was made to stand facing the shore in water as deep as his chest, then to lean forward gently on it—without splash—and to strike out with both his arms and legs together. He did it immediately, at the first trial, but of course stood up directly. Next he was told to try and make two strokes—one is easily made, but the difficulty is when drawing up the knees and bringing the hands back for the second stroke. The chin is almost certain to go under, and some spluttering to follow. Bevis did his best, and held his breath, and let his head go down well till he drew some water up his nostrils, and was compelled to sit on the rail and wait till he could breathe properly again.

Mark tried with exactly the same result. The first stroke when the feet pushed from the ground was easy; but when he endeavoured to draw up his knees for the second, down went his head.

The only orders they received were to keep on trying.

Two days afterwards they bathed again, but though they asked the governor to tell them something else he would not do so, he ordered them to try nothing but the same thing over and over again, to face the shore and strike out. If they liked they could push forward very hard with their feet, if it was done without splash, and the impetus would last through two strokes, and help to keep the body up while they drew up their knees for the second stroke. Then he went for a swim across to the Nile and left them.

They tried their very hardest, and then went on their hands on the sand to catch the idea of floating again. After that they succeeded, but so nearly together that neither could claim to be first. They pushed off from the ground hard, struck out, drew up their knees and recovered their hands, and made the second stroke. They had to hold their breath while they did it, for their mouths *would* go under, but still it was done. Shouting to the governor to come back they threw themselves at the water, bold as spaniels dashing in, wild with delight.

"You can swim," said the governor as he approached.

"Of course we *can*," said Bevis, rushing out in the field for a dance on the sward, and then back splash into the water again. That morning they could hardly be got away from it, and insisted on bathing next day whether convenient or not, so the governor was obliged to accompany them. This time he took the punt, and let them row him to the bathing-place. The lake was too deep there for poling. They had been in boats with him before, and could row well; it is remarkable that there is nothing both boys and girls learn so quickly as rowing. The merest little boy of five years old will learn to handle an oar in a single lesson. They grounded the punt and undressed on the sward where there was more room.

"Now," said the governor, as they began to swim their two strokes again, "now do this—stand up to your chest, and turn towards the rail, and when you have finished the second stroke catch hold of it."

Bevis found that this was not so easy as it sounded, but after five or six attempts he did it, and then of his own motion stood back an extra yard and endeavoured to swim three strokes, and then seize it. This was very difficult and he could not manage it that morning. Twice more the governor came with them and they had the punt, and on the second time they caught the third stroke. They pushed off, that was one stroke, swam one good stroke while floating, and made a third partly complete stroke, and seized the rail.

"That will do," said the governor. He was satisfied: his object from the beginning had been so to teach them that they could teach themselves. With a band beneath the chest he could have suspended them (one at a time) from the punt in deep water, and so taught them, but he considered it much better to let them gradually acquire a knowledge of how far the water would buoy them up, and where it would fail to do so, so as to become perfectly confident, but not *too* confident. For water, however well you can swim, is not a thing to be played with. They had seen now that everything could be done in water no deeper than the chest, and even less than that, so that he had reason to believe if left to themselves they would not venture further out till quite competent. He had their solemn promise not to go into deeper water than their shoulders. If you go up to your chin, the slightest wavelet will lift you off your feet, and in that way many too venturesome people have been drowned not twelve inches from safety.

They might go to their shoulders, always on condition of facing the shore and swimming towards it. When they thought they could swim well enough to go out of their depth he would come and watch. Both promised most faithfully, and received permission to go next time by themselves, and in a short while, if they kept their word, they should have the boat.

If any ladies should chance to read how Bevis and Mark learnt to swim, when they are at the seaside will they try the same plan? Choose a smooth sea and a low tide (only to have it shallow). Kneel in the water. Place the hands on the sand, so that the water may come almost over the shoulders—not quite, say up to them. Then let the limbs and body float. The pleasant sense of suspension without effort will be worth the little trouble it costs. On the softest couch the limbs feel that there is something solid, a hard framework beneath, and so the Sybarites put cushions on the floor under the feet of their couches. On the surface of the buoyant sea there is nothing under the soft couch. They will find that there is no pressure on the hands. They have no weight. Now let them kick with both feet together, and the propulsion will send them forward.

Next use one arm in swimming style. Next use one arm and kick at the same time. Try to use both arms, lifting the hand from the sand a little first, and presently more. Stand up to the chest in water, stoop somewhat and bend the knee, one foot in front of the other, and use the arms together, walking at the same time, so as to get the proper motion of the hands. Place the hands on the sand again, and try to use both arms once more.

Finally, stand up to the chest, face the shore, lean forward, and push off and try a stroke—the feet will easily recover themselves. Presently two strokes will become possible, after awhile three; that is swimming. The sea is so buoyant, so beautiful, that let them only once feel the sense of floating, and they will never rest till they have learned. Ladies can teach themselves so quickly, and swim better than we do. The best swimming I ever saw was done by three ladies together: the waves were large, but they swam with ease, the three graces of the sea.

Chapter Ten
Savages

Bevis and Mark went eagerly to bathe by themselves, but immediately left the direct path. Human beings must be kept taut, or, like a rope, they will slacken. The very first morning they took a leaping-pole with them, a slender ash sapling, rather more than twice their own height, which they picked out from a number in the rick-yard, intending to jump to and fro the brook on the way. But before they had got half way to the brook they altered their minds, becoming eager for the water, and raced to the bathing-place. The pole was now to be an oar, and they were to swim, supported by an oar, like shipwrecked people.

So soon as he had had a plunge or two, Bevis put one arm over the pole and struck out with the other, thinking that he should be able in that way to have a long swim. Directly his weight pressed on the pole it went under, and did not support him in the least. He put it next beneath his chest, with both arms over it, but immediately he pushed off down it went again. Mark took it and got astride, when the pole let his feet touch the bottom.

"It's no use," he said. "What's the good of people falling overboard with spars and oars? What stories they must tell."

"I can't make it out," said Bevis; and he tried again, but it was no good, the pole was an encumbrance instead of a support, for it insisted upon slipping through the water lengthways, and would not move just as he wished. In a rage he gave it a push, and sent it ashore, and turned to swimming to the rail. They did not know it, but the governor, still anxious about them, had gone round a long distance, so as to have a peep at them from the hedge on the other side of Fir-Tree Gulf by the Nile. He could tell by the post and rails that they did not go out of their depth, and went away without letting them suspect his presence.

When they got out, they had a run in the sunshine, which dried them much better than towels. The field sloped gently to the right, and their usual run was on the slope beside a nut-tree hedge towards a group of elms. All the way there and back the sward was short and soft, almost like that of the Downs which they could see, and dotted with bird's-foot lotus, over whose yellow flowers they raced. But this morning, being no longer kept taut, after they had returned from the elms with an enormous mushroom they had found there, they ran to the old quarry, and along the edge above. The perpendicular sand-cliff fell to an enclosed pool beneath, in which, on going to the very edge, they could see themselves reflected. Some hurdles and flakes—a stronger kind of hurdle—had been placed here that cattle might not wander over, but the cart-horses, who rub against everything, had rubbed against them and dislodged two or three. These had rolled down, and the rest hung half over.

While they stood still looking down over the broad waters of their New Sea, the sun burned their shoulders, making the skin red. Away they ran back to dress, and taking a short path across a place where the turf had partly grown over a shallow excavation pricked their feet with thistles, and had to limp the rest of the way to their clothes. Now, there were no thistles on their proper racecourse down to the elms and back.

As they returned home they remembered the brook, and went down to it to jump with the leaping-pole. But the soft ooze at the bottom let the pole sink in, and Bevis, who of course must take the first leap, was very near being hung up in the middle of the brook. Under his weight, as he sprang off, the pole sank deep into the ooze, and had it been a stiffer mud the pole would have stopped upright, when he must have stayed on it over the water, or have been jerked off among the flags. As it was it did let him get over, but he did not land on the firm bank, only reaching the mud at the side, where he scrambled up by grasping the stout stalk of a willow-herb. In future he felt with the butt of the pole till he found a firm spot, where it was sandy, or where the matted roots of grasses and flags had bound the mud hard. Then he flew over well up on the grass.

Mark took his turn, and as he put the butt in the water a streak of mud came up where a small jack fish had shot away. So they went on down the bank leaping alternately, one carrying the towels while the other flew over and back.

Sometimes they could not leap because the tripping was bad, undermined where cowslips in the spring hung over the stream, bored with the holes of water-rats, which when disused become covered with grass, but give way beneath the foot or the hoof that presses on them pitching leaper or rider into the current, or it was rotten from long-decaying roots, or about to slip. Sometimes the landing was bad, undermined in the same way, or higher than the tripping, when you have not only to get over, but to deliver yourself on a higher level; or swampy, where a wet furrow came to the brook; or too far, where there was nothing but mud to come on. They had to select their jumping-places, and feel the ground to the edge first.

"Here's the raft!" shouted Mark, who was ahead, looking out for a good place.

"Is it?" said Bevis, running along on the other side. They had so completely forgotten it, that it came upon them like something new. Bevis took a leap and came over, and they set to work at once to launch it. The raft slipped gradually down the shelving shore of the drinking-place, and they thrust it into the stream. Bevis put his foot on board, but immediately withdrew it, for the water rushed through twenty leaks, spurting up along the joins. Left on the sand in the sun's rays the wood of the raft shrank a little, opening the planking, while the clay they had daubed on to caulk the crevices had cracked, and the moss had dried up and was ready to crumble. The water came through every where, and the raft was half-full even when left to itself without any pressure.

"We ought to have thatched it," said Mark. "We ought to have made a roof over it. Let's stop the leaks."

"O! come on," said Bevis, "don't let's bother. Rafts are no good, no more than poles or oars when you fall overboard. We shall have a ship soon."

The raft was an old story, and he did not care about it. He went on with the leaping-pole, but Mark stayed a minute and hauled the raft on shore as far as his strength would permit. He got about a quarter of it on the ground, so that it could not float away, and then ran after Bevis.

They went into the Peninsula, and looked at all the fir-trees, to see if any would do for a mast for the blue boat they were to have. As it had no name, they called it the blue boat to distinguish it from the punt. Mark thought an ash-pole would do for the mast, as ash-poles were so straight and could be easily shaved to the right size; but Bevis would not hear of it, for masts were never made of ash, but always of pine, and they must have their ship proper. He selected a tree presently, a young fir, straight as an arrow, and started Mark for the axe, but before he had gone ten yards Mark came back, saying that the tree would be of no use unless they liked to wait till next year, because it would be green, and the mast ought, to be made of seasoned wood.

"So it ought," said Bevis. "What a lot of trouble it is to make a ship."

But as they sat on the railing across the isthmus swinging their legs, Mark remembered that there were some fir-poles which had been cut a long time since behind the great wood-pile, between it and the walnut-trees, out of sight. Without a word away they ran, chose one of these and carried it into the shed where Bevis usually worked. They had got the dead bark off and were shaving away when it was dinner-time, which they thought a bore, but which wise old Pan, who was never chained now, considered the main object of life.

Next morning as they went through the meadow, where the dew still lingered in the shade, on the way to the bathing-place, taking Pan with them this time, they hung about the path picking clover-heads and sucking the petals, pulling them out and putting the lesser ends in their lips, looking at the white and pink bramble flowers, noting where the young nuts began to show, pulling down the woodbine, and doing everything but hasten on to their work of swimming. They stopped at the gate by the New Sea, over whose smooth surface slight breaths of mist were curling, and stood kicking the ground and the stones as flighty horses paw.

"We ought to be something," said Mark discontentedly.

"Of course we ought," said Bevis. "Things are very stupid unless you are something."

"Lions and tigers," said Mark, growling, and showing his teeth.

"Pooh!"

"Shipwrecked people on an island."

"Fiddle! They have plenty to do and are always happy, and we are not."

"No; very unhappy. Let's try escaping—prisoners running away."

"Hum! Hateful!"

"Everything's hateful."

"So it is."

"This is a very stupid sea."

"There's nothing in it."

"Nothing anywhere."

"Let's be hermits."

"There's always only one hermit."

"Well, you live that side," (pointing across), "and I'll live this."

"Hermits eat pulse and drink water."

"What's pulse?"

"I suppose it's barley water."

"Horrid."

"Awful."

"You say what we shall be then."

"Pan, you old donk," said Bevis, rolling Pan over with his foot. Lazy Pan lay on his back, and let Bevis bend his ribs with his foot.

"Caw, caw!" a crow went over down to the shore, where he hoped to find a mussel surprised by the dawn in shallow water.

Bang! "Hoi! Hoo! Yah!" The discharge was half a mile away, but the crow altered his mind, and flew over the water as near the surface as he could without touching. Why do birds always cross the water in that way?

"That's Tom," said Mark. Tom was the bird-keeper. He shot first, and shouted after. He potted a hare in the corn with bits of flint, a button, three tin tacks, and a horse-stub, which scraped the old barrel inside, but slew the game. That was for himself. Then he shouted his loudest to do his duty—for other people. The sparrows had flown out of the corn at the noise of the gun, and settled on the hedge; when Tom shouted they were frightened from the hedge, and went back into the wheat. From which learn this, shoot first and shout after.

"Shall we say that was a gun at sea?" continued Mark.

"They are always heard at night," said Bevis. "Pitch black, you know."

"Everything is somehow else," said Mark. Pan closed his idle old eyes, and grunted with delight as Bevis rubbed his ribs with his foot. Bevis put his hands in his pockets and sighed deeply. The sun looked down on these sons of care, and all the morning beamed.

"Savages!" shouted Mark kicking the gate to with a slam that startled Pan up. "Savages, of course!"

"Why?"

"They swim, donk: don't they? They're always in the water, and they have catamarans and ride the waves and dance on the shore, and blow shells—"

"Trumpets?"

"Yes."

"Canoes?"

"Yes."

"No clothes?"

"No."

"All jolly?"

"Everything."

"Hurrah!"

Away they ran towards the bathing-place to be savages, but Mark stopped suddenly, and asked what sort they were? They decided that they were the South Sea sort, and raced on again, Pan keeping pace with a kind of shamble; he was too idle to run properly. They dashed into the water, each with a wood-pigeon's feather, which they had found under the sycamore-trees above the quarry, stuck in his hair. At the first dive the feathers floated away. Upon the other side of the rails there was a large aspen-tree whose lowest bough reached out over the water, which was shallow there.

Though they made such a splashing when Bevis looked over the railings a moment, he saw some little roach moving to and fro under the bough. The wavelets from his splashing rolled on to the sandy shore, rippling under the aspen. As he looked, a fly fell on its back out of the tree, and struggled in vain to get up. Bevis climbed over the rails, picked an aspen leaf, and put it under the fly, which thus on a raft, and tossed up and down as Mark dived, was floated slowly by the undulations to the strand. As he got over the rails a kingfisher shot out from the mouth of the Nile opposite, and crossed aslant the gulf, whistling as he flew.

"Look!" said Mark. "Don't you know that's a 'sign.' Savages read 'signs,' and those birds mean that there are heaps of fish."

"Yes, but we ought to have a proper language."

"Kalabala-blong!" said Mark.

"Hududu-blow-fluz!" replied Bevis, taking a header from the top of the rail on which he had been sitting, and on which he just contrived to balance himself a moment without falling backwards.

"Umplumum!" he shouted, coming up again.

"Ikiklikah," and Mark disappeared.

"Noklikah," said Bevis, giving him a shove under as he came up to breathe.

"That's not fair," said Mark, scrambling up.

Bevis was swimming, and Mark seized his feet. More splashing and shouting, and the rocks resound. The echo of their voices returned from the quarry and the high bank under the firs.

They raced presently down to the elms along the sweet soft turf, sprinkling the dry grass with the sparkling drops from their limbs, and the sunlight shone on their white shoulders. The wind blew and stroked their gleaming backs. They rolled and tumbled on the grass, and the earth was under them. From the water to the sun and the wind and the grass.

They played round the huge sycamore trunks above the quarry, and the massive boughs stretched over—from a distance they would have seemed mere specks beneath the immense trees. They raced across to a round hollow in the field and sat down at the bottom, so that they could see nothing but the sky overhead, and the clouds drifting. They lay at full length, and for a moment were still and silent; the sunbeam and the wind, the soft touch of the grass, the gliding cloud, the eye-loved blue gave them the delicious sense of growing strong in drowsy luxury.

Then with a shout, renewed, they ran, and Pan who had been waiting by their clothes was startled into a bark of excitement at their sudden onslaught. As they went homewards they walked round to the little sheltered bay where the boats were kept, to look at the blue boat and measure for the mast. It was beside the punt, half drawn up on the sand, and fastened to a willow root. She was an ill-built craft with a straight gunwale, so that when afloat she seemed lower at stem and stern than abeam, as if she would thrust her nose into a wave instead of riding it. The planks were thick and heavy and looked as if they had not been bent enough to form the true buoyant curve.

The blue paint had scaled and faded, the rowlocks were mended with a piece cut from an old rake-handle, there was a small pool of bilge water in the sternsheets from the last shower, fall of dead insects, and yellow willow leaves. A clumsy vessel put together years ago in some by-water of the far distant Thames above Oxford, and not good enough even for that unknown creek. She had drifted somehow into this landlocked pond and remained unused, hauled on the strand beneath the willows; she could carry five or six, and if they bumped her well on the stones it mattered little to so stout a frame.

Still she was a boat, with keel and curve, and like lovers they saw no defect. Bevis looked at the hole in the seat or thwart, where the mast would have to be stepped, and measured it (not having a rule with him) by cutting a twig just to the length of the diameter. Mark examined the rudder and found that the lines were rotten, having hung dangling over the stern in the water for so long. Next they stepped her length, stepping on the sand outside, to decide on the height of the mast, and where were the ropes to be fastened? for they meant to have some standing rigging.

At home afterwards in the shed, while Bevis shaved the fir-pole for the mast, Mark was set to carve the leaping-pole, for the South Sea savages have everything carved. He could hardly cut the hard dried bark of the ash, which had shrunk on and become like wood. He made a spiral notch round it, and then searched till he found his old spear, which had to be ornamented and altered into a bone harpoon. A bone from the kitchen was sawn off while in the vice, and then half through two inches from the largest end. Tapping a broad chisel gently, Mark split the bone down to the sawn part, and then gradually filed it sharp. He also filed three barbs to it, and then fitted the staff of the spear into the hollow end. While he was engraving lines and rings on the spear with his pocket-knife, the dinner interrupted his work.

Bevis, wearying of the mast, got some flints, and hammered them to split off flakes for arrowheads, but though he bruised his fingers, he could not chip the splinters into shape. The fracture always ran too far, or not far enough. John Young, the labourer, came by as he was doing this sitting on the stool in the shed, and watched him.

"I see a man do that once," said John.

"How did he do it? tell me? what's the trick?" said Bevis, impatient to know.

"Aw, I dunno; I see him at it. A' had a gate-hinge snopping um."

The iron hinge of a gate, if removed from the post, forms a fairly good hammer, the handle of iron as well as the head.

"Where was it? what did he do it for?"

"Aw, up in the Downs. Course he did it to soil um."

The prehistoric art of chipping flints lingered among the shepherds on the Downs, till the percussion-cap came in, and no longer having to get flakes for the flintlock guns they slowly let it disappear. Young had seen it done, but could not describe how.

Bevis battered his flints till he was tired; then he took up the last and hurled it away in a rage with all his might. The flint whirled over and over and hummed along the ground till it struck a small sarsen or boulder by the wood-pile, put there as a spur-stone to force the careless carters to drive straight. Then it flew into splinters with the jerk of the stoppage.

"Here's a sharp 'un," said John Young, picking up a flake, "and here's another."

Altogether there were three pointed flakes which Bevis thought would do. Mark had to bring some reeds next day from the place where they grew half a mile below his house in a by-water of the brook. They were green, but Bevis could not wait to dry them. He cut them off a little above the knot or joint, split the part above, and put the flint flake in, and bound it round and round with horsehair from the carter's store in the stable. But when they were finished, they were not shot off, lest they should break; they were carried indoors into the room upstairs where there was a bench, and which they made their armoury.

They made four or five darts next of deal shaved to the thickness of a thin walking-stick, and not quite so long. One end was split in four—once down and across that—and two pieces of cardboard doubled up thrust in, answering the purpose of feathering. There was a slight notch two-thirds up the shaft, and the way was to twist a piece of twine round it there crossed over a knot so as just to hold, the other end of the twine firmly coiled about the wrist, so that in throwing the string was taut and the point of the dart between the fingers. Hurling it the string imparted a second force, and the dart, twirling like an arrow, flew fifty or sixty yards.

Slings they made with a square of leather from the sides of old shoes, a small hole out out in the centre that the stone might not slip, but these they could never do much with, except hurl pebbles from the rick-yard, rattling up into the boughs of the oak, on the other side of the field. The real arrows to shoot with—not the reed arrows to look at—were tipped with iron nails filed to a sharp point. They had much trouble in feathering them; they had plenty of goose-feathers (saved from the Christmas plucking), but to glue them on properly was not easy.

Chapter Eleven
Savages Continued—The Catamaran

With all their efforts, they could not make a blow-tube, such as are used by savages. Bevis thought and thought, and Mark helped him, and Pan grabbed his fleas, all together in the round blue summer-house; and they ate a thousand strawberries, and a basketful of red currants, ripe, from the wall close by, and two young summer apples, far from ready, and yet they could not do it. The tube ought to be at least as long as the savage, using it, was tall. They could easily find sticks that were just the thickness, and straight, but the difficulty was to bore through them. No gimlet or auger was long enough; nor could they do it with a bar of iron, red-hot at the end; they could not keep it true, but always burned too much one side or the other.

Perhaps it might be managed by inserting a short piece of tin tubing, and making a little fire in it, and gradually pushing it down as the fire burnt. Only, as Bevis pointed out, the fire would not live in such a narrow place without any draught. A short tube was easily made out of elder, but not nearly long enough. The tinker, coming round to mend the pots, put it into their heads to set him to make a tin blow-pipe, five feet in length; which he promised to do, and sent it in a day or two. But as he had no sheet of tin broad enough to roll the tube in one piece, he had made four short pipes and soldered them together. Nothing would go straight through it because the joints were not quite perfect, inside there was a roughness which caught the dart and obstructed the puff, for a good blow-tube must be as smooth and well bored as a gun-barrel.

When they came to look over their weapons, they found they had not got any throw-sticks, nor a boomerang. Throw-sticks were soon made, by cutting some with a good thick knob; and a boomerang was made out of a curved branch of ash, which they planed down smooth one side, and cut to a slight arch on the other.

"This is a capital boomerang," said Bevis. "Now we shall be able to knock a rabbit over without any noise, or frightening the rest, and it will come back and we can kill three or four running."

"Yes, and one of the mallards," said Mark. "Don't you know?—they are always too far for an arrow, and besides, the arrow would be lost if it did not hit. Now we shall have them. But which way ought we to throw it—the hollow first, or the bend first?"

"Let's try," said Bevis, and ran with the boomerang from the shed into the field.

Whiz! Away it went, bend first, and rose against the wind till the impetus ceased, when it hung a moment on the air, and slid to the right, falling near the summer-house. Next time it turned to the left, and fell in the hedge; another time it hit the hay-rick: nothing could make it go straight. Mark tried his hardest, and used it both ways, but in vain—the boomerang rose against the wind, and, so far, acted properly, but directly the force with which it was thrown was exhausted, it did as it liked, and swept round to the left or the right, and never once returned to their feet.

"A boomerang is a stupid thing," said Bevis, "I shall chop it up. I hate it."

"No; put it upstairs," said Mark, taking it from him. So the boomerang was added to the collection in the bench-room. A crossbow was the next thing, and they made the stock from a stout elder branch, because when the pith was taken out, it left a groove for the bolt to slide up. The bow was a thick briar, and the bolt flew thirty or forty yards, but it did not answer, and they could hit nothing with it. A crossbow requires delicate adjustment, and to act well, must be made almost as accurately as a rifle.

They shot a hundred times at the sparrows on the roof, who were no sooner driven off than they came back like flies, but never hit one; so the crossbow was hung up with the boomerang. Bevis, from much practice, could shoot far better than that with his bow and arrow. He stuck up an apple on a stick, and after six or seven trials hit it at twenty yards. He could always hit a tree. Mark was afraid to throw his bone-headed harpoon at a tree, lest the head should break off; but he had another, without a bone head, to cast; and he too could generally hit a tree.

"Now we are quite savages," said Bevis, one evening, as they sat up in the bench-room, and the sun went down red and fiery, opposite the little window, filling the room with a red glow and gleaming on their faces. It put a touch of colour on the pears, which were growing large, just outside the window, as if they were ripe towards the sunset. The boomerang on the wall was lit up with the light; so was a parcel of canvas, on the floor, which they had bought at Latten town, for the sails of their ship.

There was an oyster barrel under the bench, which was to contain the fresh water for their voyage, and there had been much discussion as to how they were to put a new head to it.

"We ought to see ourselves on the shore with spears and things when we are sailing round," said Mark.

"So as not to be able to land for fear."

"Poisoned arrows," said Mark. "I say, how stupid! we have not got any poison."

"No more we have. We must get a lot of poison."

"Curious plants nobody knows anything about but us."

"Nobody ever heard of them."

"And dip our arrows and spear's in the juice."

"No one ever gets well after being shot with them."

"If the wind blows hard ashore and there are no harbours it will be awful with the savages all along waiting for us."

"We shall see them dancing and shouting with bows and throw-sticks, and yelling."

"That's you and me."

"Of course. And very likely if the wind is very hard we shall have to let down the sails, and fling out an anchor and stay till the gale goes down."

"The anchor may drag."

"Then we shall crash on the rocks."

"And swim ashore."

"You can't. There's the breakers and the savages behind them. I shall stop on the wreck, and the sun will go down."

"Red like that," pointing out of window.

"And it will blow harder still."

"Black as pitch."

"Horrible."

"No help."

"Fire a gun."

"Pooh!"

"Make a raft."

"The clouds are sure to break, or something."

"I say," said Bevis, "won't all these things," —pointing to the weapons— "do first-rate for our war?"

"Capital. There will be arrows sticking up everywhere all over the battle-field."

"Broken lances and horses without riders."

"Dints in the ground."

"Knights with their backs against trees and heaps of soldiers chopping at them."

"Flashing swords! the ground will shake when we charge."

"Trumpets!"

"Groans!"

"Grass all red!"

"Blood-red sun like that!" The disc growing larger as it neared the horizon, shone vast through some distant elms.

"Flocks of crows."

"Heaps of white bones."

"And we will take the shovels and make a tumulus by the shore."

The red glow on the wall slowly dimmed, the colour left the pear, and the song of a thrush came from the orchard.

"I want to make some magic," said Bevis, after a pause. "The thing is to make a wand."

"Genii are best," said Mark. "They do anything you tell them."

"There ought to be a black book telling you how to do it somewhere," said Bevis; "but I've looked through the bookcase and there's nothing."

"Are you sure you have quite looked through?"

"I'll try again," said Bevis. "There's a lot of books, but never anything that you want."

"I know," said Mark suddenly. "There's the bugle in the old cupboard— that will do for the war."

"So it will; I forgot it."

"And a flag."

"No; we must have eagles on a stick."

Knock! They jumped; Polly had hit the ceiling underneath with the handle of a broom.

"Supper."

When they went to bathe next morning, Bevis took with him his bow and arrows, intending to shoot a pike. As they walked beside the shore they often saw jacks basking in the sun at the surface of the water, and only a few yards distant. He had fastened a long thin string one end to the arrow and the other to the bow, so that he might draw the arrow back to him with the fish on as the savages do. Mark brought his bone-headed harpoon to try and spear something, and between them they also carried a plank, which was to be used as a catamaran.

A paddle they had made was tied to it for convenience, that their hands might not be too full. Mark went first with one end of the plank on his shoulder, and Bevis followed with the other on his, and as they had to hold it on edge it rather cut them. Coming near some weeds where they had seen a jack the day before, they put the catamaran down, and Bevis crept quietly forward. The jack was not there, but motioning to Mark to stand still, Bevis went on to where the first railings stretched out into the water.

There he saw a jack about two pounds' weight basking within an inch of the surface, and aslant to him. He lifted his bow before he went near, shook out the string that it might slip easily like the coil of a harpoon, fitted the arrow, and holding it almost up, stole closer. He knew if he pulled the bow in the usual manner the sudden motion of his arms would send the jack away in an instant. With the bow already in position, he got within six yards of the fish, which, quite still, did not seem to see anything, but to sleep with eyes wide open in the sun. The shaft flew, and like another arrow the jack darted aslant into deep water.

Bevis drew back his arrow with the string, not altogether disappointed, for it had struck the water very near if not exactly at the place the fish had occupied. But he thought the string impeded the shaft, and took it off for another trial. Mark would not stay behind; he insisted upon seeing the shooting, so leaving the catamaran on the grass, they moved gently along the shore. After a while they found another jack, this time much larger, and not less than four pounds' weight, stationary in a tiny bay, or curve of the land. He was lying parallel to the shore, but deeper than the first, perhaps six inches beneath the surface. Mark stood where he could see the dark line of the fish, while Bevis, with the bow lifted and arrow half drawn, took one, two, three, and almost another step forward.

Aiming steadily at the jack's broad side, just behind the front fins, where the fish was widest, Bevis grasped his bow firm to keep it from the least wavering (for it is the left hand that shoots), drew his arrow, and let go. So swift was the shaft, unimpeded, and drawn too this time almost to the head, in traversing the short distance between, that the jack, quick as he was, could not of himself have escaped. Bevis saw the arrow enter the water, and, as it seemed to him, strike the fish. It did indeed strike the image of the fish, but the real jack slipped beneath it.

Bevis looked and looked, he was so certain he had hit it, and so he had hit the mark he aimed at, which was the refraction, but the fish was unhurt. It was explained to him afterwards that the fish appears higher in the water than it actually is, and that to have hit it he should have aimed two inches underneath, and he proved the truth of it by trying to touch things in the water with a long stick. The arrow glanced after going two feet or so deep, and performed a curve in the water exactly opposite to that it would have traced in the air. In the air it would have curved over, in the water it curved under, and came up to the surface not very far out; the water checked it so. Bevis fastened the string again to another arrow, and shot it out over the first, so that it caught and held it, and he drew them both back.

They fetched the catamaran, and went on till they came to the point where there was a wall of stones rudely put together to shield the land from the full shock of the waves, when the west wind rolled them heavily from the Indian Ocean and the Golden Sea. Putting the plank down again, Mark went forward with his harpoon, for he knew that shoals of fish often played in the water when it was still, just beneath this rocky wall. As he expected, they were there this morning, for the most part roach, but a few perch. He knelt and crept out on all fours to the edge of the wall, leaving his hat on the sward. Looking over, he could see to the stony bottom, and as there was not a ripple, he could see distinctly.

He put his harpoon gently, without a splash, into the sunlit water, and let it sink slowly in among the shoal. The roach swam aside a yard or so from it, but showed no more fear than that it should not touch them. Mark kept his harpoon still till a larger roach came slowly by within eighteen inches of the point, when he jerked it at the fish. It passed six inches behind his tail, and though Mark tried again and again, thrusting quickly, he could not strike them with his single point. To throw it like a dart he knew was useless, they were too deep down, nor could he hit so small an object in motion. He could not do it, but some days afterwards he struck a small tench in the brook, and got him out. The tench was still, so that he could put the head of his harpoon almost on it.

They marched on, and presently launched the catamaran. It would only support one at a time astride and half in the water, but it was a capital thing.

Sitting on it, Bevis paddled along the shore nearly to the rocky wall and back, but he did not forget his promise, and was not out of his depth; he could see the stones at the bottom all the time. Mark tried to stand on the plank, but one edge would go down and pitch him off. He next tried to lie on it on his back, and succeeded so long as he let his legs dangle over each side, and so balanced it. Then they stood away, and swam to it as if it had been the last plank of a wreck.

"Look!" said Mark, after they had done this several times. He was holding the plank at arm's length with his limbs floating. "Look!"

"I see. What is it?"

"This is the way. We ought to have held the jumping-pole like this. This is the way to hold an oar and swim."

"So it is," said Bevis, "of course, that's it; we'll have the punt, and try with a scull."

Held at arm's length, almost anything will keep a swimmer afloat; but if he puts it under his arm or chest, it takes a good-sized spar. Splashing about, presently the plank forgotten for the moment slipped away, and, impelled by the waves they made, floated into deep water.

"I'm sure I could swim to it," said Bevis, and he was inclined to try.

"We promised not," said Mark.

"You stupe—I know that; but if there's a plank, that's not dangerous then."

"Stupe" was their word for stupid. He waded out till the water was over his shoulders, and tried to lift him.

"Don't—don't," said Mark. Bevis began to lean his chest on the water.

"If you're captain," cried Mark, "you ought not to."

"No more I ought," said Bevis, coming back. "Get my bow."

"What for?"

"Go and get my bow."

"I shan't, if you say it like that."

"You shall. Am I not captain?"

Mark was caught by his own argument, and went out on the sward for the bow.

"Tie the arrow on with the string," shouted Bevis. Mark did it, and brought it in, keeping it above the surface. Bevis climbed on the railings, half out of water, so that he could steady himself with his knees against the rail.

"Now, give me the bow," he said. He took good aim, and the nail, filed to a sharp point, was driven deep into the soft deal of the plank. With the string he hauled the catamaran gently back, but it would not come straight; it slipped sideways (like the boomerang in the air), and came ashore under the aspen bough.

When they came out they bathed again in the air and the sunshine; they rolled on the sward, and ran. Bevis, as he ran and shouted, shot off an arrow with all his might to see how far it would go. It went up, up, and curving over, struck a bough at the top of one of the elms, and stopped there by the rooks' nests. Mark shouted and danced on the bird's-foot lotus, and darted his spear, heedless of the bone-head. It went up into the hazel boughs of the hedge among the young nuts, and he could not get it till dressed, for the thistles.

They ran again and chased each other in and out the sycamore trunks, and visited the hollow, shouting their loudest, till the distant herd looked up from their grazing. The sunlight poured upon them, and the light air came along; they bathed in air and sunbeam, and gathered years of health like flowers from the field.

After they had dressed they took the catamaran to the quarry to leave it there (somewhat out of sight lest any one should take it for firewood), so as to save the labour of carrying it to and fro. There was a savage of another tribe in the quarry, and they crept on all fours, taking great pains that he should not see them. It was the old man who was supposed to look after the boats, and generally to watch the water. Had they not been so occupied they would have heard the thump, thump of the sculls as he rowed, or rather moved the punt up to where the narrow mound separated the New, Sea from the quarry.

He was at work scooping out some sand, and filling sacks with the best, with which cargo he would presently voyage home, and retail it to the dairymaids and at the roadside inns to eke out that spirit of juniper-berries needful to those who have dwelt long by marshy places. They need not have troubled to conceal themselves from this stranger savage; he would not have seen them if they had stood close by him. A narrow life narrows the sweep of the eye. Miserable being, he could see no farther than one of the mussels of the lake which travel in a groove. His groove led to the sanded inn-kitchen, and his shell was shut to all else. But they crept like skirmishers, dragging the catamaran laboriously behind them, using every undulation of the ground to hide themselves, till they had got it into the hollow, where they left it beside a heap of stones. Then they had to crawl out again, and for thirty yards along the turf, till they could stand up unseen.

"Let's get the poison," said Mark, as they were going home.

So they searched for the poison-plants. The woody nightshade they knew very well, having been warned long ago against the berries. It was now only in flower, and it would be some time before there were any berries; but after thinking it over they decided to gather a bundle of stalks, and soak them for the deadly juice. There were stems of arum in the ditches, tipped with green berries. These they thought would do, but shrank from touching. The green looked unpleasant and slimy.

Next they hunted for mandragora, of which John Young had given them an account. It grew in waste places, and by the tombs in the churchyard, and shrieked while you pulled it up. This they could not find. Mark said perhaps it wanted an enchanter to discover it, but he gathered a quantity of the dark green milfoil from the grass beside the hedge and paths, and crammed his pockets with it. Some of the lads had told him that it was a deadly poison. It is the reverse—thus reputation varies—for it was used to cure mediaeval sword-cuts. They passed the water-parsnip, unaware of its pernicious qualities, looking for noisome hemlock.

"There's another kind of nightshade," said Bevis; "because I read about it in that old book indoors, and it's much stronger than this. We must have some of it."

They looked a long time, but could not find it; and, full of their direful object, did not heed sounds of laughter on the other side of the hedge they were searching, till they got through a gap and jumped into the midst of a group of haymakers resting for lunch. The old men had got a little way apart by themselves, for they wanted to eat like Pan. All the women were together in a "gaggle," a semicircle of them sitting round a young girl who lounged on a heap of mown grass, with a huge labourer lying full length at her feet. She had a piece of honey suckle in her hand, and he had a black wooden "bottle" near him.

There was a courting going on between these two, and all the other women, married and single, collected round them, to aid in the business with jokes and innuendoes.

Bevis and Mark instantly recognised in the girl the one who at "Calais" had shown them the road home, and in the man at her feet the fellow who was asleep on the flint heap.

Her large eyes, like black cherries—for black eyes and black cherries have a faint tint of red behind them—were immediately bent full on Bevis as she rose and curtseyed to him. Her dress at the throat had come unhooked, and showed the line to which the sun had browned her, and where the sweet clear whiteness of the untouched skin began. The soft roundness of the swelling plum as it ripens filled her common print, torn by briars, with graceful contours. In the shadow of the oak her large black eyes shone larger, loving and untaught.

Bevis did not speak. He and Mark were a little taken aback, having jumped through the gap so suddenly from savagery into haymaking. They hastened through a gateway into another field.

"How you do keep a-staring arter they!" said the huge young labourer to the girl. "Yen you seen he afore? It's onely our young measter."

"I knows," said the girl, sitting down as Bevis and Mark disappeared through the gateway. "He put a bough on you to keep the flies off while you were sleeping."

"Did a'? Then why didn't you axe 'un for a quart?"

She had slipped along the fields by the road that day, and had seen Bevis put the bough over her lover's face as he slept on the flint heap— where she left him. The grateful labourer's immediate idea was to ask Bevis for some beer.

Behind the hedge Bevis and Mark continued their search for deadly poison. They took some "gix," but were not certain that it was the true hemlock.

"There's a sort of sorrel that's poison," said Mark.

"And heaps of roots," said Bevis.

They were now near home, and went in to extract the essence from the plants they had. The nightshade yielded very little juice from its woody bines, or stalks; the "gix" not much more: the milfoil, well bruised and squeezed, gave most. They found three small phials, the nightshade and "gix" only filled a quarter of the phials used for them: Mark had a phial three-parts full of milfoil. These they arranged in a row on the bench in the bench-room under the crossbow and boomerang, for future use in war. They did not dip their arrows or harpoon in yet, lest they should poison any fish or animal they might kill, and so render it unfit for food.

Chapter Twelve
Savages Continued—Making the Sails

The same evening, having got a great plateful of cherries, they went to work in the bench-room to cut out the sails from the parcel of canvas. There had been cherries in town weeks before, but these were the first considered ripe in the country, which is generally later. With a cherry in his mouth, Bevis spread the canvas out upon the floor, and marked it with his pencil. The rig was to be fore and aft, a mainsail and jib; the mast and gaff, or as they called it, the yard, were already finished. It took forty cherries to get it cut out properly, then they threw the other pieces aside, and placed the sails on the floor in the position they would be when fixed.

"You are sure they're not too big," said Mark, "if a white squall comes."

"There are no white squalls now," said Bevis on his knees, thoughtfully sucking a cherry-stone. "It's cyclones now. The sails are just the right size, and of course we can take in a reef. You cut off—let me see—twenty bits of string, a foot—no, fifteen inches long: it's for the reefs."

Mark began to measure off the string from a quantity of the largest make, which they had bought for the purpose.

"There's the block," he said. "How are you going to manage about the pulley to haul up the mainsail?"

"The block's a bore," mused Bevis, rolling his cherry-stone about. "I don't think we could make one—"

"Buy one."

"Pooh! There's nothing in Latten; why you can't buy anything." Mark was silent, he knew it was true. "If we make a slit in the mast and put a little wheel in off a window-blind or something—"

"That would do first-rate."

"No it wouldn't; it would weaken the mast, stupe, and the first cyclone would snap it."

"So it would. Then we should drift ashore and get eaten."

"Most likely."

"Well, bore a hole and put the cord through that; that would not weaken it much."

"No; but I know! A curtain-ring! Don't you see, you fasten the curtain-ring, it's brass, to the mast, and put the rope through, and it runs easy—brass is smooth."

"Of course. Who's that?"

Some small stones came rattling in at the open window, and two voices shouted,—

"I say. Holloa!"

Bevis and Mark went to the window and saw two of their friends, Bill and Wat, on the garden path below.

"When's the war going to begin?" asked Wat.

"Tell us about the war," said Bill.

"The war's not ready," said Bevis.

"Well how long is it going to be?"

"Make haste."

"Everybody's ready."

"Lots of them. Do you think you shall want any more?"

"I know six," said a third voice, and Tim came round the corner, having waited to steal a strawberry, "and one's a whopper."

"Let's begin."

"Now then."

"O! don't make such a noise," said Bevis. The sails and the savages had rather put the war aside, but Mark had talked of it to others, and the idea spread in a minute; everybody jumped at it, and all the cry was War!

"Make me lieutenant," said Andrew, appearing from the orchard.

"I want to carry the flag."

"Come down and tell us."

"How are we to tell you if you keep talking?" said Mark; Bevis put his head out of window by the pears, and they were quiet.

"I tell you the war's not ready," he said; "and you're as bad as rebels—I mean you're a mutiny to come here before you're sent for, and you ought to be shot,"—("Executed," whispered Mark behind him)—"executed, of course."

"How are we to know when it's ready?"

"You'll be summoned," said Bevis. "There will be a muster-roll and a trumpet blown, and you'll have to march a thousand miles."

"All right."

"And the swords have to be made, and the eagles, besides the map of the roads and the grub," —("Provisions," said Mark)—"provisions, of course, and all the rest, and how do you think a war is to be got ready in a minute, you stupes!" in a tone of great indignation.

They grumbled: they wanted a big battle on the spot.

"If you bother me much," said Bevis, "while I'm getting the fleet ready, there shan't be a war at all."

"Are you getting a fleet?"

"Here are the sails," said Mark, holding up some canvas.

"Well, you won't be long?"

"You'll let us know?"

"Shall we tell anybody else?"

"Lots," said Bevis; "tell lots. We're going to have the biggest armies ever seen."

"Thousands," said Mark. "Millions!"

"Millions!" said Bevis.

"Hurrah!" they shouted.

"Here," said Bevis, throwing the remainder of the cherries out like a shower among them.

"Are you coming to quoits?"

"O! no," said Mark, "we have so much to do; now go away." The soldiery moved off through the garden, snatching lawlessly at any fruit they saw.

"Mark," said Bevis on his knees again, "these sails will have to be hemmed, you know."

"So they will."

"We can't do it. You must take them home to Frances, and make her stitch them; roll them up and go directly."

"I don't want to go home," said Mark. "And perhaps she won't stitch them."

"I'm sure she will; she will do anything for me."

"So she will," said Mark rather sullenly. "Everybody does everything for you."

Bevis had rolled up the sails, quite indifferent as to what people did for him, and put them into Mark's unwilling hands.

"Now you can have the donkey, and mind and come back before breakfast."

"I can't catch him," said Mark.

"No; no more can I—stop. John Young's sure to be in the stable, he can."

"Ah," said Mark, brightening up a little, "that moke is a beast."

John Young, having stipulated for a "pot," went to catch the donkey; they sat down in the shed to wait for him, but as he did not come for some time they went after him. They met him in the next field leading the donkey with a halter, and red as fire from running. They took the halter and sent John away for the "pot." There was a wicked thought in their hearts, and they wanted witnesses away. So soon as John had gone, Mark looked at Bevis, and Bevis looked at Mark. Mark growled, Bevis stamped his feet.

"Beast!" said Mark.

"Wretch!" said Bevis.

"You—you—you, Thing," said Mark; they ground their teeth, and glared at the animal. They led him all fearful to a tree, a little tree but stout enough; it was an ash, and it grew somewhat away from the hedge. They tied him firmly to the tree, and then they scourged this miserable citizen.

All the times they had run in vain to catch him; all the times they had had to walk when they might have ridden one behind the other on his back; all his refusals to be tempted; all the wrongs they had endured at his heels boiled in their breasts. They broke their sticks upon his back, they cut new ones, and smashed them too, they hurled the fragments at him, and then got some more. They thrashed, thwacked, banged, thumped, poked, prodded, kicked, belaboured, bumped, and hit him, working themselves into a frenzy of rage.

Mark fetched a pole to knock him the harder as it was heavy; Bevis crushed into the hedge, and brought out a dead log to hurl at him, a log he could but just lift and swung to throw with difficulty,—the same Bevis who put an aspen leaf carefully under the fly to save it from drowning. The sky was blue, and the evening beautiful, but no one came to help the donkey.

When they were tired, they sat down and rested, and after they were cooler and had recovered from the fatigue, they loosed him—quite cowed this time and docile, and Mark, with the parcel of sails, got on his back. After all this onslaught there did not seem any difference in him except that his coat had been well dusted. This immunity aggravated them; they could not hurt him.

"Put him in the stable all night," said Bevis, "and don't give him anything to eat."

"And no water," said Mark, as he rode off. "So I will."

And so he did. But the donkey had cropped all day, and was full, and just before John Young caught him had had a draught, rather unusual for him and equal to an omen, at the drinking-place by the raft. The donkey slept, and beat them.

After Mark had gone Bevis returned to the bench-room, and fastened a brass curtain-ring to the mast, which they had carried up there. When he had finished, noticing the three phials of poison he thought he would go and see if he could find out any more fatal plants. There was an ancient encyclopaedia in the bookcase, in which he had read many curious things, such as would not be considered practical enough for modern publication, which must be dry or nothing. Among the rest was a page of chemical signs and those used by the alchemists, some of which he had copied off for magic. Pulling out the volumes, which were piled haphazard, like bricks shot out of a cart, there was one that had all the alphabets employed in the different languages, Coptic, Gothic, Ethiopic, Syriac, and so on.

The Arabic took his fancy as the most mysterious—the sweeping curves, the quivering lines, the blots where the reed pen thickened, there was no knowing what such writing might not mean. How mystic the lettering which forms the running ornament of the Alhambra! It is the writing of the Orient, of the alchemist and enchanter, the astrologer and the prophet.

Bevis copied the alphabet, and then he made a roll of a broad sheet of yellowish paper torn from the end of one of the large volumes, a fly-leaf, and wrote the letters upon it in such a manner as their shape and flowing contour arranged themselves. With these he mingled the alchemic signs for fire and air and water, and so by the time the dusk crept into the parlour and filled it with shadow he had completed a manuscript. This he rolled up and tied with string, intending to bury it in the sand of the quarry, so that when they sailed round in the ship they might land and discover it.

Mark returned to breakfast, and said that Frances had promised to hem the sails, and thought it would not take long. Bevis showed him the roll.

"It looks magic," said Mark. "What does it mean?"

"I don't know," said Bevis. "That is what we shall have to find out when we discover it. Besides the magic is never in the writing; it is what you see when you read it—it's like looking in a looking-glass, and seeing people moving about a thousand miles away."

"I know," said Mark. "We can put it in a sand-martin's hole, then it won't get wet if it rains."

They started for the bathing-place, and carefully deposited the roll in a sand-martin's hole some way up the face of the quarry, covering it with sand. To know the spot again, they counted and found it was the third burrow to the right, if you stood by the stone heap and looked straight towards the first sycamore-tree. Having taken the bearings, they dragged the catamaran down to the water, and had a swim. When they came out, and were running about on the high ground by the sycamores, they caught sight of a dog-cart slowly crossing the field a long way off, and immediately hid behind a tree to reconnoitre the new savage, themselves unseen.

"It's Jack," said Bevis; "I'm sure it is." It was Jack, and he was going at a walking pace, because the track across the field was rough, and he did not care to get to the gateway before the man sent to open it had arrived there. His object was to look at some grass to rent for his sheep.

"Yes, it's Jack," said Mark, very slowly and doubtfully. Bevis looked at him.

"Well, suppose it is; he won't hurt us. We can easily shoot him if he comes here."

"But the letter," said Mark.

"What letter?"

Mark had started for his clothes, which were in a heap on the sward, he seized his coat, and drew a note much frayed from one of the pockets. He looked at it, heaved a deep sigh, and ran with all his might to intercept Jack. Bevis watched him tearing across the field and laughed; then he sat down on the grass to wait for him.

Mark, out of breath and with thistles in his feet, would never have overtaken the dog-cart had not Jack seen him coming and stopped. He could not speak, but handed up the note in silence, more like Cupid than messengers generally. He panted so that he could not run away directly, as he had intended.

"You rascal," said Jack, flicking at him with his whip. "How long have you had this in your pocket?"

Mark tried to run away, he could only trot; Jack turned his mare's head, as if half-inclined to drive after him.

"If you come," said Mark, shaking his fist, "we'll shoot you and stick a spear into you. Aha! you're afraid! aha!"

Jack was too eager to read his note to take vengeance. Mark walked away jeering at him. The reins hung down, and the mare cropped as the master read. Mark laughed to think he had got off so easily, for the letter had been in his pocket a week, though he had faithfully promised to deliver it the same day—for a shilling. Had he not been sent home with the sails it might have remained another week till the envelope was fretted through.

Frances asked if he had given it to Jack.

Mark started. "Ah," said she, "you have forgotten it."

"Of course I have," said Mark. "It's so long ago."

"Then you did really?"

"How stupid you are," said Mark; and Frances could not press him further, lest she should seem too anxious about Jack. So the young dog escaped, but he did not dare delay longer, and had not Jack happened to cross the field meant to have ridden up to his house on the donkey. When Jack had read the note he looked at the retreating figure of Cupid and opened his lips, but caught his breath as it were and did not say it. He put his whip aside as he drove on, lest he should unjustly punish the mare.

Mark strolled leisurely back to the bathing-place, but when he got there Bevis was not to be seen. He looked round at the water, the quarry, the sycamore-trees. He ran down to the water's edge with his heart beating and a wild terror causing a whirling sensation in his eyes, for the thought in the instant came to him that Bevis had gone out of his depth. He tried to shout "Bevis!" but he was choked; he raised his hands; as he looked across the water he suddenly saw something white moving among the fir-trees at the head of the gulf.

He knew it was Bevis, but he was so overcome he sat down on the sward to watch, he could not stand up. The something white was stealthily passing from tree to tree like an Indian. Mark looked round, and saw his own harpoon on the grass, but at once missed the bow and arrows. His terror had suspended his observation, else he would have noticed this before.

Bevis, when Mark ran with the letter to Jack, had sat down on the sward to wait for him, and by-and-by, while still, and looking out over the water, his quiet eye became conscious of a slight movement opposite at the mouth of the Nile. There was a ripple, and from the high ground where he sat he could see the reflection of the trees in the water there undulate, though their own boughs shut off the light air from the surface. He got up, took his bow and arrows, and went into the firs. The dead dry needles or leaves on the ground felt rough to his naked feet, and he had to take care not to step on the hard cones. A few small bramble bushes forced him to go aside, so that it took him some little time to get near the Nile.

Then he had to always keep a tree trunk in front of him, and to step slowly that his head might not be seen before he could see what it was himself. He stooped as the ripples on the other side of the brook became visible; then gradually lifting his head, sheltered by a large alder, he traced the ripples back to the shore under the bank, and saw a moorcock feeding by the roots of a willow. Bevis waited till the cock turned his back, then he stole another step forward to the alder.

It was about ten yards to the willow which hung over the water, but he could not get any nearer, for there was no more cover beyond the alder—the true savage is never content unless he is close to his game. Bevis grasped his bow firm in his left hand, drew the arrow quick but steadily—not with a jerk—and as the sharp point covered the bird, loosed it. There was a splash and a fluttering, he knew instantly that he had hit. "Mark! Mark!" he shouted, and ran down the bank, heedless of the jagged stones. Mark heard, and came racing through the firs.

The arrow had struck the moorcock's wing, but even then the bird would have got away, for the point had no barb, and in diving and struggling it would have come out, had not he been so near the willow. The spike went through his wing and nailed it to a thick root; the arrow quivered as it was stopped by the wood. Bevis seized him by the neck and drew the arrow out.

"Kill him! Kill him!" shouted Mark. The other savage pulled the neck, and Mark, leaping down the jagged stones, took the dead bird in his eager hands.

"Here's where the arrow went in."

"There's three feathers in the water."

"Feel how warm he is."

"Look at the thick red on his bill."

"See his claws."

"Hurrah!"

"Let's eat him."

"Raw?"

"No. Cook him."

"All right. Make a fire."

Thus the savages gloated over their prey. They went back up the bank and through the firs to the sward.

"Where shall we make the fire?" said Mark. "In the quarry?"

"That old stupe may come for sand."

"So he may. Let's make it here."

"Everybody would see."

"By the hedge towards the elms then."

"No. I know, in the hollow."

"Of course, nobody would come there."

"Pick up some sticks."

"Come and help me."

"I shall dress—there are brambles."

So they dressed, and then found that Mark had broken a nail, and Bevis had cut his foot with the sharp edge of a fossil shell projecting from one of the stones. But that was nothing, they could think of nothing but the bird. While they were gathering armsful of dead sticks from among the trees, they remembered that John Young, who always paunched the rabbits and hares and got everything ready for the kitchen, said coots and moorhens must be skinned, they could not be plucked because of the "dowl."

Dowl is the fluff, the tiny featherets no fingers can remove. So after they had carried the wood they had collected to the round hollow in the field beyond the sycamore-trees, they took out their knives, and haggled the skin off. They built their fire very skilfully; they had made so many in the Peninsula (for there is nothing so pleasant as making a fire out of doors), that they had learnt exactly how to do it. Two short sticks were stuck in the ground and a third across to them, like a triangle. Against this frame a number of the smallest and driest sticks were leaned, so that they made a tiny hut. Outside these there was a second layer of longer sticks; all standing, or rather leaning against the first.

If a stick is placed across, lying horizontally, supposing it catches fire, it just burns through the middle and that is all, the ends go out. If it is stood nearly upright, the flame draws up it; it is certain to catch; it burns longer and leaves a good ember. They arranged the rest of their bundles ready to be thrown on when wanted, and then put some paper, a handful of dry grass, and a quantity of the least and driest twigs, like those used in birds'-nests, inside the little hut. Then having completed the pile they remembered they had no matches.

"It's very lucky," said Bevis. "If we had we should have to throw them away. Matches are not proper."

"Two pieces of wood," said Mark. "I know; you rub them together till they catch fire, and one piece must be hard and the other soft."

"Yes," said Bevis, and taking out his knife he cut off the end of one of the larger dead branches they had collected, and made a smooth side to it. Mark had some difficulty in finding a soft piece to rub on it, for those which touched soft crumbled when rubbed on the hard surface Bevis had prepared.

A bit of willow seemed best, and Bevis seizing it first, rubbed it to and fro till his arm ached and his face glowed. Mark, lying on the grass, watched to see the slight tongue of flame shoot up, but it did not come.

Bevis stopped, tired, and putting his hand on the smooth surface found it quite warm, so that they had no doubt they could do it in time. Mark tried next, and then Bevis again, and Mark followed him; but though the wood became warm it would not burst into flame, as it ought to have done.

Chapter Thirteen
Savages Continued—The Mast Fitted

"This is very stupid," said Bevis, throwing himself back at full length on the grass, and crossing his arms over his face to shield his eyes from the sun.

"They ought not to tell us such stupid things," said Mark. "We might rub all day."

"I know," said Bevis, sitting up again. "It's a drill; it's done with a drill. Give me my bow—there, don't you know how Jonas made the hole in Tom's gun?"

Jonas the blacksmith, a clever fellow in his way, drilled out a broken nipple in the bird-keeper's muzzle-loading gun, working the drill with a bow. Bevis and Mark, always on the watch everywhere, saw him do it.

They cut a notch or hole in the hard surface of the thicker bough, and shaped another piece of wood to a dull point to fit in it. Bevis took this, placed it against the string of his bow, and twisted the string round it. Then he put the point of the stick in the hole; Mark held the bough firm on the ground, but immediately he began to work the bow backwards and forwards, rotating the drill alternate ways, he found that the other end against which he pressed with his chest would quickly fray a hole in his jacket. They had to stop and cut another piece of wood with a hole to take the top of the drill, and Bevis now pressed on this with his left hand (finding that it did not need the weight of his chest), and worked the bow with his right.

The drill revolved swiftly, it was really very near the savages' fire-drill; but the expected flame did not come. The wood was not dry enough, or the point of friction was not accurately adjusted; the wood became quite hot, but did not ignite. You may have the exact machinery and yet not be able to use it, the possession of the tools does not make the smith. There is an indefinite something in the touch of the master's hand which is wanting.

Bevis flung down the bow without a word, heaving a deep sigh of rage.

"Flint and steel," said Mark presently.

"Hum!"

"There's a flint in the gateway," continued Mark. "I saw it just now; and you can knock it against the end of your knife—"

"You stupe; there's no tinder."

"No more there is."

"I hate it—it's horrid," said Bevis. "What's the use of trying to do things when everything can't be done?"

He sat on his heels as he knelt, and looked round scowling. There was the water—no fire to be obtained from thence; there was the broad field—no fire there; there was the sun overhead.

"Go home directly, and get a burning-glass—unscrew the telescope."

"Is it proper?" said Mark, not much liking the journey.

"It's not matches," said Bevis sententiously.

Mark knew it was of no use, he had to go, and he went, taking off his jacket before he started, as he meant to run a good part of the way. It was not really far, but as his mind was at the hollow all the while the time seemed twice as long. After he had gone Bevis soon found that the sunshine was too warm to sit in, though while they had been so busy and working their hardest they had never noticed it. Directly the current of occupation was interrupted the sun became unbearable. Bevis went to the shadow of the sycamores, taking the skinned bird with him, lest a wandering beast of prey—some weasel or jackal—should pounce on it.

He thought Mark was a very long time gone; he got up and walked round the huge trunk of the sycamore, and looked up into it to see if any immense boa-constrictor was coiled among its great limbs. He thought they would some day build a hut up there on a platform of poles. Far out over the water he saw the Unknown Island, and remembered that when they sailed there in the ship there was no knowing what monsters or what enchantments they might encounter. So he walked out from the trees into the field to look for some moly to take with them, and resist Circe.

The bird's-foot lotus he knew was not it. There was one blue spot of veronica still, and another tiny blue flower which he did not know, besides the white honeysuckle clover at which the grey bees were busy, and would scarce stir from under his footsteps. He found three button mushrooms, and put them in his pocket. Wandering on among the buttercup stalks and bunches of grass, like a butterfly drawn hither and thither by every speck of colour, he came to a little white flower on a slender stem a few inches high, which he gathered for moly. Putting the precious flower—good against sorcery—in his breast-pocket for safety, he rose from his knees, and saw Mark coming by the sycamores.

Mark was hot and tired with running, yet he had snatched time enough to bring four cherries for Bevis. He had the burning-glass—a lens unscrewed from the telescope, and sitting on the grass they focussed the sun's rays on a piece of paper. The lens was powerful and the summer sun bright, so that in a few seconds there was a tiny black speck, then the faintest whiff of bluish smoke, then a leap of flame, and soon another, till the paper burned, and their fire was lit. As the little hut blazed up they put some more boughs on, and the dead leaves attached to them sent up a thin column of smoke.

"The savages will see that," said Mark, "and come swarming down from the hills."

"We ought to have made the fire in a hole," said Bevis, "and put turf on it."

"What ever shall we do?" said Mark. "They'll be here in a minute."

"Fetich," said Bevis. "I know, cut that stick sharp at the end, tie a handful of grass on it—be quick—and run down towards the elms and stick it up. Then they'll think we're doing fetich, and won't come any nearer."

"First-rate," said Mark, and off he went with the stick, and thrust it into the sward with a wisp of grass tied to the top. Bevis piled on the branches, and when he came back there was a large fire. Then the difficulty was how to cook the bird? If they put it on the ashes, it would burn and be spoiled; if they hung it up, they could not make it twist round and round, and they had no iron pot to boil it; or earthenware pot to drop red-hot stones in, and so heat the water without destroying the vessel. The only thing they could do was to stick it on a stick, and hold it to the fire till it was roasted, one side at a time.

"The harpoon will do," said Bevis. "Spit him on it."

"No," said Mark; "the bone will burn and get spoiled—spit him on your arrow."

"The nail will burn out and spoil my arrow, and I've lost one in the elms. Go and cut a long stick."

"You ought to go and do it," said Mark; "I've done everything this morning."

"So you have; I'll go," said Bevis and away; he went to the nut-tree hedge. He soon brought back a straight hazel-rod to which he cut a point, the bird was spitted, and they held it by turns at the fire, sitting on the sward.

It was very warm in the round, bowl-like hollow, the fire at the bottom and the sun overhead, but they were too busy to heed it. Mark crept on hands and knees up the side of the hollow while Bevis was cooking, and cautiously peered over the edge to see if any savages were near. There were none in sight; the fetich kept them at a distance.

"We must remember to take the burning-glass with us when we go on our voyage," said Bevis.

"Perhaps the sun won't shine."

"No. Mind you tell me, we will take some matches, too; and if the sun shines use the glass, and if he doesn't, strike a match."

"We shall want a camp-fire when we go to war," said Mark.

"Of course we shall."

"Everybody keeps on about the war," said Mark. "They're always at me."

"I found these buttons," said Bevis; "I had forgotten them."

He put the little mushrooms, stems upwards, on some embers which had fallen apart from the main fire. The branches as they burned became white directly, coated over with a film of ash, so that except just in the centre they did not look red, though glowing with heat under the white layer. Even the flames were but just visible in the brilliant sunshine, and were paler in colour than those of the hearth. Now and then the thin column of grey smoke, rising straight up out of the hollow, was puffed aside at its summit by the light air wandering over the field. As the butterflies came over the edge of the hollow into the heated atmosphere, they fluttered up high to escape it.

"I'm sure it's done," said Mark, drawing the stick away from the fire. The bird was brown and burnt in one place, so they determined to eat it and not spoil it by over-roasting. When Bevis began to carve it with his pocket-knife he found one leg quite raw, the wings were burnt, but there was a part of the breast and the other leg fairly well cooked. These they ate, little pieces at a time, slowly, and in silence, for it was proper to like it. But they did not pick the bones clean.

"No salt," said Mark, putting down the piece he had in his hand.

"No bread," said Bevis, flinging the leg away.

"We don't do it right somehow," said Mark. "It takes such a long time to learn to be savages."

"Years," said Bevis, picking a mushroom from the embers, it burned his fingers and he had to wait till it was cooler. The mushrooms were better, their cups held some of the juice as they cooked, retaining the sweet flavour. They were so small, they were but a bite each.

"I am thirsty," said Mark. Bevis was the same, so they went down towards the water. Mark began to run down the slope, when Bevis suddenly remembered.

"Stop," he cried; "you can't drink there."

"Why not?"

"Why of course it's the New Sea. We must go round to the Nile; it's fresh water there."

So they ran through the firs to the Nile, and lapped from the brook. On the way home a little boy stepped out from the trees on the bank where it was high, and he could look down at them.

"I say!"—he had been waiting for them—"say!"

"Well!" growled Mark.

"Bevis," said the boy. Bevis looked up, he could not demean himself to answer such a mite. The boy looked round to see that he was sure of his retreat through the trees to the gap in the hedge he could crawl through, but they would find it difficult. Besides, they would have to run up the bank, which was thick with brambles. He got his courage together and shouted in his shrill little voice,—

"I say, Ted says he shan't play if you don't have war soon."

Mark picked up a dead branch and hurled it at the mite; the mite dodged it, and it broke against a tree, then he ran for his life, but they did not follow. Bevis said nothing till they reached the blue summer-house at home and sat down. Then he yawned.

"War is a bother," he said, putting his hands in his pockets, and leaning back in an attitude of weary despair at having to do something. If the rest would not have played, he would have egged them on with furious energy till they did. As they were eager he did not care.

"O! well!" said Mark, nodding his head up and down as he spoke, as much as to indicate that he did not care personally; but still, "O! well! all I know is, if you don't go to war Ted will have one all to himself, and have a battle with somebody else. I believe he sent Charlie." Charlie was the mite.

"Did he say he would have a war all to himself?" said Bevis, sitting upright.

"I don't know," said Mark, nodding his head. "They say lots of things."

"What do they say?"

"O! heaps; perhaps you don't know how to make war, and perhaps—"

"I'll have the biggest war," said Bevis, getting up, "that was ever known, and Ted's quite stupid. Mind, he doesn't have any more cherries, that's certain. I hate him—awfully! Let's make the swords."

"All right," said Mark, jumping up, delighted that the war was going to begin. He was as eager as the others, only he did not dare say so. Most of the afternoon they were cutting sticks for swords, and measuring them so as to have all the same length.

Next morning the governor went with them to bathe, as he wanted to see how they were getting on with their swimming. They had the punt, and the governor stopped it about twenty yards from the shore, to which they had to swim. Bevis dived first, and with some blowing and spluttering and splashing managed to get to where he could bottom with his feet. He could have gone further than that, but it was a new feeling to know that he was out of his depth, and it made him swim too fast and splash. Mark having seen that Bevis could do it, and knowing he could swim as far as Bevis could, did it much better.

The governor was satisfied and said they could now have the blue boat, but on two conditions, first, that they still kept their promise not to go out of their depth, and secondly, that they were to try and see every day how far they could swim along the shore. He guessed they had rather neglected their swimming; having learnt the art itself they had not tried to improve themselves. He said he should come with them once or twice a week, and see them dive from the punt so as to get used to deep water.

If they would practise along the shore in their depth till they could swim from the rocky point to the rails, about seventy yards, he would give them each a present, and they could then go out of their depth. He was obliged to be careful about the depth till they could swim a good way, because he could not be always with them, and fresh water is not so buoyant as the sea, so that young swimmers soon tire.

The same day they carried the mast up, and fitted it in the hole in the thwart. The mast was a little too large, but that was soon remedied. The bowsprit was lashed to the ring to which the painter was fastened, and at its inner end to the seat and mast. Next the gaff was tried, and drew up and down fairly well through the curtain-ring. But one thing they had overlooked—the sheets, or ropes for the jib, must work through something, and they had not provided any staples. Besides this, there was the rudder to be fitted with a tiller instead of the ropes. Somehow they did not like ropes; it did not look like a ship. This instinct was right, for ropes are not of much use when sailing; you have no power on the rudder as with a tiller.

After fitting the mast and bowsprit they unshipped them, and carried them home for safety till the sails were ready. Bevis wanted Mark to go and ask Frances to be quick, but Mark was afraid to return just yet, as Frances would now know from Jack that he had forgotten the letter. Every now and then bundles of sticks for swords, and longer ones for spears and darts, and rods for arrows, were brought in by the soldiery. All these were taken upstairs into the bench-room, or armoury, because they did not like their things looked at or touched, and there was a look and key to that room. Bevis always kept the key in his pocket now.

They could not fit a head to the oyster barrel for the fresh water on the voyage, but found a large round tin canister with a tight lid, such as contain cornflour, and which would go inside the oyster barrel. The tin canister would hold water, and could be put in the barrel, so as to look proper. More sticks kept coming, and knobbed clubs, till the armoury was crowded with the shafts of weapons. Now that Bevis had consented to go to war, all the rest were eager to serve him, so that he easily got a messenger to take a note (as Mark was afraid to go) to Frances to be quick with the stitching.

In the evening Bevis tore another broad folio page or fly-leaf from one of the big books in the parlour, and took it out into the summer-house, where they kept an old chair—the back gone—which did very well for a table. Cutting his pencil, Bevis took his hat off and threw it on the seat which ran round inside; then kneeling down, as the table was so low, he proceeded to draw his map of the coming campaign.

Chapter Fourteen
The Council of War

"I say!"

"Battleaxes—"

"Saint George is right—"

"Hold your tongue."

"Pikes twenty feet long."

"Marching two and two."

"Do stop."

"I shall be general."

"That you won't."

"Romans had shields."

"Battleaxes are best."

"Knobs with spikes."

"I say—I say!"

"You're a donkey!"

"They had flags—"

"And drums."

"I've got a flute."

"I—"

"You!"

"Yes, *me*."

"Hi!"

"Tom."

"If you hit me, I'll hit you."

"Now."

"Don't."

"Be quiet."

"Go on."

"Let's begin."

"I will," —buzz—buzz—buzz!

Phil, Tom, Ted, Jim, Frank, Walter, Bill, "Charl," Val, Bob, Cecil, Sam, Fred, George, Harry, Michael, Jack, Andrew, Luke, and half a dozen more were talking all together, shouting across each other, occasionally fighting, wrestling, and rolling over on the sward under an oak. There were two up in the tree, bellowing their views from above, and little Charlie ("Charl") was astride of a bough which he had got hold of, swinging up and down, and yelling like the rest. Some stood by the edge of the water, for the oak was within a few yards of the New Sea, and alternately made ducks and drakes, and turned to contradict their friends.

On higher ground beyond, a herd of cows grazed in perfect peace, while the swallows threaded a maze in and out between them, but just above the grass. The New Sea was calm and smooth as glass, the sun shone in a cloudless sky, so that the shadow of the oak was pleasant; but the swallows had come down from the upper air, and Bevis, as he stood a little apart listening in an abstracted manner to the uproar, watched them swiftly gliding in and out. He had convened a council of all those who wanted to join the war in the fields, because it seemed best to keep the matter secret, which could not be done if they came to the house, else perhaps the battle would be interfered with. This oak was chosen as it was known to every one.

It grew alone in the meadow, and far from any path, so that they could talk as they liked. They had hardly met ten minutes when the confusion led to frequent blows and pushes, and the shouting was so great that no one could catch more than disjointed sentences. Mark now came running with the map in his hand; it had been forgotten, and he had been sent to fetch it. As he came near, and they saw him, there was a partial lull.

"What an awful row you have been making," he said, "I heard it all across the field. Why don't you choose sides?"

"Who's to choose?" said Ted, as if he did not know that he should be one of the leaders. He was the tallest and biggest of them all, a head and shoulders above Bevis.

"You, of course," came in chorus.

"And you needn't look as if you didn't want to," shouted somebody, at which there was a laugh.

"Now, Bevis, Bevis! Sides." They crowded round, and pulled Bevis into the circle.

"Best two out of three," said Mark. "Here's a penny."

"Lend me one," said Ted.

Phil handed him the coin.

"You'll never get it back," cried one of the crowd. Ted was rather known for borrowing on the score of his superior strength.

"Bevis, you're dreaming," as Bevis stood quiet and motionless, still in his far-away mood. "Toss."

Bevis tossed, the penny spun, and he caught it on the back of his hand; Mark nudged him.

"Cry."

"Head," said Ted. Mark nudged again; but it was a head. Mark stamped his foot.

"Tail," and it was a tail; Ted won the toss.

"I told you how to do it," whispered Mark to Bevis in a fierce whisper, "and you didn't."

"Choose," shouted everybody. Ted beckoned to Val, who came and stood behind him. He was the next biggest, very easy tempered and a favourite, as he would give away anything.

"Choose," shouted everybody again. It was Bevis's turn, and of course he took Mark. So far it was all understood, but it was now Ted's turn, and no one knew who he would select. He looked round and called Phil, a stout, short, slow-speaking boy, who had more pocket-money, and was more inclined to books than most of them.

"Who shall I have?" said Bevis aside to Mark.

"Have Bill," said Mark. "He's strong."

Bill was called, and came over. Ted took another—rank and file—and then Bevis, who was waking up, suddenly called "Cecil."

"You stupe," said Mark. "He can't fight."

Cecil, a shy, slender lad, came and stood behind his leader.

"You'll lose everybody," said Mark. "Ted will have all the big ones. There, he's got Tim. Have Fred; I saw him knock George over once."

Fred came, and the choosing continued, each trying to get the best soldiers, till none were left but little Charlie, who was an odd one.

"He's no good," said Ted; "you can put him in your pocket."

"I hate you," said Charlie; "after all the times I've run with messages for you. Bevis, let me come your side."

"Take him," said Ted; "but mind, you'll have one more if you do, and I shall get some one else."

"Then he'll get a bigger one," said Mark. "Don't have him; he'll only be in the way."

Charlie began to walk off with his head hanging.

"Cry-baby," shouted the soldiery. "Pipe your eye."

"Come here," said Bevis; Charlie ran back delighted.

"Well, you have done it," said Mark in a rage. "Now Ted will have another twice as big. What's the use of my trying when you are so stupid! I never did see. We shall be whopped anyhow."

Quite heedless of these reproaches, Bevis asked Ted who were to be his lieutenants.

"I shall have Val and Phil," said Ted.

"And I shall have Mark and Cecil," said Bevis. "Let us count. How many are there on each side? Mark, write down all ours. Haven't you a pocket-book? well, do it on the back of the map. Ted, you had better do the same."

"Phil," said Ted, who was not much of a student, "you put down the names."

Phil, a reader in a slow way, did as he was bidden. There were fifteen on Bevis's side, and fourteen on Ted's, who was to choose another to make it even.

"There's the muster-roll," said Mark, holding up the map.

"But how shall we know one another?" said George.

"Who's friends, and who's enemies," said Fred.

"Else we shall all hit one another anyhow," said another.

"Stick feathers in our hats."

"Ribbons round our arms would be best," said Cecil. "Hats may be knocked off."

"Ribbons will do first-rate," said Bevis. "I'll have blue; Ted, you have red. You can buy heaps of ribbon for nothing."

"Phil," said Ted, "have you got any money?"

"Half-a-crown."

"Lend us, then."

"No, I shan't," said Phil: "I'll buy the ribbons myself."

"Let's have a skirmish now," said Bill. "Come on, Val," and he began to whirl his hands about.

"Stop that," said Bevis. "Ted, there's a truce, and if you let your fellows fight it's breaking it. Catch hold of Bill—Mark, Cecil, hold him."

Bill was seized, and hustled round behind the oak, and kept there till he promised to be quiet.

"But when are we going to begin?" asked Jack.

"Be quick," said Luke.

"War! war!" shouted half a dozen, kicking up their heels.

"Hold your noise," said Ted, cuffing one of his followers. "Can't you see we're getting on as fast as we can. Bevis, where are we going to fight?"

"In the Plain," said Bevis. "That's the best place."

"Plenty of room for a big battle," said Ted. "O, you've got it on the map, I see."

The Plain was the great pasture beside the New Sea, where Bevis and Mark bathed and ran about in the sunshine. It was some seventy or eighty acres in extent, a splendid battle-field.

"We're not going to march," said Mark, taking something on himself as lieutenant.

"We're not going to march," said Bevis. "But I did not tell you to say so; I mean we are not going to march the thousand miles, Ted; we will suppose that."

"All right," said Ted.

"But we're going to have camps," continued Bevis. "You're going to have your camp just outside the hedge towards the hills, because you live that side, and you will come that way. Here,"—he showed Ted a circle, drawn on the map to represent a camp,—"that's yours; and this is ours on this side, towards our house, as we shall come that way."

"The armies will encamp in sight of each other," said Phil. "That's quite proper. Go on, Bevis. Shall we send out scouts?"

"We shall light fires and have proper camps," said Bevis.

"And bring our great-coats and cloaks, and a hamper of grub," interrupted Mark, anxious to show that he knew all about it.

Bevis frowned, but went on. "And I shall send one of my soldiers to be with you, and you will send one of yours to be with me—"

"Whatever for?" said Ted. "That's a curious thing."

"Well, it's to know when to begin. When we are all there, we'll hoist up a flag—a handkerchief will do on a stick—and you will hoist up yours, and then when the war is to begin, you will send back my soldier, and I will send back yours, and they will cross each other as they are running, and when your soldier reaches you, and mine reaches me—"

"I see," said Ted, "I see. Then we are to march out so as to begin quite fair."

"That's it," said Bevis. "So as to begin at the same minute, and not one before the other. I have got it all ready, and you need not have sent people to worry me to make haste about the war."

"Well, how was I to know if you never said anything?" said Ted.

"And who are we to be?" said Val. "Saxons and Normans, or Crusaders, or King Arthur—"

"We're all to be Romans," said Bevis.

"Then it will be the Civil War," said Phil, who had read most history.

"Of course it will," said Bevis, "and I am to be Julius Caesar, and Ted is to be Pompey."

"I won't be Pompey," said Ted; "Pompey was beat."

"You must," said Bevis.

"I shan't."

"But you *must*."

"I won't be beaten."

"I shall beat you easily."

"That you won't," very warmly.

"Indeed I shall," said Bevis quite composedly, "as I am Caesar I shall beat you very easily."

"Of course we shall," added Mark.

"You won't; I've got the biggest soldiers, and I shall drive you anyhow."

"No, you won't."

"I've got Val and Phil and Tim, and I mean to have Ike, so now—"

"There, I told you," said Mark to Bevis. "He's got all the biggest, and Ike is a huge big donk of a fellow."

"It's no use," said Bevis, not in the least ruffled; "I shall beat you."

"Not you," said Ted, hot and red in the face. "Why I'll pitch you in the water first."

"Take you all your time," said Bevis, shutting his lips tighter and beginning to look a little dangerous. "Shut up," said Val.

"Stop," said Phil and Bill and George, pressing in.

"Hush," said Cecil. "It's a truce."

"Well, I won't be Pompey," said Ted sullenly. "Then we must have somebody who will," said Bevis sharply, "and choose again."

"I wouldn't mind," said some one in the crowd. "Nor I," said another.

"If I was general I wouldn't mind being Pompey. Let me, Bevis."

"Who's that," said Ted. "If any one says that I'll smash him." When he found he could so easily be superseded he surrendered. "Well, I'll be Pompey," he said, "but mind I shan't be beat."

"Pompey ought to win if he can," said Val; "that's only fair."

"What's the use of fighting if we are to be beat?" said Phil.

"Of course," said Bevis, "how very stupid you all are! Of course, Ted is to win if he can; he's only to be called Pompey to make it proper. I know I shall beat him, but he's to beat us if he can."

"I'm only to be called Pompey, mind," said Ted; "mind that. We are to win if we can."

"Of course;" and so this delicate point was settled after very nearly leading to an immediate battle.

"Hurrah for Pompey!" shouted George, throwing up his hat.

"Hurrah for Caesar!" said Bill, hurling up his. This was the signal for a general shouting and uproar. They had been quiet ten minutes, and were obliged to let off their suppressed energy. There was a wild capering round the oak.

"Ted Pompey," said Charlie, little and impudent, "what fun it will be to see you run away!" For which he had his ears pulled till he squealed.

"Now," shouted Mark, "let's get it all done. Come on." The noise subsided somewhat, and they gathered round as Ted and Bevis began to talk again.

"Caesar," said Phil to Bevis, "if you're Caesar and Ted's Pompey, who are we? We ought to have names too."

"I'm Mark Antony," said Mark, standing bolt upright.

"Very well," said Bevis. "Phil, you can be—let me see, Varro."

"All right, I'm Varro," said Phil; "and who's Val? Oh, I know,"—running names over in his mind,—"he's Crassus. Val Crassus, do you hear?"

"Capital," said Crassus. "I'm ready."

"Then there's Cecil," said Mark; "who's he?"

"Cecil!" said Phil. "Cecil—Cis—Cis—Scipio, of course."

"First-rate," said Mark. "Scipio Cecil, that's your name."

"Write it down on the roll," said Bevis. The names were duly registered; Pompey's lieutenants as Val Crassus and Phil Varro, and Caesar's as Mark Antony and Scipio Cecil. After which there was a great flinging of stones into the water and more shouting.

"Let's see," said Ted. "If there's fifteen each side, there will be five soldiers to each, five for captains, and five for lieutenants."

"Cohorts," said Phil. "A cohort each, hurrah!"

"Do be quiet," said Ted. "How can we go on when you make such a row? Caesar Bevis, are all the swords ready?"

"No," said Bevis. "We must fix the length, and have them all the same."

They got a stick, and after much discussion cut it to a certain length as a standard; Mark took charge of it, and all the swords were to be cut off by it, and none to be any thicker. There were to be cross-pieces nailed or fastened on, but the ends were to be blunt and not sharp.

"No sticking," said Ted. "Only knocking."

"Only knocking and slashing," said Bevis. "Stabbing won't do, and arrows won't do, nor spears."

"Why not?" said Mark, who had been looking forward to darting his javelin at Ted Pompey.

"Because eyes will get poked out," said Bevis, "and there would be a row. If anybody got stuck and killed, there would be an awful row."

"So there would," said Mark. "How stupid!" Just as if people could not kill one another without so much fuss!

"And no hitting at faces," said Bevis, "else if somebody's marked there will be a bother."

"No," said Ted. "Mind, no slashing faces. Knock swords together."

"Knock swords together," said Bevis. "Make rattling and shout."

"Shout," said Mark, bellowing his loudest.

"How shall we know when we're killed?" said Cecil.

"Well, you *are* a stupe," said Val. "Really you are." They all laughed at Cecil.

"But I don't know," said Ted Pompey. "You just think, how shall we know who's beat? Cecil's not so silly."

"No more he is," said Mark. "Bevis, how is it to be managed?"

"Those who run away are beaten," said Charlie. "You'll see Ted run fast enough." Away he scampered himself to escape punishment.

"Of course," said Bevis. "One way will be if people run away. O! I know, if the camp is taken."

"Or if the captain is taken prisoner," said Phil; "and tied up with a cord."

"Yes," continued Bevis. "If the captain is taken prisoner, and if the eagles are captured—"

"Eagles," said Ted Pompey.

"Standards," said Phil. "That's right: are we to have proper eagles, Caesar Bevis?"

"Yes," said Bevis. "Three brass rings round sticks will do. Two eagles each, don't you see, Ted, like flags, only eagles, that's proper."

"Who keeps the ground wins the victory," said Cecil.

"Right," said Ted. "I shall soon tie up Bevis—we must bring cords."

"You must catch him first," said Mark.

"Captains must be guarded," said Val. "Strong guards round them and awful fighting there," licking his lips at the thought of it.

"Captain Caesar Bevis," said Tim, who had not spoken before, but had listened very carefully. "Is there to be any punching?"

"Hum!" Bevis hesitated, and looked at Ted.

"I think so," said Ted, who had long arms and hard fists.

"If there's punching," cried Charlie from the oak, into which he had climbed for safety; "if there's punching, only the big blokes can play."

"No punching," said Mark eagerly, not that he feared, being stout and sturdy, but seizing at anything to neutralise Ted's big soldiers.

"No punching," shouted a dozen at once; "only pushing."

"Very well," said Bevis, "no punching, and no tripping—pushing and wrestling quite fair."

"Wrestling," said Ted directly. "That will do."

"Stupid," said Mark to Bevis; then louder, "Only nice wrestling, no 'scrumpshing.'"

"No 'scrumpshing,'" shouted everybody.

Ted stamped his foot, but it was of no use. Everybody was for fair and pleasant fighting.

"Never mind," said Ted. "We'll shove you out of the field."

"Yah! yah!" said Charlie, making faces at him.

"If anybody does what's agreed shan't be done," said Mark, still anxious to stop Ted's design; "that will lose the battle, even if it's won."

"It ought to be all fair," said Val, who was very big, but straightforward.

"If anything's done unfair, that counts against whoever does it," said Cecil.

"No sneaking business," shouted everybody. "No sneaking and hitting behind."

"Certainly not," said Bevis. "All quite fair."

"Somebody must watch Ted, then," said Charlie from the oak.

Ted picked up a piece of dead stick and threw it at him. He dodged it like a squirrel.

"If you say such things," said Bevis, very angry, "you shan't fight. Do you hear?"

"Yes," said Charlie, penitent. "I won't any more. But it's true," he whispered to Fred under him.

"Everything's ready now, isn't it?" said Ted.

"Yes, I think so," said Bevis.

"You haven't fixed the day," said Val.

"No, more I have."

"Let's have it to-day," said Fred.

They caught it up and clamoured to have the battle at once.

"The swords are not ready," said Mark.

"Are the eagles ready?" asked Phil.

"Two are," said Mark.

"The other two shall be made this afternoon," said Bevis. "Phil, will you go in to Latten for the blue ribbon for us; here's three shillings."

"Yes," said Phil, "I'll get both at once—blue and red, and bring you the blue."

"To-morrow, then," said Fred. "Let's fight to-morrow."

But they found that three of them were going out to-morrow. So, after some more discussion, the battle was fixed for the day after, and it was to begin in the evening, as some of them could not come before. The camps were to be made as soon after six o'clock as possible, and, this agreed to, the council broke up, though it was understood that if anything else occurred to any one, or the captains wished to make any alterations, they were to send despatches by special messengers to each other. The swords and eagles for Ted's party were to be fetched the evening before, and smuggled out of window when it was dark, that no one might see them.

"Hurrah!"

So they parted, and the oak was left in silence, with the grass all trampled under it. The cattle fed down towards the water, and the swallows wound in and out around them.

Chapter Fifteen
The War Begins

As they were walking home Mark reproached Bevis with his folly in letting Ted, who was so tall himself, choose almost all the big soldiers.

"It's no use to hit you, or pinch you, or frown at you, or anything," grumbled Mark; "you don't take any more notice than a tree. Now Pompey will beat us hollow."

"If you say any more," said Bevis, "I will hit you; and it is you who are the donk. I did not want the big ones. I like lightning-quick people, and I've got Cecil, who is as quick as anything—"

"What's the use of dreaming like a tree when you ought to have your eyes open; and if you're like that in the battle—"

"I tell you the knights were not the biggest; they very often fought huge people and monsters. And don't you remember how Ulysses served the giant with one eye?"

"I should like to bore a hole through Ted like that," said Mark. "He's a brute, and Phil's as cunning as ever he can be, and you've been and lost the battle."

"I tell you I've got Cecil, who is as quick as lightning, and all the sharp ones, and if you say any more I won't speak to you again, and I'll have some one else for lieutenant."

Mark nodded his head, and growled to himself, but he did not dare go farther. They worked all the afternoon in the bench-room, cutting off the swords to the same length, and fastening on the cross-pieces. They did not talk, Mark was sulky, and Bevis on his dignity. In the evening Phil came with the ribbons.

Next morning, while they were making two more eagles for Pompey, Val Crassus came to say he thought they ought to have telescopes, as officers had field-glasses; but Bevis said they were not invented in the time of their war. The day was very warm, still, and cloudless, and, after they had fixed the three brass rings on each long rod for standards, Bevis brought the old grey book of ballads out of the parlour into the orchard. Though he had used it so often he could not find his favourite place quickly, because the pages were not only frayed but some were broader than others, and would not run through the fingers, but adhered together.

When he had found "Kyng Estmere," he and Mark lay down on the grass under the shadow of a damson-tree, and chanted the verses, reading them first, and then singing them. Presently they came to where:—

"Kyng Estmere threwe the harpe asyde,
And swith he drew his brand;
And Estmere he, and Adler yonge,
Right stiffe in stour can stand.

"And ay their swords soe sore can byte,
Through help of gramaryè,
That soone they have slayne the Kempery men,
Or forst them forth to flee."

These they repeated twenty times, for their minds were full of battle; and Bevis said after they had done the war they would study gramaryè or magic. Just afterwards Cecil came to ask if they ought not to have bugles, as the Romans had trumpets, and Bevis had a bugle somewhere. Bevis thought it was proper, but it was of no use, for nobody could blow the bugle but the old Bailiff, and he could only get one long note from it, so dreadful that you had to put your hands to your ears if you stood near. Cecil also said that in his garden at home there was a bay-tree, and ought they not to have wreaths for the victors? Bevis said that was capital, and Cecil went home with orders from Caesar to get his sisters to make some wreaths of bay for their triumph when they had won the battle.

Soon after sunset that evening the Bailiff looked in, and said there was some sheet lightning in the north, and he was going to call back some of the men to put tarpaulins over two or three loaded waggons, as he thought, after so much dry, hot weather, there would be a great storm. The lightning increased very much, and after it grew dusk the flashes lit up the sky. Before sunset the sky had seemed quite cloudless, but now every flash showed innumerable narrow bands of clouds, very thin, behind which the electricity played to and fro.

While Bevis and Mark were watching it, Bevis's governor came out, and looking up said it would not rain and there was no danger; it was a sky-storm, and the lightning was at least a mile high. But the lightning became very fierce and almost incessant, sometimes crooked like a scimitar of flame, some times jagged, sometimes zigzag; and now and then vast acres of violet light, which flooded the ground and showed every tree and leaf and flower, all still and motionless; and after which, though lesser flashes were going on, it seemed for a moment quite dark, so much was the eye overpowered.

Bevis and Mark went up into the bench-room, where it was very close and sultry, and sat by the open window with the swords for Pompey bound up in two bundles and the standards, but they were half afraid no one would come for them. Their shadows were perpetually cast upon the white wall opposite as the flashes came and went. The crossbow and lance, the boomerang and knobbed clubs were visible, and all the tools on the bench. Now and then, when the violet flashes came, the lightning seemed to linger in the room, to fill it with a blaze and stop there a moment. In the darkness that followed one of these they heard a voice call "Bevis" underneath the window, and saw Phil and Val Crassus, who had come for the swords. Mark lowered the bundles out of window by a cord, but when they had got them they still stood there.

"Why don't you go?" said Mark.

"Lightning," said Val. "It's awful." It really was very powerful. The pears on the wall, and everything however minute stood out more distinctly defined than in daytime.

"It's a mile high," said Bevis. "It won't hurt you."

"Ted wouldn't come," said Phil. "He's gone to bed, and covered his head. You don't know how it looks out in the fields, all by yourself; it's all very well for you indoors."

"I'll come with you," said Bevis directly; up he jumped and went down to them, followed by Mark.

"Why wouldn't Ted come?" said Mark.

"He's afraid," said Phil, "and so was I till Val said he would come with me. Will lightning come to brass?" The flashes were reflected from the brass rings on the standards.

"I tell you it won't hurt," said Bevis, quite sure, because his governor had said so. But when they had walked up the field and were quite away from the house and the trees which partly obstructed the view, he was amazed at the spectacle, for all the meadow was lit up; and in the sky the streamers of flame rose in and out and over each other, till you could not tell which flash was which in the confusion of lightning. Bevis became silent and fell into one of his dream states, when, as Mark said, he was like a tree. He was lost—something seemed to take him out of himself. He walked on, and they went with him, till he came to the gate opening on the shore of the New Sea.

"O, look!" they all said at once.

All the broad, still water, smooth as glass, shone and gleamed, reflecting back the bright light above; and far away they saw the wood (where Bevis and Mark once wandered) as plain as at noontide.

"I can't go home to-night," said Phil. Val Crassus said he could sleep at his house, which was much nearer; but he, too, hesitated to start.

"It *is* awful," said Mark.

"It's nothing," said Bevis. "I like it." The continuous crackling of the thunder just then deepened, and a boom came rolling down the level water from the wooded hill. Bevis frowned, and held his lips tight together. He was startled, but he would not show it.

"I'll go with you," he said; and though Mark pointed out that they would have to come back by themselves, he insisted. They went with Pompey's lieutenants till Val's house, lit up by lightning, was in sight; then they returned. As they came into the garden, Bevis said the battle ought to be that night, because it would read so well in the history afterwards. The lightning continued far into the night, and still flashed when sleep overcame them.

Next morning Bevis sprang up and ran to the window, afraid it might be wet; but the sun was shining and the wind was blowing tremendously, so that all the willows by the brook looked grey as their leaves were turned, and the great elms by the orchard bowed to the gusts.

"It's dry," shouted Bevis, dancing.

"Hurrah!" said Mark, and they sang, —

> "Kyng Estmere threwe his harpe asyde,
> And swith he drew his brand."

This was the day of the great battle, and they were impatient for the evening.

There was a letter on the breakfast-table from Bevis's grandpa, enclosing a P.O.O., a present of a sovereign for him. He asked the governor to advance him the money in two half-sovereigns. The governor did so, and Bevis immediately handed one of them to Mark.

About dinner-time there came a special messenger from Pompey with a letter, which was in Pompey's name, but Phil's handwriting. "Ted Pompey to Caesar Bevis. Please tell me who you are going to send to be with me in my camp, and let him come to the stile in Barn Copse at half-past five, and I will send Tim to be with you till the white handkerchiefs are up. And tell me if the lieutenants are to carry the eagles, or some one else."

Bevis wrote back:—"Caesar to Pompey greeting,"—this style he copied from his books,—"Caesar will send Charlie to be with you, as he can ran quick, though he is little. The lieutenants are not to carry the eagles, but a soldier for them. And Caesar wishes you health."

Then in the afternoon Mark had to go and tell Cecil and others, who were to send on the message to the rest of their party, to meet Bevis at the gate by the New Sea at half-past five, and to mind and not be one moment later. While Mark was gone, Bevis roamed about the garden and orchard, and back again to the stable and sheds, and then into the rick-yard, which was strewn with twigs and branches torn off from the elms that creaked as the gale struck them; then indoors, and from room to room. He could not rest anywhere, he was so impatient.

At last he picked up the little book of the Odyssey, with its broken binding and frayed margin, from the chair where he had last loft it; and taking it up into the bench-room, opened it at the twenty-second book, where his favourite hero wreaked his vengeance on the suitors. With his own bow in his right hand, and the book in his left, Bevis read, marching up and down the room, stamping and shouting aloud as he came to the passages he liked best:—

"Swift as the word, the parting arrow sings,
And bears thy fate, Antinous, on its wings!

"For fate who fear'd amidst a feastful band?
And fate to numbers by a single hand?

"Two hundred oxen every prince shall pay;
The waste of years refunded in a day.
Till then thy wrath is just,—Ulysses burn'd
With high disdain, and sternly thus return'd.

"Soon as his store of flying fates was spent,
Against the wall he set the bow unbent;
And now his shoulders bear the massy shield,
And now his hands two beamy javelins wield."

Bevis had dropped his bow and seized one of Mark's spears, not hearing, as he stamped and shouted, Mark coming up the stairs. Mark snatched up one of the swords, and as Bevis turned they rattled their weapons together, and shouted in their fierce joy. When satisfied they stopped, and Mark said he had come by the New Sea, and the waves were the biggest he had ever seen there, the wind was so furious.

They had their tea, or rather they sat at table, and rushed off as soon as possible; who cared for eating when war was about to begin! Seizing an opportunity, as the coast was clear, Mark ran up the field with the eagles, which, having long handles, were difficult to hide. Cecil and Bill took the greatcoat, and a railway-rug, which Bevis meant to represent his general's cloak. He followed with the basket of provisions on his shoulder, and was just thinking how lucky they were to get off without any inquiries, when he found they had forgotten the matches to light the camp-fire. He came back, took a box, and was going out again when he met Polly the dairymaid.

"What are you doing now?" said she. "Don't spoil that basket with your tricks—we use it. What's in it?" putting her hand on the lid.

"Only bread-and-butter and ham, and summer apples. It's a picnic."

"A picnic. What's that ribbon for?" Bevis wore the blue ribbon round his arm.

"O! that's nothing."

"I've half a mind to tell—I don't believe you're up to anything good."

"Pooh! don't be a donk," said Bevis. "I'll give you a long piece of this ribbon when I come back."

Off he went, having bribed Scylla, but he met Charybdis in the gateway, where he came plump on the Bailiff.

"What's up now?" he gruffly inquired.

"Picnic."

"Mind you don't go bathing; the waves be as big as cows."

"Bathing," said Bevis, with intense contempt. "We don't bathe in the evening. Here, you—" donk, he was going to say, but forebore; he gave the Bailiff a summer apple, and went on. The Bailiff bit the apple, muttered to himself about "mischief," and walked towards the rick-yard. In a minute Mark came to meet Bevis.

"You did him?" he said.

"Yes," said Bevis, "and Polly too."

"Hurrah!" shouted Mark. "They're all there but one, and he's coming in five minutes."

Bevis found his army assembled by the gate leading to the New Sea. Each soldier wore a blue ribbon round the left arm for distinction; Tim, who had been sent by Pompey to be with them till all was ready, wore a red one.

"Two and two," said Caesar Bevis, taking his sword and instantly assuming a general's authoritative tone. He marshalled them in double file, one eagle in front, one halfway down, where his second lieutenant, Scipio Cecil, stood; the basket carried in the rear as baggage. Caesar and Mark Antony stood in front side by side.

"March," said Bevis, starting, and they followed him.

The route was beside the shore, and so soon as they left the shelter of the trees the wind seemed to hit them a furious blow, which pushed them out of order for a moment. The farther they went the harder the wind blow, and flecks of brown foam, like yeast, came up and caught against them. Rolling in the same direction as they were marching, the waves at each undulation increased in size, and when they came to the bluff Bevis walked slowly a minute, to look at the dark hollows and the ridges from whose crests the foam was driven.

But here leaving the shore he led the army, with their brazen eagles gleaming in the sun, up the slope of the meadow where the solitary oak stood, and so beside the hedge-row till they reached the higher ground. The Plain, the chosen battle-field, was on the other side of the hedge, and it had been arranged that the camps should be pitched just without the actual campaigning-ground. On this elevated place the gale came along with even greater fury; and Mark Antony said that they would never be able to light a camp-fire that side, they must get through and into shelter.

"I shall do as I said," shouted Bevis, scarcely audible, for the wind blew the words down his throat. But he kept on till he found a hawthorn bush, with brambles about the base, a detached thicket two or three yards from the hedge, and near which there was a gap. He stopped, and ordered the standard-bearer behind him to pitch the eagle there. The army halted, the eagles were pitched by thrusting the other end of the rods into the sward, the cloaks, coats, and rug thrown together in a heap, and the soldiers set to work to gather sticks for the fire. Of these they found plenty in the hedge, and piled them up in the shelter of the detached thicket.

Bevis, Mark Antony, and Scipio Cecil went through the gap to reconnoitre the enemy. They immediately saw the smoke of his camp-fire rising on the other side of the Plain, close to a gateway. The smoke only rose a little above the hedge there—the fire was on the other side—and was then blown away by the wind. None of Pompey's forces were visible.

"Ted, I mean Pompey, was here first," said Mark Antony. "He'll be ready before us."

"Be quick with the fire," shouted Caesar.

"Look," said Scipio Cecil. "There's the punt."

Behind the stony promontory at the quarry they could see the punt from the high ground where they stood; it was partly drawn ashore just inside Fir-Tree Gulf, so that the projecting point protected it like a breakwater. The old man (the watcher) had started for the quarry to get a load of sand as usual, never thinking, as how should he think? that the gale was so furious. But he found himself driven along anyhow, and unable to row back; all he could do was to steer and struggle into the gulf, and so behind the Point, where he beached his unwieldy vessel. Too much shaken to dig sand that day, and knowing that he could not row back, he hid his spade and the oars, and made for home on foot. But the journey by land was more dangerous than that by sea, for he insensibly wandered into the high road, and came to an anchor in the first inn, where, relating his adventures on the deep with the assistance of ardent liquor, he remained.

Bevis, who had gone to light the fire with the matches in his pocket, now returned through the gap, and asked if anything had been seen of Pompey's men. As he spoke a Pompeian appeared, and mounting the spars of the distant gate displayed a standard, to which was attached a white handkerchief, which fluttered in the breeze.

"They're ready," said Mark Antony. "Come on. Which way shall we march? Which way are you going?"

The smoke of Caesar's fire rose over the hedge, and swept down by the gale trailed along the ground towards Pompey's. Bevis hastened back to the camp, and tied his handkerchief to the top of an eagle, Mark followed. "Which way are you going?" he repeated. "Where shall we meet them? What are you going to do?"

"I don't know," said Caesar, angrily pushing him. "Get away."

"There," growled Mark Antony to Scipio, "he doesn't know what he's going to do, and Phil is as cunning as—"

The standard-bearer sent by Caesar pushed by him, got through the gap, and held up the white flag, waving it to attract more attention. In half a minute, Pompey's flag was hauled down, and directly afterwards some one climbed over the gate and set out running towards them. It was Charlie. "Run, Tim," said Caesar Bevis; "we're ready." Tim dashed through the gap, and set off with all his might.

"Two and two," shouted Caesar. "Stand still, will you?" as they moved towards the opening. "Take down that flag."

The eagle-bearer resumed his place behind him. Caesar signing to the legions to remain where they were, went forward and stood on the mound. He watched the runners and saw them pass each other nearly about the middle of the great field, for though little, Charlie was swift of foot, and full of the energy which is more effective than size.

"Let's go."

"Now then."

"Start."

The legions were impatient and stamped their feet, but Caesar would not move. In a minute or two Charlie reached him, red and panting with running.

"Now," shouted Bevis, "march!" and he leaped into the field; Charlie came next for he would not wait to take his place in the ranks. The legions rushed through anyhow, eager to begin the fray.

"Two and two," shouted Caesar, who would have no disorder.

"Two and two," repeated his first lieutenant, Mark Antony.

"Two and two," said Scipio Cecil, punching his men into place.

On they went, with Caesar leading, straight across the wind-swept plain for Pompey's camp. The black swifts flew about them, but just clearing the grass, and passing so close as to seem almost under foot. There were hundreds of them, they come down from the upper air, and congregate in a great gale; they glided over the field in endless turns and windings. Steadily marching, the army had now advanced a third part of the way across the field.

"Where's Pompey?" said Scipio Cecil.

"Where shall we meet and fight?" said Mark Antony.

"Silence," shouted Bevis, "or I'll degrade you from your rank, and you shan't be officers."

They were silent, but every one was looking for Pompey and thinking just the same. There was the gate in full view now, and the smoke of Pompey's camp, but none of the enemy were visible. Bevis was thinking and trying to make out whether Pompey was waiting by his camp, or whether he had gone round behind the hedge, and if so, which way, to the right towards the quarry, or to the left towards the copse, but he could not decide, having nothing to guide him.

But though uncertain in his own mind, he was general enough not to let the army suppose him in doubt. He strode on in silence, but keeping the sharpest watch, till they came to the waggon track, crossing the field from left to right. It had worn a gully or hollow way leading down to the right to the hazel hedge, where there was a gate. They came to the edge of the hollow way, where there were three thick hawthorn bushes and two small ash-trees.

"Halt!" said Caesar Bevis, as the bushes partly concealed them from view. "Stay here. Let no one move."

Bevis himself went round the trees and looked again, but he could see nothing: Pompey and his army were nowhere in sight. He could not tell what to do, and returned slowly, thinking, when looking down the hollow way an idea struck him.

"Scipio, take your men," — ("Cohort," said Antony) — "take your cohort, jump into the road, and go down to the gate there. Keep out of sight — stoop: slip through the gate, and go up inside the hedge, dart round the corner and seize Ted's camp. Quick! And mind, if they're all there, of course you're not to fight, but come back. Now — quick."

Scipio Cecil jumped into the hollow way followed by his five soldiers, and stooping so as to be hidden by the bank, ran towards the gate in the hazel hedge. They watched him till the cohort had got through the gate.

"Now what shall we do?" said Mark Antony.

"How can I tell what to do when Pompey isn't anywhere?" said Bevis, in a rage.

"Put me up a tree," said Charlie, "perhaps I could see."

"You've no business to speak," said Bevis; but he used the idea, and told two of them to "bunt" (shove) Charlie up one of the ash-trees till he could grasp a branch. Then Charlie, agile as a squirrel, was up in a minute.

"There's no one in their camp," he shouted down. "Cecil's rushing on it. Pompey, O! I can see him."

"Where?"

"There by the copse," pointing to the left and partly behind them.

"Which way is he going?" asked Bevis.

"That way," —to the left.

"Our camp," said Mark.

"That's it," said Bevis. "Come down, quick. Turn to the left," (to the army). "No, stop. Charlie, how many are there with Pompey?"

"Six, ten—oh, I can't count: I believe it's all. I can't see any anywhere else."

"Quick!" shouted Bevis, turning his legions to the left. "Quick march! Run!"

Chapter Sixteen
The Battle of Pharsalia

They left Charlie to get down how he could, and started at a sharp pace to meet and intercept Pompey. Now, if Pompey had continued his course behind the hedge all the way, he must have got to Caesar's camp first; as Caesar could not crush through the hedge. But when Pompey came to the gate, from which the waggon track issued into the field, he saw that he could make a short cut thence to the gap by Caesar's camp, instead of marching round the irregular curve of the hedge. Caesar, though running fast to meet him, was at that moment passing a depression in the ground, and was out of sight. Pompey seized so favourable an opportunity, came through the gate, and ordering "Quick march!" ran towards the gap. When Caesar came up out of the depression he saw Pompey's whole army running with their backs almost turned away from him towards the gap by the camp. They seemed to flee, and Caesar's legions beholding their enemies' backs, raised a shout. Pompey heard, and looking round, saw Caesar charging towards his rear. He halted and faced about, and at the same time saw that his own camp was in Caesar's possession; for there was an eagle at the gate there, and his baggage was being pitched over. Nothing daunted, Pompey ordered his soldiers to advance, and pushed them with his own hands into line, placing Crassus and Varro, one at either end.

As he came running, Caesar saw that the whole of Pompey's army was before them, while he had but two-thirds of his, and regretted now that he had so hastily detached Scipio's cohort. But waving his sword, he ran at the head of his men, keeping them in column. They were but a hundred yards apart, when Pompey faced about, and so short a distance was rapidly traversed.

Caesar's sword was the first to descend with a crash upon an enemy's weapon, but Antony was hardly a second later, and before they could lift to strike again, the legion behind, with a shout, pushed them by its impetus right through Pompey's line.

When Caesar Bevis stopped running, and looked round, there was a break in the enemy's army, which was divided into two parts. Bevis instantly made at the part on his left (where Phil Varro commanded), thinking, instinctively, to crush this half with all his soldiers. But as they did not know what his object was, for he had no time even to give an order, only four or five followed him. The rest paused and faced Val Crassus; and these Ted Pompey and six or seven of his men at once attacked.

Bevis met Phil Varro, and crossed swords with him. Clatter! crash! snap! thump! bang! They slashed and warded: Bevis's shoulder was stung with a sharp blow. He struck back, and his sword sliding down Varro's, broke the cross-piece, and rapped his fingers smartly. Before Varro could hit again, two others, fighting, stumbled across and interrupted the combat.

"Keep together! Keep together!" shouted Phil Varro. "Ted—Pompey, Pompey! Keep together!"

Slash! swish! crash! thump! "Hit him! Now then! He's down! Hurrah!" Crash! Crack—a sword split and flew in splinters.

"Follow Bevis!" shouted Mark, "Stick to Bevis! Fred! Bill! Quick!" He had privately arranged with these two, Fred and Bill, who were the biggest on their side, that all three should keep close to Bevis and form a guard. Mark was very shrewd, and he guessed that Ted Pompey, being so much stronger and well-supported with stout soldiers, would make every effort to seize Caesar, who was slightly built, and bind him prisoner. He did not tell Bevis that he had arranged this, for Bevis was a stickler for his imperial authority, and if Mark had told him, would be quite likely to countermand it.

Whirling his sword with terrible fury, Caesar Bevis had cut his way through all between. Slight as he was, the intense energy within him carried him through the ranks. He struck a sword from one; overthrew another rushing against him; sent a third on his knees, and reaching Phil, hit him on the arm so heavy a blow that, for a moment, he could not use his weapon, but gave way and got behind his men.

"Hurrah!" shouted Mark. "Follow Bevis! Stick to Bevis!"

"Here I am," said Bill, the young giant hitting at Varro.

"So am I," said Fred, the other giant, and slashing Varro on the side. Varro turned aside to defend himself, when Mark Antony rushed at and overturned him thump on the sward.

"Hurrah! Down they go!" Such a tremendous shout arose in another direction, that Caesar Bevis, Mark, and the rest, turned fresh from their own victory to see their companions thrashed.

"Over with them!"

Ted Pompey, Val Crassus, and the other half of the divided line had attacked the remainder of the legion, which paused, and did not follow Caesar. Separated from Bevis, they fought well, and struggled hard to regain him; and, while they could keep their assailants at sword's-length, maintained the battle. But Varro's shout, "Keep together! Keep together! Pompey! Keep together!" reminded Ted of what Phil Varro had taught him, and, signing to Crassus and his men to do the same, he crossed his arms, held his head low, and, with Crassus and the rest, charged, like bulls with eyes closed, disregarding the savage chops and blows he received. The manoeuvre was perfectly successful; their weight sent them right over Caesar's men, who rolled on the ground in all directions.

"There!" said Mark, "what did I tell you?"

"Come on!" shouted Caesar Bevis, and he ran to assist the fallen. He fell on Crassus, who chanced to be nearest, with such violence that Val gave way, when Bevis left him to attack Ted. Ted Pompey, nothing loth, lifted his sword and stepped to meet him.

"Bill! Fred!" shouted Mark; and these three, hustling before Caesar Bevis, charged under Pompey's sword, for he could not hit three ways at once; and, thump, he measured his length on the grass.

"Cords!—Ropes!" shouted Mark. "Bill—the rope. Hold him down, Fred! O! You awful stupe! O!"

He stood stock-still, mouth agape; for Bevis, pushing Fred aside as he was going to kneel on Ted as men kneel on a fallen horse's head, seized Ted by the arm and helped him up.

"Three to one's not fair," he said. "Ted, get your sword and fight *Me*."

Ted looked round for his sword, which had rolled a yard or two. At the same moment Varro, having got on his feet again, rushed up and struck Caesar a sharp blow on his left arm. He turned, Varro struck again, but Fred guarded it off on his sword. Three soldiers, with Varro, surrounded Fred and Bevis, and, for the moment, they could do nothing but fence off the blows. Ted Pompey having found his sword, ran to aid Varro, when Mark hit him: he turned to strike at Mark, but a body of soldiers, with George and Tim at their head, rushed by, fighting with others, and bore Mark and Ted before them bodily. In a second all was confusion. On both sides the leaders were separated from their troops, the battle spread out, covering forty yards or more, and twenty individual combats raged at once. All the green declivity was covered with scattered parties, and no one knew which had the better.

"Keep together! Keep together!" shouted Varro, as he struck and rushed to and fro. "I tell you, keep together! Ted! Ted! Pompey! Keep together!"

Swish! slash! clatter! thump!

"Hurrah!"

"He's down!"

"Quick!"

"You've got it!"

"Take that!" Slash! But the slain arose again and renewed the fight.

Shrewd Mark Antony having knocked his man over, paused on the higher part of the slope where he chanced to be, and looked down on the battle. He noted Phil Varro go up to Pompey and urge something. Pompey seemed to yield, and shouted, "A tail! a tail! Crassus! George! Tim! A tail!"

Mark dashed down the slope to Bevis, who was fighting on the level ground. He hastened to save the battle, for a "tail" is a terrible thing. The leader, who must be the biggest, gets in front, the next biggest behind him, a third behind him, and so on to the last, forming a tail, which is in fact a column, and so long as it keeps formation will bore a hole through a crowd. Before he could get to Caesar, for so many struck at him in passing that it took him some time to pass fifty yards, the tail was made—Pompey in front, next Val Crassus, then Varro, then Ike (a big fellow, but who had as yet done nothing, and was no good except for the weight of his body), then George, then Tim, and two more. Eight of them in a mighty line, which began to descend the slope.

"Look!" said Mark Antony at last, touching Caesar Bevis, "look there! It's a tail!"

"It doesn't matter," said Bevis, looking up.

"Doesn't matter! Why, they'll *hunt* us!"

And Pompey did hunt them, downright hunt them along. Before Fred and Bill could come at Mark's call, before they could shake themselves free of their immediate opponents, Pompey came thundering down, and swept everything before him.

"Out of the way!" cried Mark. "Bevis, out of the way! O! Now!" He wrung his hands and stamped.

Bevis stood and received the charge which Pompey led straight at him. Pompey, with his head down and arms crossed to defend it, ran with all his might. Bevis, never stirring, lifted his sword. There was a part of Pompey's bare head which his arms did not cover. It was a temptation, but he remembered the agreement, and he struck with all his strength on Pompey's left arm. So hard was the blow that the tough sword snapped, and Pompey groaned with pain, but in the same instant Caesar felt as if an oak or a mountain had fallen on him. He was hurled to the ground with stunning force, and the column passed over him, one stepping on his foot.

There he lay for half a minute, dazed, and they might easily have taken him prisoner, but they could not stop their rush till they had gone twenty or thirty yards. By that time, Mark, Fred, and Bill had dragged Bevis up, and put a sword which they snatched from a soldier into his hand. He limped, and looked pale and wild for a minute, but his blood was up, and he wanted to renew the fight. They would not let him, they pulled him along.

"It's no use," said Mark; "you can't. We must get to the trees. Here, lean on me. Run. Sycamores! Sycamores!" he shouted.

"Sycamores! trees!" shouted Fred and Bill to their scattered followers. They urged Caesar to run, he limped, but kept pace with them somehow. Pompey had turned by now, and went through a small body of Caesar's men, who had rushed towards him when they saw he was down, just as if they had been straws. Still they checked the column a little, as floating beams check heavy waves, and so gave Caesar time to get more ahead.

"Sycamores!" Mark continued to shout as he ran, and the broken legions easily understood they were to rally there. At that moment the battle was indeed lost. Pompey ranged triumphant. Leading his irresistible and victorious column with shouting, he chased the flying Caesar.

Little Charlie, left in the ash-tree, could not get down, but saw the whole of the encounter. The lowest bough was too high to drop from, the trunk too large to clasp and slide down. He was imprisoned and helpless, with the war in sight. He chafed and raged and shouted, till the tears of vexation rolled down his cheeks. Full of fiery spirit it was torture to him to see the battle in which he could not take part. For awhile, watching the first shock, he forgot everything else in the interest of the fight; but presently, when the combatants separated, and were strewn as it were over the slope, he saw how easily at that juncture any united body could have swept the field, and remembered Scipio Cecil. Why did not Cecil come?

He looked that way, and from his elevation could see Cecil standing on the gate by Pompey's camp. Having sacked the camp, put the fire out, and thrown all the coats over the gate into a heap in the field, Scipio did not know what next he ought to do, and wondered that no orders reached him from Caesar. He got up on the highest bar except one of the gate, but could see no one, the undulations of the ground completely concealing the site of the conflict. He did not know what to do; he waited a while and looked again. Once he fancied he heard shouting, but the gale was so strong he could not be certain.

Charlie in the ash-tree now seeing Pompey form the tail, or column, worked himself into a state of frenzy. He yelled, he screamed to Scipio to come, till he was hoarse, and gasped with the straining of his throat; but the howling of the tremendous wind through the trees by the gate, prevented Scipio from hearing a word. Had he known Charlie was in the tree he might have guessed there was something wrong from his frantic gestures, but he did not, and as there were so many scattered trees in the field, there was nothing to make him look at that one in particular. Charlie waved his hat, and at last flung it up into the air, waved his handkerchief—all in vain.

He could see the crisis, but could not convey a knowledge of it to the idle cohort. He looked again at the battle. Caesar was down and trampled under foot. He threw up his arms, and almost lost his balance in his excitement. The next minute Caesar was up, and he and his lieutenant were flying from Pompey. The column chased them, and the whole scene—the flight and the pursuit—passed within a short distance, half a stone's throw of the ash-tree.

Quite wild, and lost to everything but his auger, Charlie the next second was out on a bough, clinging to it like a cat. He crawled out some way, till the bough bent a little with his weight. His design was to get out till it bowed towards the ground, and so lowered him—a perilous feat! He got half a yard further, and then swung under it, out and out, till the branch gave a good way. He tried again, and looked down; the ground was still far below. He heard a shout, it stimulated him. He worked out farther, till the branch cracked loudly; it would break, but would not bend much farther. His feet hung down now; he only held by his hands. Crack! Another shout! He looked down wildly, and in that instant saw a little white knob—a button mushroom in the grass. He left hold, and dropped. The little mushroom saved him, for it guided him, steadied his drop; his feet struck it and smashed it, and his knees giving under him, down he came.

But he was not hurt, his feet, as he hung from the bowed branch, were much nearer the earth than it had looked to him from his original perch, and he alighted naturally. The shock dazed him at first, just as Bevis had been confused, a few minutes previously. In a minute he was all right, and running with all his speed towards Scipio.

As Caesar ran, with the shout of victorious Pompey close behind, he said, "If we could charge the column sideways we could break it—"

"If," snorted Mark, with the contempt of desperation; "if—of course!"

Caesar was right, but he had not got the means just then. Next minute they reached the first sycamore, not ten yards in front of Pompey. As they turned to face the enemy, with their backs to the great tree, Pompey lowered his head, crossed his arms, and the column charged. Nothing could stop that onslaught, which must have crushed them, but Bevis, quick as thought, pushed Mark and Fred one way and Bill the other, stepping after the latter. Ted Pompey, with his eyes shut, and all the force of his men thrusting behind, crashed against the tree.

Down he went recoiling, and two or three more behind him.

Thwack! thwack! The four defenders hammered their enemies before they could recover the shock.

"Quick!" cried Mark; "tie him—prisoner—quick," pulling a cord from his pocket, and putting his foot on Ted, who was lying in a heap.

Before any one could help Mark the heap heaved itself up, and Val Crassus and Phil Varro hauled their half-stunned leader back out of reach.

Crash! clatter! bang! thwack!

"Backs to trees! Stand with backs to trees!" shouted Bevis, hitting out furiously. "We shall win! Here, Bill!"

They planted themselves, these four, Bevis, Mark, Fred, and Bill, with their backs to the great trunk of the sycamore, standing a foot or two in front of it for room to swing their swords, and a little way apart for the same reason. The sycamore formed a bulwark so that none could attack them in rear.

The column, as it recoiled, widened out, and came on again in a semicircle, surrounding them.

"Give in!" shouted Val. "We're ten to one!" (that was not numerically correct.) "Give in! You'll all be prisoners in a minute!"

"That we shan't," said Bill, fetching him a side way slash.

"If we could only get Scipio up," said Mark. "Where is he? Can't we get him?"

"I forgot him," said Bevis. "There, take that," as he warded a cut and returned it. "I forgot him. Look out, Fred, that's it. Hurrah! Mark," as Mark made a successful cut. "How stupid." In the heat and constant changes of the combat they had totally forgotten Cecil and his cohort.

"Why, we've been fighting two to three," said Bill, "and they haven't done us yet."

"But we mean to," said Tim, and Bill shrank involuntarily under an unexpected knock.

"Some more of you—there," shouted Ted Pompey, as he came to himself, and saw a number of his soldiers in the rear watching the combat. "You,"—in a rage,—"you go round behind and worry them there; and some of you get up in the tree and hit down."

"O! botheration!" said Mark, as he heard the last order.

"We *must* get Cecil somehow," said Bevis.

"Now then," yelled Ted Pompey, stamping in terrible fury, "do as I tell you; go round the tree, and 'bunt' somebody up into it!"

He passed his hand across his bruised forehead, wiping off a fragment of bark which adhered indented in the skin, and rushed into the fight. Ted fought that day like a hero; twice severely punished, he returned to the war with increased determination. He was nervous at lightning, but he feared no mortal being. He was as brave as brave could be. These heavy knocks seemed only to touch him on the quick and arouse a stronger will. When he came in the combat became tremendous.

Like knights with their backs to the tree, the four received them. The swords crossed and rattled, and for two or three minutes nothing else was heard; they were too busy to shout. The eight of the column would have succeeded better had not so many of the others pressed in to get a safe knock at Bevis, hitting from behind the bigger ones so as to be themselves in safety. These impeded Val and Phil and the first line.

One and all struck at Bevis. The dust flew from his coat, his shoulders smarted, his arms were sore, his left arm, which he used as a guard like a shield, almost numb with knocks.

His face grew pale with anger. He frowned and set his lips tight together, his eyes gleamed. The hail of blows descended on him, and though his wrist began to weary, he could not repay one-tenth of that they gave him.

"Give in! Give in!" shouted Val, who was in front of him, and he put his left hand on Bevis's shoulder. With a twist of his wrist Bevis hit his right hand so sharp a knock that the sword flew out of it, and for a second Val was daunted.

"Give in! give in!" shouted Phil, pushing to Val's assistance. "You're done! It's no good. You can't help it. Hurrah!"

Two soldiers appeared in the fork of the tree above. Though so huge the trunk was short, and they began to strike down on Mark, who was forced to stand out so far from the tree that he was in great danger of being seized, and would have been, had they not been so bent on Bevis.

Bevis breathed hard and panted. So thick came the hail that he could do nothing. If he lifted his sword it was beaten down, if he struck, ten knocks came for one. He received his punishment in silence. Tim had the cord to bind him ready: they made a noose to throw, over his head.

"Stick to Bevis," shouted Mark. "Bevis—Bevis—stick to Bevis—Fred—ah!"—a smart knock made him grind his teeth, and four or five assailants rushing in separated him from Caesar.

Bevis was beaten on his knee. He crouched, his left side against the tree with his left hand against it, hitting wild and savage, and still keeping a short clear space with his sword.

"Stop!" cried Val, himself desisting. "That's enough. Stop! stop! Don't hit him! He's done. We've got him! Now, Phil."

Phil and Tim rushed in with the noose: Bevis sprang up, drove his head into Phil and sent him whirling with Tim under. Bevis made good use of the moment's breathing time he thus obtained, punishing three of his hardest thrashers.

"Keep together," shouted Phil as he got up on his knees. "If Ted would only do as I said. Hurrah!"

They had hammered Bevis by sheer dint of knocks down on his knees again. Fred and Bill in vain tried to get to him; they were attacked front and rear: Mark quite beside himself with rage, pushed, wrestled, and struck, but they encompassed him like bees. Bevis could hit no more; he warded as well as he could, he could not return.

"Shame! shame!" cried Val, pulling two back, one with each hand. "Don't hit him! He's down!"

"Why doesn't he give in, then?" said Phil, black as thunder.

Ted Pompey, who had watched this scene for a moment without moving, smiled grimly as he saw Bevis could not hit.

"Now," said he, "Phil, Tim, George—Val's too soft. Come on—keep close—in we go and have him. Hurrah! Hang it! I say!"

"Whoop!"

Volume Two

Chapter One
The Battle Continued—Scipio's Charge

Scipio's cohort rushed them clean away from the sycamore. In a mass, Scipio Cecil and his men (fetched by Charlie), with half or more of Caesar's scattered soldiers, who rallied at once to Cecil's compact party, rushed them right away. Cecil forced his men to be quiet as they ran; they saw the point, and there was not a sound till in close order they fell on Pompey. Pompey, Val, Phil, and the whole attacking party were swept away like leaves before the wind. Had they seen Scipio coming, or heard him, or in the least expected him, it would not have been so. But thus suddenly burst on from the rear, they were helpless, and carried away by the torrent.

In a second Bevis, Mark, Fred, and Bill, found themselves free. Bevis stood up and breathed again. They came to him. "Are you hurt?" said Mark.

"Not a bit," said Bevis, laughing as he shook himself together. "Look there!"

Whirled round and round by the irresistible pressure of the crowd, Pompey and his lieutenants were hurried away, shouting and yelling, but unable even to strike, so closely were they hemmed in.

"They've got my eagle," said Mark in a fury. His standard-bearer had been overthrown while he defended himself at the tree, and the eagle taken from him.

"Phil's down," said Fred. "So's Tim! And Ike! Hurrah!"

"Look at little Charlie hitting!" said Bill. "Shout for Charlie," said Bevis. "Capital!"

"My eagle," said Mark.

"Quick," said Bevis suddenly. "Mark—quick; you and Fred, and Bill, and these,"—three or four soldiers who came up now things looked better—"run quick, Mark, and get in the hollow, you know where we cooked the bird, they're going that way. See, Ted's beginning to fight again, and you will be behind him. Make an ambush, don't you see? Seize him as he goes by. Quick! I'm tired, I'll follow in a minute."

Off ran Mark, Fred, Bill, and the rest, and making a little circuit, got into the bowl-like hollow. The crowd with Scipio Cecil was still thrusting Pompey and his men before them, but Ted had worked himself free by main force, and he and Val Crassus, side by side, were fighting as they were forced backwards. Step by step they went backwards, but disputing every inch, straight back for the hollow where Mark and his party were crouching. In half a minute Ted would certainly be taken.

"Victory!" shouted Bevis, in an ecstasy of delight. He had been leaning against the sycamore: he stood up and stepped just in front of it to see better, shading his eyes (for his hat had gone long since) with his left hand, the point of his sword touched the ground. He was alone, he rejoiced in the triumph of his men. The gale blew his hair back, and brushed his cheek. His colour rose, a light shone in his eyes.

"We've won!" he shouted. Just then the hurricane smote the tree, and as there was less noise near him, he heard a bough crack above. He looked up, thinking it might fall; it did not, but when he looked back Ted was gone.

"He's down!" said Bevis. "They've got him."

He could see Mark Antony, who had risen out of the hollow; thus caught between two forces, Scipio pushing in front, the Pompeians broke and scattered to the right in a straggling line.

"Hurrah! But where's Ted? Hurrah!"

Bevis was so absorbed in the spectacle that, though the fight was only a short distance from him, the impulse to join it did not move him. He was lost in the sight.

"They're running!"

"I've got you!"

Ted Pompey pounced on him from behind the sycamore-tree; Bevis involuntarily started forward, just escaping his clutch, struck, parried, and struck again.

Pompey, while driven backwards step by step by Scipio, had suddenly caught sight of Bevis standing alone by the sycamore. He slipped from Scipio, and ran round just as Bevis looked up at the cracking bough, and Mark sprang out of the hollow. Scipio's soldiers shouted, seeing Pompey as they thought running away. Mark for a moment could not understand what had become of him, the next he was occupied in driving the Pompeians as they yielded ground. Pompey running swiftly got round behind the tree and darted on Caesar, whose strategy had left him alone, intending to grasp him and seize him by main force.

Caesar Bevis slipped from him by the breadth of half an inch.

Pompey hit hard, twice, thrice; crash, clatter. His arm was strong, and the sword fell heavy; rattle, crash. He hit his hardest, fearing help would come to Bevis. Swish! slash!

Thwack! He felt a sharp blow on his shoulder. Bevis kept him off, saw an opportunity, and cut him. With swords he was more than Ted's match. He and Mark had so often practised they had both become crafty at fencing. The harder Ted hit, overbalancing himself to put force into the blow, and the less able to recover himself quickly, the easier Bevis warded, and every three knocks gave Ted a rap. Ted danced round him, trying to get an advantage; he swung his sword to and fro in front of him horizontally. Bevis retired to avoid it past the sycamore. Finding this answer, Ted swung it all the more furiously, and Bevis retreated, watching his chance, and they passed several trees on to the narrow breadth of level short sword between the trees and the quarry.

Ted's chest heaved with the fury of his blows; Bevis could not ward them, at least not so as to be able to strike afterwards. But suddenly, as Ted swung it still fiercer, Bevis resolutely received the sword full on his left arm—thud, and stopped it. Before Ted could recover himself Bevis hit his wrist, and his sword dropped from it on the ground.

Ted instantly rushed in and grappled with him. He seized him, and by sheer strength whirled him round and round, so that Bevis's feet but just touched the sward. He squeezed him, and tried to get him across his hip to throw him; but Bevis had his collar, and he could not do it. Bevis got his feet the next instant, and worked Ted, who breathed hard, back.

The quarry was very near, they were hardly three yards from the edge of the cliff; the sward beneath their feet was short where the sheep had fed it close to the verge, and yellow with lotus flowers. Yonder far below were the waves, but they saw nothing but themselves.

The second's pause, as Bevis forced Ted back two steps, then another, then a fourth, as they glared at each other, was over. Ted burst on him again. He lifted Bevis, but could not for all his efforts throw him. He got his feet again.

"You punched me!" hissed Ted between his teeth.

"I didn't."

"You did." Ted hit him with doubled fist. Bevis instantly hit back. They struck without much parrying. At this, as at swords, Bevis's quick eye and hand served him in good stead. He kept Ted back; it was at wrestling Ted's strength was superior. Ted got a straight-out blow on the chin; his teeth rattled.

He hurled himself bodily on Bevis; Bevis stepped back and avoided the direct hug, but the cliff yawned under him. Into Ted's mind there flashed, vivid as a picture, something he had seen when two men were fighting in the road. Without a thought, it was done in the millionth of a second, he tripped Bevis. Bevis staggered, swung round, half saved himself, clutched at Ted's arm, and put his foot back over the cliff into nothing.

Ted did but see his face, and Bevis was gone. As he fell he disappeared; the edge hid him. Crash!

Ted's face became of a leaden pallor, his heart stopped boating; an uncontrollable horror seized upon him. Some inarticulate sound came from between his teeth. He turned and fled down the slope into the firs, through the fields, like the wind, for his home under the hills. He fled from his own act. How many have done that who could have faced the world! Bevis he knew was dead. As he ran he muttered to himself, constantly repeating it, "His bones are all smashed; I heard them. His bones are all smashed." He never stopped till he reached his home. He rushed upstairs, locked his door, and got into bed with all his things on.

Bevis was not dead, nor even injured. He had scarcely fallen ten feet before he was brought up by a flake, which is a stronger kind of hurdle. It was one of those originally placed along the edge of the precipice to keep cattle from falling over. It had become loose, and a horse rubbing against it sent it over weeks before. The face of the cliff there had been cut into a groove four or five feet wide years ago by the sand-seekers. This groove went straight down to a deep pool of water, which had filled up the ancient digging for the stone of the lower stratum. As the flake tumbled it presently lodged aslant the cutting, and it was in that position when Bevis fell on it.

His weight drove it down several feet farther, when the lower part caught in a ledge at that side of the groove, and it stopped with a jerk. The jerk cracked one bar of the flake, which was made much like a very slender gate, and it was this sound which Ted in his agony of mind mistook for the smashing of bones.

Bevis when he struck the flake instinctively clutched it, and it was well that he did so, or he would have rolled over into the pool. For the moment when he felt his foot go into space, he lost conscious consciousness. He really was conscious, but he had no control, or will, or knowledge at the time, or memory afterwards. That moment passed completely out of his life, till the jerk of the flake brought him to himself. He saw the pool underneath as through the bars of a grating, and clasped the flake still firmer.

In that position, lying on it, he remained for a minute, getting his breath, and recognising where he was. Then he rose up a little, and shouted "Mark!" The gale took his voice out over the New Sea, whose waves were rolling past not more than twenty yards from the base of the cliff.

"Mark!" No one answered. He sat upon the flake still holding it, and began to try and think what he should do if Mark did not come.

His first thought was to climb up somehow, but when he looked he saw that the sand was as straight as a wall. Steps might be cut in the soft sand, and he put his hand in his pocket for his knife, when he reflected that steps for the feet would be of no use unless he had something to hold to as well. Then he looked down, inclined for the moment to drop into the water, which would check his fall, and bring him up without injury. Only the sides of the pool were as steep as the cliff itself, so that any one swimming in it could not climb up to get out.

He recollected the frog which he and Mark put in the stone trough, to see how it swam, and how it went round and round, and could not escape. So he should be if he fell into the pool. He could only swim round and round until his strength failed him. If the flake broke, or tipped, or slipped again, that was what would happen.

Bevis sat still, and tried to think; and while he did so he looked out over the New Sea. The sun was now lower, and all the waves were touched with purple, as if the crests had been sprinkled with wine. The wind blew even harder, as the sun got nearer the horizon, and fine particles of sand were every now and then carried over his head from the edge of the precipice.

What would Ulysses have done? He had a way of getting out of everything; but try how he would, Bevis could not think of any plan, especially as he feared to move much, lest the insecure platform under him should give way. He could see his reflection in the pool beneath, as if it were waiting for him to come in reality.

While he sat quite still, pondering, he thought he heard a rumbling sound, and supposed it to be the noise of tramping feet, as the legions battled above. He shouted again, "Mark! Mark!" and immediately wished he had not done so, lest it should be a party fetched by Pompey to seize him; for if he was captured the battle would be lost. He did not know that Pompey had fled, and feared that his shout would guide his pursuers, forgetting in his excitement that if he could not get up to them, neither could they get down to him. He kept still looking up, thinking that in a minute he should see faces above.

But none appeared, and suddenly there was another rumbling noise, and directly afterwards a sound like scampering, and then a splash underneath him. He looked, and some sand was still rolling down sprinkling the pool. "A rabbit," thought Bevis. "It was a rabbit and a weasel. I see—of course! Yes; if it was a rabbit then there's a ledge, and if there's a ledge I can get along."

Cautiously he craned his head over the edge of the flake, carefully keeping his weight as well back as he could. There was a ledge about two feet lower than the flake, very narrow, not more than three or four inches there; but having seen so many of these ledges in the quarry before, he had no doubt it widened. As that was the extreme end, it would be narrowest there. He thought he could get his foot on it, but the difficulty was what to hold to.

It was of no use putting his foot on a mere strip like that unless there was something for his hand to grasp. Bevis saw a sand-martin pass at that moment, and it occurred to him that if he could find a martin's hole to put his hand in, that would steady him. He felt round the edge of the groove, when, as he extended himself to do so, the flake tipped a little, and he drew back hastily. His chest thumped with sudden terror, and he sat still to recover himself. A humble-bee went by round the edge of the groove, and presently a second, buzzing close to him, and seeing these two he remembered that one had passed before, making three humble-bees.

"There must be thistles," said Bevis to himself, knowing that humble-bees are fond of thistle-flowers, and that there were quantities of thistles in the quarry. "If I can catch hold of some thistles, perhaps I can do it." He wanted to feel round the perpendicular edge again, but feared that the flake would tip. In half a minute he got his pocket-knife, opened the largest blade, and worked it into the sand farthest from the edge—in the corner—so as to hold the flake there like a nail.

Then with the utmost caution, and feeling every inch of his way, he put his hand round the edge, and moving it about presently felt a thistle. Would it hold? that was the next thing; or should he pull it up if he held to it? How could he hold it tight, the prickles would hurt so. He knew that thistles generally have deep roots, and are hard to pull up, so he thought it would be firm, and besides, if there was one there were most likely several, and three or four would be stronger.

Taking out his handkerchief, he put his hand in it, and twisted it round his wrist to make a rough glove, then he knelt up close to the sand wall, and steadied himself before he started. The flake creaked under these movements, and he hesitated. Should he do it, or should he wait till Mark missed him and searched? But the battle—the battle might be lost by then, and Mark and all his soldiers driven from the field, and Pompey would triumph, and fetch long ladders, and take him prisoner.

Bevis frowned till a groove ran up the centre of his forehead, then he moved towards the verge of the flake, and slowly put his foot over till he felt the narrow ledge, at the same time searching about with his hand for the thistle. Now he had his foot on the ledge, and his hand on the stem of the thistle; it was very stout, which reassured him, but the prickles came through the handkerchief. A moment's pause, and he sprang round and stood upright on the ledge.

His spring broke the blade of the knife, and the flake upset and crashed down splash into the pool.

The prickles of the thistle dug deep into his hand, causing exquisite pain.

He clung to the thistle, biting his lips, till he had got his other foot on. One glance showed him his position.

The moment he had his balance he let go of the thistle, and ran along the ledge, which widened to about nine inches or a foot, tending downwards. Running kept him from falling, just as a bicycle remains upright while in motion.

In four yards he leapt down from the ledge to a much broader one, ran along that six or seven yards, still descending, sprang from it down on a wide platform, thence six or eight feet on to an immense heap of loose sand, into which he sank above his knees, struggled slipping as he went down its yielding side, and landed on his hands and knees on the sward below, while still the wavelets raised by the fall of the flake were breaking in successive circles against the sides of the pool.

He was up in a moment, and stamped his feet alternately to shake the sand off; then he pulled out some of the worst of the thistle points stuck in his hand, and kicked his heels up and danced with delight.

Without looking back he ran up on the narrow bank between the excavation and the New Sea, as the nearest place to look round from. The punt was just there inside the headland. He saw that the waves, though much diminished in force by the point, had gradually worked it nearly off the shore. He could see nothing of the battle, but remembering a place where the ascent of the quarry was easy, and where he and Mark had often run up the slope, which was thinly grown with grass, he started there, ran up, and was just going to get out on the field when he recollected that he was alone, and had no sword, so that if Pompey had got a party of his soldiers, and was looking for him, they could easily take him prisoner. He determined to reconnoitre first, and seeing a little bramble bush and a thick growth of nettles, peered out from beside this cover. It was well that he did so.

Val Crassus, with a strong body of Pompeians, was coming from the sycamores direct towards him. They were not twenty yards distant when Bevis saw them, and instantly crouched on hands and knees under the brambles. He heard the tramp of their feet, and then their voices.

"Where can he be?"

"Are you sure you looked all through the firs?"

"Quite sure."

"Well, if he isn't in the firs, nor behind the sycamores, nor anywhere else, he *must* be in the quarry," said Crassus.

"So I think."

"I'm sure."

"Ted's got him down somewhere."

"Perhaps he's hiding from Ted."

"Can you see him now in the quarry?"

They crowded on the edge, looking over Bevis into the excavated hollow beneath. Now Bevis had not noticed when he crouched that he had put his hand almost on the mouth of a wasp's nest, but suddenly feeling something tickle the back of his hand, he moved it, and instantly a wasp, which had been crawling over it, stung him. He pressed his teeth together, and shut his eyes in the endeavour to repress the exclamation which rose; he succeeded, but could not help a low sound in his chest. But they were so busy crowding round and talking they did not hear it.

"I can't see him."

"He's not there."

"He may be hidden behind the stone-heaps. There's a lot of nettles down there," said Crassus.

"Yes," said another, and struck at the nettles by Bevis, cutting down three or four with his sword.

"Anyhow," said Crassus, "we're sure to have him, he can't get away; and Mark's a mile off by this time."

"Look sharp then; let's go down and hunt round the stone heaps."

"There's the old oak," said some one; "it's hollow; perhaps he's in that."

"Let's look in the oak as we go round to get down, and then behind the stones. Are there any caves?"

"I don't know," said Crassus. "Very likely. We'll see. March."

They moved along to the left; Bevis opened his eyes, and saw the sting and its sheath left sticking in his hand. He drew it out, waited a moment, and then peered out again from the brambles. Crassus and the cohort were going towards the old hollow oak, which stood not far from the quarry on low ground by the shore of the New Sea, so that their backs were towards him. Bevis stood out for a second to try and see Mark. There was not a sign of him, the field was quite deserted, and he remembered that Crassus had said Mark was a mile away. "The battle's lost," said Bevis to himself. "Mark has fled, and Pompey's after him, and they'll have me in a minute."

He darted down the slope into the hollow which concealed him for the time, and gave him a chance to think. "If I go out on the Plain they'll see me," he said to himself; "if I ran to the firs I must cross the open first; if I hide behind the stones, they're coming to look. What shall I do? The New Sea's that side, and I can't. O!"

He was over the bank and on the shore in a moment. The jutting point was rather higher than the rest of the ground there, and hid him for a minute. He put his left knee on the punt, and pushed hard with his right foot. The heavy punt, already loosened by the waves, yielded, moved, slid off the sand, and floated. He drew his other knee on, crept down on the bottom of the punt, and covered himself with two sacks, which were intended to hold sand. He was, too, partly under the seat, which was broad. The impetus of his push off and the wind and waves carried the punt out, and it was already fifteen or twenty yards from the land when Crassus and his men appeared.

Chapter Two
The Battle Continued—Mark Antony

They had found the oak empty, and were returning along the shore to search the quarry. The wind brought their voices out over the water.

"Mind, he'll fight if he's there."

"Pooh! we're ten to one."

"Well, he hits hard."

"And he can run. We shall have to catch him when we find him; he can run like a hare."

"Look!"

"The punt's loose."

"So it is."

"Serves the old rascal right. Hope it will sink."

"It's sure to sink in those big waves," said Crassus. "Come on," and down he went into the quarry, where they looked behind the stone heaps and every place they could think of, in vain. Next some one said that perhaps even now Bevis might be in the sycamores, up in the boughs, so they went there and looked, and actually pushed a soldier up into one tree to see the better. After which they went down to the lower ground and searched along the nut tree hedge, some one side, some another, and two up in the mound itself.

"Wherever *can* he be?" said Crassus. "It's extraordinary. And Pompey, too."

"Both of them nowhere."

"I can't make it out. Thrust your sword into those ferns." So they continued hunting the hedge.

Now the way Val Crassus and his cohort came to hunt for Caesar Bevis was like this: At the moment when Pompey pounced on Caesar, the rest of the Pompeians, a little way off, were scattering before Mark Antony and Scipio Cecil, who had attacked them front and rear. Mark Antony, though he had (to him unaccountably) missed Ted, saw the eagle which he had lost before him, and, calling to Cecil, pursued with fury. So terrific was their onslaught, especially as Scipio's cohort was quite fresh, that the Pompeians gave way and ran, not knowing where their general was, and some believing they had seen him fly the combat. This pursuit continued for a good distance, almost down to the group of elms to which Bevis and Mark used to run when they came out from their bath.

As the Pompeians ran, Val Crassus, driven along by the throng, caught his foot against one who had tumbled, and fell. When he got up he found the rest had gone on and left him behind with several stragglers who had escaped at the side of the crowd. As he stood, dubious what to do, and looking round for Pompey, several more stragglers gathered about him, till by-and-by he had a detachment. Still he was uncertain what to do, whether to go after Mark and endeavour to check the rout, or whether to stay there and rally the Pompeians, if possible, to him.

By this time the fugitives, with Antony and Scipio hot on their rear, had gone through the gate to which the hollow way or waggon-track led, and were out of sight. Val Crassus moved towards the rising ground to view what happened in the meadows beyond, when two Pompeians came running to him, and said that Pompey had got Caesar Bevis prisoner.

These were the two who had been hoisted up into the sycamore-tree, at Pompey's order, to slash down at the four defenders. So long as Bevis stood there afterwards watching Scipio drive his recent assailants away, they dared not descend. They had seen Bevis fight like a paladin; and though he was alone they dared not come down. But when Pompey pounced on him, and they went fencing at each other, past the tree, and some distance, they slipped out of the tree, which was very large, but equally short, so that they had not half the depth to fall that Charlie had.

They dreaded to go near the two leaders, for the moment, but watched the main fight, and hesitated to go near it, too, as their friends were in distress. When they turned, Pompey and Caesar were both gone: they looked the other way, and the Pompeians were in full flight. They hid for a few minutes in the bowl-like hollow, where the moor-cock was cooked; and when they ventured to peep out, saw Val Crassus, with the soldiers who had rallied around him. They ran to him with the story of Caesar's capture, and that Ted was holding him, and could but just manage it.

Val Crassus immediately hastened to the sycamores, but when he arrived, found no one, for Pompey had fled, and Bevis was on the flake. Val turned angrily on the two who had brought him this intelligence, but they maintained their story, and being now in for it, added various other particulars; how Caesar had got up once, and how Ted pulled him down again, so that, most likely, Bevis had got away again, and Ted was chasing him.

Crassus shouted, but received no answer; then he went through the firs, and came back to the sycamores, and next to the quarry, where he stood within a yard or two of Bevis without seeing him. Unable to discover either Pompey or Bevis, Crassus was now minutely searching the broad mound of the nut tree hedge.

While he had been thus engaged, Antony and Scipio followed close in the rear of the fugitives across two meadows, Mark forgetting Bevis in his eagerness to recover his standard. As they ran, presently Phil Varro stopped, sat down on the grass, and was instantly taken prisoner. He was short and stout and so overcome with his exertions that he could make no resistance, as they tied his hands behind him.

Antony still continued to pursue, shouting to the soldier with the eagle to surrender. He did not do so, but, looking back and seeing Varro taken, threw it down, the better to escape. So Antony recovered it, and at last, pausing, found himself alone, having outstripped all the rest. He now returned to where Varro was prisoner, and Scipio Cecil came up with another eagle, which he had taken, and which had been carried before Phil Varro.

"Hurrah!" shouted Mark, sitting down to recover breath; and they all rested a minute or two.

"Wreaths!" said Cecil, panting. "Wreaths for the victors!"

"How many did you have made?"

"Two or three. Hurrah! we'll put them on presently."

"Where's Bevis?" said Mark, as he got over his running.

"I haven't seen him," said Cecil.

"Nor I!"

"It's curious."

"Have you seen him?" — to the others.

"Not for a long time."

"No—nor Pompey." Every one remarked on the singular absence of the two leaders.

"Crassus," said Mark. "Bevis is hunting Crassus and Pompey: that's it. Come on. Let's help. March."

He marched along the winding hedge-row towards the Plain, and, turning round a corner, presently came to the gate in the nut tree mound just as Crassus, who had been searching it, opened the gate.

"Charge!" shouted Mark, and they dashed on the Pompeians. Crassus drew back, but before he could get quite through, Mark jammed him with the gate, between the gate and the post.

"Fred! Bill!" For Crassus struggled, and was very strong. Bill rushed to Mark's assistance: together they squeezed Val tight.

"O! My side! You dogs!" Crassus hit at them with his sword: they pressed him harder.

"Give in," said Bill. "You're caught—give in."

"I shan't," gasped Val. "If I could only reach you,"—he hit viciously, but they were just an inch or two beyond his arm.

"Charge, Cecil!—Scipio, charge!" shouted Mark. Scipio had charged already, and the Pompeians, being divided into three parties, one on each side of the mound, and the third up in it, were easily scattered. Scipio himself found their eagle in the brambles, where the bearer had left it, as he jumped out of the hedge to run.

"Yield," said Bill. "Give in—we've got your eagle."

"All the eagles," said Scipio, returning. "Every one—our two and Pompey's two."

"And Varro's a prisoner—there he is," said Mark. "Give in, Val."

"I won't. Let me out. Come near and hit then. If I could get at you!"

"But you can't!"

"O!"—as they pressed him.

"Give in!"

"No! Not if I'm squashed:—no, that I won't," said Val, frantically struggling.

"What's the use?" said Scipio. "You may just as well—the battle's won, and it's no use your fighting."

"Where's Pompey?" asked Val Crassus.

"Run away," said Mark promptly.

"Then where's Bevis?"

"After him of course," said Mark.

"I don't believe it; did any one see Pompey run? Phil, did you?"—to the prisoner.

"Don't know," said Varro, sullenly. "Don't care. If he had done as I said he would have won. Yes, I saw him leave the fight."

"Now will you give in?" said Mark. "Or must we chop you till you do."

"Chop away," said Val defiantly.

"Don't hit him," said Scipio. "Val, really it's no good, you've lost the battle."

"I suppose we have," said Val. "Well, let some one take Varro on the hill, and let him tell me if he can see Pompey anywhere."

They did so. Cecil and three others as guards took Varro on the rising ground; Varro was obliged to own that Pompey was not in sight.

"Take it then," said Crassus, hurling his sword at them. "Well, I never thought Ted would have run. If he had not, I would not have given in for fifty of you."

"But he did run," said Mark, unable to suppress his joy.

"You won't tie me," said Crassus, as they let him out. Mark did not tie him, and then as they were now ten to one they loosened Varro too. Mark led them up on the higher ground towards the sycamores, fully expecting to see Bevis every moment. When he got there, and could not see him anywhere, he could not understand it. Then Crassus told him of the search he had made. Mark went to the quarry and looked down—no one was there. He halted while two of his men ran through the firs shouting, but of course came back unsuccessful.

"I know," said Scipio, "he's gone to the camp."

"Of course," said Mark. "How stupid of us—of course he's at the camp. Let him see us come properly. Two and two, now—prisoners two and two half-way down, that's it. Eagles in front. Right. March."

He marched, with Scipio beside him, the four eagles behind, and the prisoners in the centre. Never was there a prouder general than Mark at that moment. He had captured both the enemy's eagles, recovered his own, and taken Pompey's lieutenants captive. Pompey himself and all his soldiers had fled: looking round the Plain there was not one in sight. Mark Antony was in sole possession of the battlefield. Proudly he marched, passing every now and then broken swords on the ground, and noticing the trampled grass where fierce combats had occurred. How delighted Bevis would be to see him! How he looked forward to Bevis's triumph! All his heart was full of Bevis, it was not his own success, it was Bevis's victory that he rejoiced in.

"Bevis! Bevis!" he shouted, as they came near the camp, but there was no answer. When they entered the camp, and found the fire still smouldering, but no Bevis, Mark's face became troubled. The triumph faded away, he grew anxious.

"Where ever can he be?" he said. "I hope there's nothing wrong. Bevis!" shouting at the top of his voice. The gale took the shout with it, but nothing came but the roaring of the wind. The sun was now sinking and cast a purple gleam over the grass.

Chapter Three
Bevis in the Storm

In the punt Bevis remained quite still under the sacks while Crassus searched the quarry for him, then looked up in the sycamores, and afterwards went to the hazel hedge. Bevis, peeping out from under the broad seat, saw him go there, and knew that he could not see over the New Sea from the lower ground, but as others might at any moment come on the hill, he considered it best to keep on the bottom of the boat. The punt at first floated slowly, and was sheltered by the jutting point, but still the flow of the water carried it out, and in a little time the wind pushed it more strongly as it got farther from shore. Presently it began to roll with the waves, and Bevis soon found some of the inconveniences of a flat-bottomed vessel.

The old punt always leaked, and the puntsman being too idle to bale till compelled, the space between the veal and the false bottom was full of water. As she began to roll this water went with a sound like "swish" from side to side, and Bevis saw it appear between the edge of the boards and the side. When she had drifted quite out of the gulf and met the full force of the waves every time they lifted her, this bilgewater rushed out over the floor. Bevis was obliged to change his position, else he would soon have been wet through. He doubled up the two sacks and sat on them, reclining his arms on the seat so as still to be as low down and as much concealed as possible.

This precaution was really needless, for both the armies were scattered, the one pursuing and the other pursued, in places where they could not see him, and even had they moved by the shore they would never have thought of looking for him where he was. He could not know this, and so sat on the sacks. The punt was now in the centre of the storm, and the waves seemed immense to Bevis. Between them the surface was dark, their tops were crested with foam, which the wind blew off against him, so that he had to look in the direction he was going and not back to escape the constant shower of scud in his face.

Now up, now down, the boat heaved and sank, turning slowly round as she went, but generally broadside on. With such a hurricane and such waves she floated fast, and the shore was already far behind. When Bevis felt that he was really out on the New Sea a wild delight possessed him. He shouted and sang how—

"Estmere threw his harpe asyde, And swith he drew his brand!"

The dash of the waves, the "wish" of the gust as it struck him, the flying foam, the fury of the storm, the red sun almost level with the horizon and towards which he drifted, the dark heaving waters in their wrath lifted his spirit to meet them. All he wished was that Mark was with him to share the pleasure. He was now in the broadest part of the New Sea where the rollers having come so far rose yet higher. Bevis shouted to them, wild as the waves.

The punt being so cumbrous and heavy did not rise buoyantly as the waves went under, but hung on them, so that the crests of the larger waves frequently broke over the gunwale and poured a flood of water on board. There were crevices too in her sides, which in ordinary times were not noticed, as she was never loaded deep enough to bring them down to the water-line. But now the waves rising above these found out the chinks, and rushed through in narrow streams.

The increase of the water in the punt again forced Bevis to move, and he sat up on the seat with his feet on the sacks. The water was quite three inches above the false bottom, and rushed from side to side with a great splash, of course helping to heel her over. Bevis did not like this at all; he ceased singing, and looked about him.

It seemed a mile (it was not so far) back to the quarry, such a waste of raging waves and foam! On either side the shore was a long, long way, he could not swim a tenth as far. He recognised the sedges where he and Mark had wandered on his left, and found that he was rapidly coming near the two islands. He began to grow anxious, thinking that the boat would not keep afloat very much longer. The shore in front beyond the islands was a great way, and from what he knew of it he believed it was encumbered far out with weeds through which, if the punt foundered, he could not swim, so that his hope was that she would strike either the Unknown Island or Serendib.

Both were now near, and he tried to discover whether the current and wind would throw him on them. A long white streak parallel to the course of the storm marked the surface of the water rising and falling with the waves like a ribbon, and this seemed to pass close by Serendib. The punt being nearly on the streak he hoped he should get there. If he only had something to row with! The Old Man of the Sea had hidden the sculls, and had not troubled to bring the movable seat with him, as he did not want it.

The movable seat would have made a good paddle. As for the stretcher it was fixed, nailed to the floor.

He could do nothing paddling with his hand, in calm weather he might, but not in such a storm of wind. If he only had something to paddle with he could have worked the punt into the line so as to strike on Serendib. As it was he could do nothing; if he had only had his hat he could have baled out some of the water, which continued to rise higher.

Drifting as the waves chose he saw that Serendib was a low, flat island. The Unknown Island rose into a steep sand bluff at that end which faced him. Against this bluff the waves broke with tremendous fury, sending the spray up to the bushes on the top. Bevis watched to see where the punt would ground, or whether it would miss both islands and drift through the narrow channel between them.

He still thought it might hit Serendib, when it once more rotated, and that brought it in such a position that the waves must take it crash against the low steep cliff of the Unknown Island. Bevis set his teeth, and prepared to dig his nails into the sand, when just as the punt was within three waves of the shore, it seemed to pause. This was the reflux—the undertow, the water recoiling from the bank—so that the boat for half a moment was suspended or held between the two forces.

Before he had time to think what was best to do the punt partly swung round, and the rush of the current, setting between the islands, carried it along close beside the shore. The bluff now sloped, and the waves rushed up among the bushes and trees. Bevis watched, saw a chance, and in an instant stepped on the seat, and leaped with all his might. It was a long way, but he was a good jumper, and his feet landed on the ground. He would even then have fallen back into the water had he not grasped a branch of alder.

For a moment he hung over the waves, the next he drew himself up, and was safe. He stepped back from the edge, and instinctively put his left arm round the alder trunk, as if clinging to a friend. Leaning against the tree he saw the punt, pushed out by the impetus from his spring, swing round and drift rapidly between the islands. It went some distance, and then began to settle, and slowly sank.

Bevis remained holding the tree till he had recovered himself, then he moved farther into the island, and went a little way up the bluff, whence he saw that the sun had set. He soon forgot his alarm, and as that subsided began to enjoy his position. "What a pity Mark was not with me!" he said to himself. "I am so sorry. Only think, I'm really shipwrecked. It's splendid!"

He kicked up his heels, and a startled blackbird flew out of a bramble bush and across the water.

Bevis watched him fly aslant the gale till he lost sight of him in the trees on shore. Looking that way—north-west—his quick eyes found out a curious thing. On that side of the island there was a broad band of weeds stretching towards the shore, and widening the farther it extended.

These weeds were level with the surface, and as the waves rolled under they undulated like a loose green carpet lifted by a strong draught. As they proceeded the undulations became less and less, till on emerging into an open channel on the other side of the weeds, they were nothing more than slow ripples. Still passing on the slow ripples gently crossed, and were lost in a second band of weeds. He could hear the boom of the waves as they struck the low cliff and dashed themselves to pieces, yet these furious waves were subdued by the leaves and stalks of the weeds, any of which he knew he could pull up with his hand.

Watching the green undulations he looked farther and saw that at some distance from the island there were banks covered with sedges, and the channel between the weeds (showing deeper water) wound in among these. Next he went up on the top of the cliff, and found a young oak-tree growing on the summit, to which he held while thus exposed to the full strength of the wind, and every now and then the spray flew up and sprinkled him.

Shading his eyes with his hand, for the wind seemed to hurt them, he looked towards the quarry, which appeared yellow at this distance. He saw a group of people, as he supposed Pompey's victorious army, passing by the sycamores.

"It's no use, Ted," he said to himself, "you can't find me, and you can't win. I've done you."

The group was really Mark and the rest searching for him. After a while they went over the hill, and Bevis could not see them.

Bevis came down from the cliff, and thought he would see how large the island was, so he went all round it, as near the edge as he could. It was covered with wood, and there were the thickest masses of bramble he had ever seen. He had to find a way round these, so that it took him some time to get along. Some firs too obstructed his path, and he found one very tall spruce. At last he reached the other extremity, where the ground was low, and only just above the water, which was nearly smooth there, being sheltered by the projecting irregularities of the shore.

Returning he had in one place to climb over quantities of stones, for the bank just there was steeper, and presently compelled him to go more inland. The island seemed very large, in shape narrow and long, but so thickly overgrown with bushes and trees that he could not see across it. The surface was uneven, for he went down into a hollow which seemed beneath the level of the water, and afterwards came to a steep bank, on rounding which he was close to the place from which he started.

Not having had anything to eat since dinner (for they shirked their tea), and having gone through all these labours, Bevis began to feel hungry, but there was nothing to eat on his island, for the berries were not yet ripe. First he whistled, then he wished Mark would come, then he walked up to the cliff and climbed into the oak on the summit.

"Mark is sure to come," he said to himself. Just then he saw the full moon, which had risen above the distant hills, and shining over the battlefield touched the raging waves with tarnished silver.

He looked at the great round shield on which the heraldic markings were dimmed by its own gleam. He almost fancied he could see it move, so rapidly did it sweep upwards. It was clear and bright as if wind-swept, as if the hurricane had brushed it. Bevis watched it a little while, and then he thought of Mark. The possibility that Mark would not know where he was never entered his mind, nor did it occur to him that perhaps even Mark would hesitate to venture out in such a tempest of wind: so strong was his faith in his companion.

The wind blew so hard up in the tree, he presently got down, and descended the slope till the ridge sheltered him. He sat on the rough grass, put his hands in his pockets, and whistled again to assure himself that he liked it. But he was hungry, and the time seemed very slow, and he could not quite suppress an inward feeling that shipwreck when one was quite alone was not altogether so splendid. It was so dull.

He got up, picked up some stones, and threw them into the shadowy bushes, just for something to do. They fell with a crash, and one or two birds fluttered away. He wished he had his knife to cut and whittle a stick. He thought he would make up his mind to go to sleep, and extended himself on the ground, when, looking up as he lay on his back, he saw there were stars. Not in the least sleepy, up he jumped again.

"Kaack! kaack!" like an immensely exaggerated and prolonged "quack" without the "qu;" a harsh shriek resounding over the water even above the gale.

"A heron," thought Bevis. "If I only had a gun, or my bow now." He took a stone, and peered out over the water on the side the cry came from, which was where the weeds were. The surface was dim and shadowy in that direction, and he could not see the heron. He returned and sat down on the grass. He could not think of anything to do, till at last he resolved to build a hut of branches, as shipwrecked people did. But when he came to pull at the alder branches, those of any size were too tough; the aspen were too high up; the firs too small.

"Stupid," he said to himself. "This *is* stupid." Once more he returned to the foot of the slope, and sat down on the grass.

Before him there were the shadowy trees and bushes, and behind he could hear the boom of the waves, yet it never occurred to him how weird the place was. All he wanted was to be at something. "Why ever doesn't Mark come?" he repeated to himself. Just then he chanced to put his hand in his jacket-pocket, and instantly jumped up delighted. "Matches!" He took out the box, which he had used to light the camp-fire, and immediately set about gathering materials for a fire. "The proper thing to do," he thought. "The very thing!"

He soon began to make a pile of dead wood, when he stopped, and, lifting the bundle in his arms, carried it up the slope nearly to the top of the cliff, where he put it down behind a bramble bush. He thought that if he made the fire on the height it would be a guide to Mark, but down in the hollow no one could see it. To get together enough sticks took some time; for the moon, though full and bright only gave light where the beams fell direct. In the shadow he could hardly see at all.

Having arranged the pile, and put all the larger sticks on one side, ready to throw on presently, he put some dry leaves and grass underneath, as he had no straw or paper, struck a match and held, it to them. Some of the leaves smouldered, one crackled, and the dry grass lit a little, but only just where it was in contact with the flame of the match. The same thing happened with ten matches, one after the other. The flame would not spread. Bevis on his knees thought a good while, and then he set to work and gathered some more leaves, dry grass, and some thin chips of dry bark. Then he took out the sliding-drawer of the match-box, and placed it under these, as the deal of which it was made would burn like paper. The outer case he was careful to preserve, because they were safety matches, and lit only on the prepared surface.

In and around the little drawer he arranged half-a-dozen matches, and then lit them, putting the rest in his pocket. The flame caught the deal, which was as thin as a wafer, then the bark and tiny twigs, then the dry grass and larger sticks. It crept up through the pile, crackling and hissing. In three minutes it had hold of the boughs, curling its lambent point round them, as a cow licks up the grass with her tongue. The bramble bush sheltered it from the gale, but let enough wind through to cause a draught.

Up sprang the flames, and the bonfire began to cast out heat, and red light flickering on the trees. Bevis threw on more branches, the fire flared up and gleamed afar on the wet green carpet of undulating weeds. He hauled up a fallen pole, the sparks rose as he hurled it on.

"Hurrah!" shouted Bevis, dancing and singing:

"Kyng Estmere threwe his harpe asyde,
And swith he drew his brand;
And Estmere he, and Adler yonge,
Right stiffe in stour can stand!"

"Adler will be here in a minute." He meant Mark.

Chapter Four
Mark is put in Prison

But Adler was himself in trouble. After they had waited some time in the camp, thinking that Bevis would be certain to return there sooner or later, finding that he did not come, the whole party, with Mark at their head, searched and re-searched the battlefield and most of the adjacent meadows, not overlooking the copse. Mark next ran home, hoping that Bevis for some reason or other might have gone there, and asked himself whether he had offended him in any way, and was that why he had left the fight? But he could not recollect that he had done anything.

Bevis, of course, was not at home, and Mark returned to the battlefield, every minute now adding to his anxiety. It was so unlike Bevis that he felt sure something must be wrong.

"Perhaps he's drowned," said Val.

"Drowned," repeated Mark, with intense contempt; "why he can swim fifty yards."

Fifty yards is not far, but it would be far enough to save life on many occasions. Val was silenced, still Mark, to be certain, went along the shore, and even some way up the Nile. By now the others had left, one at a time, and only Val, Cecil, and Charlie remained.

The four hunted again, then they walked slowly across the field, trying to think. Mark picked up Bevis's hat, which had fallen off in the battle; but to find Bevis's hat was nothing, for he had a knack of leaving it behind him.

"Perhaps he's gone to your place," said Charlie, meaning Mark's home.

Mark shook his head. "But I wish you would go and see," he said; he dared not face Frances.

"So I will," said Charlie, always ready to do his best, and off he went.

Charlie's idea gave rise to another, that Bevis might be gone to Jack's home in the Downs, and Val offered to go and inquire, though it was a long, long walk.

He set out, Cecil went with him, and Mark, left to himself, walked slowly home, hoping once more Bevis might have returned. As he came in with Bevis's hat in his hand, the servants pounced upon him. Bevis was missed, there had been a great outcry, and all the people were inquiring for him. Several had come to the kitchen to gossip about it. The uproar would not have been so great so soon but it had got out that there had been a battle.

"You said it was a picnic," said Polly, shaking Mark.

"You told I so," said the Bailiff, seizing his collar.

"Let me go," shouted Mark, punching.

"Well, what have you done with him? Where is he?"

Mark could not tell, and between them, four or five to one, they hustled him into the cellar.

"You must go to gaol," said the Bailiff grimly. "Bide there a bit."

"How can you find Bevis without me!" shouted Mark, who had just admitted he did not know where Bevis was. But the Bailiff pushed him stumbling down the three stone steps, and he heard the bolt grate in the staple. Thus the general who had just won a great battle was thrust ignominiously into a cellar.

Mark kicked and banged the door, but it was of solid oak, without so much as a panel to weaken it, and though it resounded it did not even shake. He yelled till he was hoarse, and hit the door till his fists became numbed. Then suddenly he sat down quite quiet on the stone steps, and the tears came into his eyes. He did not care for the cellar, it was about Bevis—Bevis was lost somewhere and wanted him, and he *must* go to Bevis.

Dashing the tears away, up he jumped, and looked round to see if he could find anything to burst the door open. There was but one window, deep set in the thick wall, with an iron upright bar inside. The glass was yellowish-green, in small panes, and covered with cobwebs, so that the light was very dim. He could see the barrels, large and small, and as his eyes became accustomed to the semi-darkness some meat—a joint—and vegetables on a shelf, placed there for coolness. Out came his pocket-knife, and he attacked the joint savagely, slashing off slices anyhow, for he (like Bevis) was hungry, and so angry he did not care what he did.

As he ate he still looked round and round the cellar and peered into the corners, but saw nothing, though something moved in the shadow on the floor, no doubt a resident toad. Mark knew the cellar perfectly, and he had often seen tools in it, as a hammer, used in tapping the barrels, but though he tried hard he could not find it. It must have been taken away for some purpose. He stamped on the stone floor, and heard a rustle as a startled mouse rushed into its hole.

The light just then seemed to increase, and turning towards the window he saw the full round moon. As it crossed the narrow window the shadow of the iron bar fell on the opposite wall, then moved aside, and in a very few minutes the moon began to disappear as she swept up into the sky. He watched the bright shield still himself for awhile, then as he looked down he thought of the iron bar, and out came his knife again.

The bar was not let into the stonework, the window recess inside was encased with wood, and the bar, flattened at each end, was fastened with three screws. Mark endeavoured to unscrew these, he quickly broke the point of his knife, and soon had nothing but a stump left. The stump answered better than the complete blade, and he presently got the screws out. He then worked the bar to and fro with such violence that he wrenched the top screws clean away from the wood there. But just as he lifted the bar to smash all the panes and get out, he saw that the frame was far too narrow for him to pass through.

Inside the recess was wide enough, but it was not half so broad where the glass was. The bar was really unnecessary; no one could have got in or out, and perhaps that was why it had been so insecurely fastened, as the workmen could hardly have helped seeing it was needless.

Mark hurled the bar to the other end of the cellar, where it knocked some plaster off the wall, then fell on an earthenware vessel used to keep vegetables in, and cracked it. He stamped up and down the cellar, and in his bitter and desperate anger, had half a mind to set all the taps running for spite.

"Let me out," he yelled, thumping the door with all his might. "Let me out; you've no business to put me in here. If the governor was at home, I know he wouldn't, and you're beasts—you're *beasts*."

He was right in so far that the governor would not have locked him in the cellar; but the governor was out that evening, and Bevis's mamma, so soon as she found he was missing, had had the horse put in the dog-cart, and went to fetch him. So Mark fell into the hands of the merciless. No one even heard him howling and bawling and kicking the heart of oak, and when he had exhausted himself he sat down again on a wooden frame made to support a cask. Presently he went to the door once more, and shouted through the keyhole, "Tell me if you have found Bevis!"

There was no answer. He waited, and then sat down on the frame, and asked himself if he could get up through the roof. By standing on the top of the largest cask he thought he could touch the rafters, but no more, and he had no tool to cut his way through with. "I know," he said suddenly, "I'll smash the lock." He searched for the iron bar, and found it in the earthenware vessel.

He hit the lock a tremendous bang, then stopped, and began to examine it more carefully. His eyes were now used to the dim light, and he could see almost as well as by day, and he found that the great bolt of the lock, quite three inches thick, shot into an open staple driven into the door-post, a staple much like those used to fasten chains to.

In a minute he had the end of the iron bar inside the staple. The staple was strong, and driven deep into the oaken post, but he had a great leverage on it. The bar bent, but the staple came slowly, then easier, and presently fell on the stones. The door immediately swung open towards him.

Mark dashed out with the bar in his hand, fully determined to knock any one down who got in his way, but they were all in the road, and he reached the meadow. He dropped the bar, and ran for the battlefield. Going through the gate that opened on the New Sea, something pushed through beside him against his ankles. It would have startled him, but he saw directly it was Pan. The spaniel had followed him: it may be with some intelligence that he was looking for his master.

"Pan! Pan!" said Mark, stooping to stroke him, and delighted to get some sympathy at last. "Come on."

Together they raced to the battlefield.

Then from the high ground Mark saw the beacon on the island, and instantly knew it was Bevis. He never doubted it for a moment. He looked at the beacon, and saw the flames shoot up, sink, and rise again; then he ran back as fast as he could to the head of the water, where the boats were moored in the sandy corner. Fetching the sculls from the tumbling shed where they were kept, he pushed off in the blue boat which they were fitting up for sailing, never dreaming that the first voyage in it would be like this. Pan jumped in with him.

In his haste, not looking where he was going, he rowed into the weeds, and was some time getting out, for the stalks clung to the blade of the scull as if an invisible creature in the water were holding it. Soon after he got free he reached the waves, and in five minutes, coming out into the open channel, the boat began to dance up and down. With wind and wave and oar he drove along at a rapid pace, past the oak where the council had been held, past the jutting point, and into the broad waters, where he could see the beacon, if he glanced over his shoulder.

The boat now pitched furiously, as it seemed to him rising almost straight up, and dipping as if she would dive into the deep. But she always rose again, and after her came the wave she had surmounted rolling with a hiss and bubble eager to overtake him. The crest blew off like a shower in his face, and just as the following roller seemed about to break into the stern-sheets it sank. Still the wave always came after him, row as hard as he would, like vengeance, black, dire, and sleepless.

Lit up by the full moon, the raging waters rushed and foamed and gleamed around him. Though he afterwards saw tempests on the ocean, the waves never seemed so high and so threatening as they did that night, alone in the little boat. The storms, indeed, on inland waters are full of dangers, perhaps more so than the long heaving billows of the sea, for the waves seem to have scarcely any interval between, racing quick, short and steep, one after the other.

This great black wave—for it looked always the same—chased him eagerly, overhanging the stern. Pan sat there on the bottom as it looked under the wave. Mark rowed his hardest, trying to get away from it. Hissing, foaming, with the rush and roar of the wind, the wave ran after. When he ventured to look round he was close to the islands, so quickly had he travelled.

Bevis was standing on the summit of the cliff with a long stick burning at the end in his hand. He held it out straight like the arm of a signal, then waved it a little, but kept it pointing in the same direction. He was shouting his loudest, to direct Mark, who could not hear a sound, but easily guessed that he meant him to bear the way he pointed. Mark pulled a few strokes and looked again, and saw the white spray rushing up the cliff, though he could not hear the noise of the surge.

Bevis was frantically waving the burning brand; Mark understood now, and pulled his left scull, hardest. The next minute the current setting between the islands seized the boat, and he was carried by as if on a mountain torrent. Everything seemed to whirl past, and he saw the black wave that had followed him dashed to sparkling fragments against the cliff.

He was taken beyond the island before he could stay the boat, then he edged away out of the rush behind the land, where the water was much smoother, and was able presently to row back to it in the shelter. Bevis came out from the trees to meet him, and taking hold of the stem of the boat drew it ashore. Mark stepped out, and Pan, jumping on Bevis, barked round him.

Bevis told him how it had all happened, and danced with delight when he heard how Mark had won the battle, for he insisted that Mark had done it. They went to the beacon fire, and then Mark, now his first joy was over, began to grumble because Bevis had been really shipwrecked and he had not. He wished he had smashed his boat against the cliff now. Bevis said they could have another great shipwreck soon. Mark wanted to stop all night on the island, but Bevis was hungry.

"And besides," said he, "there's the governor; he will be awfully frightened about us, and he ought to know."

"So he did," said Mark. "Very well; but, mind, there is to be a jolly shipwreck."

Scamps as they were, they both disliked to give pain to those who loved them. It was the knowledge that the governor would never have put him in the cellar that stopped Mark from the spiteful trick of turning on the taps. Bevis was exceedingly angry about Mark having been locked up. He stamped his foot, and said the Bailiff should know.

They got into the boat, and each took a scull, but when they were afloat they paused, for it occurred to both at once that they could not row back in the teeth of the storm.

"We shall have to stop on the island now," said Mark, not at all sorry. Bevis, however, remembered the floating breakwater of weeds, and the winding channel on that side, and told Mark about it. So they rowed between the weeds, and so much were the waves weakened that the boat barely rocked. Now the boat was steady, Pan sat in front, and peered over the stem like a figure-head. Presently they came to the sand or mudbanks where the water was quite smooth, and here the heron rose up.

"We ought to have a gun," said Bevis; "it's a shame we haven't got a gun."

"Just as if we didn't know how to shoot," said Mark indignantly.

"Just as if," echoed Bevis; "but we will have one, somehow."

The boat as he spoke grounded on a shallow; they got her off, but she soon grounded again, and it took them quite three-quarters of an hour to find the channel, so much did it turn and wind. At last they were stopped by thick masses of weeds, and a great bunch of the reed-mace, often called bulrushes, and decided to land on the sandbank. They hauled the boat so far up on the shore that she could not possibly get loose, and then walked to the mainland.

There the bushes and bramble thickets again gave them much trouble, but they contrived to get through into the wildest-looking field they had over seen. It was covered with hawthorn-trees, bunches of thistles, bramble bushes, rushes, and numbers of green ant-hills, almost as high as their knees. Skirting this, as they wound in and out the ant-hills, they startled some peewits, which rose with their curious whistle, and two or three white tails, which they knew to be rabbits, disappeared round the thistles.

It took them some time to cross this field; the next was barley, very short; the next wheat, and then clover; and at last they reached the head of the water, and got into the meadows. Thence it was only a short way home, and they could see the house illuminated by the moonlight.

The authorities were wroth, though secretly glad to see them. Nothing was said; the wrath was too deep for reproaches. They were ordered to bed that instant. They did not dare disobey, but Mark darted a savage look, and Bevis shouted back from the top of the staircase that he was hungry. "Be off, sir," was the only reply. Sullenly they went into their room and sat down. Five minutes afterwards some one opened the door a little way, put in a plate and a jug, and went away. On the plate were three huge slices of bread, and in the jug cold water.

"I won't touch it," said Bevis; "it's hateful."

"It's hateful," said Mark.

"After we came home to tell them, too," said Bevis. "Horrid!"

But by-and-by his hunger overcame him; he ate two of the huge slices, and Mark the other. Then after a draught of the cold water, they undressed, and fell asleep, quick and calm, just as Aurora was beginning to show her white foot in the East.

Chapter Five
In Disgrace—Visit to Jack's

"As if we were dogs," said Bevis indignantly.

"Just as if," said Mark. "It's hateful. And after coming home from the island to tell them."

"All that trouble."

"I could have brought you some stuff to eat," said Mark, "and we could have stopped there all night, quite jolly."

"Hateful!"

They were in the blue-painted summer-house the next day talking over the conduct of the authorities, whose manner was distant in the extreme. The governor was very angry. They thought it unjust after winning such a mighty victory, and actually coming home on purpose to save alarm.

"I do not like it at all," said Bevis.

"Let's go back to the island," said Mark eagerly.

"They would come and look there for us the first thing," said Bevis. "I've a great mind to walk to Southampton, and see the ships. It's only sixty miles."

"Well, come on," said Mark, quite ready, "The road goes over the hills by Jack's. O! I know!"

"What is it?" for Mark had jumped up.

"Jack's got a rifle," said Mark. "He'll lot us shoot. Let's go and stop with Jack."

"First-rate," said Bevis. "But how do you know he has a rifle? There wasn't one when I was there last—you mean the long gun."

"No, I don't; he's got a rifle. I know, because he told Frances. He tells Frances everything. Stupids always tell girls everything. Somebody wanted to sell it, and he bought it."

"Are you quite sure?" said Bevis, getting up.

"Quite."

"What sort is it?"

"A deer rifle."

"Come on."

Off they started without another word, and walked a mile in a great hurry, when they recollected that if they did not appear in the evening there would be a hunt for them.

"Just as if we were babies," said Mark.

"Such rubbish," said Bevis. "But we won't have any more such stuff and nonsense. Let's find Charlie, and send him back with a message."

They found him, and sent him home with a piece of paper, on with Bevis wrote, "We are gone to Jack's, and we shall not be home to-night." It was quite an hour's walk to Jack's, whose house was in a narrow valley between two hills. Jack was away in the fields, but when he returned he showed them the rifle, a small, old-fashioned muzzle-loader, and they spent a long time handling it, and examining the smallest detail.

"Let's have a shot," said Bevis.

"Yes," said Mark. "Now do, Jack." They begged and teased and worried him, till he almost yielded. He thought perhaps Bevis's governor would not like shooting, but on the other hand he knew Frances was fond of Bevis, and Mark was her brother, with whom, for various reasons, he wished to keep especially friendly. At last he said they would go and try and shoot a young rabbit, and took down his double-barrel.

They did not take any dogs, meaning to stalk the rabbits and shoot them sitting, as neither Mark nor Bevis could kill anything moving. Jack went down to some little enclosed meadows at the foot of the Downs where the rabbits came out as the sun began to sink. Every now and then he made them wait while he crept forward and peered through gaps or over gates.

Presently he came quietly back from a gap by a hollow willow, and giving Bevis the gun (which he had hitherto carried himself, being very anxious lest an accident should happen), whispered to him that there were three young rabbits out in the grass.

"Aim at the shoulder," said Jack, thinking Bevis might miss the head. "And be sure you don't pull both triggers at once, and—I say—" But Bevis had started. Bevis stepped as noiselessly as a squirrel, and glancing carefully round the willow saw the rabbits' ears pricked up in the grass. They had heard or seen him, but being so young were not much frightened, and soon resumed feeding.

He lifted the gun, which was somewhat heavy, having been converted from a muzzle-loader, and old guns were made heavier than is the custom now. One of the rabbits moving turned his back to him, so that he could not see the shoulder; the other was behind a bunch of grass; but in a minute the third moved, and Bevis aimed at him. The barrels would not at first keep quite steady, the sight, just as he had got it on the rabbit, jumped aside or drooped, so that he had to try twice before he was satisfied.

"What a time he is," whispered Mark, when Bevis pulled the trigger, and they all ran forward. Jack jumped through the gap and picked up the rabbit, which was kicking in the grass. Bevis rubbed his shoulder and felt his collar-bone.

"Hurt?" said Jack, laughing. "Kicked? I was going to tell you only you were in such a hurry. You should have held the stock tight to your shoulder, then it would not kick. There, like this; now try."

Bevis took the gun and pressed it firm to his bruised shoulder.

"Got it tight?" said Jack. "Aim at that thistle, and try again."

"But he'll frighten the rabbits, and it's my turn," said Mark.

"All gone in," said Jack, "every one; you'll have to wait till they come out again. Shoot."

Bevis shot, and the thistle was shattered. It scarcely hurt him at all, it would not have done so in the least, only his shoulder was tender now.

"It's a very little rabbit," said Mark.

"That it's not," said Bevis. "How dare you say so?"

"It looks little."

"The size of a kitten," said Jack. "As sweet as a chicken," he added, "when cooked, and as white. You shall have it to-morrow for dinner— just the right size to be nice;" he saw that Bevis was rather inclined to be doubtful, and wished to reassure him. Jack was a huge, kind-hearted giant.

"Are you sure it will be nice?"

"The very thing," said Jack, "if Mark can only shoot another just like it; it wants two for a pudding."

About half an hour afterwards Mark did shoot another, and then there was a long discussion as to which was the biggest, which could not be decided, for, in fact, being both about the same age, one could hardly be distinguished from the other, except that Mark's had a shot-hole in the ear, and Bevis's had not. On the way home a cloud of sparrows rose out of some wheat and settled on the hedge, and Bevis had a shot at these, bringing down three. Afterwards he missed a yellow-hammer that sat singing happily on a gate.

He wanted the yellow-hammer because it had so fine a colour. The yellow-hammer sang away while he aimed, repeating the same note, as he perched all of a heap, a little lump of feathers on the top bar. The instant the flash came the bird flew, and as is its habit in starting drooped, and so was shielded by the top bar. The bar was scarred with shot, and a dozen pellets were buried in it; but the yellow-hammer was not hurt.

Mark was delighted that Bevis had missed. There was an elm near the garden, and up in it Mark, on the look-out for anything, spied a young thrush. He took steady aim, and down came the thrush. They were disposed to debate as to who had shot, best, but Jack stopped it, and brought out the quoits. After they had played some time, and it was growing dusky, Ted entered the field.

"Halloa! Pompey," said Mark. "Pompey!"

"Pompey," said Jack, not understanding.

Ted walked straight up to Bevis.

"Where did you go," said Bevis, "after I fell over?"

"But aren't you angry?" said Ted.

"Angry—why?"

"Because I sent you over."

"But you didn't do it purposely."

"No, *that* I didn't," said Ted, with all his might.

From that moment they were better friends than they had ever been before, though it was some time before Ted could really believe that Bevis was not angry about it. In fact, the idea had never entered Bevis's mind. Ted stopped with them to supper, and everything was explained to Jack, who was delighted with the battle, and could not hear enough about it. But they did not press Ted as to what had become of him, seeing how confused he was whenever the subject was approached.

Quite beside himself with terror and misery, poor Ted had pretended illness and remained in his room, refusing to see any one, and dreading every footstep and every knock at the door, lest it should be the constable come to arrest him. Towards the afternoon Val, who had already been down to Bevis's house and found he was all right, strolled up to see Pompey. Ted would not open the door even to him, and Val taunted him for being such a coward all that time after the battle. Still, Ted would not unlock it till Val happened to say that there was a row about the war, and Bevis had gone up to Jack's. Open came the door directly.

"Where's Bevis?" said Ted, grasping at Val's arm.

"At Jack's."

"Not killed?"

"Killed—no. How could he be killed?"

As soon as he understood that Bevis was really alive, not even hurt, Ted started off, to Val's amazement, and never stopped till he entered the field where they were picking up the quoits as it grew too dark to play well. So Caesar and Pompey sat down to supper very lovingly, and talked over Pharsalia. Big Jack made them tell him the story over and over again, and wished he could have taken part in the combat. Like Mark, too, he envied Bevis's real shipwreck. Now seeing Jack so interested they made use of his good-humour, and coaxed him till at last he promised to let them shoot with the rifle on the morrow in the evening, after he had finished in the fields.

All next day they rambled about the place, now in the garden, then in the orchard, then in the rick-yard or the stables, back again into the house, and up into the lumber-room at the top to see if they could find anything; down into the larder, where Jack's dear old mother did her best to surfeit them with cakes and wines, and all the good things she could think of, for they reminded her of Jack when he was a boy and, in a sense, manageable. As for Jack's old father, who was very old, he sat by himself in the parlour almost all day long, being too grim for anybody to approach.

He sat with his high hat on, aslant on his head, and when he wanted anything knocked the table or the floor as chance directed with a thick stick. When he walked out, every one slipped aside and avoided him, hiding behind the ricks, and Jack's pointer slunk into his house, drooping his tail.

In the orchard Bevis and Mark squailed at the pears with short sticks. If they hit one it was bruised that side by the blow; then as it fell it had another good bump; but it is well-known that such thumping only makes pears more juicy. Tired of this they walked down by the mill-pool, in which there were a few small trout, Jack's especial pets. The water was so clear that they could see the bottom of the pool for some distance; it looked very different to that of the New Sea below in the valley.

"We ought to have some of this water in our water-barrel when we go on our voyage," said Bevis. "It's clearer than the Nile."

"The water-barrel must be got ashore somehow when we have the shipwreck," said Mark, "or perhaps we shall not have any to drink."

They were rather inclined to have a swim in the pool, but did not know how Jack would like it, as he was so jealous of his trout, and angry if they were disturbed. They would have had a swim though all the same, if the miller had not been looking over the hatch of his door. There he stood white and floury, blinking his eyes, and watching them.

"How anybody can be so stupid as to stand stock still, and stare, stare, stare, I can't think," said Mark, quite loud enough for the miller to hear. He did not smile nor stir; he did not even understand that he was meant; so sidelong a speech was beyond his comprehension. It would have needed very severe abuse indeed, hurled straight at his head, to have made him so much as lift his hand to dust the flour from his sleeve—the first thing he did when he began to feel a little.

Next they went indoors and had a look at the guns and rifle on the rack, which they dared not touch. Hearing the quick clatter of hoofs they ran out, and saw a labourer riding a pony bare back. He had been sent out to a village two miles away for some domestic requirement, and carried a parcel under his arm, while his heels but just escaped scraping the ground. The pony came up as sharp as he could, knowing his stable.

But no sooner was the labourer off, than Bevis was up, and forced him to go round the pasture below the house. When Bevis wearied, Mark mounted, and so by turns they rode the pony round and round the field, making him leap a broad furrow, and gallop his hardest. By-and-by, as Bevis got off and Mark had put his hand on before he sprang up, the pony gave a snort and bolted, throwing up his heels as he flew for his stable.

Such an experience was new to him, and he was some time before he quite understood; so soon as he did, and found out into what hands he had fallen, the pony made use of the first opportunity. They followed, but he showed his heels so viciously they thought it best to let him alone; so hurling the sticks with which they had thrashed him round the field at his head, they turned away. After dinner they took to another game.

This was sliding down the steep down just behind the house, on a short piece of broad plank with a ridge in front. The way is to lie down with the chest on the plank head first, trailing the toes behind, legs extended as rudders to keep the course straight. A push with the feet starts the board, and the pace increasing, you presently travel at a furious velocity. Nothing can be nicer. They worked at it for hours. The old gentleman came out into the garden and watched them, no doubt remembering when he used to do it himself; but as for the performers, all they thought about him was that they would like to squail a stick at his high and ancient hat aslant on his head.

Presently they rambled into a nut copse over the hill. The nuts were not ripe, and there was nothing much to be done there, but it was a copse, and copses are always pleasant to search about in. Mark returned to the sliding, Bevis sat down on the summit, and at first looked on, but after a while he became lost in his dreamy mood.

Far away the blue-tinted valley went out to the horizon, and the sun was suspended over it like a lamp hung from the ceiling, as it seemed no higher than the hill on which he sat. Underneath was the house, and round the tiled gables the swallows were busy going to and fro their nests. The dovecot and the great barn, the red apples in the orchard, the mill-pool and the grey mill, he could almost put his hand out on them.

Beyond these came the meads, and then the trees closed together like troops at the bugle call, making a limitless forest, and in this was a narrow bright gleam, like a crooked reaping-hook thrown down. It was the New Sea. After which there was no definition, surface only, fainter and fainter to the place where the white clouds went through the door of distance and disappeared. He did not see these, and only just knew that the wheat at his back rustled as the light wind came over. It was the vast aerial space, and the golden circle of the sun. He did not think, he felt, and listened to it.

Mark shouted presently that Jack was coming home; so he ran down, and they went to meet him. Jack put up the target after tea. It was a square of rusty sheet-iron, on which he drew a circle with chalk six inches in diameter, and outside that another about two feet. This he placed against the steep hill—the very best of butts—keeping it upright with two stakes, which he drove in the sward. He measured a hundred yards by stepping, and put three flints in a row to mark the spot. The rifle was loaded and the bullet rammed home with the iron ramrod, which had a round smooth handle at the end, so that you might force the lead into the grooves.

Jack fired, and missed; fired again, and missed; shot a third time after longer aim, and still there was no ringing sound and no jagged hole in the sheet-iron. Bevis tried, and Mark tried, and Jack again, but they could not hit it. More powder was used, and then less powder; the bullet was jammed home hard by knocking the ramrod with a fragment of post (the first thing that came handy), and then it was only just pushed down to the powder. All in vain. The noise of the reports had now brought together a number of labourers and cottage boys, who sat on the summit of the hill in a row.

They fired standing up, kneeling down, lying at full length. A chair was fetched, and the barrel was placed on the rung at the back as a rest, but not a single hole was made in the target. Mark wanted to go nearer and try at fifty yards, but Jack would not; the rifle was made to kill deer at a hundred yards, and at a hundred yards he intended to use it. He was getting very angry, for he prided himself on his shooting, and was in fact a good shot with the double-barrel; but this little rifle—a mere toy—defied him; he could not manage it. They fired between thirty and forty shots, till every bullet they had ready cast was gone.

The earth was scored by the target, cut up in front of it, ploughed to the right and left, drilled over it high up, but the broad sheet-iron was untouched.

Jack threatened to pitch the rifle into the mill-pool, and so disgusted was he that very likely he would have done it had not Bevis and Mark begged him earnestly not to do so. He put it up on the rack, and went off, and they did not see him till supper-time. He was as much out of temper as it was possible for him to be.

When they went to their bedroom that night, Bevis and Mark talked it over, and fully agreed that if they only had the rifle all to themselves they could do it.

"I'm sure we could," said Bevis.

"Of course we could," said Mark. "There's only something you have to find out."

"As easy as nothing," said Bevis.

Chapter Six
Sailing

At Bevis's home the authorities were still more wroth when they received the scrap of paper sent by Charlie, who scampered off before he could be questioned. There was more wrath about the battle than any of their previous misdeeds, principally because it was something novel. No one was hurt, and no one had even had much of a knock, except the larger boys, who could stand it. There was more rattling of weapons together than wounds. Ted's forehead was bruised, and Bevis's ankle was tender where some one had stepped on it while he was down. This was nothing to the bruises they had often had at football.

The fall over the quarry indeed might have been serious, so too the sinking of the punt; but both those were extrinsic matters, and they might have fought twenty Pharsalias without such incidents. All of them had had good sense enough to adhere to the agreement they had come to before the fighting. They could not anyhow have hurt themselves more than they commonly did at football, so that the authorities were perhaps a little too bitter about it. If only they had known what was going on, and had had it explained, if it had not been kept secret, so that the anxiety about Bevis being lost might not have been so great, there would not have been much trouble.

But now Bevis and Mark were in deep disgrace. As for their going away they might go and stay away if they wished. For the first day, indeed, it was quite a relief, the house was so quiet and peaceful; it was like a new life altogether. It would be a very good plan to despatch these rebels to a distance, where they would be fully employed, and under supervision. How peaceful it would be! The governor and Bevis's mother thought with such a strain removed they should live fully ten years longer.

But next day somehow it did not seem so pleasant. There was a sense of emptiness about the house. The rooms were vacant, and occasional voices sounded hollow. No one chattered at breakfast. At dinner-time Pan was called in that there might be some company, and in the stillness they could hear the ring, ring of the blacksmith's hammer on his anvil. When Bevis was at home they could never hear that.

The governor rode off in the afternoon, and Bevis's mother thought now these tormentors were absent it would be a good time to sit down calmly at some needlework.

Every five minutes she got up and looked out of window. Who was that banged the outer gate? Was it Bevis? The familiar patter of steps on the flags, the confused murmur which came before them did not follow. It was only John Young gone out into the road. The clock ticked so loud, and Pan snored in the armchair, and looked at her reproachfully when she woke him. By-and-by she went upstairs into their bedroom. The bed was made, but no one had slept in it.

There was a gimlet on the dressing-table, and Bevis's purse on the floor, and the half-sovereign in it. A great tome, an ancient encyclopaedia, which Bevis had dragged upstairs, was lying on a chair, open at "Magic." Mark's pocket-knife was stuck in the bed-post, and in his best hat there were three corn-crake's eggs, blown, of course, and put there for safety, as he never wore it.

She went to the window, and the swallows came to their nests above under the eaves. Bevis's jackets and things were lying everywhere, and as she left the room she saw a curious mark on the threshold, all angles and points. He had been trying to draw the wizard's foot there, inking the five angles, to keep out the evil spirits and witches, according to the proper way, lest they should take the magician by surprise.

Next she went to the bench-room—their armoury—and lifted the latch, but it was locked, the key in Bevis's pocket. The door rattled hollow. She looked through the keyhole, and could see the crossbow and the rigging for the ship. Downstairs again, sitting with her needlework, she heard the carrier's van go by, marking the time to be about four. There was the booing of distant cows, and then a fly buzzed on the pane. She took off her thimble and looked at old Pan in the armchair—old Pan, Bevis's friend.

It was deadly quiet. No shout, and bang, and clatter upstairs. No loud "I must," "I will." No rushing through the room, upsetting chairs, twisting tables askew. No "Ma, where's the hammer?" "Ma, where's my bow?" "Ma, where's my hat?"

She rang the bell, and told Polly to go down and ask Frances to come and take tea with her, as she was quite alone. Frances came, and all the talk was about Bevis, and Mark, and big Jack. So soon as she had heard about the battle Frances immediately took their part, and thought it was very ingenious of Bevis to contrive it, and brave to fight so desperately. Then mamma discovered that it was very good of Mark, and very affectionate, and very brave to row all up the water in the storm to fetch Bevis from the island.

When the governor returned, to his surprise, he found two ladies confronting him with reasons why Bevis and Mark were heroes instead of scamps. He did not agree, but it was of no use; of course he had to yield, and the result was the dog-cart was sent for them on the following morning. But Bevis was not in the least hurry to return, not a bit. He was disposed, on the contrary, to disobey, and remain where he was. Mark persuaded him not to do this, but still he kept the dog-cart waiting several hours, till long after dinner.

They tried hard to get Jack to let them take the rifle with them, unsuccessfully, for he thought the authorities would not like it. At last Bevis deigned to get up, and they were driven home, for in his sullen mood Bevis would not even touch the reins, nor let Mark. He was very much offended. The idea of resentment against Ted had never entered his mind. Ted was his equal for one thing, in age.

But he hated to be looked at with a severe countenance as if he had been a rogue and stolen sixpence by the authorities against whom he did not feel that he had done anything. He burned against them as the conspirators abroad burn with rage against the government which rules them. They were not Ted, and equal; they had power and used it over him. Bevis was wrong and very unjust, for they were the tenderest and kindest of home authorities.

At home there was a dessert waiting on the table for them, and some Burgundy. The Burgundy, a wine not much drunk in the country, had been got a long time ago to please Bevis, who had read that Charles the Bold was fond of and took deep draughts of it. Bevis fancied he should like it, and that it would make him bold like Charles. Mamma poured him out a glassful, Mark took his, and said "Thank you."

Bevis drank in silence.

"Aren't you glad to come home?" said mamma.

"No, *that* I'm not," said Bevis, and marched off up into the bench-room. Mamma saw that Mark wanted to follow, so she kissed him, recollecting that he had ventured through the storm after Bevis, and told him to do as he liked.

"The sails ought to be finished by now," said Bevis, as Mark came up.

"Yes," said Mark, "they're sure to be. But you know I can't go."

"You ought to fetch them," said Bevis, "you're lieutenant; captains don't fetch sails." He was ready for any important exertion, but he had a great idea of getting other people to do these inferior things for him.

"I can't go," said Mark, "Frances hates me."

"O! very well," said Bevis savagely, and ready to quarrel with anybody on the least pretext. The fact was, though resentful, he did not feel quite certain that he approved of his own conduct to his mother. He could have knocked any one down just to recover confidence. He pushed by Mark, slammed the door, and started to get the sails.

Frances laughed when she saw him. "Ah!" she said, "Mark did not care to come, did he?" She brought out the sails nicely hemmed—they had been ready some days—and made them into a parcel for him.

"So you ran away from the battle," she said.

"I didn't," said Bevis rudely.

"You sailed away—floated away."

"Not to run away."

"Yes, you did. And you were called Caesar."

She liked to tease him, being fond of him; she stroked his short golden curls, pinched his arm, kissed him, taunted him, and praised him; walked with him as he went homewards, asked him why he did not offer her his arm, and when he did, said she did not take boys' arms—*boys* with emphasis— till he grew scarlet with irritation. Then she petted him, asked him about the battle, and said it was wonderful, and he must show her over the battlefield. She made him promise to take her for a sail, and looked so delicious Bevis could not choose but smile.

She had her hat in her hand, such a little hand and so white, like a speck of sunshine among shadows. Her little feet peeped out among the grass and the blue veronica flowers. Her rounded figure, not too tiny at the waist, looked instinct with restless life, buoyant as if she floated. The bright light made her golden brown hair gleam. She lifted her long eyelashes, and looked him through and through with her grey eyes. Delicate arched eyebrows, small regular features, pouting lips, and impudent chin.

"You're very little," said Bevis, able to speak again. "I believe I could lift you over the stile."

She was little—little and delicious, like a wild strawberry, daintily tinted, sweet, piquant, with just enough acid to make you want some more, rare, and seldom found.

"As you are so impertinent," said she, "I shall not come any farther."

Bevis got over the stile first to be safe, then he turned, and said,—

"Jack will have you some day, and he's big, and he'll manage you."

"O!" said Frances, dropping her hat, "O!" Her little foot was put forward, she stood bolt upright with open lips. Scorn, utter, complete, perfect scorn was expressed from head to foot. Jack manage her! The idea! Before she could recover her breath, Bevis, who had immediately started running, was half across the next field.

Next morning they set to work to fix up the blue boat for sailing, and first stepped the mast and wedged it tight with a chip. A cord came down each side aslant to the gunwale, and was fastened there—these were the backstays to strengthen the mast when the wind blew rough. The bowsprit was lashed firmly at the bow, and the sheets or cords to work the foresail put through the staples, after which the tiller was fixed on instead of the lines. They had two sails—mainsail (without a boom) and foresail. Bevis once thought of having a topsail, but found it very awkward to contrive it without the ropes (they always called their cords ropes) becoming entangled.

The rigging and sails were now up, and Mark wanted to unfurl them and see how they answered, but Bevis, who was in a sullen mood, would not let him, till everything was completed. They had to put in the ballast, first bricks placed close together on the bottom, then two small bags of sand, and a large flat stone, which they thought would be enough. All this occupied a great deal of time, what with having to go backwards and forwards to the house for things and tools that had been forgotten, and the many little difficulties that always arise when anything new is being done.

Nothing fits the first time, and it all has to be done twice. So that when the last thing of all, the oyster-barrel with the tin canister inside, was put on board, it was about four in the afternoon. When they began to push the boat off the ground and get her afloat, they found that the wind had sunk. In the morning it had blown steadily from the westward, and busy at their work they had not noticed that after noon it gently declined. They pushed off, and rowed a hundred yards, so as to be out of the shelter of the trees on the shore, but there was no more breeze there than in the corner which they called the harbour.

The surface was smooth, and all the trees were reflected in it. Bevis had been sullen and cross all day, and this did not improve his temper. It was very rare for him to continue angry like this, and Mark resented it, so that they did not talk much. Bevis unfurled the sails and hoisted them up. The foresail worked perfectly, but the mainsail would not go up nor come down quickly. It was fastened to the mast by ten or twelve brass rings for travellers, and these would not slip, though they looked plenty large enough. They stuck, and had to be pushed by hand before the sail could be hoisted.

This was not at all proper, sails ought to go up and down easily and without a moment's delay, which might indeed be dangerous in a squall. Bevis pulled out his knife, and cut a number of them off, leaving only three or four, and the sail then worked much better. Next they tried reefing, they had put in two rows, but when the second was taken in the sail looked rather shapeless, and Bevis angrily cut off the second row. He told Mark to row back while he furled, and Mark did so. After they had fastened the boat by the painter to the willow root, and picked up their tools, they went homewards, leaving the rigging standing ready for use on the morrow.

"There's two things now," said Mark, "that ought to be done."

"What's that?" crossly.

"There ought to be an iron ring and staple to tie the ship to—a ship ought not to be tied to a root."

"Get a ring, then."

"And another thing—two more things."

"That there are not."

"That there are. You want a bowl to bale the water out, the waves are sure to splash over."

"That's nothing."

"Well, then," said Mark savagely, "you've forgotten the anchor."

Bevis looked at him as if he could have smashed him, and then went up into the bench-room without a word.

"You're a bear," shouted Mark from the bottom of the staircase. "I shan't come;" and he went to the parlour and found a book. For the remainder of the day, whenever they met, in a minute they were off at a tangent, and bounded apart. Bevis was as cross as a bear, and Mark would not conciliate him, not seeing that he had given him the least reason. At night they quarrelled in their bedroom, Bevis grumbling at Mark for throwing his jacket on the chair he generally used, and Mark pitching Bevis's waistcoat into a corner.

About ten minutes after the candle was out, Bevis got up, slipped on his trousers and jacket, and went downstairs barefoot in the dark.

"Glad you're gone," said Mark.

Bevis opened the door of the sitting-room where his mother was reading, walked up to her, kissed her, and whispered, "I'm sorry; tell the governor," and was off before she could answer. Next morning he was as bright as a lark, and every thing went smoothly again. The governor smiled once more, and asked where they intended to sail to first.

"Serendib," said Mark.

"A long voyage," said the governor.

"Thousands of miles," said Bevis. "Come on, Mark; what a lot you do eat."

Mark came, but as they went up the meadow he said that there ought to be an anchor.

"So there ought," said Bevis. "We'll make one like that in the picture—you know, with a wooden shaft, and a stone let through it."

"Like they used to have when they first had ships," said Mark.

"And went cruising along the shore—"

"We've forgotten the compass."

"Of course, that's right; they had no compass when we lived."

"No; they steered by the sun. Look, there's a jolly wind."

The water was rippling under a light but steady and pleasant summer breeze from the north-west. They pushed out, and while the boat slowly drifted, set the sails. Directly the foresail was up she turned and moved bow first, like a horse led by the bridle. When the mainsail was hoisted she began to turn again towards the wind, so that Bevis, who steered, had to pull the tiller towards him, or in another minute they would have run into the weeds. He kept her straight before the wind till they had got out of the bay where the boats were kept, and into the open water where the wind came stronger. Then he steered up the New Sea, so that the wind blew right across the boat, coming from the right-hand side.

It was a beautiful breeze, just the one they wanted, not too strong, and from the best direction, so that they could sail all the way there and back without trouble, a soldier's wind, out and home again.

Mark sat by the mast, both of them on the windward side, so as to trim the boat by their weight and make her stiffer. He was to work the foresail if they had to tack, or let down the mainsail if a white squall or a tornado struck the ship. The ripples kissed the bow with a merry smack, smack, smack; sometimes there was a rush of bubbles, and they could feel the boat heel a little as the wind for a moment blew harder.

"How fast we're going!" said Mark. "Hurrah!"

"Listen to the bubbles? Don't the sails look jolly?" said Bevis. The sunshine shone on the white canvas hollowed out by the wind; as the pilot looked up he could see the slender top of the mast tracing a line under the azure sky. Is there anything so delicious as the first sail in your own boat that you have rigged yourself?

Away she slipped, and Mark began to hum, knocking the seat with his knuckles to keep time. Then Bevis sang, making a tune of his own, leaning back and watching the sails with the sheet handy to let go if a puff came, for were they not voyaging on unknown seas? Bevis sang the same two verses over and over:—

> "Telling how the Count Arnaldos,
> With his hawk upon his hand,
> Saw a fair and stately galley,
> Steering onward to the land.
>
> 'Learn the secret of the sea?
> Only those who brave its dangers,
> Comprehend its mystery!'"

Mark sang with him, till by-and-by he said, "There's the battlefield; what country's that?"

"Thessaly," said Bevis. "It's the last land we know; now it's all new, and nobody knows anything."

"Except us."

"Of course."

"Are you going all round or straight up?" said Mark presently, as they came near Fir-Tree Gulf.

"We ought to coast," said Bevis. "They used to; we mustn't go out of sight of land."

"Steer into the gulf then; mind the stony point; what's that, what's the name?"

"I don't know," said Bevis. "It's a dreadful place; awful rocks—smash, crash, ship's side stove in—no chance for any body to escape there."

"A raft would be smashed."

"Lifeboats swamped."

"People jammed on the rocks."

"Pounded into jelly-fish."

"But it ought to have a name? Is it Cape Horn?"

"I don't think so, that's the other way round the world; we're more the India way, I think."

"Perhaps it's Gibraltar."

"As if we shouldn't know Gibraltar!"

"Of course we should, I forgot. Look! There's a little island and a passage—a channel. Mind how you steer—"

"It's Scylla and Charybdis," said Bevis. "I can see quite plain."

"Steer straight," said Mark. "There's not much room, rocks one side, shoal the other; it's not a pistol-shot wide—"

"Not half a pistol-shot."

"We're going. Hark! bubbles!"

Chapter Seven
Sailing Continued—"There She Lay, All The Day!"

Bevis had eased off, and the boat was sailing right before the wind, which blew direct into the gulf. Mark crawled up more into the bow to see better and shout directions to the pilot.

"Left—left."

"Port."

"Well, port."

"Starboard, now—that side. There, we scraped some weeds." The weeds made a rustling sound as the boat passed over them.

"Right—right—starboard, that side," holding out his hand, "you'll hit the rocks; you're too close."

"Pooh!" said Bevis. "It's deeper under the rocks, don't you remember." He prided himself on steering within an inch; the boat glided between the sandy island and the rocky wall, so close to the wall that the sail leaning over the side nearly swept it. Then he steered so as to pass along about three yards from the shore. The quarry opened out, and they went by it on towards the place where they bathed.

"Kails," said Mark, "mind the rails." By the bathing-place the posts and rails which were continued into the water were partly under the surface, so that a boat might get fixed on the top. Bevis pushed the tiller over, and the boat came round broadside to the wind, and began to cross the head of Fir-Tree Gulf.

The ripples here increased in size, and became wavelets as the breeze, crossing a wider surface of water, blew straight on shore, and seemed to rush in a stronger draught through the trees. These wavelets were not large enough to make the boat dance, but they caused more splashing at the bow, and she heeled a little to the wind. They slipped across the head of the gulf, some two hundred yards, at a good pace, steering for the mouth of the Nile.

"Tack," said Bevis, as they came near. "It's almost time. Get ready."

Mark unfastened the cord or sheet on the left side, against which the foresail was pulling, and held it in his hand. "I'm ready," he said, and in a minute, — "Quick, we shall be on shore."

Bevis pushed the tiller down hard to the left, at the same time telling Mark to let go. Mark loosened the foresheet, and the boat turning to the right was carried by her own impetus and the pressure of the mainsail up towards the wind. Bevis expected her to do as he had seen the yachts and ships at the seaside, and as he had read was the proper way, to come round slowly facing the wind, till just as she passed the straight line as it were of the breeze, Mark would have to tighten the foresheet, and the wind would press on the foresail like a lever and complete the turn.

He watched the foresail eagerly, for the moment to shout to Mark; the boat moved up towards the wind, then paused, hung, and began to fall back again. The wind blew her back. Bevis jammed the tiller down still harder, rose from his seat, bawled, "Mark! Mark!" but he was jerked back in a moment as she took the ground.

Mark seized a scull to push her off, when letting go the sheet the foresail flapped furiously, drawing the cord or rope through the staple as if it would snap it. Bevis, fearing the boat would turn over, let go the mainsheet, and then the mainsail flew over the left side, flapping and shaking the mast, while the sheet or rope struck the water and splashed it as if it were hit with a whip.

"Pull down the mainsail," shouted Bevis, stumbling forward.

"Hold tight," shouted Mark, giving a great shove with the scull. The boat came off, and Bevis was thrown down on the ballast. The wind took her before they could scramble into their places, and she drifted across the mouth of the Nile and grounded again.

"Down with the sail, I tell you," shouted Bevis in a rage. "Not that one — the big one."

Mark undid the cord or halyard, and down fell the mainsail into the boat, covering Bevis, who had to get out from under it before he could do anything.

"Did you ever see such a bother?" said Mark.

"Is anything broken?" said Bevis.

"No. You ought to have tacked sooner."

"How could I tell? She wouldn't come round."

"You ought to have had room to try twice."

"So we will next time."

"Let's go up the Nile and turn round, and get the sails up there," said Mark. "It will be such a flapping here."

Bevis agreed, and they pushed the boat along with the sculls a few yards up the Nile which was quite smooth there, while at the mouth the quick wavelets dashed against the shore. The bank of the river and the trees on it sheltered them while they turned the boat's head round, and carefully set the sails for another trial.

"We'll have two tries this time," said Bevis, "and we're sure to do it. If we can't tack, it's no use sailing."

When everything was ready, Mark rowed a few strokes with one oar till the wind began to fill the sails; then he shipped it, and sat down on the ballast on the windward side. The moment she was outside the Nile the splashing began, and Mark, to his great delight, felt a little spray in his face. "This is real sailing," he said.

"Now we're going," said Bevis, as the boat increased her speed. "Lot's see how much we can gain on this tack." He kept her as close to the wind as he could, but so as still to have the sails well filled and drawing. He let the mainsail hollow out somewhat, thinking that it would hold the wind more and draw them faster.

"Hurrah!" said Mark; "we're getting a good way up; there's the big sarsen—we shall get up to it."

There was a large sarsen or boulder, a great brown stone, lying on the shore on the quarry side of the gulf, about thirty yards above the bathing-place. If they could get as high up as the boulder, that would mean that in crossing the gulf on that tack they had gained thirty yards in direct course, thirty yards against the wind. To Mark it looked as if they were sailing straight for the boulder, but the boat was not really going in the exact direction her bow pointed.

She inclined to the right, and to have found her actual course he ought to have looked not over the stem but over the lee bow. The lee is the side away from the wind. That is to say, she drifted or made leeway, so that when they got closer they were surprised to see she was not so high up as the boulder by ten yards. She was off a bunch of rushes when Bevis told Mark to be ready. He had allowed space enough this time for two trials.

"Now," said Bevis, pushing the tiller over to the right; "let go."

Mark loosened the foresail, that it might not offer any resistance to the wind, and so check the boat from turning.

Bevis pushed the tiller over still harder, and as she had been going at a good pace the impetus made her answer the rudder better.

"She's coming," shouted Mark. "Jam the rudder."

The rudder was jammed, but when the bow seemed just about to face the wind, and another foot would have enabled Mark to tighten the foresail, and let it draw her quite round like a lever, she lost all forward motion.

"O! dear!" said Bevis, stamping with vexation. The boat stopped a moment, and then slowly fell back. "Pull tight," said Bevis, meaning refasten the foresheet. Mark did so, and the boat began to move ahead again.

"We're very close," said Mark almost directly.

"Tack," said Bevis. "Let go."

He tried to run her up into the wind again, but this time, having less weigh or impetus, she did not come nearly so far round, but began to pay off, or fall back directly, and, before Mark could get a scull out, bumped heavily against the shore, which was stony there.

"Let's row her head round," said Mark.

"Sculls ought not to be used," said Bevis. "It's lubberly."

"Awful lubberly," said Mark. "But what are we to do?"

"Pull away, anyhow," said Bevis.

Mark put out the scull, pushed her off, and after some trouble pulled till her head came round. Then he shipped the scull, and they began to sail again.

"We haven't got an inch," said Bevis. "Just look; there are the rails."

They had made about twenty yards, but in missing stays twice, drifting, and rowing round, had lost it all before the boat could get right again, before the sails began to draw well.

"What ever is it?" said Mark. "What is it we don't do?"

"I can't think," said Bevis. "It's very stupid. That's better."

There was a hissing and bubbling, and the boat, impelled by a stronger puff, rushed along, and seemed to edge a way up into the wind.

"Splendid," said Mark. "We shall get above the Nile this time, we shall get to the willow."

A willow-tree stood on the shore that side some way up. The boat appeared to move direct for it.

"I shall tack soon," said Bevis, "while we've got a good wind."

"Tack now," said Mark. "It doesn't matter about going right across."

"All right—now; let go."

They tried again, just the same; the boat paused and came back: then again, and still it was of no use.

"Row," said Bevis. "Bother!"

Mark rowed with a scull out on the lee side, and got her round.

"Now, just look," said Bevis. "Just look!"

He pointed at the Nile. They had drifted so that when they at last turned they were nearly level with the mouth of the river from which they had started.

"Let me row quicker next time," said Mark. "Let me row directly. It's hateful, though."

"It's hateful," said Bevis. "Sailing without tacking is stupid. Nobody would ever think we were sailors to see us rowing round."

"What's to be done?" said Mark. "Now try."

Bevis put the tiller down, and Mark pulled her head round as quick as he could. By the time the sails had begun to draw they had lost more than half they had gained, and in crossing as the breeze slackened a little lost the rest, and found themselves as before, just off the mouth of the Nile.

"I don't think you keep her up tight enough," said Mark, as they began to cross again. "Try her closer. Close-hauled, you know."

"So I will," said Bevis; and the breeze rising again he pulled the mainsheet tighter (while Mark tightened the foresheet), and pushed the tiller over somewhat.

The boat came closer to the wind, and seemed now to be sailing straight for the quarry.

"There," said Mark, "we shall get out of the gulf in two tacks."

"But we're going very slow," said Bevis.

"It doesn't matter if we get to the quarry."

The boat continued to point at the quarry, and Bevis watched the mainsail intently, with his hand on the tiller, keeping her so that the sail should not shiver, and yet should be as near to it as possible.

"Splendid," said Mark, on his knees on the ballast, looking over the stem. "Splendid. It's almost time to tack."

He lifted the foresail, and peered under it at the shore.

"I say—well, Bevis!"

"What is it?" asked Bevis. "I'm watching the mainsail; is it time?"

"We haven't got an inch—we're going—let's see—not so far up as the rushes."

All the while the boat's head pointed at the quarry she had been making great leeway, drifting with the wind and waves. The sails scarcely drew, and she had no motion to cut her way into the wind. Instead of edging up into it, she really crossed the gulf in nearly a straight line, almost level with the spot whence she started. When Bevis tried to get her found, she would not come at all. She was moving so slowly she had no impetus, and the wind blew her back. Mark had to row round again.

"That's no use," he said. "But it looked as if it was."

"She won't sail very near the wind," said Bevis, as they crossed again towards the Nile. "We must let her run free, and keep the sails hollow."

They crossed and crossed five times more, and still came only just above the mouth of the Nile, and back to the bunch of rushes.

"I believe it's the jib," said Bevis, as they sailed for the quarry side once more. "Let's try without the jib. Perhaps it's the jib won't let her come round. Take it down."

Mark took the foresail down, and the boat did show some disposition to run up into the wind; but when Bevis tried to tack she went half-way, and then payed off and came back, and they nearly ran on the railings, so much did they drift. Still they tried without the foresail again; the boat they found did not sail so fast, and it was not the least use, she would not come round. So they re-set the foresail. Again and again they sailed to and fro, from the shore just above the Nile to the bunch of rushes, and never gained a foot, or if they did one way they lost it the other. They were silent for some time.

"It's like the Bay of Biscay," said Mark.

"'There she lay, all the day,
In the Bay of Biscay, O!'

"And the sails look so jolly too."

"I can't make it out," said Bevis. "The sails are all proper, I'm sure they are. What can it be? We shall never get out of the gulf."

"And after all the rowing round too," said Mark. "Lubberly."

"Horrid," said Bevis. "I hope there's no other ship about looking at us. The sailors would laugh so. I know—Mark!"

"Yes."

"Don't row next time; we'll wear ship."

"What's that?"

"Turn the other way—with the wind. Very often the boom knocks you over or tears the mast out."

"Capital, only we've no boom. What must I do?"

"Nothing; you'll see. Sit still—in the middle. Now."

Bevis put the tiller over to windward. The boat paid off rapidly to leeward, and described a circle, the mainsail passing over to the opposite side, and as it took the wind giving a jerk to the mast.

Mark tightened the other foresheet, and they began to sail back again.

"But just look!" said he.

"Horrid," said Bevis.

In describing the circle they had lost not only what they had gained, but were level with the mouth of the Nile, and not five yards from the shore at the head of the gulf. It was as much this tack as they could do to get above the railings; they were fifteen yards at least below the rushes, when Bevis put the tiller up to windward, and tried the same thing again. The boat turned a circle to leeward, and before she could get right round and begin to sail again, they had gone so near the shore, drifting, that Mark had to put out the scull in case they should bump. In crossing this time the wind blew so light that they could not get above the mouth of the Nile.

"It's no use wearing ship," said Mark.

"Not a bit; we lose more than ever. You'd better row again," said Bevis reluctantly.

Mark pulled her round again, and they sailed to and fro three times more, but did but keep their position, for the wind was perceptibly less as the day went on, and it became near noon.

"I hate those rushes," said Mark, as he pulled her head round once more.

Bevis did not reply, but this time he steered straight across to the Nile and up it till the bank sheltered them from the wind. There they took down the sails, quite beaten, for that day at least, and rowed back to harbour.

Next morning when they arrived at the New Sea they found that the wind came more down the water, having turned a little to the south, but it was the same in force. They started again, and sailed very well till they were opposite the hollow oak in which on the day of battle it was supposed Bevis had hidden. Here the wind was a head-wind, against which they could only work by tacking, and when they came to tack they found just the same difficulty as yesterday.

All the space they gained during the tack was lost in coming round before the boat could get weigh on her. They sailed to and fro from the hollow oak to some willow bushes on the other side, and could not advance farther. Sometimes they got above the oak, but then they fell back behind the willow bushes; sometimes they worked up twenty yards higher than the willow bushes, but dropped below the oak.

Bevis soon discovered why they made better tacks now and then; it was because the wind shifted a little, and did not so directly oppose them. The instant it returned to its usual course they could not progress up the sea. By the willow bushes they could partly see into Fir-Tree Gulf; yesterday they could not sail out of the gulf, and to-day, with all their efforts, they could not sail into it.

After about twenty trials they were compelled to own that they were beaten, and returned to harbour. Bevis was very much troubled with this failure, and as soon as they had got home he asked Mark to go up in the bench-room, or do anything he liked, and leave him by himself while he looked at the old encyclopaedia.

Mark did as he was asked, knowing that Bevis always learnt anything best by himself. Bevis went up into the bedroom, where the great book remained open on the chair, knelt down, and set to work to read everything there was in it on ships and navigation. There was the whole history of boats and ships, from the papyrus canoes of the Nile, made by plaiting the stalks, the earthenware boats, hide boats, rafts or skins, hollowed trees, bark canoes, catamarans, and proas. There was an account of the triremes of Rome, and on down to the caravels, bilanders, galliots, zebecs, and great three-deckers. The book did not quite reach to the days of glorious Nelson.

It laid down the course supposed to have been followed by Ulysses, and described the voyages of the Phoenicians to Britain. The parts of a three-decker were pictured, and the instruments of navigation were explained with illustrations. Everything was there except what Bevis wanted, for in all this exhaustive and really interesting treatise, there were no plain directions how to tack.

There were the terms and the very orders in nautical language, but no explanation as to how it was done. Bevis shut the book up, and rose with a sigh, for he had become so occupied with his search that he had unconsciously checked his breathing. He went down to the bookcase and stood before it thoughtfully. Presently he recollected that there was something about yachting in a modern book of sports. He found it and read it carefully, but though it began about Daedalus, and finished with the exact measurement of a successful prize-winning yacht, he could not make out what he wanted.

The account was complete even to the wages of the seamen and the method of signalling with flags. There was a glossary of terms, but nothing to tell him how to tack, that is, nothing that he could understand. He put the book away, and went out into the blue-painted summer-house to think it over again.

What you really want to know is never in a book, and no one can tell you. By-and-by, if you keep it steadily in memory and ever have your eyes open, you hit on it by accident. Some mere casual incident throws the solution right into your hands at an unexpected moment.

Bevis had fitted up his boat according to his recollections of those he had seen in the pictures.

There was no sailing-boat that he could go and see nearer than forty miles. As he sat thinking it over Mark rushed up. He, too, had been thinking, and he had found something.

"I know," he said.

"What?"

"We have not got enough ballast," said Mark. "That's it—I'm sure that's it. Don't you remember how the boat kept drifting?"

"Very likely," said Bevis. "Yes, that's it; how stupid we were. Let's get some more directly. I know; I'll ask the governor for a bag of shot."

The governor allowed them to take the bag, which weighed twenty-eight pounds, on condition that they put it inside a small sack, so as to look like sand, else some one might steal it. They also found two pieces of iron, scraps, which made up the fresh ballast to about forty pounds. The wind had now gone down as it did soon after midday, and they could do nothing.

But next morning it blew again from the south, and they were afloat directly after breakfast. The effect of the ballast was as Mark had anticipated; the boat did not drift so much, she made less leeway, and she was stiffer, that is, she stood up to the wind better. They did not lose so much quite, but still they did not gain, nor would she come round without using a scull; indeed, she was even worse in this respect, and more obstinate, she would not come up into the wind, the weight seemed to hold her back.

After two hours they were obliged to give it up for the third time. The following day there was no wind. "Let's make the anchor," said Mark, "and while we're making the anchor perhaps we shall think of something about tacking."

So they began to make the anchor, after the picture of one in the old folio. They found a square piece of deal, it was six inches by four, and sawed off about two feet. In the middle they cut a long hole right through, and after much trouble found a flat stone to fit it. This was wedged in tight, and further fastened with tar-cord. Near one end a small square hole was cut, and through this they put a square rod of iron, which the blacksmith sold them for a shilling—about three times its value.

The rod was eighteen inches long, and when it was through it was bent up, or curved, and the ends filed to a blunt point. It fitted tight, but they wedged it still firmer with nails, and it was put the opposite way to the stone, so that when the stone tried to sink flat on the bottom, one or other of the points of the bar would stick in the ground. Mark thought there ought to be a cross-piece of wood or iron as there is in proper anchors, but so far as they could make out, this was not attached to the ancient stone-weighted ones, and so they did not put it.

Lastly, a hole was bored at the other end of the shaft, and the rope or cable (a stout cord) inserted and fastened. Looking eagerly out of window in the morning to see if there was a wind they were delighted to see the clouds drifting from the north-north-west. This was a capital wind for them as they could not tack. It was about the same that had been blowing the first day when they sailed into Fir-Tree Gulf and could not get out, but it would have taken them to the very end of the New Sea had they not considered it proper to coast round. This time they meant to sail straight up the centre and straight back.

Chapter Eight
Sailing Continued—Voyage to the Unknown Island

After breakfast they got afloat, and when away from the trees the boat began to sail fast, and every now and then the bubbles rushed from under the bow. Mark sat on the ballast, or rather reclined, and Bevis steered. The anchor was upon the forecastle, as they called it, with twenty-five feet of cable. Sailing by the bluff covered with furze, by the oak where the council was held, past the muddy shore lined with weeds where the cattle came down to drink, past the hollow oak and the battlefield, they saw the quarry and Fir-Tree Gulf, but did not enter it. As they reached the broader water the wind came fresher over the wide surface, and the boat careening a little hastened on. They were now a long way from either shore in the centre of the widest part.

"This is the best sail we've had," said Mark, putting his legs out as far as he could, leaning his back against the seat and his head against the mast. "It's jolly."

Bevis got off the stern-sheets and sat down on the bottom so that he too could recline, he had nothing to do but just keep the tiller steady and watch the mainsail, the wind set the course for them. They could feel the breeze pulling at the sails, and the boat drawn along.

"Is it rough?" said Mark.

"Shall we take in a reef?" said Bevis.

"No," said Mark. "Let's capsize."

"Right," said Bevis. "It doesn't matter."

"Not a bit. Isn't she slipping along?"

"Gurgling and guggling."

"Bubbling and smacking. That was spray."

"There's a puff. How many knots are we going?"

"Ten."

"Pooh! twenty. No chance of a pirate catching us."

"In these unknown seas," said Mark, "you can't tell what proas are waiting behind the islands, nor how many Malays with creeses."

"They're crooked the wrong way," said Bevis. "The most curious knives I ever saw."

"Or junks," went on Mark. "Are these the Chinese Seas?"

"Jingalls," said Bevis, "they shoot big bullets, almost cannon-balls, as big as walnuts. I wish we had one in the forecastle."

"We ought to have a cannon."

"Of course we did."

"As if we couldn't manage a cannon!"

"As if!"

"Or a double-barrel gun."

"Or anything."

"Anything."

"People *are* stupid."

"Idiotic."

"We must have a gun."

"We must."

They listened again to the gurgling and "guggling," the bubbles, and kiss, kiss of the wavelets.

"We're a long way now," said Mark presently. "Can we see land?"

"See land! We lost sight of land months ago. I should think not. Look up there."

Bevis was watching the top of the mast, tracing its line along the sky, where white filmy clouds were floating slowly. Mark opened his drowsy eyes and looked up too.

"No land in sight," said he. "Nothing but sky and clouds," said Bevis. "How far are we from shore?"

"Six thousand miles."

"It's the first time anybody has ever sailed out of sight of land in our time," said Mark. "It's very wonderful, and we shall be made a great deal of when we get home."

"Yes, and put in prison afterwards. That's the proper way."

"We shall bring home sandal-wood, and diamonds as big as—as apples—"

"And see unknown creatures in the sea, and butterflies as huge as umbrellas—"

"Catch fevers and get well again—"

"We must make notes of the language, and coax the people to give us some of their ancient books."

"O! I say," said Mark, "when you were on the Unknown Island did you see the magician with long white robes, and the serpent a hundred feet long he keeps in a cave under the bushes?"

"No," said Bevis, "I forgot him." So he had. His imagination ran so rapidly, one thing took the place of the other as the particles of water take each other's place in a running brook. "We shall find him, I dare say."

"Let's land and see."

"So we will."

"Are you sure you're steering right?"

"O! yes; it's nothing to do, you only have to keep the wind in the sails."

"I wonder what bird that is?" said Mark, as a dove flew over. He knew a dove well enough on land.

"It's a sort of parrot, no doubt."

"I wonder how deep it is here."

. "About a million fathoms."

"No use trying to anchor."

"Not the least."

"It's very warm."

"In these places ships get burnt by the sun sometimes."

Another short silence. "Is it time to take a look-out, captain?"

"Yes, I think so," said the captain. Mark crept up in the bow.

"You're steering too much to the right—that way," he cried, holding out his right arm. "Is that better?"

"More over."

"There."

"Right."

As the boat fell off a little from the wind obeying the tiller, Bevis, now the foresail was out of his line of sight could see the Unknown Island. They were closer than they had thought.

"Shall we land on Serendib?"

"O! no—on your island," said Mark. "Steer as close to the cliff as you can."

Bevis did so, and the boat approached the low sandy cliff against which the waves had once beat with such fury. The wavelets now washed sideways past it with a gentle splashing, they were not large enough to make the boat dance, and if they had liked they could have gone up and touched it.

"It looks very deep under it," said Mark, as Bevis steered into the channel, keeping two or three yards from shore.

"Ready," he said; "get ready to furl the mainsail."

Mark partly unfastened the halyard, and held it in his hand. Almost directly they had passed the cliff they were in the lee of the island which kept off the wind. The boat moved, carried on by its impetus through the still water, but the sails did not draw. In a minute Bevis told Mark to let the mainsail down, and as it dropped Mark hauled the sail in or the folds would have fallen in the water. At the same moment Bevis altered the course, and ran her ashore some way below where he had leaped off the punt, and where it was low and shelving. Mark was out the instant she touched with the painter, and tugged her up on the strand. Bevis came forward and let down the foresail, then he got out.

"Captain," said Mark, "may I go round the island?"

"Yes," said the captain, and Mark stepped in among the bushes to explore. Bevis went a little way and sat down under a beech. The hull of the boat was hidden by the undergrowth, but he could see the slender mast and some of the rigging over the boughs. The sunshine touched the top of the smooth mast, which seemed to shine above the green leaves. There was the vessel; his comrade was exploring the unknown depths of the wood; they were far from the old world and the known countries. He sat and gloated over the voyage, till by-and-by he remembered the tacking.

They could not do it, even yet they were only half mariners, and were obliged to wait for a fair wind. If it changed while they were on the island they would have to row back. He was no longer satisfied; he went down to the boat, stepped on board, and hoisted the sails. The trees and the island itself so kept off the wind that it was perfectly calm, and the sails did not even flutter. He stepped on shore, and went a few yards where he could look back and get a good view of the vessel, trying to think what it could be they did not do, or what it could be that was wrong.

He looked at her all over, from the top of the mast to the tiller, and he could not discover anything. Bevis walked up and down, he worked himself quite into a fidget. He went into the wood a little way, half inclined to go after Mark as he felt so restless. All at once he took out his pocket-book and pencil and sat down on the ground just where he was, and drew a sailing-boat such as he had seen. Then he went back to the shore, and sketched their boat on the other leaf. His idea was to compare the sailing-boats he had seen with theirs.

When he had finished his outline drawing he saw directly that there were several differences. The mast in the boat sketched from memory was much higher than the mast in the other. Both sails, too, were larger than those he had had made. The bowsprit projected farther, but the foresail was not so much less in proportion as the mainsail. The foresail looked almost large enough, but the mainsail in the boat was not only smaller, it was not of the same shape.

In his sketch from memory the gaff or rod at the top of the sail rose up at a sharper angle, and the sail came right back to the tiller. In the actual boat before him the gaff was but little more than horizontal to the mast, and the sail only came back three-fourths of the distance it ought to have done.

"It must be made bigger," Bevis thought. "The mainsail must be made ever so much larger, and it must reach to where I sit. That's the mistake— you can see it in a minute. Mark! Mark!" He shouted and whistled.

Mark came presently running. "I've been all round," he said panting, "and I've—"

"This is it," said Bevis, holding up his pocket-book.

"I've seen a huge jack—a regular shark. I believe it was a shark—and three young wild ducks, and some more of those parrots up in the trees."

"The mainsail—"

"And something under the water that made a wave, and went along—"

"Look, you see it ought to come—"

"What could it have been that made the wave and went along?"

"O! nothing—only a porpoise, or a seal, or a walrus—nothing! Look here—"

"But," said Mark, "the wave moved along, and I could not tell what made it."

"Magic," said Bevis. "Very likely the magician. Did you see him?"

"No; but I believe there's something very curious about this island—"

"It's enchanted, of course," said Bevis. "There's lots of things you know are there, and you can't find," said Mark; "there's a tiger, I believe, in the bushes and reeds at the other end. If I had had my spear I should have gone and looked, and there's boa-constrictors and a hippopotamus was here last night, and heaps of jolly things, and I've found a place to make a cave. Come and see," (pulling Bevis).

"I'll come," said Bevis, "in a minute. But just look, I've found out what was wrong—"

"And how to tack?"

"Yes."

"Then let's do it, and tack and get shipwrecked, and live here. If we only had Jack's rifle."

"But we must sail properly first," said Bevis. "I shan't do anything till we can sail properly: now this is it. Look."

He showed Mark the two sketches, and how their mainsail did not reach back far enough towards the stern.

"Frances must make it larger," said Mark. "Of course that's it—it's as different as possible. And the mast ought to be higher—it would crack better, and go overboard—whop!"

"I don't know," said Bevis; "about the mast; yes, I think I will. We will make one a foot or eighteen inches higher—"

"Bigger sails will go faster, and smash the ship splendidly against the rocks," said Mark. "There'll be a crash and a grinding, and the decks will blow up, and there'll be an awful yell as everybody is gulped up but you and me."

"While we're doing it, we'll make another bowsprit, too—longer," said Bevis.

"Why didn't we think of it before," said Mark. "How stupid! Now you look at it, you can see it in a minute. And we had to sail half round the world to find it."

"That's just it," said Bevis. "You sail forty thousand miles to find a thing, and when you get there you can see you left it at home."

"We have been stupes," said Mark. "Let's do it directly. I'll shave the new mast, and you take the sails to Frances. And now come and see the place for the cave."

Bevis went with him, and Mark took him to the bank or bluff inside the island which Bevis had passed when he explored it the evening of the battle. The sandy bank rose steeply for some ten or fifteen feet, and then it was covered with brambles and fern. There was a space at the foot clear of bushes and trees, and only overgrown with rough grasses. Beyond this there were great bramble thickets, and the trees began again about fifty yards away, encircling the open space. The spot was almost in the centre of the island, but rather nearer the side where there was a channel through the weeds than the other.

"The sand's soft and hard," said Mark. "I tried it with my knife; you can cut it, but it won't crumble."

"We should not have to prop the roof," said Bevis.

"No, and it's as dry as chips; it's the most splendid place for a cave that ever was."

"So it is," said Bevis. "Nobody could see us."

He looked round. The high bank shut them in behind, the trees in front and each side. "Besides, there's nobody to look. It's capital."

"Will you do it," said Mark.

"Of course I will—directly we can sail properly."

"Hurrah!" shouted Mark, hitting up his heels, having caught that trick from Bevis. "Let's go home and begin the sails. Come on."

"But I know one thing," said Bevis, as they returned to the boat; "if we're going to have a cave, we must have a gun."

"That's just what I say. Can't we borrow one? I know, you put up Frances to make Jack lend us his rifle. She's fond of you—she hates me."

"I'll try," said Bevis. "How ought you to get a girl to do anything?"

"Stare at her," said Mark. "That's what Jack does, like a donk at a thistle when he can't eat any more."

"Does Frances like the staring?"

"She pretends she doesn't, but she does. You stare at her, and act stupid."

"Is Jack stupid?"

"When he's at our house," said Mark. "He's as stupid as an owl. Now she kisses you, and you just whisper and squeeze her hand, and say it's very tiny. You don't know how conceited she is about her hand—can't you see—she's always got it somewhere where you can see it; and she sticks her foot out so," (Mark put one foot out); "and don't you move an inch, but stick close to her, and get her into a corner or in the arbour. Mind, though, if you don't keep on telling her how pretty she is, she'll box your ears. That's why she hates me—"

"Because you don't tell her she's pretty. But she is pretty."

"But I'm not going to be always telling her so—I don't see that she's anything very beautiful either—you and I should look nice if we were all the afternoon doing our hair, and if we walked like that and stuck our noses up in the air; and kept grinning, and smacked ourselves with powder, and scent, and all such beastly stuff. Now Jack's rifle—"

"We could make it shoot," said Bevis, "if we had it all to ourselves, and put bullets through apples stuck up on a stick, or smash an egg—"

"And knock over the parrots up in these trees."

"I *will* have a gun," said Bevis, kicking a stone with all his might. "Are you sure Frances could get Jack—"

"Frances get Jack to do it! Why, I've seen him kiss her foot."

They got on board laughing and set the sails, but as the island kept the wind off, Mark had to row till they were beyond the cliff. Then the sails filled and away they went.

"Thessaly," said Mark presently. "See! we're getting to places where people live again. I say, shall we try the anchor?"

"Yes. Let down the mainsail first."

Mark let it down, and then put the anchor over. It sank rapidly, drawing the cable after it. The flat stone in the shaft endeavoured as it sank to lie flat on the bottom, and this brought one of the flukes or points against the ground, and the motion of the boat dragging at it caused it to stick in a few inches. The cable tightened, and the boat brought up and swung with her stem to the wind. Mark found that they did not want all the cable; he hauled it in till there was only about ten feet out; so that, allowing for the angle, the water was not much more than five or six feet deep. They were off the muddy shore, lined with weeds. Rude as the anchor was, it answered perfectly. In a minute or two they hauled it up, set the mainsail, and sailed almost to the harbour, having to row the last few yards because the trees kept much of the breeze off. They unshipped the mast, and carried it and the sails home.

In the evening Mark set to work to shave another and somewhat longer pole for the new mast, and Bevis took the sails and some more canvas to

Frances. He was not long gone, and when he returned said that Frances had promised to do the work immediately.

"Did you do the cat and mouse?" said Mark. "Did you stare?"

"I stared," said Bevis, "but there were some visitors there—"

"Stupes?"

"Stupes, so I couldn't get on very well. She asked me what I was looking at, and if she wasn't all right—"

"She meant her flounces; she thinks of nothing but her flounces. Some of the things are called gores."

"But I began about the rifle, and she said perhaps, but she really had no influence with Jack."

"O!" said Mark with a snort. "Another buster."

"And she couldn't think why you didn't come home. She had forgiven you a long time, and you were always unkind to her, and she was always forgiving you."

"Busters," said Mark. "She's on telling stories from morning to night."

"I don't see why you should be afraid of her; she can't hurt you."

"Not hurt me! Why if you've done anything—it's niggle-niggle, niggle-naggle, and she'll play you every nasty trick, and set the Old Moke on to look cross; and then when Jack comes, it's 'Mark, dear Mark,' and wouldn't you think she was a sweet darling who loved her brother!"

Mark tore off a shaving.

"One thing though," he added. "Won't she serve Jack out when he's got her and obliged to have her. As if I didn't know why she wants me to come home. All she wants is to send some letters to him."

"Postman. I see," said Bevis.

"But I'll go," said Mark. "I'll go and fetch the sails to-morrow. I should like to see the jolly Old Moke; and don't you see? if I take the letters she'll be pleased and get the rifle for us."

It was exceedingly disrespectful of Mark to speak of his governor as the Old Moke; his actual behaviour was very different to his speech, for in truth he was most attached to his father. The following afternoon Mark walked over and got the sails, and as he had guessed Frances gave him a note for Jack, which he had to deliver that evening. They surprised the donkey; Mark mounted and rode off.

Bevis went on with the mast and the new gaff and bowsprit, and when Mark got back about sunset he had the new mast and rigging fitted up in the shed to see how it looked. The first time they made a mast it took them a long while, but now, having learned exactly how to do it, the second had soon been prepared. The top rose above the beam of the shed, and the mainsail stretched out under the eave.

"Hoist the peak up higher," said the governor. Being so busy they had not heard him come. "Hoist it up well, Mark."

Mark gave another pull at the halyard, and drew the peak, or point of the gaff, up till it stood at a sharp angle.

"The more peak you can get," said the governor, "the more leverage the wind has, and the better she will answer the rudder."

He was almost as interested in their sailing as they were themselves, and had watched them from the bank of the New Sea concealed behind the trees. But he considered it best that they should teach themselves, and find out little by little where they were wrong. Besides which he knew that the greatest pleasure is always obtained from inferior and incomplete instruments. Present a perfect yacht, a beautiful horse, a fine gun, or anything complete to a beginner, and the edge of his enjoyment is dulled with too speedy possession. The best way to learn to ride is on a rough pony, to sail in an open ill-built boat, because by encountering difficulties the learner comes to understand and appreciate the perfect instrument, and to wield or direct it with fifty times more power than if he had been born to the purple.

From the shore the governor had watched them vainly striving to tack, and could but just refrain from pointing out the reason. When he saw them fitting up the enlarged sails and the new mast, he exulted almost as much as they did themselves. "They will do it," he said to himself, "they will do it this time."

Then to Bevis, "Pull the mainsail back as far as you can, and don't let it hollow out, not hollow and loose. Keep it taut. It ought be as flat as a board. There—" He turned away abruptly, fearing he had told them too much.

"As flat as a board," repeated Bevis. "So I will. But we thought it was best hollow, didn't we?" There was still enough light left to see to step the mast, so they carried the sails and rigging up to the boat, and fitted them the same evening.

Chapter Nine
Sailing Continued—The Pinta—New Formosa

In the morning the wind blew south, coming down the length of the New Sea. Though it was light and steady it brought larger waves than they had yet sailed in, because they had so far to roll. Still they were not half so high as the day of the battle, and came rolling slowly, with only a curl of foam now and then. The sails were set, and as they drifted rather than sailed out of the sheltered harbour, the boat began to rise and fall, to their intense delight.

"Now it's proper sea," said Mark.

"Keep ready," said Bevis. "She's going. We shall be across in two minutes."

He hauled the mainsheet taut, and kept it as the governor had told him, as flat as a board. Smack! The bow hit a wave, and threw handfuls of water over Mark, who knelt on the ballast forward, ready to work the foresheets. He shouted with joy, "It's sea, it's real sea!"

Smack! smack! His jacket was streaked and splotched with spray; he pushed his wet hair off his eyes. Sish! sish! with a bubbling hiss the boat bent over, and cut into the waves like a knife. So much more canvas drove her into the breeze, and as she went athwart the waves every third one rose over the windward bow like a fountain, up the spray flew, straight up, and then horizontally on Mark's cheek. There were wide dark patches on the sails where they were already wet.

Bevis felt the tiller press his hand like the reins with a strong fresh horse. It vibrated as the water parted from the rudder behind. The least movement of the tiller changed her course. Instead of having to hold the tiller in such a manner as to keep the boat's head up to the wind, he had now rather to keep her off, she wanted to fly in the face of the breeze, and he had to moderate such ardour. The broad mainsail taut, and flat as a board, strove to drive the bow up to windward.

"Look behind," said Mark. "Just see."

There was a wake of opening bubbles and foam, and the waves for a moment were smoothed by their swift progress. Opposite the harbour the New Sea was wide, and it had always seemed a long way across, but they had hardly looked at the sails and the wake, and listened to the hissing and splashing, than it was time to tack.

"Ready," said Bevis. "Let go."

Mark let go, and the foresail bulged out and fluttered, offering no resistance to the wind. Bevis pushed the tiller over, and the mainsail having its own way at last drove the head of the boat into the wind, half round, three-quarters; now they faced it, and the boat pitched. The mainsail shivered; its edge faced the wind.

"Pull," said Bevis the next moment.

Mark pulled the foresheet tight to the other side. It drew directly, and like a lever brought her head round, completing the turn. The mainsail flew across. Bevis hauled the sheet tight. She rolled, heaved, and sprang forward.

"Hurrah! We've done it! Hurrah!"

They shouted and kicked the boat. Wish! the spray flew, soaking Mark's jacket the other side, filling his pocket with water, and even coming back as far as Bevis's feet. Sish! sish! The wind puffed, and the rigging sang; the mast leaned; she showed her blue side; involuntarily they moved as near to windward as they could.

Wish! The lee gunwale slipped along, but just above the surface of the water, skimming like a swallow. Smack! Such a soaker. The foresail was wet; the bowsprit dipped twice. Swish! The mainsail was dotted with spray. Smack! Mark bent his head, and received it on his hat.

"Ready!" shouted the captain.

The foresheet slipped out of Mark's hand, and flapped, and hit him like a whip till he caught the rope. The mainsail forced her up to the wind; the foresail tightened again levered her round. She rolled, heaved, and sprang forward.

Next time they did it better, and without a word being spoken. Mark had learned the exact moment to tighten the sheet, and she came round quicker than ever. In four tacks they were opposite the bluff, the seventh brought them to the council oak. As the wind blew directly down the New Sea each tack was just the same.

Bevis began to see that much depended upon the moment he chose for coming about, and then it did not always answer to go right across. If he waited till they were within a few yards of the shore the wind sometimes fell, the boat immediately lost weigh, or impetus, and though she came round it was slowly, and before she began to sail again they had made a little leeway.

He found it best to tack when they were sailing full speed, because when he threw her head up to windward she actually ran some yards direct against the wind, and gained so much. Besides what they had gained coming aslant across the water at the end of the tack she shot up into the eye of the wind, and made additional headway like that. So that by watching the breeze, and seizing the favourable opportunity, he made much more than he would have done by merely travelling as far as possible.

The boat was badly built, with straight, stiff lines, a crank, awkward craft. She ought to have been a foot or so broader, and more swelling, when she would have swung round like a top.

Bevis might then have crossed to the very shore, though the wind lessened, without fear of leeway. But she came round badly even at the best. They thought she came round first-rate, but they were mistaken. Had she done so, she would have resumed the return course without a moment's delay, instead of staggering, rolling, heaving, and gradually coming to her work again. Bevis had to watch the breeze and coax her.

His eye was constantly on the sail, he felt the tiller, handling it with a delicate touch like a painter's brush. He had to calculate and decide quickly whether there was space and time enough for the puff to come again before they reached the shore, or whether he had better sacrifice that end of the tack and come round at once. Sometimes he was wrong, sometimes right. In so narrow a space, and with such a boat, everything depended upon coming round well.

His workmanship grew better as they advanced. He seemed to feel all through the boat from rudder to mast, from the sheet in his hand to the bowsprit. The touch, the feeling of his hand, seemed to penetrate beyond the contact of the tiller, to feel through wood and rope as if they were a part of himself like his arm. He responded to the wind as quickly as the sail. If it fell, he let her off easier, to keep the pace up; if it blew, he kept her closer, to gain every inch with the increased impetus. He watched the mainsail hauled taut like a board, lest it should shiver. He watched the foresail, lest he should keep too close, and it should cease to draw. He stroked, and soothed, and caressed, and coaxed her, to put her best foot foremost.

Our captains have to coax the huge ironclads. With all the machinery, and the science, and the elaboration, and the gauges, and the mathematically correct everything, the iron monsters would never come safe to an anchorage without the most exquisite coaxing. You must coax everything if you want to succeed; ironclads, fortune, Frances.

Bevis coaxed his boat, and suited her in all her little ways; now he yielded to her; now he waited for her; now he gave her her head and let her feel freedom; now, he hinted, was the best moment; suddenly his hand grew firm, and round she came.

Do you suppose he could have learnt wind and wave and to sail like that if he had had a perfect yacht as trim as the saucy Arethusa herself? Never. The crooked ways of the awkward craft brought out his ingenuity.

As they advanced the New Sea became narrower, till just before they came opposite the battlefield the channel was but a hundred yards or so wide. In these straits the waves came with greater force and quicker; they wore no higher, but followed more quickly, and the wind blew harder, as if also confined. It was tack, tack, tack. No sooner were the sheets hauled, and they had begun to forge ahead, than they had to come about. Flap, flutter, pitch, heave, on again. Smack! smack! The spray flew over. Mark buttoned his jacket to his throat, and jammed his hat down hard on his head.

The rope, or sheet, twisted once round Bevis's hand, cut into his skin, and made a red weal. He could not give it a turn round the cleat because there was no time. The mainsail pulled with almost all its force against his hand. Just as they had got the speed up, and a shower of spray was flying over Mark, round she had to come. Pitch, pitch, roll, heave forward, smack! splash! bubble, smack!

On the battlefield side Bevis could not go close to the shore because it was lined with a band of weeds; and on the other there were willow bushes in the water, so that the actual channel was less than the distance from bank to bank. Each tack only gained a few yards, so that they crossed and recrossed nearly twenty times before they began to get through the strait. The sails were wet now, and drew the better; they worked in silence, but without a word, each had the same thought.

"It will do now," said Mark.

"Once more," said Bevis.

"Now," said Mark, as they had come round.

"Yes!"

From the westward shore Bevis kept her close to the wind, and as the water opened out, he steered for Fir-Tree Gulf. He calculated that he should just clear the stony promontory. Against the rocky wall the waves dashed and rose up high above it, the spray was carried over the bank and into the quarry. The sandbank or islet in front was concealed, the water running over it, but its site was marked by boiling surge.

The waves broke over it, and then met other waves thrown back from the wall; charging each other, they sprang up in pointed tips, which parted and fell. Over the grassy bank above rolled brown froth, which was then lifted and blown away. This was one of those places where the wind always seems to blow with greater force. In a gale from the southwest it was difficult to walk along the bank, and even now with only a light breeze the waves ran at the stony point as if they were mad. Bevis steered between Scylla and Charybdis, keeping a little nearer the sunken islet this time, the waves roared and broke on each side of them, froth caught against the sails, the boat shook as the reflux swept back and met the oncoming current; the rocky wall seemed to fly by, and in an instant they were past and in the gulf.

Hauling into the wind, the boat shot out from the receding shore, and as they approached the firs they were already half across to the Nile. Returning, they had now a broad and splendid sea to sail in, and this tack took them up so far that next time they were outside the gulf. It was really sailing now, long tacks, or "legs," edging aslant up into the wind, and leaving the quarry far behind.

"It's splendid," said Mark. "Let me steer now."

Bevis agreed, and Mark crept aft on hands and knees, anxious not to disturb the trim of the boat; Bevis went forward and took his place in the same manner, buttoning his jacket and turning up his collar.

Mark steered quite as well. Bevis had learned how to work the boat, to coax her, from the boat and the sails themselves. Mark had learned from Bevis, and much quicker. It requires time, continued observation, and keenest perception to learn from nature. When one has thus acquired the art, others can learn from him in a short while and easily. Mark steered and handled the sheet, and brought her round as handily as if he had been at it all the time.

These lengthened zigzags soon carried them far up the broad water, and the farther they went the smaller the waves became, having so much the less distance to come, till presently they were but big ripples, and the boat ceased to dance. As the waves did not now oppose her progress so much, there was but little spray, and she slipped through faster. The motive power, the wind, was the same; the opposing force, the waves, less. The speed increased, and they soon approached Bevis's island, having worked the whole distance up against the wind. They agreed to land, and Mark brought her to the very spot where they had got out before. Bevis doused the mainsail, leaped out, and tugged her well aground. After Mark had stepped ashore they careened the boat and baled out the water.

There was no tree or root sufficiently near to fasten the painter to, so they took out the anchor, carried it some way inland, and forced one of the flukes into the ground. The boat was quite safe and far enough aground not to drift off, but it was not proper to leave a ship without mooring her. Mark wanted to go and look at the place he thought so well adapted for a cave, so they walked through between the bushes, when he suddenly remembered that the vessel in which they had just accomplished so successful a voyage had not got a name.

"The ship ought to have a name," he said. "Blue boat sounds stupid."

"So she ought," said Bevis. "Why didn't we think of it before? There's Arethusa, Agamemnon, Sandusky, Orient—"

"Swallow, Viking, Saint George—but that won't do," said Mark. "Those are ships that sail now and some have steam; what were old ships—"

"Argo," said Bevis. "I wonder what was the name of Ulysses' ship—"

"I know," said Mark, "Pinta—that's it. One of Columbus's ships, you know. He was the first to go over there, and we're the first on the New Sea."

"So we are; it shall be Pinta, I'll paint it, and the island ought to have a name too."

"Of course. Let's see: Tahiti?" said Mark. "Loo-choo?"

"Celebes?"

"Carribbees?"

"Cyclades? But those are a lot of islands, aren't they?"

"Formosa is a good name," said Bevis. "It sounds right. But I don't know where it is—it's somewhere."

"Don't matter—call it New Formosa."

"Capital," said Bevis. "The very thing; there's New Zealand and New Guinea. Right. It's New Formosa."

"Or the Land of Magic."

"New Formosa or the Magic Land," said Bevis. "I'll write it down on the map we made when we get home."

"Here's the place," said Mark. "This is where the cave ought to be," pointing at a spot where the sandy cliff rose nearly perpendicular; "and then we ought to have a hut over it."

"Poles stuck in and leaning down and thatched."

"Yes, and a palisade of thick stakes stuck in, in front of the door."

"So that no one could take us by surprise at night."

"And far enough off for us to have our fire inside."

"Twist bushes in between the stakes."

"Quite impassable to naked savages."

"How high?"

"Seven feet."

"Or very nearly."

"We could make a bed, and sleep all night."

"Wouldn't it be splendid to stop here altogether?"

"First-rate; no stupid sillinesses."

"No bother."

"Have your dinner when you like."

"Nobody to bother where you've been to."

"Let's live here."

"All right. Only we must have a gun to shoot birds and things to eat," said Bevis. "It's no use unless we have a gun; it's not proper, nor anything."

"No more it is," said Mark; "we *must* have a gun. Go and stare at Frances."

"But it takes such a time, and then you know how slow Jack is. It would take him three months to make up his mind to lend us the rifle."

"So it would," said Mark; "Jack's awful slow, like his old mill-wheel up there."

"Round and round," said Bevis. "Boom and splash and rumble," — swinging his arm — "round and round, and never get any farther."

"Not an inch," said Mark. "Stop; there's Tom's gun." He meant the bird-keeper's.

"Pooh!" said Bevis, "that's rotten old rusty rubbish. Isn't there anybody we could borrow one of?"

"Nobody," said Mark; "they're all so stupid and afraid."

"Donks."

"Awful donks! Let's sell our watches, and buy one," said Mark. "Only they would ask what we had done with our watches."

"I know," said Bevis, suddenly kicking up his heels, then standing on one foot and spinning round—"I know!"

"What is it! Quick! Tell me!"

"Make one," said Bevis.

"Make one?"

"A matchlock," said Bevis. "Make a matchlock. And a matchlock is quite proper, and just what they used to have—"

"But the barrel?"

"Buy an iron tube," said Bevis. "They have lots at Latten, at the ironmonger's; buy an iron pipe, and stop one end—"

"I see," said Mark. "Hurrah!" and up went his heels, and there was a wild capering for half a minute.

"The bother is to make the breech," said Bevis. "It ought to screw, but we can't do that."

"Ask the blacksmith," said Mark; "we need not let him know what it's for."

"If he doesn't know we'll find out somehow," said Bevis. "Come on, let's do it directly. Why didn't we think of it before."

They returned towards the boat.

"Just won't it be splendid," said Mark. "First, we'll get everything ready, and then get shipwrecked proper, and be as jolly as anything."

"Matchlocks are capital guns," said Bevis; "they're slow to shoot with, you know, but they kill better than rifles. They have long barrels, and you put them on a rest to take steady aim, and we'll have an iron ramrod too, so as not to have the bother of making a place to put the rod in the stock, and to ram down bullets to shoot the tigers or savages."

"Jolly!"

"The stock must be curved," said Bevis; "not like the guns, broad and flat, but just curved, and there must be a thing to hold the match; and just remind me to buy a spring to keep the hammer up, so that it shall not fall till we pull the trigger—it's just opposite to other guns, don't you see? The spring is to keep the match up, and you pull against the spring. And there's a pan and a cover to it—a bit of tin would do capital—and you push it open with your thumb. I've seen lots of matchlocks in glass cases, all inlaid gold and silver."

"We don't want that."

"No all we want is the shooting. The match is the bother—"

"Would tar-cord do?"

"We'll try; first let's make the breech. Take up the anchor."

Mark picked up the anchor, and put it on board. They launched the Pinta, and set sail homewards, Mark steering. As they were running right before the wind, the ship went at a great pace.

"That's the Mozambique," said Bevis, as they passed through the strait where they had had to make so many tacks before.

"Land ho!" said Mark, as they approached the harbour. "We've had a capital sail."

"First-rate," said Bevis. "But let's make the matchlock."

Now that he had succeeded in tacking he was eager to go on to the next thing, especially the matchlock-gun. The hope of shooting made him three times as ready to carry out Mark's plan of the cave on the island. After furling the sails, and leaving everything ship-shape, they ran home and changed their jackets, which were soaked.

Chapter Ten
Making a Gun—The Cave

Talking upstairs about the barrel of the gun, they began to think it would be an awkward thing to bring home, people would look at them walking through the town with an iron pipe, and when they had got it home, other people might ask what it was for. Presently Mark remembered that John Young went to Latten that day with the horse and cart to fetch things; now if they bought the tube, Young could call for it, and bring it in the cart and leave it at his cottage. Downstairs they ran, and up to the stables, and as they came near, heard the stamp of a cart-horse, as it came over. Mark began to whistle the tune,—

> "John Young went to town
> On a little pony,
> Stuck a feather in his hat,
> And called him Macaroni."

"Macaroni!" said he, as they looked in at the stable-door. "Macaroni" did not answer; the leather of the harness creaked as he moved it.

"Macaroni!" shouted Mark. He did not choose to reply to such a nickname.

"John!" said Bevis.

"Eez—eez," replied the man, looking under the horse's neck, and meaning "Yes, yes."

"Fetch something for us," said Mark.

"Pint?" said John laconically.

"Two," said Bevis.

"Ar-right," ("all right") said John, his little brown eyes twinkling. "Ar-right, you." For a quart of ale there were few things he would not have done: for a gallon his soul would not have had a moment's consideration, if it had stood in the way.

Bell, book, and candle shall not drive me back When pewter tankard beckons to come on!

They explained to him what they wanted him to do.

"Have you got a grate in your house?" said Bevis.

"A yarth," said John, meaning an open hearth. "Burns wood."

"Can you make a hot fire—very hot on it?"

"Rayther. Boilers." By using the bellows. "What could we have for an anvil?"

"Be you going a blacksmithing?"

"Yes—what will do for an anvil?"

"Iron quarter," said John. "There's an ould iron in the shed. Shall I take he whoam?" An iron quarter is a square iron weight weighing 28 pounds: it would make a useful anvil. It was agreed that he should do so, and they saw him put the old iron weight, rusty and long disused, up in the cart.

"If you wants anybody to blow the bellers," said he, "there's our Loo— she'll blow for yer. Be you going to ride?"

"No," said Bevis; "we'll go across the fields."

Away they went by the meadow foot-path, a shorter route to the little town, and reached it before John and his cart. At the ironmonger's they examined a number of pipes, iron and brass tubes. The brass looked best, and tempted them, but on turning it round they fancied the join showed, and was not perfect, and of course that would not do. Nor did it look so strong as the iron, so they chose the iron, and bought five feet of a stout tube—the best in the shop—with a bore of 5-eighths; and afterwards a brass rod, which was to form the ramrod. Brass would not cause a spark in the barrel.

John called for these in due course, and left them at his cottage. The old rogue had his quart, and the promise of a shilling, if the hearth answered for the blacksmithing. In the evening, Mark, well primed as to what he was to ask, casually looked in at the blacksmith's down the hamlet. The blacksmith was not in the least surprised; they were both old frequenters; he was only surprised one or both had not been before.

Mark pulled some of the tools about, lifted the sledge which stood upright, and had left it's mark on the iron "scale" which lay on the ground an inch deep. Scale consists of minute particles which fly off red-hot iron when it is hammered—the sparks, in fact, which, when they go out, fall, and are found to be metal; like the meteors in the sky, the scale shooting from Vulcan's anvil, which go out and drop on the earth. Mark lifted the sledge, put it down, twisted up the vice, and untwisted it, while Jonas, the smith, stood blowing the bellows with his left hand, and patting the fire on the forge with his little spud of a shovel.

"Find anything you want," he said presently.

"I'll take this," said Mark. "There's sixpence."

He had chosen a bit of iron rod, short, and thicker than their ramrod. Bevis had told him what to look for.

"All right, sir—anything else?"

"Well," said Mark, moving towards the door, "I don't know,"—then stopping with an admirable assumption of indifference. "Suppose you had to stop up one end of a pipe, how should you do it?"

"Make it white-hot," said the smith. "Bring it to me."

"Will white-hot shut tight?"

"Quite tight—it runs together when hit. Bring it to me. I say, where's the punt?" grinning. His white teeth gleamed between his open lips—a row of ivory set in a grimy face.

"The punt's at the bottom," said Mark, with a louring countenance.

"Nice boys," said the smith. "You're very nice boys. If you was mine—" He took up a slender ash plant that was lying on the bench, and made it ply and whistle in the air.

Mark tossed his chin, kicked the door open, and walked off.

"I say!—I say!" shouted the smith. "Bring it to me."

"Keep yourself to yourself," said Mark loftily.

Boys indeed! The smith swore, and it sounded in his broad deep chest like the noise of the draught up the furnace. He was angry with himself—he thought he had lost half-a-crown, at least, by just swishing the stick up and down. If you want half-a-crown, you must control your feelings.

Mark told Bevis what the smith had said, and they went to work, and the same evening filed off the end of the rod Mark had bought. Bevis's plan was to file this till it almost fitted the tube, but not quite. Then he meant to make the tube red-hot—almost white—and insert the little block. He knew that heat would cause the tube to slightly enlarge, so that the block being cold could be driven in; then as the tube cooled it would shrink in and hold it tight, so that none of the gas of the powder could escape.

The block was to be driven in nearly half an inch below the rim; the rim was to be next made quite white-hot, and in that state hammered over till it met in the centre, and overlapped a little. Again made white-hot, the overlapping (like the paper of a paper tube doubled in) was to be hammered and solidly welded together. The breech would then be firmly closed, and there would not be the slightest chance of its blowing out. This was his own idea, and he explained it to Mark.

They had now to decide how long the barrel should be: they had bought rather more tube than they wanted. Five, or even four feet would be so long, the gun would be inconvenient to handle, though with a rest, and very heavy. In a barrel properly built up, the thickness gradually decreases from the breech to the muzzle, so that as the greatest weight is nearest the shoulder the gun balances. But this iron tube was the same thickness from one end to the other, and in consequence, when held up horizontally, it seemed very heavy at the farther extremity.

Yet they wanted a long barrel, else it would not be like a proper matchlock. Finally, they fixed on forty inches, which would be long, but not too long; with a barrel of three feet four inches they ought, they considered, to be able to kill at a great distance. Adding the stock, say fifteen inches, the total length would be four feet seven.

Next morning, taking their tools and a portable vice in a flag-basket, as they often did to the boat, they made a détour and went to John Young's cottage. On the door-step there sat a little girl without shoes or stockings; her ragged frock was open at her neck. At first, she looked about twelve years old, as the original impression of age is derived from height and size. In a minute or two she grew older, and was not less than fourteen. The rest of the family were in the fields at work, Loo had been left to wait upon them. Already she had a huge fire burning on the hearth, which was of brick; the floor too was brick. With the door wide open they could hardly stand the heat till the flames had fallen. Bevis did not want so much flame; embers are best to make iron hot. Taking off their jackets they set to work, put the tube in the fire, arranged the anvil, screwed the vice to the deal table, which, though quite clean, was varnished with grease that had sunk into the wood, selected the hammer which they thought would suit, and told Loo to fetch them her father's hedging-gloves.

These are made of thick leather, and Mark thought he could hold the tube better with them, as it would be warm from one end to the other. The little block of iron, to form the breech, was filed smooth, so as to just *not* fit the tube. When the tube was nearly white-hot, Mark put on the leather gloves, seized and placed the colder end on the anvil, standing the tube with the glowing end upwards.

Bevis took the iron block, or breech-piece, with his pincers, inserted it in the white-hot tube, and drove it down with a smart tap. Some scale fell off and dropped on Mark's shirt-sleeve, burning little holes through to his skin. He drew his breath between his teeth, so sudden and keen was the pain of the sparks, but did not flinch. Bevis hastily threw his jacket over Mark's arms, and then gave the block three more taps, till it was flush with the top of the tube.

By now the tube was cooling, the whiteness superseded by a red, which gradually became dull. Mark put the tube again in the fire, and Loo was sent to find a piece of sacking to protect his arm from the sparks. His face was not safe, but he had sloped his hat over it, and hold his head down. There were specks on his hat where the scale or sparks had burnt it. Loo returned with a sack, when Bevis, who had been thinking, discovered a way by which Mark might escape the sparks.

He pulled the table along till the vice fixed to it projected over the anvil. Next time Mark was to stand the tube upright just the same, but to put it in the vice, and tighten the vice quickly, so that he need not hold it. Bevis had a short punch to drive the block or breech-piece deeper into the tube. Loo, blowing at the embers, with her scorched face close to the fire, declared that the tube was ready. Mark drew it out, and in two seconds it was fixed in the vice, but with the colder end in contact with the anvil underneath. Bevis put his punch on the block and tapped it sharply till he had forced it half an inch beneath the rim.

He now adjusted it for the next heating himself, for he did not wish all the end of the tube to be so hot; he wanted the end itself almost white-hot, but not the rest. While it was heating they went out of doors to cool themselves, leaving Loo to blow steadily at the embers. She watched their every motion as intent as a cat a mouse; she ran with her naked brown feet to fetch and carry; she smiled when Mark put on the leather gloves, for she would have held it with her hands, though it had been much hotter.

She would have put her arm on the anvil to receive a blow from the hammer; she would have gone down the well in the bucket if they had asked her. Her mind was full of this wonderful work—what could they be making? But her heart and soul was filled with these great big boys with their beautiful sparkling eyes and white arms, white as milk, and their wilful, imperious ways. How many times she had watched them from afar! To have them so near was almost too great a joy; she was like a slave under their feet; they regarded her less than the bellows in her hands.

Directly the tube was white-hot at the extremity, she called them. Mark set the tube up; Bevis carefully hammered the rim over, folding it down on the breech block. Another heating, and he hammered the yielding metal still closer together, welding the folds. A third heating, and he finished it, deftly levelling the projections. The breech was complete, and it was much better done than they had hoped. As it cooled the tube shrank on the block; the closed end of the tube shrank too, and the breech-piece was incorporated into the tube itself. Their barrel was indeed far safer at the breech than scores of the brittle guns turned out cheap in these days.

Loo, seeing them begin to put their tools in the flag-basket, asked, with tears in her eyes, if they were not going to do any more? They had been there nearly three hours, for each heating took some time, but it had not seemed ten minutes to her. Bevis handed the barrel to her, and told her to take great care of it; they would come for it at night. It was necessary to smuggle it up into the armoury at home, and that could not be done by day. She took it. Had he given it in charge of a file of soldiers it could not have been safer; she would watch it as a bird does her nest.

Just then John came in, partly for his luncheon, partly out of curiosity to see how they were getting on. "Picters you be!" said John.

Pictures they were—black and grimy, not so much from the iron as the sticks and logs, half burnt, which they had handled; they were, in fact, streaked and smudged with charcoal. Loo instantly ran for a bowl of water for them to wash, and held the towel ready. She watched them down the hill, and wished they had kicked her or pulled her hair. Other boys did; why did not they touch her? They might have done so. Next time she thought she would put her naked foot so that they would step on it; then if she cried out perhaps they would stroke her.

In the afternoon they took two spades up to the boat. The wind had fallen as usual, but they rowed to New Formosa. The Pinta being deep in the water and heavy with ballast, moved slowly, and it was a long row. Mark cut two sticks, and these were driven into the face of the sand cliff, to show the outline of the proposed cave. It was to be five feet square, and as deep as they could dig it.

They cleared away the loose sand and earth at the foot in a few minutes, and began the excavation. The sand at the outside was soft and crumbled, but an inch deep it became harder, and the work was not anything like so easy as they had supposed. After pecking with the spades for a whole hour, each had only cut out a shallow hole.

"This is no good," said Mark; "we shall never do it like this."

"Pickaxes," said Bevis.

"Yes; and hatchets," said Mark. "We could chop this sand best."

"So we could," said Bevis. "There are some old hatchets in the shed; we'll sharpen them; they'll do."

They worked on another half-hour, and then desisted, and cutting some more sticks stuck them in the ground in a semicircle before the cliff, to mark where the palisade was to be fixed. The New Sea was still calm, and they had to row through the Mozambique all the way to the harbour.

In the evening they ground two old hatchets, which, being much worn and chipped, had been thrown aside, and then searched among the quantities of stored and seasoned wood and poles for a piece to make the stock of the matchlock. There was beech, oak, elm, ash, fir—all sorts of wood lying about in the shed and workshop. Finally, they selected a curved piece of ash, hard and well seasoned. The curve was nearly what was wanted, and being natural it would be much stronger. This was carried up into the armoury to be shaved and planed into shape.

At night they went for the barrel. Loo brought it, and Bevis, as he thought, accidentally stepped on her naked foot, crushing it between his heel and the stones at the door. Loo cried out.

"O dear!" said he, "I am so sorry. Here—here's sixpence, and I'll send you some pears."

She put the sixpence in her mouth and bit it, and said nothing. She indented the silver with her teeth, disappointed because he had not stroked her, while she stood and watched them away.

They smuggled the barrel up into the armoury, which was now kept more carefully locked than ever, and they even put it where no one could see it through the keyhole. In the morning, as there was a breeze from the westward, they put the hatchets on board the Pinta, and sailed away for New Formosa. The wind was partly favourable, and they reached the island in three tacks. The hatchets answered much better, cutting out the sand well, so that there soon began to be two holes in the cliff.

They worked a little way apart, each drilling a hole straight in, and intending to cut away the intervening wall afterwards, else they could not both work at once. By dinner-time there was a heap of excavated sand and two large holes. The afternoon and evening they spent at work on the gun. Mark shaved at the stock; Bevis filed a touch-hole to the barrel; he would have liked to have drilled the touch-hole, but that he could not do without borrowing the blacksmith's tools, and they did not want him to know what they were about.

For four days they worked with their digging at the cave in the morning, and making the matchlock all the rest of the day. The stock was now ready—it was simply curved and smoothed with sand-paper, they intended afterwards to rub it with oil, till it took a little polish like the handles of axes.

The stock was almost as long as the barrel, which fitted into a groove in it, and was to be fastened in with copper wire when all was ready.

Bevis at first thought to cut a mortise in the handle of the stock to insert the lock, but on consideration he feared it would weaken the stock, so he chiselled a place on the right side where the lock could be counter-sunk. The right side of the stock had been purposely left somewhat thicker for the pan. The pan was a shallow piece of tin screwed on the stock and sunk in the wood, one end closed, the other to be in contact with the barrel under the touch-hole. In this pan the priming was to be placed. Another piece of tin working on a pivot formed of a wire nail (these nails are round) was to cover the pan like a slide or lid, and keep the priming from dropping out or being blown off by the wind.

Before firing, the lid would have to be pushed aside by the thumb, and the outer corner of it was curled over like a knob for the thumb-nail to press against. The lock was most trouble, and they had to make many trials before they succeeded. In the end it was formed of a piece of thick iron wire. This was twisted round itself in the centre, so that it would work on an axle or pivot.

It was then, heated red-hot, and beaten flat or nearly, this blacksmith's work they could do at home, for no one could have guessed what it was for. One end was bent, so that though fixed at the side of the stock, it would come underneath for the trigger, for in a matchlock trigger and hammer are in a single piece. The other end curved over to hold the match, and this caused Bevis some more thought, for he could not split it like the match-holders of the Indian matchlocks he had seen in cases.

Bevis drew several sketches to try and got at it, and at last twisted the end into a spiral of two turns. The match, which is a piece of cord prepared to burn slowly, was to be inserted in the spiral, the burning end slightly projecting, and as at the spiral the iron had been beaten thin, if necessary it could be squeezed with thumb and finger to hold the cord tighter, but Bevis did not think it would be necessary to do that.

Next the spring was fixed behind, and just above the trigger end in such a way as to hold the hammer end up. Pulling the trigger you pulled against the spring, and the moment the finger was removed the hammer sprang up—this was to keep the lighted match away from the priming till the moment of firing. The completed lock was covered with a plate of brass screwed on, and polished till it shone brightly. Bevis was delighted after so much difficulty to find that it worked perfectly. The brass ramrod had been heated at one end, and enlarged there by striking it while red-hot, which caused the metal to bulge, and they now proceeded to prove the barrel before fastening it in the stock.

Chapter Eleven
Building the Hut

Powder was easily got from Latten; they bought a pound of loose powder at three halfpence the ounce. This is like black dust, and far from pure, for if a little be flashed off on paper or white wood it leaves a broad smudge, but it answered their purpose very well. While Bevis was fretting and fuming over the lock, for he got white-hot with impatience, though he would and did do it, Mark had made a powder-horn by sawing off the pointed end of a cow's horn, and fitting a plug of wood into the mouth. For their shot they used a bag, and bought a mould for bullets.

The charger to measure the powder was a brass drawn cartridge-case, two of which Mark had chanced to put in his pocket while they were at Jack's. It held more than a charge, so they scratched a line inside to show how far it was to be filled. At night the barrel was got out of the house, and taken up the meadows, three fields away, to a mound they had chosen as the best place. Mark brought a lantern, which they did not light till they arrived, and then put it behind the bushes, so that the light should not show at a distance.

The barrel was now charged with three measures of powder and two of shot rammed down firm, and then placed on the ground in front of a tree. From the touch-hole a train of powder was laid along the dry ground round the tree, so that the gun could be fired while the gunner was completely protected in case the breech blew out.

A piece of tar-cord was inserted in a long stick split at the end. Mark wished to fire the train, and having lit the tar-cord, which burned well, he stood back as far as he could and dropped the match on the powder. Puff—bang! They ran forward, and found the barrel was all right. The shot had scored a groove along the mound and lost itself in the earth; the barrel had kicked back to the tree, but it had not burst or bulged, so that they felt it would be safe to shoot with. Such a thickness of metal, indeed, would have withstood a much greater strain, and their barrel, rude as it was, was far safer than many flimsy guns.

The last thing to be made was the rest. For the staff they found a straight oak rod up in the lumber-room, which had once been used as a curtain-rod to an old-fashioned four-poster. Black with age it was hard and rigid, and still strong; the very thing for their rest. The fork for the barrel to lie in was a difficulty, till Bevis hit on the plan of forming it of two pieces of thick iron wire. These were beaten flat at one end, a hole was bored in the top of the staff, and the two pieces of wire driven in side by side, when their flatness prevented them from moving. The wires were then drawn apart and hammered and bent into a half-circle on which the stock would rest.

The staff was high enough for them to shoot standing, but afterwards it was shortened, as they found it best to aim kneeling on one knee. When the barrel was fastened in the stock by twisting copper wire round, it really looked like a gun, and they jumped and danced about the bench-room till the floor shook. After handling it for some time they took it to pieces, and hid it till the cave should be ready, for so long a weapon could not be got out of the house very easily, except in sections. Not such a great while previously they had felt that they must not on any account touch gunpowder, yet now they handled it and prepared to shoot without the least hesitation. The idea had grown up gradually. Had it come all at once it would have been rejected, but it had grown so imperceptibly that they had become accustomed to it, and never questioned themselves as to what they were doing.

Absorbed in the details and the labour of constructing the matchlock, the thinking and the patience, the many trials, the constant effort had worn away every other consideration but that of success. The labour made the object legitimate. They gloried in their gun, and in fact, though so heavy, it was a real weapon capable of shooting, and many a battle in the olden times was won with no better. Bevis was still making experiments, soaking cord in various compositions of saltpetre, to discover the best slow match.

By now the cave began to look like a cave, for every morning, sailing or rowing to New Formosa, they chopped for two or three hours at the hard sand. This cave was Mark's idea, but once started at work Bevis became as eager as he, and they toiled like miners. After the two headings had been driven in about five feet, they cut away the intervening wall, and there was a cavern five feet square, large enough for both to sit down in.

They had intended to dig in much deeper, but the work was hard, and, worse than that, slow, and now the matchlock was ready they were anxious to get on the island. So they decided that the cave was now large enough to be their store-room, while they lived in the hut, to be put up over the entrance. Bevis drew a sketch of the hut several times, trying to find out the easiest way of constructing it. The plan they selected was to insert long poles in the sand about three feet higher up than the top of the cave. These were to be placed a foot apart; and there were to be nine of them, all stuck in holes made for the purpose in a row, thus covering a space eight feet wide and eight high. From the cliff the rafters were to slope downwards till the lower and outward ends were six feet above the ground. That would give the roof a fall of two feet in case of rain.

Two stout posts were to be put up with a long beam across, on which the outer ends of the rafters were to rest. Two lesser posts in the middle were to mark the doorway. The roof was to be covered with brushwood to some thickness, and then thatched over that with sedges and reed-grass.

The walls they meant to make of hurdles stood on end, and fastened with tar-cord to upright stakes. Outside the hurdles they intended to pile up furze, brushwood, faggots, bundles of sedges—anything, in short. A piece of old carpeting was to close the door as a curtain. The store-room was five feet square, the hut would be eight, so that with the two they thought they should have plenty of space.

The semi-circular fence or palisade starting from the cliff on one side, and coming to it on the other, of the hut was to have a radius of ten yards, and so enclose a good piece of ground, where they could have their fire and cook their food secure from wild beasts or savages. A gateway in the fence was to be just wide enough to squeeze through, and to be closed by two boards nailed to a frame.

It took some time to settle all these details, for Bevis would not begin till he had got everything complete in his mind, but the actual work did not occupy nearly so long as the digging of the cave. There were plenty of poles growing on the island, which Mark cut down with Bevis's own hatchet, not the blunt ones they had used for excavating, but the one with which he had chopped at the trees in the Peninsula.

As Mark cut them down, some ash, some willow, and a few alder, Bevis stripped off the twigs with a billhook, and shortened them to the proper length. All the poles were ready in one morning, and in the afternoon coming again they set up the two stout corner posts. Next day the rafters were fitted, they had to bring a short ladder to get at the cliff over the mouth of the cave. Then the hurdles were brought and set up, and the brushwood cut and thrown on the top.

Sedges grew in quantities at the other end of the island, where the ground sloped till it became level with the water. In cutting them they took care to leave an outer fringe standing, so that if any one passed, or by any chance looked that way from the shore, he should not see that the sedges had been reaped. They covered the roof two feet thick with brushwood, sedges, and reed-grass, which they considered enough to keep out any ordinary shower.

Of course if the tornadoes common to these tropical countries should come they must creep into the inner cave. Against such fearful storms no thatch they could put up would protect them. The walls took a whole day to finish, as it required such a quantity of brushwood, and it had to be fastened in its place with rods, thrust into the ground, and tied at the top to the outside rafters.

At last the hut was finished, and they could stand up, or walk about in it; but when the carpet-curtain was dropped, it was dark, for they had forgotten to make a window. But in the daytime they would not want one, as the curtain could be thrown aside, and the doorway would let in plenty of light, as it faced the south. At night they would have a lantern hung from the roof.

"It's splendid," said Mark; "we could live here for years."

"Till we forgot what day it was, and whether it was Monday or Saturday," said Bevis.

"And our beards grow down to our waists." Their chins were as smooth as possible.

"Ships would be sent out to search for us."

"And when we come home everybody would come to see us," said Mark. "Just think of all the wonders we shall have to tell them!"

"I wish Ted could see it," said Bevis, "and Charlie, and Val."

"Wouldn't they be jealous if they knew," said Mark. "They'd kill us if we did not let them come too."

"It's a great secret," said Bevis; "we must be very careful. There may be mines of gold in this island, don't you see."

"Diamonds."

"There's a pearl fishery, I'm sure."

"Birds of Paradise."

"Spices and magic things."

"It's the most wonderful island ever found out."

"Hurrah!"

"Let's have a sail."

"So we will."

"Not work any more this afternoon."

"No; let's sail up farther—"

"Beyond the island?"

"Yes; unknown seas, don't you know. Come on."

Away they ran to the Pinta. The wind lately had blown lightly from the east, and continued all day. These light easterly summer breezes are a delight to those who watch the corn, for they mean fine weather and full wheat-ears. Mark took the tiller, and they sailed southwards through the channel, between New Formosa and Serendib. Not far beyond, Bevis, looking over the side, saw the sunken punt. She was lying in six or seven feet of water, but the white streak on her gunwale could be clearly seen. He told Mark.

"I hope the governor won't get her up yet," said Mark. "Lucky he's so busy—"

"Why?"

"Don't you see," said shrewd Mark, "while the punt's at the bottom nobody can come to our island to see what we're at."

"Ah!" said Bevis. "What a jolly good thing I was shipwrecked."

As they went southwards they passed several small islands or sandbanks, and every now and then a summer snipe flew up and circled round them, just above the water, returning to the same spot.

"Those are the Coral Isles," said Bevis. "They're only just above the surface."

"Tornadoes would sweep right over them," said Mark. "That's why there are no cocoa-nut trees."

Another sandbank some way on the left they named Grey Crow Island, because a grey or hooded crow rose from it.

"Do you see any weeds?" said Mark presently. "You know that's a sign of land."

"Some," said Bevis, looking over the side into the ripples. "They are brown and under water; I suppose it's too deep for them to come to the top."

The light breeze carried them along pleasantly, though slowly.

"Swallows," said Bevis; "I can see some swallows, high up, there. That's another sign of land."

"Heave the lead," said Mark.

"We've forgotten it; how stupid! Mind you remember it next time."

New Formosa was a long way in the rear now.

"That's Pearl Island," said Mark, pointing to a larger sandbank. "Can't you see the shells glistening; it's mother-of-pearl."

"So it is."

The crows had carried the mussels up on the islet, and left the shells strewn about. The inner part reflected the sunlight. If examined closely there are prismatic colours.

"There's that curious wave," said Mark, standing up and pointing to an undulation of the water on the other side of a small patch of green weeds. The undulation went away from them till they lost sight of it. "What is it?"

"There are all sorts of curious things in the tropic seas," said Bevis. "Some of them are not found out even yet. Nobody can tell what it is."

"Perhaps it's magic," said Mark.

"Lots of magic goes on in the south," said Bevis. "I believe we're very nearly on the equator; just feel how hot the gunwale is,"—the wood was warm from the sunshine—"and the sun goes overhead every day, and it's so, light at night. We will bring the astrolabe and take an observation—I say!"

The Pinta brought up with a sudden jerk. They had run on a shoal.

"Wrecked!" shouted Mark joyfully. "But there are no waves. It's no good with these ripples."

Bevis pushed the Pinta off with a scull, and so feeling the bottom, told Mark to ease the tiller and sail more to the right. Two minutes afterwards they grounded again, and again pushed off. On the left, or eastern side, they saw a broad channel leading up through the weeds. Bevis told Mark to tack up there. Mark did so, and they slowly advanced with the weeds each side. The tacks were short, and as the wind was so light they made little progress. Presently the channel turned south; then they ran faster; next it turned sharp to the east, and came back. In trying to tack here Mark ran into the weeds.

"Stupe!" said Bevis.

"That I'm not," said Mark. "You can't do it."

"Can't I?" said Bevis contemptuously.

"Try then," said Mark, and he left the tiller. Bevis took it and managed two tacks very well. At the third he too ran into the weeds, for in fact the channel was so narrow there was no time to get weigh on the ship.

"Stupe yourself," said Mark.

He tried to row out, but every time he got a pull the wind blew them back, and they had to let the mainsail down.

"It wants a canoe," said Bevis.

"Of course it does. It's no use going on unless you're going to row."

"No; but look!" Bevis pointed to a small branch which was floating very slowly past them.

"There's a current," said Mark.

"River," said Bevis. "In the sedges somewhere."

"What is it? I know; it's the Orinoco."

"No, I don't think so."

"Amazon?"

"No."

"Hoang-Ho?"

"How can we tell, till we get the astrolabe and take an observation? Most likely it's a new river, the biggest ever found."

"It must be a new river," said Mark. "This is the New Sea. We're drifting back a little."

"We'll come again in a canoe, or something," said Bevis.

They rowed out of the channel, set the mainsail, and sailed back, past Pearl Island, Grey Crow Island, the Coral Isles, and approached New Formosa. Mark looked over the side, and watched to see the sunken punt.

"It's a wreck," said he presently, as they passed above the punt. "She foundered."

"It's a Spanish galley," said Bevis. "She's full of bullion, gold and silver—"

"Millions of broad gold pieces."

"Doubloons."

"Pistoles."

"Ingots."

"You can see the skeletons chained at the oar-benches."

"Yes—just as they went down."

"There are strange sounds here at night."

"Bubbles come up, and shouts, and awful shrieks."

"Hope we shan't hear them when we're in our hut."

"No; it's too far."

They sailed between New Formosa and Serendib, and homewards through Mozambique to the harbour. The east wind, like the west, was a there-and-back wind, and they could reach their island, or return from it, in two or three tacks, sometimes in one stretch.

Chapter Twelve
Provisioning the Cave

Next day they took an iron bar with them, and pitched the stakes for the fence or stockade. Between the stakes they wove in willow rods and brushwood, so that thus bound together, it was much stronger than it looked, and no one could have got in without at least making a great noise. The two boards, nailed together for the gate, were fastened on one side to a stouter stake with small chains like rude hinges. On the other there was a staple and small padlock.

"It's finished," said Mark, as he turned the key and locked them in.

"No," said Bevis, "there's the bedstead. The ground's dry," (it was sand), "but it's not proper to sleep on the ground."

They put off preparing the bedstead till next day, when they approached on a spanking south east wind—half a breeze—against which they had to tack indeed, but spun along at a good speed. The waves were not large enough to make the Pinta roll, but some spray came over now and then.

"It's almost shipwreck weather," said Mark. "Just see—" He pointed at the cliff where there was a little splashing, as the waves swept sideways along the base of the cliff. "If you run her against the cliff the bowsprit will be knocked in. Would the mast go by the board?"

"Not enough wind," said Bevis, as he steered past, and they landed at the usual place. The bedstead was made by placing five or six thick poles sawn off at four feet on the floor on the left side of the hut, like the sleepers of a railway. Across these lengthways they laid lesser rods, then still more slender rods crossways, and on these again boughs of spruce fir, one on the other to a foot or more in depth. The framework of logs and rods beneath kept the bed above the ground, and the boughs of the spruce fir, being full of resinous sap, gave out a slight fragrance. On this mattress a rug and some old great-coats were to be thrown, and they meant to cover themselves with more rugs and coats. The bedstead took up much of the room, but then it would answer in the daytime instead of chairs to sit on.

"It's finished now, then," said Mark.

"Quite finished," said Bevis. "All we have now to do is to bring our things."

"And get wrecked," said Mark. "These chips and boughs," pointing to the heap they had cut from the poles and stakes, "will do for our fire. Come on. Let's go up and look at the cliff where we are to be dashed to pieces."

They climbed up the cliff to the young oak on the summit, and went to the edge. The firm sand bore them safely at the verge.

"It looks very deep," said Bevis. "The sand goes down straight."

"Fathomless," said Mark. "Just think how awful. It ought to happen at night—pitch black! I know! Some savages ought to light a fire up here and guide us to destruction."

"We could not scramble up this cliff out of the water—I mean if we have to swim."

"Of course we shall have to swim, clinging to oars."

"Then we must get round that corner, somehow."

"The other side is all weeds; that wouldn't do."

"Very likely the waves would bang us against the cliff. Don't you remember how Ulysses clung to the rock?"

"His hands were torn."

"Nearly drowned."

"Tired out."

"Thumped and breathless."

"Jolly!"

"But I say! There's one thing we've forgotten," said Bevis. "If we smash our ship against a cliff like this she'll go to the bottom—"

"Well, that's just what we want."

"Ah, but it's not like rocks or shoals; she'll go straight down, right under where we can't get at her—"

"All the better."

"But then our things will go down too—gun, and powder, and provisions, and everything."

"Put them on the island first and wreck ourselves afterwards."

"So we could. Yes, we could do that, but then," said Bevis, imagining what would happen, "when the Pinta was missed from the harbour and did not come back, there would be a search, and they would think something had happened to us."

"I see," said Mark, "that's very awkward. What a trouble it is to get wrecked! Why can't people let us be jolly?"

"They must not come looking after us," said Bevis, "else it will spoil everything."

"Perhaps we had better put the wreck off," said Mark, in a dejected tone. "Do the island first, and have the wreck afterwards."

"It seems as if we must," said Bevis, "and then it's almost as awkward—"

"Why?"

"We shall have to come here in the Pinta, and yet we must not keep her here, else she will be missed."

"The ship must be here and at home too."

"Yes," said Bevis; "she must be at New Formosa on the equator and at home in the harbour. It's a very difficult thing."

"Awfully difficult," said Mark. "But you can do it. Try! Think! Shall I tickle you?"

"It wants magic," said Bevis. "I ought to have studied magic more; only there are no magic books now."

"But you can think, I know. Now, think hard—*hard*."

"First," said Bevis slowly, tracing out the proceedings in his imagination; "first we must bring all our things—the gun and powder, and provisions, and great-coats, and the astrolabe, and spears, and leave them all here."

"Pan ought to come," said Mark, "to watch the hut."

"So he did; he shall come, and besides, if we shoot a wild duck he can swim out and fetch it."

"Now go on," said Mark. "First, we bring everything and Pan."

"Tie him up," said Bevis, "and row home in the boat. Then the thing is, how are we to get to the island?"

"Swim," said Mark.

"Too far."

"But we needn't swim all up the New Sea. Couldn't we swim from where we landed that night after the battle?"

"Ever so much better. Let's go and look," said Bevis.

Away they went to the shore on that side of the island, but they saw in a moment that it was too far. It was two hundred yards to the sedges on the bank where they had landed that night. They could not trust themselves to swim more than fifty or sixty yards; there was, too, the risk of weeds, in which they might get entangled.

"I know!" said Bevis, "I know! You stop on the island with Pan. I'll sail the Pinta into harbour, then I'll paddle back on the catamaran."

"There!" said Mark, "I knew you could do it if you thought hard. We could bring the catamaran up in the boat, and leave it in the sedges there ready."

"I can leave half my clothes on the island," said Bevis, "and tie the rest on my back, and paddle here from the sedges in ten minutes. That will be just like the savages do."

"I shall come too," said Mark. "I shan't stop here. Let Pan be tied up, and I'll paddle as well."

"The catamaran won't bear two."

"Get another. There's lots of planks. I will come—it's much jollier paddling than sitting here and doing nothing."

"Capital," said Bevis. "We'll have two catamarans, and paddle here together."

"First-rate. Let's be quick and get the things on the island."

"There will be such a lot," said Bevis. "The matchlock, and the powder, and the flour, and—"

"Salt," said Mark. "Don't you remember the moorhen. Things are not nice without salt."

"Yes, salt and matches, and pots for cooking, and a lantern, and—"

"Ever so many cargoes," said Mark. "As there's such a lot, and as we can't go home and fetch anything if it's forgotten, hadn't you better write a list?"

"So I will," said Bevis. "The pots and kettles will be a bother, they will want to know what we are going to do."

"Buy some new ones."

"Right; and leave them at Macaroni's."

"Come on. Sail home and begin."

They launched the Pinta, and the spanking south-easterly breeze carried them swiftly into harbour. At home there was a small parcel, very neatly done up, addressed to "Captain Bevis."

"That's Frances's handwriting," said Mark. Bevis cut the string and found a flag inside made from a broad red ribbon cut to a point.

"It's a pennant," said Bevis. "It will do capitally. How was it we never thought of a flag before?"

"We were so busy," said Mark. "Girls have nothing to do, and so they can remember these sort of stitched things."

"She shall have a bird of paradise for her hat," said Bevis. "We shall be sure to shoot one on the island."

"I shouldn't give it to her," said Mark. "I should sell it. Look at the money."

In the evening they took a large box (which locked) up to the boat, carrying it through the courtyard with the lid open—ostentatiously open—and left it on board. Next morning they filled it with their tools. Bevis kept his list and pencil by him, and as they put in one thing it suggested another, which he immediately wrote down. There were files, gimlets, hammers, screw-drivers, planes, chisels, the portable vice, six or seven different sorts of nails, every tool indeed they had. The hatchet and saw were already on the island. Besides these there were coils of wire and cord, balls of string, and several boxes of safety and lucifer matches. This was enough for one cargo, they shut the lid, and began to loosen the sails ready for hoisting.

"You might take us once."

"You never asked us."

Tall Val and little Charlie had come along the bank unnoticed while they were so busy.

"I wish you would go away," said Mark, beginning to push the Pinta afloat. The ballast and cargo made her drag on the sand.

"Bevis," said Val, "let us have one sail."

"All the times you've been sailing," said Charlie, "and all by yourselves, and never asked anybody."

"And after we banged you in the battle," said Val. "If you did beat us, we hit you as hard as we could."

"It was a capital battle," said Bevis hesitatingly. He had the halyard in his hand, and paused with the mainsail half hoisted.

"Whopping and snopping," said Charlie.

"Charging and whooping and holloaing," said Val.

"Rare," said Bevis. "Yes; you fought very well."

"But you never asked us to have a sail."

"Not once—you didn't."

"Well, it's not your ship. It's our ship," said Mark, giving another push, till the Pinta was nearly afloat.

"Stop," cried Charlie, running down to the water's edge. "Bevis, do take us—"

"It's very selfish of you," said Val, following.

"So it is," said Bevis. "I say, Mark—"

"Pooh!" said Mark, and with a violent shove he launched the boat, and leaped on board. He took a scull, and began to row her head round. The wind was north and light.

"I bate you," said Charlie. "I believe you're doing something. What's in that box."

"Ballast, you donk," said Mark.

"That it isn't, I saw it just before you shut the lid. It's not ballast."

"Let's let them come," said Bevis irresolutely.

"You awful stupe," said Mark, under his breath. "They'll spoil everything."

"And why do you always sail one way?" said Val. "We've seen you ever so many times."

"I won't be watched," said Bevis angrily: he, unconsciously, endeavoured to excuse his selfishness under rage.

"You can't help it."

"I tell you, I won't."

"You're not General Caesar now."

"I hate you," pulling up the mainsail. Mark took the rope and fastened it; Bevis sat down to the tiller.

"You're a beast," screamed little Charlie, as the sails drew and the boat began to move: the north wind was just aft.

"I never thought you were so selfish," shouted Val. "Go on—I won't ask you again."

"Take that," said Charlie, "and that—and that."

He threw three stones, one after the other, with all his might: the third, rising from the surface of the water, struck the Pinta's side sharply.

"Aren't they just horrid?" he said to Val.

"I never saw anything like it," said Val. "But we'll pay them out, somehow."

On the boat, Bevis looked back presently, and saw them still standing at the water's edge.

"It's a pity," he said; "Mark, I don't like it: shall we have them?"

"How can we? Of course they would spoil everything; they would tell everybody, and we could never do it; and, besides, the new island would not be a new island, if everybody was there."

"No more it would."

"We can take them afterwards—after we've done the island. That will be just as well."

"So it will. They will watch us, though."

"It's very nasty of them to watch us," said Mark. "Why should we take them for sails when they watch us?"

"I hate being watched," said Bevis.

"They will just make everything as nasty for us as they can," said Mark; "and we shall have to be as cunning as ever we can be."

"We will do it, though, somehow."

"That we will."

The light north wind wafted the Pinta gently up the New Sea: the red pennant, fluttering at the mast, pointed out the course before them. They disposed of their first cargo in the store-room, or cave, placing the tools in a sack, though the cave was as dry as the box, that there might not be the least chance of their rusting. The return voyage was slow, for they had to work against the wind, and it was too light for speed. They looked for Charlie and Val, but both were gone.

Another cargo was ready late in the afternoon. They carried the things up in the flag-basket, and, before filling the box, took care to look round and behind the shed where the sculls were kept, lest any one should be spying. Hitherto they had worked freely, and without any doubt or suspicion: now they were constantly on the watch, and suspected every tree of concealing some one. Bevis chafed under this, and grew angry about it. In filling the box, too, they kept the lid towards the shore, and hoisted the mainsail to form a screen.

Mark took care that there should be some salt, and several bags of flour, and two of biscuits, which they got from a whole tinful in the house. He remembered some pepper too, but overlooked the mustard. They took several tins of condensed milk. From a side of bacon, up in the attic, they cut three streaky pieces, and bought some sherry at the inn; for they thought if they took one of the bottles in the house, it would be missed, and that the servants would be blamed. Some wine would be good to mix with the water; for though they meant to take a wooden bottle of ale, they knew it would not keep.

Then there was a pound of tea, perhaps more; for they took it from the chest, and shovelled it up like sand, both hands full at once. A bundle of old newspapers was tied up, to light the fire; for they had found, by experience, that it was not easy to do so with only dry grass. Bevis hunted about till he discovered the tin mug he had when he was a little boy, and two tin plates. Mark brought another mug. A few knives and forks would never be missed from the basketful in the kitchen; and, in choosing some spoons, they were careful not to take silver, because the silver was counted every evening.

They asked if they could have a small zinc bucket for the boat; and when they got it, put three pounds or more of knob sugar in it, loose; and covered it over with their Turkish bathing-towels, in which they had wrapped up a brush and comb. Just as they were about to start, they remembered soap and candles. To get these things together, and up to the Pinta, took them some hours, for they often had to wait awhile till people were out of the way before they could get at the cupboards. In the afternoon, as they knew, some of the people went upstairs to dress, and that was their opportunity. By the time they had landed, and stowed away this cargo, the sun was declining.

Chapter Thirteen
More Cargoes—All Ready

Next morning the third cargo went; they had to row, for the New Sea was calm. It consisted of arms. Bevis's favourite bow, of course, was taken, and two sheaves of arrows; Mark's spears and harpoon; the crossbow, throw-sticks, the boomerang and darts; so that the armoury was almost denuded.

Besides these there were fish-hooks (which were put in the box), fishing-rods, and kettles; an old horn-lantern, the old telescope, the astrolabe, scissors and thread (which shipwrecked people always have); a bag full of old coins, which were to be found in the sand on the shore, where a Spanish galleon had been wrecked (one of those the sunken galley had been convoying when the tornado overtook them); a small looking-glass, a piece of iron rod, six bottles of lemonade, a cribbage-board and pack of cards, and a bezique pack; a basket of apples, and a bag of potatoes. The afternoon cargo was clothes, for they thought they might want a change if it was wet; so they each took one suit, carefully selecting old things that had been disused, and would not be missed.

Then there were the great-coats for the bed; these were very awkward to get up to the boat, and caused many journeys, for they could only take one coat each at a time.

"What a lot of rubbish you are taking to your boat," said mamma once. "Mind you don't sink it: you will fill your boat with rubbish till you can't move about."

"Rubbish!" said Bevis indignantly. "Rubbish, indeed!"

They so often took the rugs that there was no need to conceal them. Mark hit on a good idea and rolled up the barrel of the matchlock in one of the rugs, and with it the ramrod. In the other they hid the stock and powder-horn, and so got them to the boat; chuckling over Mark's device, by which they removed the matchlock in broad daylight.

"If Val's watching," said Bevis, as they came up the bank with the rugs, the last part of the load, "he'll have to be smashed."

"People who spy about ought to be killed," said Mark. "Everything ought to be done openly," carefully depositing the concealed barrel in the stern-sheets. This was the most important thing of all. When they had got the matchlock safe in the cave, they felt that the greatest difficulty was surmounted.

John Young had brought their anvil, the 28 pound weight, for them to the bank, and it was shipped. He bought a small pot for boiling, the smallest size made, for them in Latten, also a saucepan, a tin kettle, and teapot. One of the wooden bottles, like tiny barrels, used to send ale out to the men in the fields, was filled with strong ale. Mark drew it in the cellar which had once been his prison, carefully filling it to the utmost, and this John got away for them rolled up in his jacket. The all-potent wand of the enchanter Barleycorn was held over him; what was there he would not have done for them?

He was all the more ready to oblige them because since Mark's imprisonment in the cellar, Bevis and Mark had rather taken his part against the Bailiff, and got him out of scrapes. Feeling that he had powerful friends at court, John did not trouble to work so hard. They called at the cottage for the pot and the other things, which were in a sack ready for them. Loo fetched the sack, and Bevis threw it over his shoulder.

"I scoured them well," said Loo. "They be all clean."

"Did you?" said Bevis. "Here," searching his pocket. "O! I've only a fourpenny piece left." He gave it to her.

"I can cook," said Loo wistfully, "and make tea." This was a hint to them to take her with them; but away they strode unheeding. The tin kettle and teapot clashed in the sack.

"I believe I saw Val behind that tree," said Bevis.

"He can't see through a sack though," said Mark.

The wind was still very light, and all the morning was occupied in delivering this cargo. The cave or store-room was now crammed full, and they could not put any more without shelves.

"That's the last," said Mark, dragging the heavy anvil in. "Except Pan."

"And my books," said Bevis, "and ink and paper. We must keep a journal of course."

"So we must," said Mark. "I forgot that. It will make a book."

"'Adventures in New Formosa,'" said Bevis.

"We'll write it every evening after we've done work, don't you see."

When they got home he put his books together—the Odyssey, Don Quixote, the grey and battered volume of ballads, a tiny little book of Shakespeare's poems, of which he had lately become very fond, and Filmore's rhymed translation of Faust. He found two manuscript books for the journal; these and the pens and ink-bottle could all go together in the final cargo with Pan.

All the while these voyages were proceeding they had been thinking over how they should get away from home without being searched for, and had concluded that almost the only excuse they could make would be that they were going to spend a week or two with Jack. This they now began to spread about, and pretended to prepare for the visit. As they expected, it caused no comment. All that was said was that they were not to stop too long. Mamma, did not much like the idea of being left by herself, but then it was quite different to their being away in disgrace.

But she insisted upon Bevis writing home. Bevis shrugged his shoulders, foreseeing that it would be difficult to do this as there was no post-office on New Formosa; but it was of no use, she said he should not go unless he promised to write.

"Very well," said Bevis. "Letters are the stupidest stupidity stupes ever invented."

But now there arose a new difficulty, which seemed as if it could not be got over. How were they to tell while they were away on the island, and cut off from all communication with the mainland, what was going on at home; whether it was all right and they were supposed to be at Jack's, or whether they were missed? For though so intent on deceiving the home authorities, and so ingenious in devising the means, they stopped at this.

They did not like to think that perhaps Bevis's governor and mamma, who were so kind, would be miserable with anxiety on finding that they had disappeared. Mark, too, was anxious about his Jolly Old Moke. With the usual contradiction of the mind they earnestly set about to deceive their friends, and were equally anxious not to give them any pain. After all their trouble, it really seemed as if this would prevent the realisation of their plans. A whole day they walked about and wondered what they could do, and got quite angry with each other from simple irritation.

At last they settled that they must arrange with some one so as to know, for if there was any trouble about them they meant to return immediately. Both agreed that little Charlie was the best they could choose; he was as quick as lightning, and as true as steel.

"Just remember," said Bevis, "how he fetched up Cecil in the battle."

"That just made all the difference," said Mark. "Now I'll manage it with him; don't you come, you leave him to me; you're so soft—"

"Soft!—Well, I like that."

"No; I don't mean stupid—so easy. There, don't look like that. You tell me—you think what Charlie must do—and I'll manage him."

Bevis thought and considered that Charlie must give them a signal— wave a handkerchief. Charlie must stand on some conspicuous place visible from New Formosa; by the quarry would be the very place, at a certain fixed time every day, and wave a white handkerchief, and they could look through the telescope and see him. If anything was wrong, he could take his hat off and wave that instead. Mark thought it would do very well, and set out to find and arrange with Charlie.

Being very much offended because he had not been taken for a sail, Charlie was at first very off-hand, and not at all disposed to do anything. But when shrewd Mark let out as a great secret that he and Bevis were going to live in the wood at the end of the New Sea for a while like savages, Charlie began to relent, for all his sympathies went with the idea.

Mark promised him faithfully that when he and Bevis had done it first, he should come too if he would help them. Charlie gave in and agreed, but on condition that he should be taken for a sail first. Eager as Mark was for the island, it was no good trying to persuade Charlie, he adhered to his stipulation, and Mark had to yield. However, he reflected that if they took Charlie for a sail he would be certain to do as he promised, and besides that it would make Val jealous, and he and Charlie would quarrel, and so they would not be always watching.

So it was settled—Charlie to have a sail, and then every afternoon at four o'clock he was to stand just above the quarry and wave a white handkerchief if all was right. If Bevis and Mark were missed he was to take off his hat, and wave that. As he had no watch, Charlie was to judge the time by the calling of the cows to be milked—the milkers make a great hullabaloo and shouting, which can be heard a long distance off.

"I said we were going to live in the wood," Mark told Bevis when he came back. "Then he won't think we're on the island. If he plays us any trick he'll go and try and find us in the wood."

While Mark was gone about the signal, Bevis, thinking everything over, remembered the letter he had promised to write home. To post the letter one or other of them must go on the mainland, if by day some one would very likely see them and mention it, and then the question would arise why they came near without going home? Bevis went up to the cottage, and told Loo to listen every evening at ten o'clock out of her window, which looked over the field at the back, and if she heard anybody whistle three notes, "Foo-tootle-too," to slip out, as it would be them.

"That I will," said Loo, delighted. "I'll come in a minute."

Charlie had his sail next morning, but they took care not to go near the island. Knowing how sharp his eyes were, they tacked to and fro in Mozambique and Fir-Tree Gulf. Charlie learned to manage the foresail in five minutes, then the tiller, and to please him the more they let him act as captain for a while. He promised most faithfully to make the signal every day, and they knew he would do it.

In the afternoon they thought and thought to see if there was anything they had forgotten, and to try and call things to mind, wandered all over the house, but only recollected one thing—the gridiron. There were several in the kitchen. They took an old one, much burnt, which was not used. With this and Bevis's books they visited New Formosa, rowing up towards evening, and upon their return unshipped the mast, and took it and the sails home, else perhaps Val or some one would launch the Pinta and try to sail in their absence. They meant to padlock the boat with a chain, but if the sails were in her it would be a temptation to break the lock. There was now nothing to take but Pan, and they were so eager for the morning that it was past midnight before they could go to sleep.

The morning of the 3rd of August—the very day Columbus sailed—the long desired day, was beautifully fine, calm, and cloudless. They were in such haste to start they could hardly say "Good-bye."

"Good-bye," said Polly the dairymaid.

"Don't want to see you," said Bevis. Polly was not yet forgiven for the part she had taken in hustling Mark into the cellar. They had got out into the meadow with Pan, when Bevis's mother came running after.

"Have you any money?" she asked, with her purse in her hand.

They laughed, for the thought instantly struck them that they could not spend money on New Formosa, but they did not say they did not want any. She gave them five shillings each, and kissed them again. She watched them till they went through the gateway with Pan, and were hidden from sight.

Pan leaped on board after them, and they rowed to the island. It was so still, the surface was like glass. The spaniel ran about inside the stockade, and sniffed knowingly at the coats on the bedstead, but he did not wag his tail or look so happy when Bevis suddenly drew his collar three holes tighter and buckled it. Bevis knew very well if his collar was not as tight as possible Pan would work his head out. They fastened him securely to the post at the gateway in the palisade, and hastened away.

When Pan realised that they were really gone, and heard the sound of the oars, he went quite frantic. He tugged, he whined, he choked, he rolled over, he scratched, and bit, and shook, and whimpered; the tears ran down his eyes, his ears were pulled over his head by the collar, against which he strained. But he strained in vain. They heard his dismal howls almost down to the Mozambique.

"Poor Pan!" said Bevis. "He shall have a feast the first thing we shoot."

They had left their stockings on the island, and everything else they could take off so as not to have very large bundles on their backs while paddling, and took their pocket-knives out of their trouser's pockets and left them, knowing things are apt to drop out of the pockets. The Pinta was drawn up as far as she would come on the shore at the harbour, and then fastened with a chain, which they had ready, to a staple and padlocked. Mark had thought of this, so that no one could go rowing round, and he had a piece of string on the key with which he fastened it to a button-hole of his waistcoat that it might not be lost.

This done, they got through the hedge, and retraced the way they had come home on the night of the battle, through the meadows, the cornfields, and lastly across the wild waste pasture or common. From there they scrambled through the hedges and the immense bramble thickets, and regained the shore opposite their island.

They went down the marshy level to the bank, and along it to the beds of sedges, where, on the verge of the sea, they had hidden the catamarans. There they undressed, and made their clothes and boots into bundles, and slung them over their shoulders with cord. Then they hauled their catamarans down to the water.

Chapter Fourteen
New Formosa

Splash!

"Is it deep?"

"Not yet."

Bevis had got his catamaran in and ran out with it some way, as the water was shallow, till it deepened, when he sat astride and paddled. "Come on," he shouted. Splash! "I'm coming."

Mark ran in with his in the same manner, and sitting astride paddled about ten yards behind.

"Weeds," said Bevis, feeling the long rough stalks like string dragging against his feet. "Where? I can't see."

"Under water. They will not hurt."

"There goes a flapper," (a young wild duck). "I hope we shan't see the magic wave."

"Pooh!"

"My bundle is slipping."

"Pull it up again."

"It's all right now."

"Holloa! Land," said Bevis, suddenly standing up.

He had reached a shallow where the water was no deeper than his knees.

"A jack struck. There," said Mark, as he too stood up, and drew his catamaran along with his hand.

Splash!

Bevis was off again, paddling in deeper water. Mark was now close behind.

"There's a coot; he's gone into the sedges."

"Parrots," said Mark, as two wood-pigeons passed over.

"Which is the right channel?" said Bevis, pausing.

They had now reached the great mass of weeds which came to the surface, and through which it was impossible to move. There were two channels, one appeared to lead straight to the island, the other wound about to the right.

"Which did we come down in the Pinta, when we hid the catamarans?" said Mark.

"Stupe, that's just what I want to know."

"Go straight on," said Mark; "that looks clearest."

So it did, and Bevis went straight on; but when they had paddled fifty yards they both saw at once that they could not go much farther that way, for the channel curved sharply, and was blocked with weeds.

"We must go back," said Mark.

"We can't turn round."

"We can't paddle backwards. There I'm in the weeds."

"Turn round on the plank."

"Perhaps I shall fall off."

"Sit sideways first."

"The plank tips."

"Very well, I'll do it first," said Bevis.

He turned sideways to try and get astride, looking the other way. The plank immediately tipped and pitched him into the water, bundle and all.

"Ah!" said Mark. "Thought you could do it so easy; didn't you?"

Bevis threw his right arm over the plank, and tried to get on it; but every time he attempted to lift his knee over, the catamaran gave way under him. His paddle floated away. The bundle of clothes on his back, soaked and heavy, kept him down.

Mark paddled towards him, and tried to lift him with one hand, but nearly upset himself. Bevis struggled hard to get on, and so pushed the plank sideways to the edge of the weeds. He felt the rough strings again winding round his feet.

"You'll be in the weeds," said Mark, growing alarmed. "Come on my plank. Try. I'll throw my bundle off." He began to take it from his back. "Then it will just keep you up. O!"

Bevis put his hands up, and immediately sank under the surface, but he had done it purposely, to free himself from his bundle. The bundle floated, and the cord slipped over his head. Bringing his hands down Bevis as instantly rose to the surface, bumping his head against the catamaran.

"Now I can do it," he said, blowing the water from his nostrils.

He seized the plank, and laid almost all along in the water, so as to press very lightly on it, his weight being supported by the water, then he got his knee over and sat up.

"Hurrah!"

The bundle was slowly settling down when Mark seized it.

"Never mind about the things being wet," he said. "Sit still; I'll fetch your paddle."

Dragging the bundle in the water by the cord, Mark went after, and recovered Bevis's paddle. To come back he had to back water, and found it very awkward even for so short a distance. The catamaran would not go straight.

"O! what a stupe I was," said Bevis. "I've got on the same way again."

In his hurry he had forgotten his object, and got astride facing the island as before.

"Well, I never," said Mark. "Stop—don't."

Bevis slipped off his catamaran again, but this time not being encumbered with the bundle he was up on it again in half a minute, and faced the mainland.

"There," said he. "Now you can come close. That's it. Now give me your bundle."

Mark did so. Afterwards Bevis took the cord of his own bundle, which being in the water was not at all heavy. "Now you can turn."

Mark slipped off, but managed so that his chest was still on the plank. In that position he worked himself round and got astride the other way.

"Done very well," said Bevis; "ever so much better than I did. Here."

Mark slung his bundle, and they paddled back to the shallow water, Bevis towing his soaked dress. They stood up in the shallow and rested a few minutes, and Bevis fastened his bundle to his plank just in front of where he sat.

"Come on." Off he went again, following the other channel this time. It wound round a bank grown with sedges, and then led straight into a broader and open channel, the same they had come down in the boat. They recognised it directly, and paddled faster.

"Hark! there's Pan," said Mark.

As they came near the island, Pan either scented them or heard a splashing, for he set up his bark again. He had choked himself silent before.

"Pan! Pan!" shouted Bevis, whistling.

Yow—wow—wow!

"Hurrah!"

"Hurrah!"

They ran up on the shore of New Formosa, and began to dance and caper, kicking up their heels.

Yow-wow—wow-wow!

"Pan! I'm coming," said Bevis, and began to run, but stopped suddenly.

Thistles in the grass and trailing briars stayed him. He put on his wet boots, and then picking his way round, reached the hut. He let Pan loose. The spaniel crouched at his feet and whimpered, and followed him, crawling on the ground. Bevis patted him, but he could not leap up as usual, the desertion had quite broken his spirit for the time. Bevis went into the hut, and just as he was, with nothing on but his boots, took his journal and wrote down "Wednesday."

"There," said he to Mark, who had now come, more slowly, for he carried the two bundles, "there, I've put down the day, else we shall lose our reckoning, don't you see."

They were soon dressed. Bevis put on the change he had provided in the store-room, and spread his wet clothes out to dry in the sun. Pan crept from one to the other; he could not get enough patting, he wanted to be continually spoken to and stroked. He would not go a yard from them.

"What's the time?" said Bevis, "my watch has stopped." The water had stopped it.

"Five minutes to twelve," said Mark. "You must write down, 'We landed on the island at noon.'"

"So I will to-night. My watch won't go; the water is in it."

"Lucky mine did not got wet too."

"Hang yours up in the hut, else perhaps it will get stopped somehow, then we shan't know the time."

Mark hung his watch up in the hut, and caught sight of the wooden bottle.

"The first thing people do is to refresh themselves," he said. "Let's have a glass of ale: splendid thing when you're shipwrecked—"

"A libation to the gods," said Bevis. "That's the thing; you pour it out on the ground because you've escaped."

"O!" said Mark, opening the bottle. "Now just look! And I filled it to the brim so that I could hardly get the cork in."

"John," said Bevis.

"The rascal."

"Ships' provisions are always scamped," said Bevis; "somebody steals half, and puts in rotten biscuits. It's quite proper. Why, there's a quart gone."

John Young, carrying the heavy bottle, could not resist just taking out the cork to see how full it was. And his mouth was very large.

"Here's a mug," said Mark, who had turned over a heap of things and found a tin cup. They each had a cupful.

"Matchlock," said Bevis.

"Matchlock," said Mark. For while they drank both had had their eyes on their gun-barrel.

"Pliers," said Bevis, taking it up. "Here's the wire; I want the pliers."

It was not so easy to find the pliers under such a heap of things.

"Store-room's in a muddle," said Mark.

"Put it right," said the captain.

"I've got it."

Bevis put the barrel in the stock, and began twisting the copper wire round to fasten it on. Mark searched for the powder-horn and shot-bag. Three strands were twisted neatly and firmly round the barrel and stock— one near the breech, one half-way up, the third near the muzzle. It was then secure.

"It looks like a real gun now," said Mark.

"Put your finger on the touch-hole," said Bevis. Mark did so, while he blew through the barrel.

"I can feel the air," said Mark; "the barrel is clear. Shall I measure the powder?"

"Yes."

Bevis shut the pan, Mark poured out the charge from the horn and inserted a wad of paper, which Bevis rammed home with the brass ramrod.

Bow-wow—bow-yow!

Up jumped Pan, leaped on them, tore round the hut, stood at the doorway and barked, ran a little way out, and came back again to the door, where, with his head over his shoulder, as if beckoning to them to follow, he barked his loudest.

"It's the gun," said Mark. Pan forgot his trouble at the sound of the ramrod.

Next the shot was put in, and then the priming at the pan. A piece of match or cord prepared to burn slowly, about a foot and a half long, was wound round the handle of the stock, and the end brought forward through the spiral of the hammer. Mark struck a match and lit it.

"What shall we shoot at?" said Bevis, as they went out at the door. Pan rushed before and disappeared in the bramble bushes, startling a pair of turtle-doves from a hawthorn.

"Parrakeets," said Mark. "They're smaller than parrots; you can't shoot flying with a matchlock. There's a beech; shoot at that."

The sunshine fell on one side of the trunk of a beech, lighting up the smooth bark. They walked up till they thought they were near enough, and planted the staff or rest in the ground. Bevis put the matchlock on it, pushed the lid of the pan open with his thumb, and aimed at the tree. He pulled the trigger; the match descended on the powder in the pan, which went puff! The report followed directly.

"Never kicked a bit," said Bevis, as the sulphury smoke rose; the barrel was too heavy to kick.

"Hit!" shouted Mark, who had run to the tree. "Forty dozen shots everywhere."

Bevis came with the gun, and saw the bark dotted all over with shot. He measured the distance back to the rest left standing in the ground, by pacing steadily.

"Thirty-two yards."

"My turn," said Mark.

The explosion had extinguished the match, so shutting the pan-lid they loaded the gun again. Before Mark shot, Bevis went to the tree, and fastened a small piece of paper to the bark with a pin. Mark fired and put three shots through the paper. Pan raced and circled round to find the game, and returned with his back covered with cleavers which stuck to his coat. After shooting three times each they thought they would try bullets, but with ball they could do nothing. Four times they each fired at the beech and missed it, though every time they took a more careful aim.

"The staff's too high," said Mark, "I'm sure that's it. We ought to kneel, then it would be steadier."

Bevis cut the staff shorter, not without some difficulty, for the old black oak was hard like iron. The next was Mark's turn. He knelt on one knee, aimed deliberately, and the ball scored the trunk, making a groove along the bark. Bevis tried but missed, so did Mark next time; then again Bevis fired, and missed.

"That's enough," said Bevis; "I shan't have any more shooting with bullets."

"But I hit it once."

"But you didn't hit it twice."

"You never hit it once."

"It wants a top-sight," said Bevis, not very well pleased. "Nobody can shoot ball without a sight."

"You can't put one," said Mark.

"I don't know." The sight was the only defect of the weapon; how to fasten that on they did not know.

"I hit it without a sight," said Mark.

"Chance."

"That it wasn't."

"It's time to have dinner, I'm sure," said Bevis. "The gun is to be put away now. I'll take it in; you get some sticks for the fire."

"O! very well," said Mark shortly. "But there's plenty of sticks inside the stockade!"

He followed Bevis and began to make a pile in their enclosed courtyard. Bevis having left the gun in the hut came out and helped him silently.

"It's very hot here."

"Awful!"

"Tropics."

"The sun's overhead."

"Sun-stroke."

"The fire ought to be made in the shadow."

"There's no shadow here."

"Let us go into the wood then."

"Very well—under the beech."

They went out, and collected a heap of sticks in the shade of the beech at which they had been shooting. Mark lit the fire; Bevis sat down by the beech and watched the flame rise.

"Pot," he said.

"Pot—what?" said Mark, still sulky.

"Fetch the water."

"What?"

"Fetch the water."

"O! I'm not Polly."

"But I'm captain."

"Hum!"

However, Mark fetched the pot, filled it at the shore, and presently came back with it, and put it on. Then he sat down too in the shade.

"You've not finished," said Bevis.

"What else?"

"What else; why the bacon."

"Get it yourself."

"Aren't you going?"

"No."

Bevis went to the hut, cut off a slice of bacon, and put it on.

Mark went to the hut, fetched a handful of biscuits and two apples, and began to eat them.

"You never brought me any," said Bevis.

"You never ordered me, captain."

"Why can't you be agreeable?"

"Why can't you ask anybody, and do something yourself, too."

"Don't be a stupe," said Bevis, "so I will. But get me a biscuit, now do." At this Mark fetched the bag for him.

"We shall have to wait a long time for our dinner," he said. "They're just having a jolly one at home."

"While they're at home and comfortable we're on an island seven thousand miles from anywhere."

"Savages all round."

"Magic things."

"If they only knew, wouldn't they be in a state."

"Ships fitted out to find us. But they would not know which way to sail."

"No charts."

"Nothing."

"Never find us. I say, get a fork and try the bacon."

"Don't look done."

"Put some more sticks on. I say; we forgot the potatoes."

"O! bother. It's hot; don't let's have any. Let's sit still."

"Right."

Pan looked from one to the other, ran round and came back, went into the underwood and came out again, but finding that it was of no use, and that the gun was really put aside, he presently settled down like them in the shade, and far enough from the fire not to feel any heat from it.

"Oaks are banyans, aren't they?" said Mark. "They used to be, you know," remembering the exploration of the wood.

"Banyans," said Bevis.

"What are beeches?"

"O! teak."

"That's China; aren't we far from China?"

"Ask me presently when I've got the astrolabe."

"What are elms? Stop, now I remember; there are no elms!"

"How do you know?"

"Didn't I go round the island one day? Besides, you could see them if there were, from the cliff."

"So we could; there are no elms. That shows how different this country is from any other country ever found."

"Poplars?" said Mark in an interrogative tone.

"Palms, of course. You can see them miles away like palms in a desert."

"Pictures," said Mark. "Yes, that's it. You always see the sun going down, camels with long shadows, and palm-trees. Then I suppose it's Africa?"

"You must wait till we have taken an observation. We shall see too by the stars."

"Firs?" said Mark. "They're cedars, of course."

"Of course. Willows are blue gums."

"Then it's near Australia. I expect it is; because, don't you know, there were no animals in Australia except kangaroos, and there are none here at all. So it's that sort of country."

"But there are tigers in the reeds."

"Ah, I forgot them."

"Huge boa-constrictors. One of them would reach from here to Serendib. Did you hear that rustling? Most likely that was one."

"Do elephants swim? They might come off here."

"Hippopotami."

"A black rhinoceros; they're rogues."

"Hyenas."

"Giraffes. They can nibble half-way up the palm-trees."

"Pumas."

"Panthers."

"'Possums."

"Yaks."

"Grizzlies."

"Scorpions."

"Heaps of things on your bed and crawling on the ceiling."

"Jolly!"

"Fork up the bacon."

Mark forked it up.

"It looks queer," he said, dropping it in again. "Ought the pot to be on the ashes?"

"There's an iron rod for the kettle to swing on," said Bevis. "It's somewhere in the store-room. Is it eight bells yet?"

"I expect so," said Mark. "Rations are late. A mutton chop now, or a fowl—"

"Don't grow here," said Bevis. "You cut steaks from buffaloes while they're alive, or fry elephants, or boil turkeys. There are no fowls."

"It seems to me," said Mark, "that we ought to have the gun here. Suppose some savages were to land from canoes and get between us and the hut? It's twenty yards to the stockade; more I should think."

"I never thought of that," said Bevis. "There may be fifty canoes full of them in the reeds, and proas flying here almost. Fetch the gun—quick."

Mark ran and brought it.

"Load with ball," said Bevis.

The ball was rammed home. Pan set up a joyous bark.

"Kick him," said Bevis, languidly raising himself on one arm. He had been lying on his back. "He'll bring the savages, or the crocodiles."

Pan was kicked, and crouched.

Mark leaned the gun against the teak-tree, and sat down again.

"Awfully hot," he said.

"Always is in the tropics."

"Ought to have an awning," said Mark; "and hammocks."

"So we did," said Bevis, sitting up. "How stupid to forget the hammocks. Did you ever see anything like it?"

"We can make an awning," said Mark. "Hang up one of the rugs by the four corners."

"Capital. Come on."

They fastened four pieces of cord to the corners of the rug, but found that the trees did not grow close enough together, so they had to set up two poles near the teak, and tie the cords at one end of the rug to these. The others were tied to a branch of the teak. By the time this was done they had worked themselves hot again putting up the awning to get cool. There was not a breath of wind, and it was very warm even in the double shadow of the teak and the awning.

"Bacon must be done," said Bevis.

"Must," said Mark.

They could not rest more than a quarter of an hour. They forked it out, and Mark held it on the fork, while Bevis ran to the hut for a piece of board to put it on, as they had forgotten dishes. Setting the bacon on the board, they put it on the ground under the awning (Pan wanted to sniff at it), and tried a slice. It was not exactly nice, nor disagreeable, considering that they had forgotten to scrape it, or take the rind off. But biscuits were not so good as bread.

"We must make some dampers," said Mark; "you know, flour cakes: we can't bake, we haven't got an oven."

"Dampers are proper," said Bevis. "That's gold-mining. Very likely there are heaps of nuggets here somewhere—"

"Placers."

"And gold-dust in the river."

"No mustard. And I recollected the salt!" said Mark. "I say; is this bacon quite nice?"

"Well, no; not quite."

"I don't like it."

"No, I don't."

"Wish we could have brought some meat."

"Can't keep meat under the tropics."

"Shall we chuck it to Pan?"

"No, not all. Here, give him a slice. Pooh! He sniff's at it. Just see! He's pampered; he won't eat it. Here, take the board, Mark, and put it in the store-room."

Mark took the board with the bacon on it; and went to the hut. He came back with a mug full of ale, saying they had better drink it before it got quite stale.

"We must shoot something," said Bevis. "We can't eat much of that stuff."

"Let's go round the island," said Mark, "and see if there's anything about. Parrots, perhaps."

"Pigeon-pie," said Bevis.

"Parrot-pie; just the thing."

"Hammer Pan, or he'll run on first and spoil everything."

Chapter Fifteen
New Formosa—First Day

Bevis lit the match, and they went quietly into the wood. Pan had to he hammered now and then to restrain him from rushing into the brambles. They knew the way now very well, having often walked round while building the hut looking for poles, and had trampled out a rough path winding about the thorns. The shooting at the teak-tree and the noise of Pan's barking had alarmed all the parrots; and though they looked out over the water in several places, no wild-fowl were to be seen.

As they came round under the group of cedars to the other side of the island Mark remembered the great jack or pike which he had seen there, almost as big as a shark. They went very softly, and peering round a blue gum bush, saw the jack basking in the sun, but a good way from shore, just at the edge of some weeds. The sunshine illumined the still water, and they could see him perfectly, his long cruel jaws, his greenish back and white belly, and powerful tail.

Drawing back behind the blue gum, Bevis prepared the matchlock, blow the match so that the fire might be ready on it, opened the pan, and pushed the priming up to the touch-hole, from which it had been shaken as he walked, and then advanced the staff or rest to the edge of the bush. He put the heavy barrel on it, and knelt down. The muzzle of the long matchlock protruded through the leafy boughs.

"Ball cartridge," whispered Mark, holding Pan by the collar. "Steady."

"All right."

Bevis aimed up the barrel, the strands of wire rather interfered with his aim, and the glance passed from one of these to the other, rather than along the level of the barrel. The last strand hid the end of the barrel altogether. It wanted a sight. He looked along, and got the gun straight for the fish, aiming at the broadest part of the side; then he remembered that a fish is really lower in the water than it appears, and depressed the muzzle till it pointed beneath the under-line of the jack.

Double-barrel guns with their hammers which fall in the fiftieth of a second, driven by a strong spring directly the finger touches the trigger, translate the will into instant action. The gunner snatches the second when his gun is absolutely straight, and the shot flies to its destination before the barrel can deviate the thirty-second part of an inch. When Bevis's finger first pressed the trigger of the matchlock he had the barrel of his gun accurately pointed. But while he pulled the match down to the pan an appreciable moment of time intervened; and his mind too—so swift is its operation—left the fish, his mark and object, and became expectant of the explosion. The match touched the priming. Puff!

So infinitely rapid is the mind, so far does it outstrip gunpowder, that the flash from the pan and its tiny smoke seemed to Bevis to occur quite a little time before the great discharge, and in that little time his mind left the barrel, and came to look at the tiny puff of smoke.

Bang! the ball rushed forth, but not now in the course it would have taken had a hair-trigger and a spring instantly translated his original will into action. In these momentary divisions of time which had elapsed since he settled his aim, the long barrel, resting on the staff and moving easily on its pivot, had imperceptibly drooped a trifle at the breech and risen as much at the muzzle.

The ball flew high, hit the water six inches beyond the fish, and fired at so low an angle ricochetted, and went skipping along the surface, cutting out pieces of weed till the friction dragged it under, and it sank. The fish swished his tail like a scull at the stern of a boat or the screw of a steamer, but swift as was his spring forward, he would not have escaped had not the ball gone high. He left an undulation on the surface as he dived unhurt.

Bevis stamped his foot to think he had missed again.

"It was the water," said Mark. "The bullet went duck and drake; I saw it."

He was too just to recall the fact of his having hit the teak-tree, the tree was so much larger than the fish. As he did not recall his success at the tree, Bevis's irritation went no farther.

"We must have a top-sight," he said.

"We won't use bullets again till we have a sight."

"No, we won't. But I'm sure I had the gun straight."

"So we had the rifle straight, but it did not hit."

"No, no more did it. There's something peculiar in bullets—we will find out. I wanted that jack for supper."

As they had not brought the powder-horn with them, they walked back to the hut.

"It's not the gun's fault, I'm sure," said Mark. "It shoots beautiful; it's my turn next."

"Yes; you shall shoot. O! no, it's not the gun. They can shoot sparrows in India with a single ball," said Bevis; "and matchlocks kill tigers better than rifles. Matchlocks are splendid things."

"Splendid things," said Mark, stroking the stock of the gun, which he now carried on his shoulder, as if it had been a breathing pet that could appreciate his affection.

"This is a curious groove," said Bevis, looking at the score in the bark of the teak where Mark's bullet had struck it. "Look, it goes a little round; the bullet stuck to the tree and went a little way round, instead of just coming straight, so."

"So it did," said Mark. "It curved round the tree."

"My arrow would have glanced off just the other way," said Bevis, "if it had hit here."

"The ball goes one way and the arrow the other."

"One sticks to the tree as long as it can and the other shoots aside directly."

Bullets have been known in like manner to strike a man's head in the front part and score a track half round it, and even then not do much injury.

"We ought to keep the gun loaded," said Mark, as they reached the hut.

"Yes; but it ought to be slung up, and not put anywhere where it might be knocked over."

"Let's make some slings for it."

After loading the gun this time with a charge of shot, and ramming it home with the brass ramrod—Mark enjoyed using the ramrod too much to hurry over it—they set to work and drove two stout nails into the uprights on the opposite side to the bed. To one of these nails a loop of cord was fastened; to the other a similar piece was tied at one end, the other had a lesser loop, so as to take on or off the nail. When off it hung down, when on it made a loop like the other. The barrel of the gun was put through the first loop, and the stock then held up while the other piece of cord was hitched to its nail, when the long gun hung suspended.

"It looks like a hunter's hut now," said Bevis, contemplating the matchlock. "I'll put my bow in the corner." He leaned his bow in the corner, and put a sheaf of arrows by it.

"My spear will go here," said Mark.

"No," said Bevis. "Put the spear by the bee head."

"Ready for use in the night?"

"Yes; put a knobstick too. That's it. Now look."

"Doesn't it look nice?"

"Just doesn't it!"

"Real hunting."

"Real as real."

"If Val, and Cecil, and Ted could see!"

"And Charlie."

"They would go wild."

"The store-room *is* a muddle."

"Shall we put it straight?"

"And get things ship-shape?"

"Yes."

They began to assort the heaped-up mass of things in the cave, putting tools on one side, provisions on the other, and odd things in the centre. After awhile Mark looked up at his watch.

"Why, it's past five! Tea time at home."

"I don't know," said Bevis. "I expect the time's different—it's longitude."

"We are hours later, then?"

"While it's tea time here, it's breakfast there."

"When we go to bed, they get up. Here's the astrolabe. Take the observation."

"So I will."

The sun was lower now, just over the tops of the trees. Bevis hung the circle to the gate-post of the stockade and moved the tube till he could see the sun through it. It read 20 degrees on the graduated disc.

"Twenty degrees north latitude," he said. "It's not on the equator."

"But it's in the tropics."

"O, yes!—it's in Cancer, right enough. It's better than the Equator: they are obliged to lie still there all day long; and it's all swamps and steaming moisture and fevers and malaria."

"Much nicer here."

"O! Much nicer."

"How lucky! This island is put just right."

"The very spot!"

"There ought to be a ditch outside the palisade," said Mark. "Like they have outside tents to run the water away when it rains. I've seen them round tents."

"So there ought. We'll dig it."

They fetched the spades and shovelled away half an hour, but it was very warm, and they sat down presently inside the fence, which began to cast a shadow.

"We ought to have some blacks to do this sort of work," said Mark.

"White people can't slave in the tropics," said Bevis. "Let's do nothing now for a while."

"Lemonade," said Mark. Bevis nodded; and Mark fetched and opened a bottle, then another.

"There are only four left," he said.

"A ship ought to come every year with these kind of things," said Bevis.

"It ought to be wrecked, and then we could get the best things from the wreck. Shall we do some more shooting?"

"Practising. We ought to practise with ball; but we said we would not till we had a sight."

"But it's loaded with shot, and it's my turn; and there's nothing for supper, or dinner to-morrow."

"No more there is. One thing, though, if we practise shooting, we shall frighten all the birds away."

"Ducks," said Mark, "flappers and coots, and moorhens, they're all about in the evening. The sun's going down: let's shoot one."

"Very well."

Mark got down the matchlock, and lit the match. He went first, and Bevis followed, two or three yards behind, with Pan. They walked as quietly as possible along the path they had made round the island, glancing out over the water at intervals. As they approached the other end of the island, where the ground was low and thick with reed-grass and sedges, they moved still more gently. They saw two young ducks, but they were too far;

and whether they heard or suspected something swam in among a bed of rushes on a shoal. Mark stooped, and went down to the water's edge. Bevis stooped and followed, and there they set up the gun on the rest, hidden behind the fringe of sedges and reed-grass they had left when cutting them for the roof.

The muzzle almost, but not quite, protruded through the sedges, and they sat down to wait on some of the dry grasses they had reaped, but did not carry, not requiring all they had cut. The ground so near the edge was soft and yielding, and this dry hay of sedge and flag better to sit on. Bevis held Pan by the collar, and they waited a long time while the sun sank to the north-westwards, almost in front, of them.

"No twilight in the tropics," whispered Mark.

"But there's the moon," said Bevis. The moon being about half full, was already high in the sky, and her light continued the glow of the sunset. Restless as they were, they sat still, and took the greatest care in slightly changing their positions for ease not to rustle the dry sedges. Pan did not like it, but he reconciled himself after awhile. Presently Mark, who was nearest the standing sedges, leaned forward and moved the gun, Bevis glanced over his shoulder and saw a young wild duck among the weeds by the shoal. "Too far," he whispered. It looked a long way. Mark did not answer; he was aiming. Puff—bang! Bow-wow! Pan was in the water, dashing through the smoke before they could tell whether the shot had taken effect or not. The next moment they saw the duck struggling and splashing unable to dive. "Lu—lu!"

"Go on, Pan!"

"Catch him!"

"Fetch him!"

"He's got him!"

"He's in the weeds."

"Look—he can't get back—the duck drags in the weeds."

"Pan! Pan! Here—here!"

"He can't do it."

"He's caught."

"He'll sink."

"Not he."

"But he will."

"No."

After striving his hardest to bring the duck back through the thick weeds, Pan suddenly turned and swam to the shoal where the rushes grew. There he landed and stood a moment with the duck's neck in his mouth: the bird still flapped and struggled.

"Here—here!" shouted Bevis, running along to attract the spaniel to a place where the weeds looked thinner. Mark whistled: Pan plunged in again; and this time, having learned the strength of the weeds, he swam out round them and laid the bird at their feet.

"It's a beauty."

"Look at his webbed feet!"

"But he's not very big!"

"But he's a young one."

"Of course: the feathers are very pretty."

"He kicks still."

"Kill him. There; now we must pluck him this evening. Some of the feathers will do for Frances."

"O! Frances! She's no use," said Mark, carrying his bird by the legs.

The head hung down, and Pan licked it. Plucking they found a tedious business. Each tried in turn till they were tired, and still there seemed no end to the feathers.

"There are thousands of them," said Bevis.

"Just as if they could not have a skin."

"But the feathers are prettier."

"Well, you try now."

Bevis plucked awhile. Then Mark tried again. This was in the courtyard of the hut. The moonlight had now quite succeeded to the day. By the watch it was past nine. Out of doors it was light, but in the hut Bevis had to strike a match to see the time.

"It's supper-time," he said.

"Now they are having breakfast at home, I suppose."

"I dare say we're quite forgotten," said Bevis. "People always are. Seven thousand miles away they're sure to forget us."

"Altogether," said Mark. "Of course they will. Then some day they'll see two strange men with very long beards and bronzed faces."

"Broad-brimmed Panama bats."

"And odd digger-looking dresses."

"And revolvers in their pockets out of sight, come strolling up to the door and ask for—"

"Glasses of milk, as they're thirsty, and while they're sipping—as they don't really like such stuff—just ask quietly if the governor's alive and kicking—"

"And the Jolly Old Moke asleep in his armchair—"

"And if mamma's put up the new red curtains."

"Then they'll stare—and shriek—"

"Recognise and rumpus."

"Huge jollification!"

"Everybody tipsy and happy."

"John Young tumbling in the pond."

"Bells ringing."

"I say, ought we to forgive the Bailiff and Polly?"

"Hum! I suppose so. But that's a very long time yet?"

"O! a very long time. This duck will never be done."

"We forgot to have tea," said Mark.

"So we did; and tea would be very nice. With dampers like the diggers," said Bevis. "Let's have tea now."

"Finish the horrid duck to-morrow," said Mark. "I'll hang him up."

"Fire's gone out," said Bevis, looking from the gateway. "Can't see any sparks."

"Gone out long ago," said Mark. "Pot put it out."

They had left the pot on the ashes.

"It would be a good plan to light a fire inside the stockade now," said Bevis. "It will do to make the tea, and keep things away in the night."

"Lions and tigers," said Mark. "If they want to jump the fence they won't dare face the fire. But it's very warm; we must not make it by the hut."

"Put it on one side," said Bevis, "in the corner under the cliff. Bring the sticks."

They had plenty of wood in the stockade, piled up, from the chips and branches and ends of the poles with which they had made the roof and fence. The fire was soon lit. Bevis got out the iron rod to swing the kettle. Mark went down and dipped the zinc bucket full of water.

"Are there any things about over the New Sea?" he said when he came back. "It's dark as you go through the wood, and the water looks all strange by moonlight."

"Very curious things are about I dare say," said Bevis, who had lit the lantern, and was shaking tea into the tin teapot in the hut. "Curious magic things."

"Floating round; all misty, and you can't see them."

"But you know they're there."

"Genii."

"Ghouls."

"Vampires. Look, there's a big bat—and another; they're coming back again."

"That's nothing; everything's magic. Mice are magic, especially if they're red. I'll show you in Faust. If they're only dun they're not half so much magic."

"More mousey."

"Yes. Besides, if you were in the wood you would see things behind the trees; you might think they were shadows, but they're not: and lights moving about—sparks—"

"Magic?"

"Magic. Stars are magic. There's one up there. And there are things in trees, and satyrs in the fern, and those that come out of the trees and out of the water are ladies—very beautiful, like Frances—"

"Frances is very plain."

"That she's not."

"She's so short."

"Well, the tree-ladies are not very large. If I had a hook of secret lore, that's the right name—"

"A magic hook?"

"I'd make them come and dance and sing to us."

"But are there no monsters?" said Mark, stirring the fire.

Chapter Sixteen
New Formosa—Morning in the Tropics

The flames darted up, and mingling with the moonlight cast a reddish-yellow glare on the green-roofed hut, the yellowy cliff of sand, throwing their shadows on the fence, and illuming Pan, who sat at the door of the hut. The lantern, which Bevis had left on the floor, was just behind the spaniel. Outside the stockade the trees of the wood cast shadows towards them; the moon shone high in the sky. The weird calls of water-fowl came from a distance; the sticks crackled and hissed. Else all was silent, and the smoke rose straight into the still air.

"Green eyes glaring at you in the black wood," said Bevis. "Huge creatures, with prickles on their backs, and stings: the ground heaves underneath, and up they come; one claw first—you see it poking through a chink—and then hot poisonous breath—"

"Let's make a circle," said Mark. "Quick! Let's lock the gate."

"Lock the gate!" Mark padlocked it. "I'll mark the wizard's foot on it. There,"—Bevis drew the five-angled mark with his pencil on the boards—"there, now they're just done."

"They can't come in."

"No."

"But we might see them?"

"Perhaps, yes."

"Let's play cards, and not look round."

"All right. Bezique. But the kettle's boiling. I'll make the tea." He took the kettle off and filled the teapot. "We ought to have a damper," he said.

"So we did: I'll make it." Mark went into the hut and got some flour, and set to work and made a paste: you see, if you are busy, you do not know about things that look like shadows, but are not shadows. He pounded away at the paste; and after some time produced a thick flat cake of dough, which they put in the ashes and covered over.

They put two boards for a table on the ground, in front of the hut door and away from the fire, and set the lantern at one end of the table. Bevis brought the teapot and the tin mugs, for they had forgotten cups and saucers, and made tea; while Mark buttered a heap of biscuits.

"Load the matchlock," said Bevis. Mark loaded the gun, and leaned it by the door-post at their backs, but within reach. Bevis put his bow and two arrows close at his side, as he sat down, because he could shoot quicker with his bow in case of a sudden surprise, than with the matchlock. The condensed milk took a few minutes to get ready, and then they began. The corner of the hut kept off the glow from the fire; they leaned their backs against the door-posts, one each side, and Pan came in between. He gobbled up the buttered biscuits, being perfectly civilised; now from one, now from the other, as fast as they liked to let him.

"This is the jolliest tea there ever was," said Mark. "Isn't it jolly to be seven thousand miles from anywhere?"

"No bothers," said Bevis, waving his hand as if to keep people at a distance.

"Nothing but niceness."

"And do as you please."

"Had enough?"

"Yes. Bezique."

"I'll deal."

"No—no; cat."

The cards were dealt on the two rough boards, and they played, using the old coins they had brought with them as counters. Pan watched a little while, then he retired, finding there was nothing more to eat, and stretched himself a few yards away. The fire fell lower, flickered, blazed again: the last sticks thrown on burning off in the middle broke and half rolled off one side and half the other; the smoke ceased to rise, the heated vapour which took its place was not visible. By-and-by the moon's white light alone filled the interior of the stockade, and entered in at the doorway of the hut, for the glimmer of the horn-lantern did not reach beyond the boards of their tables. At last the candle guttered and went out, but they played on by the moonlight.

"Ah, ah!" said Bevis presently.

"Double bezique!" shouted Mark; "and all the money's mine!"

Pan looked up at the noise.

"The proper thing is, to shoot you under the table," said Bevis: "that's what buccaneers do."

"But there were no revolvers when we lived," said Mark; "only matchlocks."

"Shovel them up," said Bevis. "Broad gold pieces, but you won't have them long. I'm tired to-night. I shall win them to-morrow, and your estate, and your watch, and your shirt off your back, and your wife—"

"I shan't have a wife," said Mark, yawning as he pocketed the coins, which were copper. "I don't want a Frances—O, no! thank you very much!"

"What's the time?"

"Nearly twelve."

"I'm tired."

"Make the bed."

They began to make it, and recollected that one of the rugs was under the teak-tree, where they had hoisted it up for an awning. Bevis took his bow and arrow; Mark his spear. They called Pan, and thus, well armed and ready for the monsters, marched across to the teak, glancing fearfully around, expectant of green blazing eyes and awful coiling shapes; quite fearless all the time, and aware that there was nothing. They had to pull up the poles to get the awning down. On returning to the stockade, the gate was padlocked and the bed finished. The lantern, in which a fresh candle had been placed, was hung to a cord from the ceiling, but they found it much in the way.

"If there's an alarm in the night," said Mark, "and anybody jumps up quick, he'll hit his head against the lantern. Let's put it on the box."

"Chest," said Bevis; "it's always chest."

Mark dragged the chest to the bed-side, and put the lantern on it, and a box of matches handy. The matchlock was hung up; the teapot and mugs and things put away, and the spear and bow and knobstick arranged for instant use. Bevis let down the carpet at the doorway, and it shut out the moonlight like a curtain. They took off their boots and got on the bed with their clothes on. Just as Bevis was about to blow out the candle, he remembered something.

"Mark—Lieutenant, how's the barometer?"

"Went down in the ship, sir."

"How's the weather then? Look out and see if a tornado's brewing."

"Ay, ay, sir."

Mark stepped under the curtain, looked round, and came in again.

"Sky's clear," he said. "Only the moon and a little shooting star, a very little one, a mere flicker just like striking a lucifer when it doesn't light."

"Streak of light on the wall."

"Yes."

"No tornado?"

"No."

"Thirty bells," said the captain. "Turn in. Lights out." He blew out the candle and they made themselves comfortable.

"What's that?" said Mark in a minute. A corner of the curtain was lifted, and let the moonlight in on the floor.

"Only Pan."

Finding he was alone outside, Pan came in and curled up by the chest.

"Good-night."

"Good-night."

"Good-night, Pan," said Bevis, putting out his hand and touching Pan's rough neck. Almost before he could bring his hand back again they were both firm asleep. Quite tired out by such a long, long day of exertion and change, they fell asleep in a second, without any twilight of preliminary drowsiness. Change wearies as much as labour; a journey, for instance, or looking up at rows of pictures in different colours. They slept like buccaneers or humming-tops, only unconsciously throwing the covering rug partly off, for the summer night was warm. The continuance of easterly breezes had caused the atmosphere to become so dry that there was no mist, and the morning opened clear, still, and bright.

After a while Pan stretched himself, got up, and went out. He could not leap the fence, but looking round it found a place where it joined the cliff, not quite closed up. They knew this, but had forgotten all about it. Pan pushed his head under, struggled, and scratched, till his shoulders followed as he lay on his side, and the rest followed easily. Roaming round, he saw the pot in which the bacon had been boiled still on the grey ashes of the fire under the teak. The lid was off, thrown aside, and he ran to the pot, put his paws on the rim, and lapped up the greasy liquor with a relish.

Loo, the cottage girl, could she have seen, would have envied him, for she had but a dry crust for breakfast, and would have eagerly dipped it in. Pan roamed round again, and came back to the hut and waited. In an hour's time he went out once more, lapped again, and again returned to watch the sleepers.

By-and-by he went out the third time and stayed longer. Then he returned, thrust his head under the curtain and uttered a short bark of impatient questioning, "Yap!"

"The genie," said Mark, awaking. He had been dreaming.

"What's the time?" said Bevis, sitting up in an instant, as if he had never been asleep. Pan leaped on the bed and barked, delighted to see them moving.

"Three o'clock," said Mark. "No; why it's stopped!"

"It's late, I know," said Bevis, who had gone to the doorway and lifted the curtain. "The sun's high; it's eight or nine, or more."

"I never wound it up," said Mark, "and—well I never! I've left the key at home."

"It was my key," said Bevis. One did for both in fact.

"Now we shan't know what the time is," said Mark. "Awfully awkward when you're seven thousand miles from anywhere."

"Awful! What a stupe you were; where did you leave the key?"

"On the dressing-table, I think; no, in the drawer. Let's see, in my other waistcoat: I saw it on the floor; now I remember, on the mantelpiece, or else on the washing-stand. I know, Bevis; make a sundial!"

"So I will. No, it's no use."

"Why not?"

"I don't know when to begin."

"When to begin?"

"Well the sundial must have a start. You must begin your hours, don't you see."

"I see; you don't know what hour to put to the shadow."

"That's it."

"But can't you find out? Isn't the sun always south at noon?"

"But which is quite south?"

"Just exactly proper south?"

"Yes, meridian is the name. I know, the north star!"

"Then we must wait till night to know the time to-day."

"And then till the sun shines again—"

"Till to-morrow."

"Yes."

"I know!" said Mark; "Charlie. You make the sundial, and he'll wave the handkerchief at four o'clock."

"Capital," said Bevis. "Just the very thing—like Jupiter's satellites; you know, they hide behind, and the people know the time by seeing them. Charlie will set the clock for us. There's always a dodge for everything. Pan, Pan, you old rascal."

Bevis rolled him over and over. Pan barked and leaped on them, and ran out into the sunshine.

"Breakfast," said Mark; "what's for breakfast?"

"Well, make some tea," said Bevis, putting on his boots. "That was best. And, I say, we forgot the damper."

"So we did. It will do for breakfast."

The damper was raked out of the ashes, and having been left to itself was found to be well done, but rather burned on one side. When the burnt part had been scraped off, and the ashes blown from it, it tasted very fair, but extremely dry.

"The butter won't last long," said Mark presently, as they sat down to breakfast on the ground at their two boards. "We ought to have another shipload."

"Tables without legs are awkward," said Bevis, whose face was heated from tending the fire they had lit and boiling the kettle. "The difficulty is, where to put your knees."

"Or else you must lie down. We could easily make some legs."

"Drive short stakes into the ground, and put the boards on the top," said Bevis. "So we will presently. The table ought to be a little one side of the doorway, as we can't wheel it along out of the way."

"Big stumps of logs would do for stools," said Mark. "Saw them off short, and stand them on end."

"The sun's very warm," said Bevis.

The morning sunshine looked down into their courtyard, so that they had not the least shade.

"The awning ought to be put up here over our table."

"Let's put it up, then. I say, how rough your hair looks."

"Well, you look as if you had not washed. Shall we go and have a swim?"

"Yes. Put the things away; here's the towels."

They replaced their breakfast things anywhere, leaving the teapot on the bed, and went down to the water, choosing the shore opposite Serendib, because on that side there were no weeds.

As they came down to the strand, already tearing off their coats, they stopped to look at the New Sea, which was still, smooth, and sunlit. Though it was so broad it did not seem far to-day to the yellow cliff of the quarry, to the sward of the battlefield, and the massive heads of the sycamores under which the war had raged.

There was not a breath of wind, but the passage of so much air coming from the eastwards during the last week or so had left the atmosphere as clear as it is in periods of rain. The immense sycamores stood out against the sky, with the broad green curve of their tops drawn along the blue. Except a shimmer of uncertain yellow at the distant shore they could not see the reflection of the quarry which was really there, for the line of vision from where they stood came nearly level with the surface of the water, so that they did not look into it but along it.

Beneath their feet they saw to the bottom of the New Sea, and slender shapes of fish hovering over interstices of stones, now here, now gone. There was nothing between them and the fish, any more than while looking at a tree. The mere surface was a film transparent, and beneath there seemed nothing. Across on Serendib the boughs dipped to the boughs that came up under to meet them. A moorhen swam, and her imago followed beneath, unbroken, so gently did she part the water that no ripple confused it. Farther the woods of the jungle far away rose up, a mountain wall of still boughs, mingled by distance into one vast thicket.

Southwards, looking seawards, instead of the long path of gold which wavelets strew before him, the sun beamed in the water, throwing a stream of light on their faces, not to be looked at any more than the fire which Archimedes cast from his mirrors melting the ships. All the light of summer fell on the water, from the glowing sky, from the clear air, from the sun. The island floated in light, they stood in light, light was in the shadow of the trees, and under the thick brambles; light was deep down in the water, light surrounded them as a mist might; they could see far up into the illumined sky as down into the water.

The leaves with light under them as well as above became films of transparent green, the delicate branches were delineated with finest camel's hair point, all the grass blades heaped together were apart, and their edges apparent in the thick confusion; every atom of sand upon the shore was sought out by the beams, and given an individual existence amid the inconceivable multitude which the sibyl alone counted. Nothing was lost, not a grain of sand, not the least needle of fir. The light touched all things, and gave them to be.

The tip of the shimmering poplar had no more of it than the moss in the covert of the bulging roots. The swallows flew in light, the fish swam in light, the trees stood in light. Upon the shore they breathed light, and were silent till a white butterfly came fluttering over, and another white butterfly came under it in the water, when looking at it the particular released them from the power of the general.

"Magic," said Bevis. "It's magic."

"Enchantment," said Mark; "who is it does it—the old magician?"

"I think the book says its Circe," said Bevis; "in the Ulysses book, I mean. It's deep enough to dive here."

In a minute he was ready, and darted into the water like an arrow, and was sent up again as an arrow glances to the surface. Throwing himself on his side he shot along. "Serendib!" he shouted, as Mark appeared after his dive under.

"Too far," said Mark.

"Come on."

Mark came on. The water did not seem to resist them that morning, it parted and let them through. With long scoops of their arms that were uppermost, swimming on the side, they slipped on still between the strokes, the impetus carrying them till the stroke came again. Between the strokes they glided buoyantly, lifted by the water as swallows glide on the plane of the air. From the hand thrust out in front beyond the head to the feet presently striking back—all the space between the hands and feet they seemed to grasp. All this portion of the water was in their power, and its elasticity as their strokes compressed it threw them forward.

At each long sweep Bevis felt a stronger hold, his head shot farther through above the surface like the stem of the Pinta when the freshening breeze drove her. He did not see where he was going, his vision was lost in the ecstasy of motion; all his mind was concentrated in the full use of his limbs. The delicious delirium of strength—unconsciousness of reason, unlimited consciousness of force—the joy of life itself filled him.

Presently turning on his chest for the breast-stroke he struck his knee, and immediately stood up:

"Mark!"

Fortunately there were no stones, or his knee would have been grazed; the bottom was sand. Hearing him call Mark turned on his chest and stood up too. They waded some way, and then found another deep place, swam across that more carefully, and again walked on a shallow which continued to the shore of Serendib, where they stood by the willow boughs.

"Pan!"

Chapter Seventeen
New Formosa—Planning the Raft

Pan had sat on the strand watching them till they appeared about to land on the other side, then at the sound of his name he swam to them. Now you might see how superior he was, for the two human animals stood there afraid to enter the island lest a rough bough should abrade their skins, a thorn lacerate, or a thistle prick their feet, but Pan no sooner reached the land than he rushed in. His shaggy natural coat protected him.

In a minute out came a moorhen, then another, and a third, scuttling over the surface with their legs hanging down. Two minutes more and Pan drove a coot out, then a young duck rose and flew some distance, then a dab-chick rushed out and dived instantaneously, then still more moorhens, and coots.

"Why, there are hundreds!" said Mark. "What a place for our shooting!"

"First-rate," said Bevis. "It's full of moorhens and all sorts."

So it was. The island of Serendib was but a foot or so above the level of the water, and completely grown over with willow osiers (their blue gum), the spaces between the stoles being choked with sedges and reed-grass, vast wild parsnip stalks or "gix," and rushes, in which mass of vegetation the water-fowl delighted. They had been undisturbed for a very long time, and they looked on Serendib as theirs; they would not move till Pan was in the midst of them.

"We must bring the matchlock," said Mark. "But we can't swim with it. Could we do it on the catamarans?"

"They're awkward if you've got anything to carry," said Bevis, remembering his dip. "I know—we'll make a raft."

"Then we can go to all the islands," said Mark, "that will be ever so much better; why we can shoot all round them everywhere."

"And go up the river," said Bevis, "and go on the continent, the mainland, you know, and see if it's China, or South America—"

"Or Africa or Australia, and shoot elephants—"

"And rabbits and hares and peewits, and pick up the pearls on Pearl Island, and see what there is at the other end of the world up there," pointing southwards.

"We've never been to the end yet," said Mark. "Let's go back and make the raft directly."

"The catamaran planks will do capital," said Bevis, "and some beams, and I'll see how Ulysses made his, and make ours like it—he had a sail somehow."

"We could sail about at night," said Mark, "nobody would see us."

"No; Val or Charlie would be sure to see in the daytime; the stars would guide us at night, and that would be just proper."

"Just like they used to—"

"Yes, just like they used to when we lived three thousand years ago."

"Capital. Let's begin."

"So we will."

"Pan! Pan!"

Pan was so busy routing out the hitherto happy water-fowl that he did not follow them until they had begun to swim, having waded as far as they could. The shoals reduced the actual distance they had to swim by quite half, so that they reached New Formosa without any trouble, and dressed. They went to the hut that Bevis might read how Ulysses constructed his ship or raft, and while they were looking for the book saw the duck which they had plucked the evening before.

This put them in mind of dinner, and that if they did not cook it, it would not be ready for them as it used to be at home. They were inclined to let dinner take its chance, but buttered biscuits were rather wearisome, so they concluded to cook the dinner first, and make the raft afterwards. It was now very hot in the stockade, so the fire was lit under the teak-tree in the shade, the duck singed, and hung on a double string from a hazel rod stuck in the ground. By turning it round the double string would wind up, and when left to itself unwind like a roasting-jack.

The heat of the huge fire they made, added to that of the summer sun, was too great—they could not approach it, and therefore managed to turn the duck after a fashion with a long stick. After they had done this some time, working in their shirtsleeves, they became impatient, and on the eve of quarrelling from mere restlessness.

"It's no use our both being here," said Mark. "One's enough to cook."

"One's enough to be cooked," said Bevis. "Cooking is the most hateful thing I ever knew."

"Most awful hateful. Suppose we say you shall do it to-day and I do it to-morrow, instead of being both stuck here by this fire?"

"Why shouldn't you do it to-day, and *I* do it to-morrow?"

"Toss up, then," said Mark, producing a penny. "Best two out of three."

"O! no," said Bevis. "You know too many penny dodges. No, no; I know—get the cards, shuffle them and cut, and who cuts highest goes off and does as he likes—"

"Ace highest?"

"Ace."

The pack was shuffled, and Mark cut a king. Bevis did not got a picture-card, so he was cook for that day.

"I shall take the matchlock," said Mark.

"That you won't."

"That I shall."

"You won't, though."

"Then I won't do anything," said Mark, sulking. "It's not fair; if you had cut king you would have had the gun."

Bevis turned his duck, poking it round with the stick, then he could not help admitting to himself that Mark was right. If he had cut a king he would have taken the gun, and it was not fair that Mark should not do so.

"Very well," he said. "Take it; mind it's my turn to-morrow."

Mark went for the matchlock, and came out of the stockade with it. But before he had gone many yards he returned into the hut, and put it up on the slings. Then he picked out his fishing-rod from the store-room, and his perch-line and hooks, mixed some mustard and water in his tin mug, and started off. Bevis, who had sat down far enough from the fire to escape the heat, did not notice him the second time.

Mark walked into the wood till he found a moist place, there he poured his mixture on the ground, and the pungent mustard soon brought some worms up. These he secured, but he did not know how to carry them, for the mug he used for drinking from, and did not like to put them in it. Involuntarily feeling his pockets as people do when in difficulty, he remembered his handkerchief; he put some moss in it, and so made a bundle. He had but one mug, but he had several handkerchiefs in the store-room, and need not use this one again.

Looking round the island for a place to fish, he came to a spot where a little headland projected on the Serendib side, but farther down than where they had bathed. At the end of the headland a willow trunk or blue gum hung over the water, and as he came near a kingfisher flew off the trunk and away round Serendib. Mark thought this a likely spot, as the water looked deep, and the willow cast a shadow on one side, and fish might come for anything that fell from the boughs. He dropped his bait in, and sat down in the shade to watch his blue float, which was reflected in the still water.

He had not used his right to take the matchlock, because when he came out with it and saw Bevis, whose back was turned, he thought how selfish he was, for he knew Bevis liked shooting better than anything. So he put the gun back, and went fishing.

Against his own wishes Bevis acknowledged Mark's reason and right; against his own wishes Mark forbore to use his right that he might not be selfish.

While Mark watched his float Bevis alternately twisted up the duck, and sat down under the teak-tree with the Odyssey, in which he read that—

On the lone island's utmost verge there stood
Of poplars, pines, and firs a lofty wood,

from which Ulysses selected and felled enough for his vessel, and,—

At equal angles these disposed to join;
He smooth'd and squared them by the rule and line.

Long and capacious as a shipwright forms
Some bark's broad bottom to outride the storms,
So large he built the raft: then ribb'd it strong
From space to space, and nail'd the planks along;
These form'd the sides: the deck he fashioned last;
Then o'er the vessel raised the taper mast,
With crossing sailyards dancing in the wind,
And to the helm the guiding rudder join'd.

Pondering over this Bevis planned his raft, intending to make it of six or eight beams of poplar, placed lengthways; across these a floor of short lesser poles put close together; thirdly, a layer of long poles; and above these the catamaran planks for the deck. He had not enough plank to make the sides so he proposed to fix uprights and extend a railing all round, and wattle this with willows, which would keep off some of the wash of the waves, like bulwarks. Even then, perhaps, the sea might flush the deck; so he meant to fasten the chest in the store-room on it as a locker, to preserve such stores as they might take with them.

A long oar would be the rudder, working it on the starboard side, and there would be a mast; but of course such a craft could only sail before the wind—she could not tack. In shallow water—they could pole along like a punt better than row, for the raft would be cumbrous. Arranging this in his mind, he let the duck burn one side; it had a tendency to burn, as he could not baste it. Soon after he had sat down again he wondered what the time was, and recollected the sundial.

This must be made at once, because it must be ready when Charlie made the signal. He looked up at the sun, whose place he could distinguish, because the branches sheltered his eyes from the full glare. The sun seemed very high, and he thought it must be already noon. Giving the duck a twist, he ran to the hut, and fetched a piece of board, his compasses, and a gimlet. Another twist, and then under the teak-tree he drew a circle with the compasses on the board, scratching with the steel point in the wood.

With the gimlet he bored two holes aslant to each other, and then ran for two nails and a file. In his haste, having to get back to turn the roast, he did not notice that the matchlock was hung up in the hut. He filed the heads off the nails, and then tapped them into the gimlet holes; they wanted a little bending, and then their points met, forming a gnomon, like putting the two forefingers together.

Then he bored two holes through the board, and inserted other nails half through, ready for hammering into the post. The post he cut from one of the poles left from the fence; it was short and thick, and he sharpened it at one end, leaving the top flat as sawn off. Fetching the iron bar, he made a hole in the ground, put the post in, and gave it one tap; then the duck wanted turning again.

As he returned to his work he remembered that in the evening the teak and the other trees of the wood cast long shadows towards the hut, which would blot out the time on the sundial. It ought to be put where the full beams would fall on it from sunrise to sunset. The cliff was the very place. He ran up and chose a spot which he could see would be free from shadow, pitched the post, and ran down to the duck.

Next he carried up the dial, and nailed it to the top of the post; the two nails kept it from moving if touched, and were much firmer than one. The gnomon at once cast a pointed shadow on that side of the circle opposite the sun, but there were as yet no marks for the hours. He could not stay to look at his work, but went down to the teak, and began to wonder why he did not hear Mark shoot, though very likely in the heat of the day the water-fowl did not cross the open water to the island.

Thinking of shooting reminded him of the sight so much wanted at the top of the barrel. He could not solder anything on, nor drill a hole, and so fix it, nor was it any use to file a notch, because nothing would stick in the notch, as iron is not like wood. Perhaps sealing-wax would—a lump of sealing-wax—but he had none in the store-room; it would not look proper either, and was sure to get chipped off directly. Could he tie anything on? The barrel was fastened into the stock with wire, why not twist two pieces of wire round, and put a nail head (the nail filed off very short) between them, very much as hats are hung with the brim between two straps.

That would do, but presently he thought of a still easier way, which was to put a piece of wire round the barrel and fasten it, but not tight, so that it was like a loose ring. Then with the pliers seize the part at the upper side of the barrel and twist it, forming a little loop of the loose wire; this would tighten the ring, then twisting the upper loop round it would make a very short and tiny coil upon itself, and this coil would do capitally for a sight.

He wished Mark would come with the matchlock, that he might put the sight on at once. He looked at the duck; it seemed done, but he was not certain, and sat down to rest again in the shadow. A cooing came from the wood, so there were doves which had not yet finished nesting. Bevis was very tired of turning the roast, and determined to try if they could not make an earth oven. The way he thought was to dig a hole in the ground, put in a layer of hot embers, then the meat; then another layer of hot embers; so that the meat was entirely surrounded with them: and finally, a cover of clay placed over to quite confine the heat.

One little hole lets out the steam or gas: it is made by standing a small stick in the oven, and then when all is finished, drawing it out so as to leave a tube. He was not certain that this was quite right, but it was all he could remember, and it would be worth trying. This horrible cooking took up so much time, and made him so hot and uncomfortable: shipwrecked people wanted a slave to do the cooking. But he thought he should soon whistle for Mark. Pan had gone with him, but now came back, as Bevis supposed, weary of waiting in ambush; but, in fact, with an eye to dinner.

Mark's float did not move: it stood exactly upright, it did not jerk, causing a tiny ripple, then come up, and then move along, then dive and disappear, going down aslant. It remained exactly upright, as the shot-weight on the line kept it. There was no wind, so the line out of the water did not blow aside and cause the float to rotate. Long since he had propped his rod on a forked stick, and weighted the butt with a flat stone, to save himself the trouble of holding it.

He sat down, and Pan sat by him: he stroked Pan and then teased him; Pan moved away and watched, out of arm's reach. By-and-by the spaniel extended himself and became drowsy. Mark's eyes wearied of the blue float, and he too stretched himself, lying on his side with his head on his arm, so that he could see the float, if he opened his eyes, without moving. A wagtail came and ran along the edge of the sand so near that with his rod he could have reached it. Jerking his tail the wagtail entered the still water up to the joints of his slender limbs, then came out, and ran along again.

Mark's head almost touched the water: his hair (for his hat was off, as usual) was reflected in it, and a great brown water-beetle passed through the reflection. A dove—his parrakeet—came over and entered the wood; it was the same Bevis afterwards heard cooing. Mark half opened his eyes, and thought the wagtail's tiny legs were no thicker than one of Frances's hair-pins.

The moorhens and coots had now recovered from the fright Pan had given them. As he gazed through the chinks of his eyelids along the surface of the water, he could see them one by one returning towards Serendib, pausing on the way among the weeds, swimming again, with nodding heads, turning this side and that to pick up anything they saw; but still, gradually approaching the island opposite. They all came from one direction, and he remembered that when Pan hunted them out, they all scuttled the same way. So did the wild duck; so did the kingfisher. "I believe they all go to the river," Mark thought; "the river that flows out through the weeds. Just wait till we have got our raft."

Something swam out presently from the shore of New Formosa; something nearly flush with the water, and which left a wake of widening ripples behind it, by which Mark knew it was a rat: for water-fowl, though they can move rapidly, do not cause much undulation. The rat swam out a good way, then turned and came in again. This coasting voyage he repeated down the shore several times.

To look along the surface, as Mark did, was like kneeling and glancing over a very broad and well polished table, your eyes level with it. The slightest movement was visible a great way—a little black speck that crossed was seen at once. The little black speck was raised a very small degree above the surface, and there was something in the water not visible following it.

The water undulated, but less than behind the rat; now the moorhens nod their heads to and fro, as you or I nod: but this black speck waved itself the other way, from side to side, as it kept steadily onwards. Mark recognised a snake, swimming swiftly, its head (black only from distance and contrast with the gleam of the crystal top of the polished table) just above the surface, and sinuous length trailing beneath the water. He did not see whence the snake started, but he saw it go across to the weeds at the extreme end of Serendib, and there lost it.

He thought of the huge boa-constrictors hidden in the interior of New Formosa, they would be basking quite still in such heat, but he ought to have brought his spear with him. You never ought to venture from the stockade in these unknown places without a spear. By now the shadows had moved, and his foot was in the sunshine: he could feel the heat through the leather. Two bubbles came up to the surface close to the shore: he saw the second one start from the sand and rise up quickly with a slight wobble, but the sand did not move, and he could not see anything in it.

His eyes closed, not that he slept, but the gleam of the water inclined them to retire into the shadow of the lids. After some time there was a shrill pipe. Mark started, and lifted his head, and saw the kingfisher, which had come back towards his perch on the willow trunk. He came within three yards before he saw Mark; then he shot aside, with a shrill whistle of alarm, rose up and went over the island.

In starting up, Mark moved his foot, and a butterfly floated away from it: the butterfly had settled in the sunshine on the heated leather. With three flutters, the butterfly floated with broad wings stretched out over the thin grass by the shore. It was no more effort to him to fly than it is to thistledown.

The same start woke Pan. Pan yawned, licked his paw, got up and wagged his tail, looked one way and then the other, and then went off back to Bevis. The blue float was still perfectly motionless. Mark sat up, took his rod and wound up the winch, and began to wander homewards too, idly along the shore. He had gone some way when he saw a jack basking by a willow bush aslant from him, so that the markings on his back were more visible than when seen sideways, for in this position the foreshortening crowded them together. They are like the water-mark on paper, seen best at a low angle, or the mark on silk, and somewhat remind you of the mackerel.

Chapter Eighteen
New Formosa—Kangaroos

So soon as he was sure the jack had not noticed him, Mark drew softly back, and with some difficulty forced a way between the bramble thickets towards the stockade. He thus entered a part they had not before visited, for as the trees and bushes were not so thick by the water, their usual path followed the windings of the shore. Trampling over some and going round others, Mark managed to penetrate between the thickets, having taken his rod to pieces, as it constantly caught in the branches.

Next he came to a place where scarcely anything grew, everything having been strangled by those Thugs of the wood, the wild hops, except a few scattered ash-poles, up which they wound, indenting the bark in spirals. The ground was covered with them, for, having slain their supports, they were forced to creep, so that he walked on hops; and from under a bower of them, where they were smothering a bramble bush, a nightingale "kurred" at him angrily.

He came near the nightingale's young brood, safely reared. "Sweet kur-r-r!" The bird did not like it. These wild hops are a favourite cover with nightingales. A damp furrow or natural ditch, now dry, but evidently a watercourse in rain, seemed to have stopped the march of this creeping, twining plant, for over it he entered among hazel-bushes; and then seeing daylight, fancied he was close to the stockade; but to his surprise, stepped out into an open glade with a green knoll on one side.

The knoll did not rise quite so high as the trees, and there was a quantity of fern about the lower part, then an open lawn of grass, a little meadow in the midst of the wood. He saw a white tail disappear among the fern—there were then rabbits here.

"Bevis!" said Mark aloud. In his surprise he called to Bevis, as he would have done had Bevis been present. He ran to the knoll, and as he ran, more white tails—little ones—raced into the fern, where he saw burries and sand-heaps thrown out.

On the top of the knoll there were numerous signs of rabbits—places worn bare, and "runs," or footpaths, leading down across the grass. He looked round, but could see nothing but trees, which hid the New Sea and the cliff at home.

Eager to tell Bevis of the discovery, and especially of the rabbits, which would furnish them with food, and were, above all, something fresh to shoot at, he ran down the hill so fast that he could not stop himself, though he saw something white in the grass. He returned, and found it was mushrooms, and he gathered between twenty and thirty in a few minutes—"buttons," full grown mushrooms, and overgrown ketchup ones. How to carry them he did not know, having used his handkerchief already, and left his coat at home, till he thought of his waistcoat, and took it off and made a rough bundle of them in it. Then he heard Bevis's whistle, the well-known notes they always used to call each other, and shouted in reply, but the shout did not penetrate so far as the shrill sound had done.

The whistle came from a different direction to that in which he supposed the cave to be, for in winding in and out the brambles he had lost the true course and had forgotten to look at the sun. He found he could not go straight home, for the brambles were succeeded by blackthorn, through which nothing human can move, and hardly a spaniel, when thick as it was here. He had to go all round by the opposite shore of the island, the weed-grown side, and so to the fire under the teak-tree.

"Where's the gun?" said Bevis, coming to meet him.

"I left it at home."

"No, you had it."

"I put it back as you were not coming."

"I never saw it."

"It's in the hut."

"Didn't you really take it?"

"No—really. We'll both go with the gun—"

"So we will." Bevis regretted now that he had made any difficulty. "No, it's your turn; you shall have it."

"I shan't," said Mark. "Look here,"—showing the mushrooms—"splendid for supper, and I've found some rabbits!"

"Rabbits!"

"And a little green hill, and a kingfisher, and a jack. Come and get the gun, and let's shoot him. Quick."

Mark began to run for the matchlock, and they left the duck to itself. Bevis ran with him, and Mark told him all about it as they went.

They talked so much by sign and mere monosyllables in this short run to the hut that I cannot transcribe it in words, though they understood each other better than had they used set speech. For two people always together know the exact meaning of a nod, the indication of a glance, and a motion of the lip means a page of conversation.

Having got the gun as they came back, Mark said perhaps Pan would eat the duck. Bevis called him, but he did not need the call. Gluttonous epicure as he was, Pan, at a whistle from Bevis, would have left the most marrowy bone in the world; but Bevis with a gun! why, Polly with a broom-stick could not have stopped him.

Before they got to the willow bush it had been settled that Mark should shoot at the jack, as the matchlock was loaded with shot, and Bevis wanted to shoot with ball, and reserved his turn for the time when he had made the new sight. Bevis held Pan while Mark went forward. The jack was there, but Mark could not get the rest in a position to take a steady aim, because the willow boughs interfered so.

So Bevis knelt down, still holding Pan, and Mark rested the long heavy barrel on his shoulder. The shot plunged into the water, and the jack floated, blown a yard away, dead on his back; his head shattered, but the long body untouched. Pan fetched him out, and they laughed at the spaniel, he looked so odd with the fish in his mouth. Bevis wanted to see the glade and the rabbit's burries, but Mark said, if the duck was done, it would burn to a cinder, so they went home to their dinner. By the time they reached the teak-tree, the duck was indeed burned one side.

It was dry and hard for lack of basting, when they cut it up, but not unsavoury; and what made it nicer was, that every now and then they found shots—which their teeth had flattened—shots from their own gun. These they saved, and Mark put them in his purse; there were six altogether. Mark gloried in the number, as it was a long shot at the duck, and they showed that he had aimed straight. The ale in the wooden bottle was now stale, so they drank water, with a little sherry in it; and then started to see the discovery Mark had made. Pan went with them. The old spaniel had been there long before, for he found out the rabbits the first stroll he took after landing from the Pinta, but could not convey his knowledge to them.

Bevis marked out a tree, behind which they could wait in ambush to shoot at the rabbits, as it was within easy range of their burries; and then, as they felt it was now afternoon, they returned to the stockade, got the telescope and went up on the cliff to watch for Charlie's signal. The shadow of the gnomon on the dial had moved a good way since Bevis set it up. They had not the least idea of the hour, but somehow they felt that it was afternoon.

Long habit makes us clocks, if we pause, or are forced to consult ourselves. Slow changes in the frame proceed till they are recognised by the mind, or rather by the subtle connexion between the mind and the body; for there seems a nexus, or medium, which conveys this kind of eighth sense from the flesh to the mental consciousness. Birds and animals know the time without a clock or dial, and the months or seasons almost to a day; and so, too, the human animal, if driven from the conveniences of civilisation, which save him the trouble of thinking soon reverts to these original and indefinable indications.

For instance (though in a different way), you can set the clock of your senses to awake exactly at any hour you choose in the morning. If you put your watch aside, reversing the process, and listen to the senses, they will tell you when it is afternoon.

The sandy summit of the cliff was very warm, and the bramble bushes were not high enough to give them any shade; so that, to escape the sun, they reclined on the ground in front of the young oak-tree, and between it and the edge. Bevis looked through the telescope, and could see the sand-martins going in and out of their holes in the distant quarry.

Charlie was not on the hill, or, if so, he was behind a sycamore and out of sight; but they knew he had not yet made the signal, because the herd of cows was down by the hollow oak, some standing in the water. They had not yet been called by the milkers. Sweeping the shore of Fir-Tree Gulf, and down the Mozambique to the projecting bluff which prevented farther view, he saw a crow on the sand, and another perched on a rail; another sign that there was no one about.

"Any savages?" said Mark.

"Not one."

"Proas hauled up somewhere out of sight."

Mark carefully felt his way to the very verge, and there sat with his legs dangling over. He said the cliff was quite safe; and Bevis joined him. Underneath they could see deep into the water; but though so still, they could not distinguish the bottom. Clear at the surface, the water seemed to thicken to a dense shadow, which could not be seen through. It was deep there; they thought they should like a dive, only it was too far for them to plunge. There was a ball of thistledown on the surface, floating on the tips of its delicate threads; the spokes with which it flies as a wheel rolls.

"How did the rabbits—I mean the kangaroos—get here?" said Bevis presently. "I don't think they could swim so far."

"Savages might bring them," said Mark. "But they don't very often carry pets with them: they eat everything so."

"Nibbling men like goats nibbling hedges," said Bevis. "We must take care: but how did the kangaroos get on the island?"

"It is curious," said Mark. "Perhaps it wasn't always an island—joined to the mainland and the river cut a way through the isthmus."

"Or a volcano blew it up," said Bevis. "We will see if we can find the volcano."

"But it will be gone out now."

"O! yes. All those sort of things happened when there was no one to see them."

"Before we lived."

"Or anybody else."

A large green dragon-fly darted to and fro now under their feet and between them and the water; now overhead, now up to the top of the oak, and now round the cliff and back again; weaving across and across a warp and weft in the air. As they sat still he came close, and they saw his wings revolving, and the sunlight reflected from the membrane. Every now and then there was a slight snap, as he seized a fly, and ate it as he flew: so eager was he that when a speck of wood-dust fell from the oak, though he was yards away, he rushed at it and intercepted it before it could reach the ground. It was rejected, and he had returned whence he started in a moment.

"The buffaloes are moving," said Mark. "They're going up the hill. Get ready. Here, put it on my shoulder."

The herd had begun to ascend the green slope from the water's edge, doubtless in response to the milker's halloo which they could not hear on the island. Bevis rested the telescope on Mark's shoulder, and watched. In point of fact it was not so far but that they could have seen any one by the quarry without a glass, but the telescope was proper.

"There he is," said Mark.

Bevis, looking through the telescope, saw Charlie come out from behind a sycamore, where he had been lying in the shadow, and standing on the edge of the quarry, wave his white handkerchief three times, with an interval between.

"It's all right. White flag," said Bevis. "He's looking. He can't see us, can he?"

"No, there are bushes behind us. If we stood up against the sky perhaps he might."

"I'll crawl to the dial," said Bevis, and he went on hands and knees to the sundial, where he could stand up without being seen, as there were brambles and the oak between him and the cliff. He drew a line with his pencil where the shadow of the gnomon fell on the circle, that was four o'clock. Mark came after, creeping too.

"We won't sit there again," said Mark, "when it's signal-time. He keeps staring. You can see his face through the telescope. We will keep behind the tree."

"There ought to be a crow's nest up in it," said Bevis. "Suppose we make one. Lash a stout stick across two boughs, or tie cords across and half round, so as to be able to sit and watch up there nicely."

"So we will. Then we can see if the savages are prowling round."

"The sedges are very thick that side," said Bevis, pointing to the eastern shore where they had had such a struggle through them. "They would hide five thousand savages."

They went down to the hut, and Bevis made the sight for the matchlock. The short spiral of copper wire answered perfectly, and he could now take accurate aim. But after he had put the powder in, and was just going to put a bullet, he recollected the kangaroos. If he shot off much at a target with bullets at that time in the afternoon it would alarm everything on the island, for the report would be heard all over it. Kangaroos and water-fowl are generally about more in the evening than the morning, so he put off the trial with ball and loaded with shot.

It was of no use going into ambush till the shadows lengthened, so he set about getting the tea while Mark sawed off two posts, and drove them into the ground at one side of the doorway of the hut. Each post had a cross-piece at the top, and the two boards were placed on these, forming a table. Bevis made four dampers, and at Mark's suggestion buried a number of potatoes in the embers of the fire, so as to have them baked for supper, and save more cooking.

The mushrooms were saved for breakfast, and the jack, which was about two pounds' weight, would do for dinner. When he had finished the table, Mark went to the teak-tree, and fetched the two poles that had been set up there for the awning. These he erected by the table, and stretched the rug from them over the table, fastening the other two edges to the posts of the hut.

They had found the nights so warm that more than one rug was unnecessary, and the other could be spared for a permanent awning under which to sit at table. Some tea was put aside to be drunk cold, miner fashion, and it was then time to go shooting. Mark was to have the gun, but he would not go by himself, Bevis must accompany him.

They had to go some distance round to get at the glade, and made so much noise pushing aside branches, and discussing as to whether they were going the right way, that when they reached it if any kangaroos had been out feeding, they had all disappeared.

"I will bring the axe," said Bevis, "and blaze the trees, then we shall know the way in a minute."

Fixing the rest so that he could command the burries on that side of the knoll, Mark sat down under the ash-tree they had previously selected, and leaned the heavy matchlock on the staff. They chose this tree because some brake fern grew in front of it and concealed them. Pan had now come to understand this manner of hunting, and he lay down at once, and needed no holding. Bevis extended himself at full length on his back just behind Mark, and looked up at the sky through the ash branches.

The flies would run over his face, though Mark handed him a frond of fern to swish them with, so he partly covered himself with his handkerchief. The handkerchief was stretched across his ear like the top of a drum, and while he was lying so quiet a fly ran across the handkerchief there, and he distinctly heard the sound of its feet. It was a slight rustle, as if its feet caught a little of the surface of the handkerchief. This happened several times.

The sun being now below the line of the tree-tops, the glade was in the shadow, except the top of the knoll, up which the shadow slowly rose like a tide as the sun declined. Now the edge of the shadow reached a sand-heap thrown out from a burrow; now a thicker bunch of grass; then a thistle; at last it slipped over the top in a second.

Mark could see three pairs of tiny, sharp-pointed ears in the grass. He knew these were young rabbits, or kangaroos, too small for eating. They were a difficulty, they were of no use, but pricked up and listened, if he made the least movement, and if they ran in would stop larger ones from coming out. There was something moving in the hazel stoles across the glade which he could not make out, and he could not ask Bevis to look and see because of these minute kangaroos.

Ten minutes afterwards a squirrel leaped out from the hazel, and began to dart hither and thither along the sward, drawing his red tail softly over the grass at each arching leap as lightly as Jack drew the tassel of his whip over his mare's shoulder when he wished to caress and soothe her. Another followed, and the two played along the turf, often hidden by bunches of grass.

Mark dared not touch Bevis or tell him, for he fancied a larger rabbit was sitting on his haunches at the mouth of a hole fringed with fern. Bevis under his handkerchief listened to Pan snapping his teeth at the flics, and looked up at the sky till four parrots (wood-pigeons) came over, and descended into an oak not far off. The oak was thick with ivy, and was their roost-tree, though they did not intend to retire yet.

Presently he saw a heron floating over at an immense height. His wings moved so slowly he seemed to fly without pressure on the air—as slowly as a lady fans herself when there is no one to coquet with. The heron did not mean to descend to the New Sea, he was bound on a voyage which he did not wish to complete till the dusk began, hence his deliberation. From his flight you might know that there was a mainland somewhere in that direction.

Bang! Mark ran to the knoll, but Pan was there before him, and just in time to seize a wounded kangaroo by the hindquarter as he was paddling into a hole by the fore paws. Mark had seen the rabbit behind the fringe of fern move, and so knew it really was one, and so gently had he got the matchlock into position, moving it the sixteenth of an inch at a time, that Bevis did not know he was aiming. By the new sight he brought the gun to bear on a spot where he thought the rabbit's shoulder must be, for he could not see it, but the rabbit had moved, and was struck in the haunch, and would have struggled out of reach had not Pan had him.

The squirrel had disappeared, and the four parrots had flown at the report.

"This island is full of things," said Bevis, when Mark told him about the squirrel. "You find something new every hour, and I don't know what we shan't find at last. But you have had all the shooting and killed everything."

"Well, so I have," said Mark. "The duck, and the jack, and the kangaroo. You *must* shoot something next."

VOLUME THREE

Chapter One
New Formosa—Bevis's Zodiac

They returned to the hut and prepared the kangaroo and the fish for boiling on the morrow; the fish was to be coiled up in the saucepan, and the kangaroo in the pot. Pan had the paunch, and with his great brown eyes glaring out of his head with gluttony, made off with it to his own private larder, where, after eating his full, he buried the rest. Pan had his own private den behind a thicket of bramble, where he kept some bones of a duck, a bacon bone, and now added this to his store. Here he retired occasionally from civilisation, like the king of the Polynesian island, to enjoy nature, away from the etiquette of his attendance at court on Bevis and Mark.

Next, Mark with one of the old axes they had used to excavate the store-room, cut a notch in the edge of the cave, where it opened on the hut, large enough to stand the lantern in, as the chest would be required for the raft. They raked the potatoes out of the ashes, and had them for supper, with a damper, the last fragment of a duck, and cold tea, like gold-diggers.

Bevis now recollected the journal he had proposed to keep, and got out the book, in which there was as yet only one entry, and that a single word, "Wednesday." He set it on the table under the awning, with the lantern open before him. Outside the edge of the awning the moon filled the courtyard with her light.

"Why, it's only Thursday now," said Mark. "We've only been here one full day, and it seems weeks."

"Months," said Bevis. "Perhaps this means Wednesday last year."

"Of course: this is next year to that. How we must have altered! Our friends would not know us."

"Not even our mothers," said Bevis.

"Nor our jolly old mokes and governors."

"Shot a kangaroo," said Bevis, writing; "shot a duck and a jack—No. Are they jacks? That's such a common name?"

"No; not jacks: jack-sharks."

"No; sun-fish: they're always in the sun."

"Yes; sun-fish."

"Shot a sun-fish: saw two squirrels, and a heron, and four parrots—"

"And a kingfisher—"

"Halcyon," said Bevis, writing it down—"a beautiful halcyon; made a table and a sun-dial. I must go up presently and mark the meridian by the north star."

"Saw one savage."

"Who was that?"

"Why, Charlie."

"O yes, one savage; believe there are five thousand in the jungle on the mainland."

"Seven thousand miles from anywhere. Put it down," said Mark.

"Twenty degrees north latitude; right. There, look; half a page already!"

"We ought to wash some sand to see if there's any gold," said Mark— "in a cradle, you know."

"So we did. We ought to have looked in the duck's gizzard; tiny nuggets get in gizzards sometimes."

"Everything goes to the river beyond the weeds," said Mark; "that ought to be written."

"Does everything go to the river?"

"Everything. While I was fishing I saw them all come back to Serendib from it."

"We must make haste with the raft."

"Like lightning," said Mark.

"Let me see," said Bevis, leaning his arm on the table and stroking his hair with the end of the penholder. "There are blue gum trees, and palms, and banyans."

"Reeds—they're canes."

"Sedges are papyrus."

"The big bulrushes are bamboos." He meant the reed-mace.

"Yes, bamboos. I've put it down. There ought to be a list of everything that grows here—cedars of course; that's something else. Huge butterflies—"

"Very huge."

"Heaps of flies."

"And a tiger somewhere."

"Then there ought to be the names of all the fossils, and metals, and if there's any coal," said Bevis; "and when we have the raft we must dredge up the anemones and pearl oysters, and—"

"And write down all the fish."

"And everything. The language of the natives will be a bother. I must make a new alphabet for it. Look! that will do for A,"—he made a tiny circle; "that's B, two dots."

"They gurgle in their throats," said Mark.

"That's a gurgle," said Bevis, making a long stroke with a dot over and under it; "and they click with their tongues against the roofs of their mouths. No: it's awkward to write clicks. I know: there, CK, that's for click, and this curve under it means a tongue—the way you're to put it to make a click."

"Click! Click!"

"Guggle!"

"Then there's the names of the idols," said Mark. "We'd better find some."

"You can cut some," said Bevis; "cut them with your knife out of a stick, and say they're models, as they wouldn't let you take the real ones. The names; let's see—Jog."

"Hick-kag."

"Hick-kag; I've put it down. Jog and Hick-kag are always quarrelling, and when they hit one another, that's thunder. That's what they say."

"Noodles."

"Natives are always noodles."

"But they can do one thing capital though."

"What's that?"

"Stick up together."

"How? Why?"

"If you take a hatchet and chop a big notch in them, they stick up together again directly."

"Join up."

"Like glue."

"Then the thing is, how did the savages get here? Nobody has ever been here before us; now where did they come from? There are sure to be grand ruins in the jungle somewhere," said Bevis, "all carved, and covered with inscriptions."

"Huge trees growing on the top."

"Magic signs chipped out on stones, and books made of string with knots instead of writing."

Kaak! kaak! A heron was descending. The unearthly noise made them look up.

"Are there any tidal waves?" said Mark.

"Sometimes—a hundred feet high. But the thing is how did they get here? How did anybody ever get anywhere?"

"It's very crooked," said Mark, "very crooked: you can't quite see it, can you? Suppose you go and do the sun-dial: I'm sleepy."

"Well, go to bed; I can do it."

"Good-night!" said Mark. "Lots of chopping to do to-morrow. We ought to have brought a grindstone for the axes. You have got the plan ready for the raft?"

"Quite ready."

Mark went into the hut, placed the lantern in the niche, and threw himself on the bed. In half a minute he was firm asleep. Bevis went out of the courtyard, round outside the fence, and up on the cliff to the sun-dial. The stars shone brighter than it is usually thought they do when there is no moon; but in fact it is not so much the moon as the state of the atmosphere. There was no haze in the dry air, and he could see the Pole Star distinctly.

He sat down—as the post on which the dial was supported was low— on the southern side, with it between him and the north. He still had to stoop till he had got the tip of the gnomon to cover the North Star. Closing one eye, as if aiming, he then put his pencil on the dial in the circle or groove scratched by the compass. The long pencil was held upright in the groove, and moved round till it intercepted his view of the star. The tip of the gnomon, the pencil, and the Pole Star were in a direct line, in a row one behind the other.

To make sure, he raised his head and looked over the gnomon and pencil to the star, when he found that he had not been holding the pencil upright; it leaned to the east, and made an error to the west in his meridian. "It ought to be a plumb-line," he thought. "But I think it's straight now."

He stooped again, and found the gnomon and pencil correct, and pressing on the pencil hard, drew it towards him out of the groove a little way. By the moonlight when he got up he could see the mark he had left, and which showed the exact north. To-morrow he would have to draw a line from that mark straight to the gnomon, and when the shadow fell on that line it would be noon. With the fixed point of noon and the fixed point of four o'clock, he thought he could make the divisions for the rest of the hours.

The moonlight cast a shadow to the east of the noon-line, as she had crossed the meridian. Looking up, he saw the irregular circle of the moon high in the sky, so brilliant that the scored relievo work enchased upon her surface was obscured by the bright light reflected from it.

Behind him numerous lights glittered in the still water, near at hand they were sharp clean points, far away they were short bands of light drawn towards him. Bevis went to the young oak and sat down under it. Cassiopeia fronted him, and Capella; the Northern Crown, was faint and low; but westward great Arcturus shone, though the moon had taken the redness from him. The cross of Cygnus was lying on its side as it was carried through the eastern sky; beneath it the Eagle's central star hung over the Nile. Low in the south, over the unknown river Antares, too, had lost his redness.

Up through the branches of the oak he saw Lyra, the purest star in the heavens, white as whitest and clearest light may be, gleaming at the zenith of the pale blue dome. But just above the horizon northwards there was a faint white light, the faintest aurora, as if another moon was rising there. By these he knew his position, and that he was looking the same way as if he had been gazing from the large northern window of the parlour at home, or if he had been lying on the green path by the strawberries, as he sometimes did in the summer evenings.

Then the North Star, minute but clear—so small, and yet chosen for the axle and focus of the sky, instead of sun-like Sirius—the North Star always shone just over the group of elms by the orchard. Summer and winter, spring and autumn, it was always there, always over the elms—whether they were reddening with the buds and flowers of February, whether they were dull green now in the heats of August, whether they were yellow in October.

Dick and his Team, whose waggon goes backwards, swung round it like a stone in a sling whirled about the shoulders. Sometimes the tail of the Bear, where Dick bestrides his second horse, hung down behind the elms into the vapour of the horizon. Sometimes the Pointers were nearly overhead. If they were hidden by a cloud, the Lesser Bear gave a point; or you could draw a line through Cassiopeia, and tell the North by her chair of stars.

The comets seemed to come within the circle of Bootes—Arcturus you always know is some way beyond the tail of the Bear. The comets come inside the circle of the stars that never set. The governor had seen three or four appear there in his time, just over the elms under the Pole. Donati's, which perhaps you can remember, came there—a tiny thing twelve inches long from nucleus to tail to look at, afterwards the weird sign the world stood amazed at. Then there was another not long after, which seemed to appear at once as a broad streak across the sky.

Like the sketches in old star-maps, it did indeed cross the whole sky for a night or two, but went too quickly for the world to awake at midnight and wonder at. Lately two more have come in the enchanted circle of the stars that never set.

All the stars from Arcturus to Capella came about the elms by the orchard; as Arcturus went down over the place of sunset in autumn, Capella began to shine over another group of elms—in the meadow to the north-east. Capella is sure to be seen, because it begins to become conspicuous just as people say the sky is star-lit as winter sends the first frost or two. But Capella is the brightest star in the northern sky in summer, and it always came up by the second or north-east group of elms.

Between these two groups of tall trees—so tall and thick that they were generally visible even on dark nights—the streamers of the Aurora Borealis shot up in winter, and between them in summer the faint reflection of the midnight sun, like the lunar dawn which precedes the rising of the moon always appeared. The real day-dawn—the white foot of Aurora—came through the sky-curtain a little to the right of the second group, and about over a young oak in the hedge across the road, opposite the garden wall.

When the few leaves left on this young oak were brown, and rustled in the frosty night, the massy shoulder of Orion came heaving up through it—first one bright star, then another; then the gleaming girdle, and the less definite scabbard; then the great constellation stretched across the east. At the first sight of Orion's shoulder Bevis always felt suddenly stronger, as if a breath of the mighty hunter's had come down and entered into him.

He stood upright; his frame enlarged; his instep lifted him as he walked, as if he too could swing the vast club and chase the lion from his lair. The sparkle of Orion's stars brought to him a remnant of the immense vigour of the young world, the frosty air braced his sinews, and power came into his arms.

As the constellation rose, so presently new vigour too entered into the trees, the sap moved, the buds thrust forth, the new leaf came, and the nightingale travelling up from the south sang in the musical April nights. But this was when Orion was south, and Sirius flared like a night-sun over the great oak at the top of the Home Field.

Sirius rose through the young oak opposite the garden wall, passed through a third group of elms, by the rick-yard, gleaming through the branches—hung in the spring above the great oak at the top of the Home Field, and lowered by degrees westwards behind the ashes growing at that end of the New Sea by the harbour. After it Arcturus came, and lorded the Midsummer zenith, where now lucent Lyra looked down upon him.

Up, too, through the little oak came Aldebaran the red Bull's-Eye, the bent rod of Aries, and the cluster of the Pleiades. The Pleiades he loved most, for they were the first constellation he learned to know. The flickering Pleiades, the star-dusted spot in Cancer, and Leo, came in succession. Antares, the harvest-star, scarcely cleared the great oak southwards in summer. He got them all from a movable planisphere, the very best star-maps ever made, proceeding step by step, drawing imaginary lines from one to the other, as through the Pointers to the Pole, and so knew the designs on our northern dome.

He transferred them from the map to the trees. The north group of elms, the north-east group, the east oak, the south-east elms, the southern great oak, the westward ashes, the orchard itself north-west,—through these like a zodiac the stars moved, all east to west, except the enchanted circle about the Pole. For the Bear and the Lesser Bear sometimes seemed to move from west to east when they were returning, swinging under to what would have been their place of rising.

Fixing them thus by night, he knew where many were by day; the Pole Star was always over the north elms—when the starlings stayed and whistled there before they flew to the housetop, when the rooks called there before the sun set on their way home to the jungle, when the fieldfares in the gloomy winter noon perched up there. The Pole Star was always over the elms.

In the summer mornings the sun rose north of east, between the second group of elms and the little oak—so far to the north that he came up over the vale instead of the downs. The morning beams then lit up the northern or outer side of the garden wall, and fell aslant through the narrow kitchen window, under the beam of the ceiling. In the evening the sun set again northwards of the orchard, between it and the north elms, having come round towards the place of rising, and shining again on the outside of the garden wall, so that there seemed but a few miles between. He did not sink, but only dipped, and the dawn that travelled above him indicated his place, moving between the north and north-east elms, and overcoming the night by the little oak. The sun did not rise and sink; he travelled round an immense circle.

In the winter mornings the sun rose between the young oak and the third group of elms, red and vapour hung, and his beams presently shot through the window to the logs on the kitchen hearth. He sank then between the south-westerly ashes and the orchard, rising from the wall of the Downs, and sinking again behind it. At noon he was just over, only a little higher than the great southern oak. All day long the outer side of the garden wall was in shadow, and at night the northern sky was black to the horizon. The travelling dawn was not visible: the sun rose and sank, and was only visible through half of the great circle. The cocks crowed at four in the afternoon, and the rooks hastened to the jungle.

But by-and-by, when the giant Orion shone with his full width grasping all the sky, then in the mornings the sun's rising began to shift backwards— first to the edge of the third group of elms, then straight up the road, then to the little oak. In the afternoon, the place of setting likewise shifted backwards to the north, and came behind the orchard. At noon he was twice as high as the southern oak, and every day at noontide the shadows gradually shortened. The nightingale sang in the musical April night, the cowslips opened, and the bees hummed over the meadows.

Last of all, the sweet turtle-doves cooed and wooed; beauteous June wearing her roses came, and the sun shone at the highest point of his great circle. Then you could not look at him unless up through the boughs of a tree. Round the zodiac of the elms, and the little oak, the great oak, the ashes, and the orchard, the sun revolved; and the house, and the garden path by the strawberries—the best place to see—were in the centre of his golden ring.

The sward on the path on which Bevis used to lie and gaze up in the summer evening, was real, and tangible; the earth under was real; and so too the elms, the oak, the ash-trees, were real and tangible—things to be touched, and known to be. Now like these, the mind, stepping from the one to the other, knew and almost felt the stars to be real and not mere specks of light, but things that were there by day over the elms as well as by night, and not apparitions of the evening departing at the twittering of the swallows. They were real, and the touch of his mind felt to them.

He could not, as he reclined on the garden path by the strawberries, physically reach to and feel the oak; but he could feel the oak in his mind, and so from the oak, stepping beyond it, he felt the stars. They were always there by day as well as by night. The Bear did not sink, the sun in summer only dipped, and his reflection—the travelling dawn—shone above him, and so from these unravelling out the enlarging sky, he felt as well as knew that neither the stars nor the sun ever rose or set. The heavens were always around and with him. The strawberries and the sward of the garden path, he himself reclining there, were moving through, among, and between the stars; they were as much by him as the strawberry leaves.

By day the sun, as he sat down under the oak, was as much by him as the boughs of the great tree. It was by him like the swallows.

The heavens were as much a part of life as the elms, the oak, the house, the garden and orchard, the meadow and the brook. They were no more separated than the furniture of the parlour, than the old oak chair where he sat, and saw the new moon shine over the mulberry-tree. They were neither above nor beneath, they were in the same place with him; just as when you walk in a wood the trees are all about you, on a plane with you, so he felt the constellations and the sun on a plane with him, and that he was moving among them as the earth rolled on, like them, with them, in the stream of space.

The day did not shut off the stars, the night did not shut off the sun; they were always there. Not that he always thought of them, but they were never dismissed. When he listened to the greenfinches sweetly calling in the hawthorn, or when he read his books, poring over the Odyssey, with the sunshine on the wall, they were always there; there was no severance. Bevis lived not only out to the finches and the swallows, to the far-away hills, but he lived out and felt out to the sky.

It was living, not thinking. He lived it, never thinking, as the finches live their sunny life in the happy days of June. There was magic in everything, blades of grass and stars, the sun and the stones upon the ground.

The green path by the strawberries was the centre of the world, and round about it by day *and* night the sun circled in a magical golden ring.

Under the oak on New Formosa that warm summer night, Bevis looked up as he reclined at the white pure light of Lyra, and forgot everything but the consciousness of living, feeling up to and beyond it. The earth and the water, the oak, went away; he himself went away: his mind joined itself and was linked up through ethereal space to its beauty.

Bevis, as you know did not think: we have done the thinking, the analysis for him. He felt and was lost in the larger consciousness of the heavens.

The moon moved, and with it the shadow of the cliff on the water beneath, a planet rose eastwards over their new Nile, water-fowl clucked as they flew over.

Kaak! Kaak! Another heron called and his discordant piercing yell sounded over the water, seeming to penetrate to the distant and shadowy shores. The noise awoke him, and he went down to the hut. Mark was firm asleep, the lantern burned in the niche; Pan had been curled up by the bedside, but lifted his head and wagged his tail, thumping the floor as he entered. Bevis let down the curtain closing the doorway, put out the lantern, and in three minutes was as firm as Mark. After some time, Pan rose quietly and went out, slipping under the curtain, which fell back into its place when he had passed.

Chapter Two
New Formosa—The Raft

They did not get up till the sun was high, and when Mark lifted the curtain a robin flew from the table just outside, where he had been picking up the crumbs, across to the gate-post in the stockade. The gate had not been shut—Pan was lying by it under the fence, which cast a shadow in the morning and evening.

"Pan!" said Mark; the lazy spaniel wagged his tail, but did not come.

"I shall go and finish the sun-dial while you get the breakfast," said Bevis. It was Mark's turn to-day, and as he went out at the gate he stooped and patted Pan, who looked up with speaking affection in his eyes, and stretched himself to his full length in utter lassitude.

Bevis drew the line from the gnomon to the mark he had made the night before, this was the noon or meridian. Then he drew another from the mark where the shadow had fallen at four o'clock in the afternoon. The space between the two he divided into four equal divisions and drew lines for one, two, and three o'clock. They were nearly two inches apart, and having measured them exactly he added four more beyond, up to eight o'clock, as he thought the sun set about eight; and then seven more on the other side where the shadow would fall in the morning, as he supposed the sun rose about five.

His hours, therefore, ranged from five till eight, and he added half lines to show the half-hours. When it was done the shadow of the gnomon touched the nine, so he shouted to Mark that it was nine o'clock. He knew that his dial was not correct, because the hour lines ought to be drawn so as to show the time every day of the year, and his would only show it for a short while.

How often he had drawn a pencil-mark along the edge of the shadow on the window-frame in the south window of the parlour! In the early spring, while the bitter east wind raged, he used to sit in the old oak chair at the south window, where every now and then the warm sunshine fell from a break in the ranks of the marching clouds. Out of the wind the March sun was warm and pleasant, and while it lasted he dreamed over his books, his Odyssey, his Faust, his Quixote, his Shakespeare's poems.

About eleven the sunshine generally came, and he drew a line on the frame to mark the hour. But in two days the verge of the shadow had gone on, and at eleven left the pencil-mark behind. He marked it again and again, it went on as the sun, coming up higher and higher, described a larger ring. So with his pencil-lines on the window-frame he measured the spring and graduated the coming of summer, till the eggs in the goldfinch's nest in the apple-tree were hard set. From this he knew that his sun-dial was not correct, for as the sun now each day described a circle slightly less than before, the shadow too would change and the error increase. Still the dial would divide the day for them, and they could work and arrange their plans by it.

Had they had the best chronometer ever made it would have been of no further use. All time is artificial, and their time was correct to them.

Mark shouted that breakfast was ready, so he went down, and they sat at the table under the awning.

"Pan's been thieving," said Mark. "There was half a damper on the table last night, and it was gone this morning, and two potatoes which we left, and I put the skin of the kangaroo on the fence, and that's gone—"

"He couldn't eat the skin, could he?" said Bevis. "Pan, come here, sir."

"Look at him," said Mark, "he's stuffed so full he can hardly crawl—if he was hungry he would come quick."

"So he would. Pan, you old rascal! What have you done with the kangaroo skin, sir?"

Pan wagged his tail and looked from one to the other; the sound of their voices was stern, but he detected the goodwill in it, and that they were not really angry.

"And the damper?"

"And the potatoes? And just as if you could eat leather and fur, sir!"

Pan put his fore-paws on Bevis's knee, and looked up as if he had done something very clever.

"Pooh! Get away," said Bevis, "you're a false old rascal. Mark, cut him some of that piece of bacon presently."

"So I will—and I'll put the things higher up," said Mark. "I'll drive some nails into the posts and make a shelf, then you'll be done, sir."

Pan, finding there was nothing more for him to eat, walked slowly back to the fence and let himself fall down.

"Too lazy to lie down properly," said Bevis.

After breakfast they put up the shelf, and placed the eatables on it out of Pan's reach, and then taking their towels started for their bath.

"It might have been a rat," said Mark; "that looks gnawn." He kicked the jack's head which had been cut off, being shattered with the shot, and thrown down outside the gate. "But Pan's very full, else he would come," for the spaniel did not follow as usual. So soon as they had gone the robin returned to the table, took what he liked, ventured into the hut for a minute, and then perched on the fence above Pan before returning to the wood.

Bevis and Mark swam and waded to Serendib again. There was a light ripple this morning from the south-east, and a gentle breeze which cooled the day. They said they would hasten to construct the raft, so as to be able to shoot the water-fowl, but Bevis wanted first to try the matchlock with ball now he had fitted it with a sight. He fired three times at the teak-tree, to which Mark pinned a small piece of paper as a bull's-eye, and at thirty yards he hit the tree very well, but not the paper. The bullets were all below, the nearest about four inches from the bull's-eye. Still it was much better shooting.

He then loaded the gun with shot, and took it and a hatchet—the two were a good load—intending to look in the wood for suitable timber, and keep the gun by him for a possible shot at something. But just as he had got ready, and Pan shaking himself together began to drag his idle body after him, he thought Mark looked dull. It was Mark's turn to cook, and he had already got the fire alight under the teak.

"I won't go," he said; "I'll stop and help you. Things are stupid by yourself."

"Fishing is very stupid, by yourself," said Mark.

"Let's make a rule," said Bevis. "Everybody helps everybody instead of going by themselves."

"So we will," said Mark, only too glad, and the new rule was agreed to, but as they could not both shoot at once, it was understood that in this the former contract was to stand, and each was to have the matchlock a day to himself. The pot and the saucepan, with the kangaroo and the jack were soon on, and they found that boiling had one great advantage over roasting, they could pile on sticks and go away for some time, instead of having to watch and turn the roast.

They found a good many small trees and poles such as they wanted not far from home, and among the rest three dead larches which had been snapped by a tornado. These dry trees were lighter and would float better than green timber. For the larger beams, or foundation of the raft, they chose aspen and poplar, and for the cross-joists firs, and by dinner-time they had collected nearly enough.

It was half-past one by the sun-dial when Mark began to prepare the table; Bevis had gone to haul the catamaran planks up to the place where the raft was to be built. Under one of the planks, as he turned it over, there was a little lizard; the creature at first remained still as if dead, then not being touched ran off quickly, grasping the grass sideways with its claws as a monkey grasps a branch. With the end of a plank under each arm Bevis hauled these across to the other materials.

This time they had a nicer meal than any they had prepared: fish and game; the kangaroo was white and juicy, almost as white as a chicken, as a young summer rabbit is if cooked soon after it is shot. It is the only time indeed when a rabbit does not taste like a rabbit. If you tasted a young one fresh shot in summer, you would not care to eat them in winter, and discover that the frost improvement theory is an invention of poulterers who cannot keep their stock unless it is bitterly cold. There was sufficient left for supper, and a bone or two for Pan. The chopping they had done made them idle, and they agreed not to work again till the evening; they lounged about like Pan till the time appointed to look for Charlie's signal.

When they went up on the cliff it was a quarter-past three by the dial, so they sat down in the shade of the oak where the brambles behind would prevent their being seen against the sky line. After awhile Mark crept on all fours to the sun-dial, and said it was half-past three, and suddenly exclaimed that the time was going backwards.

The shadow of the gnomon slipped the wrong way; he looked up and saw a light cloud passing over the sun. Bevis had often seen the same thing in March, sitting by the southern window, when the shadow ran back from his pencil-line on the window-frame as the clouds began again to cover up the blue roof. Charlie was rather late to-day, but he gave the signal according to promise: they saw him look a long while and then move away.

Presently, while Mark was preparing the tea, Bevis got the matchlock to practise again. They were always ready for tea, and it is a curious fact that those who live much out of doors and work hard, like gold-diggers abroad, and our own reapers at home labouring among the golden wheat, prefer it to anything while actually engaged and in the midst of their toil; but not afterwards.

Bevis set up the rest in the gateway of the stockade, and took aim at the piece of paper pinned on the teak-tree, which was between fifty and sixty yards distant. Twice he fired and missed the teak: then he let Mark try, and Mark also missed; and a third time he fired himself. None of the four bullets struck either the tree or the branches; so, though they could hit it at thirty yards, they could not rely on their gun at sixty.

Directly after tea they began to work again at the preparations for the raft, cutting some more poles and sawing up those they had already into the proper lengths. Sawing is very hard work, causing a continual strain upon the same muscles, with no change of position as possible while chopping, and they were obliged to do it by shifts, one working so long and then the other. The raft was to be twelve feet long and five wide. The beams for the foundation gave them most trouble to procure, being largest, and not every tree was exactly the size they wished.

They laboured on into the moonlight, which grew brighter every night as the moon increased, and did not cease till all the materials were ready; the long beams of aspen and poplar placed side by side (on rollers) and near these short cross-pieces of fir with holes bored for the nails, then a row of long fir poles, and the short lengths of plank to form the deck. Everything was just ready for fitting together. It cost them some self-denial to wait till all was thus prepared instead of at once beginning to nail the frame together.

There is something in driving in a nail tempting to the wrist; when the board is ready, the gimlet-hole made, and the hammer at hand, the physical mind desires to complete the design. They resisted it, because they knew that they should really complete the raft much quicker by getting every portion of the frame ready before commencing to fix it. They did not recognise how tired they were till they started for the hut; their backs, so long bent over the sawing, had stiffened in that position, and pained them as they straightened the sinews to stand upright; their fingers were crooked from continually grasping the handles; they staggered about as they walked, for their stiff limbs were not certain of foothold, and jerked them where the ground was uneven.

Mark sat down to light the fire in the courtyard, for they wanted some more tea; Bevis sat by him. They were dog-tired. Looking in the larder to lay out the supper, Mark saw the mushrooms which had been forgotten; he hunted out the gridiron, and put two handsful of them on. Now the sight of these savoury mushrooms raised their fainting spirits more than the most solid food, and they began to talk again. While these were doing, Bevis cut Pan a slice of the cooked bacon on the shelf; it was rather fat, and pampered Pan, after mumbling it over in his chops, carried it just outside the fence, and came back trying to look as if he had eaten it.

With the mushrooms they made a capital supper, but they were still very tired. Bevis got out his journal, but he only wrote down "Friday," and then put it away, remarking that he must soon write a letter home.

Even cards could not amuse them, they were so tired; but the cry of a heron roused Bevis a little, and he took the matchlock and loaded it with shot, to see if he could shoot it and get the plumes.

"Heron's plumes were thought a good deal of in our day where we lived, you know. Didn't the knights use to wear them?" he said. "Herons are very hard to shoot."

Mark came with him and the spaniel, and they walked softly down the path, now well-worn, and peered over the moonlit water, but the heron was not on the island, nor in sight. He was probably on some of the lesser islets among the shallows, so they returned home and immediately went to bed, quite knocked up. Pan curled round by the bedside for about an hour, then he got up and slipped out under the curtain into the moonlight.

In the morning when they went to bathe there was a mist over the water, which curled along and gathered thicker in places, once quite hiding Serendib, and then clearing away and drawing towards the unknown river. The water was very warm.

They then began to nail the raft together. On the long thick beams they placed short cross-pieces of fir close together and touching; over these long poles of fir lengthways, also touching; lastly, short planks across making the deck. There were thus four layers, for they knew that rafts sink a good deal and float deep, especially when the wood is green, as you may see a bough, or a tree-trunk in the brook quite half immersed as it goes by on the current. It was built on rollers, because Bevis, consulting his book, read how Ulysses rigged his vessel:—

And roll'd on levers, launch'd her in the deep.

And, reflecting, he foresaw that the raft being so heavy would be otherwise difficult to move.

The spot where they had built her was a little below where Bevis leaped on shore on the evening of the battle. The ground sloped to the water, which was rather deep. By noon the raft was ready—for they had decided to complete the rigging, bulwarks, and fittings when she was afloat—and with levers they began to heave her down.

She moved slowly, rumbling and crushing the rollers into the sward. By degrees with a "Yeo! Heave-ho!" at which Pan set up a barking, the raft approached the water, and the forward part entered it. The weight of the rest prevented the front from floating, forcing it straight under the surface till the water rose a third of the way along the deck.

"Yeo! Heave-ho!"

Yow-wow-wow! Pan, who had been idle all the morning lying on the ground, jumped round and joined the chorus.

"Now! Heave-ho! She's going! Now!"

"Stop!"

"Why?"

"She'll slip away—right out!"

"So she will."

"Run for a rope."

"All right."

Mark ran for a piece of cord from the hut. The raft as it were hung on the edge more than half in and heaving up as the water began to float her, and they saw that if they gave another push she would go out and the impetus of her weight would carry her away from the shore out of reach. Mark soon returned with the cord, which was fastened to two stout nails.

"Ready?"

"Go!"

One strong heave with the levers and the raft slid off the last roller, rose to the surface, the water slipping off the deck each side, and floated. Seizing the cord as it ran out, they brought her to, and Mark instantly jumped on board. He danced and kicked up his heels—Pan followed him and ran round the edge of the raft, sniffing over at the water. The raft floated first-rate, and the deck, owing to the three layers under it, was high above the surface. These layers, too, gave the advantage that they could walk to the very verge without depressing it to the water. Mark got off and held the cord while Bevis got on, then they both shouted, "Serendib!"

They pushed off with long poles, like punting, Pan swam out so soon as they had started, and was hauled on board. A short way from shore the channel was so deep the poles would not reach the bottom, but the raft had way on her and continued to move, and paddling with the poles they kept up the slow movement till they reached the shallows. Thence to Serendib they poled along, one each side. The end of the raft crashed in among the willow boughs, and the jerk as it grounded almost threw them down. Pan leaped off directly, and they followed, fastening the raft by the cord or painter to the willows.

"Nothing but blue gums," said Mark, who led the way. "What are these?" pointing to the wild parsnips or "gix" which rose as high as their heads, with hollow-jointed stalks and broad heads of minute white flowers.

"It's a new kind of bamboo," said Bevis. "Listen! Pan's hunting out the moorhens again. This is some kind of spice—you sniff—the air is heavy with the scent, just as it always is in the tropics."

As they pushed along they shook the meadowsweet flowers which grew very thickly, and the heavy perfume rose up. In a willow stole or blue gum Mark found the nest of a sedge bird, but empty, the young birds hatched long since.

"Mind you don't step on a crocodile," said Mark, "you can't see a bit."

The ground was so matted with vegetation that their feet never touched the earth at all, they trampled on grasses, rushes, meadowsweet, and triangular fluted carex sedges. Sometimes they approached the shore and saw several empty nests of moorhens and coots, but just above the level of the water. Sometimes their uncertain course led them in the interior to avoid thickets of elder. If they paused a moment they could hear the rustling as water-fowl rushed away. Pan had gone beyond hearing now. Presently they came on a small pool surrounded with sedges—a black-headed bunting watched them from a branch opposite.

"No fish," said Bevis: they could see the bottom of the shallow water. "Herons and kingfishers have had them of course."

Crashing through the new bamboos they at last reached the southern extremity of the island, where the shallow sea was covered with the floating leaves of weeds, over which blue dragon-flies flew to and fro.

"Everything's gone to the river again," said Mark; "and where's Pan? He's gone too, I dare say."

A short bark in that direction in a few minutes made them look at an islet round which reed-mace rose in a tall fringe, and there was Pan creeping up out of the weeds, dragging his body after him on to the firm ground. He set up a great yelping on the islet.

"Something's been there," said Bevis. "Perhaps it's the thing that makes the curious wave. Pan! Pan!"—whistling. Pan would not come: he was too excited. "We must come here in the evening," said Bevis, "and make an ambush. There's heaps of moorhens."

As there was nothing else to see on Serendib they worked a way between the blue gums back to the raft, and re-embarked for New Formosa. Just before they landed Pan dashed into the water from Serendib and swam to them. He did not seem quite himself, he looked as if he had done something out of the common and could not tell them.

"Was it a crocodile?" said Mark, stroking him. Pan whined, as much as to say, "I wish I could tell you," and then to give vent to his excitement he rushed into the wood.

Chapter Three
New Formosa—No Hope of Returning

After fastening the raft they returned towards the hut, for they were hungry now, and knew it was late, when Pan set up such a tremendous barking that they first listened, and then went to see. The noise led them to the green knoll where the rabbit burries were, and they saw Pan running round under the great oak thickly grown with ivy, in which Bevis had seen the wood-pigeons alight.

They went to the oak, it was very large and old, the branches partly dead and hung with ivy; they walked round and examined the ground, but could see no trace of anything. Mark hurled a fragment of a dead bough up into the ivy, it broke and came rustling down again, but nothing flew out. There did not seem to be anything in the tree.

"The squirrels," said Bevis, suddenly remembering.

"Why, of course," said Mark. "How stupid of us—Pan, you're a donk."

They left the oak and again went homewards: now Pan had been quite quiet while they were looking on the ground and up into the tree, but directly he understood that they had given up the search he set up barking again and would not follow. At the hut Bevis went in to cut some rashers from the bacon which had not been cooked and Mark ran up on the cliff to see the time.

It was already two o'clock—the work on the raft and the voyage to Serendib had taken up the morning. Bevis showed Mark where some mice had gnawed the edge of the uncooked bacon which had been lying in the store-room on the top of a number of thing's. Mark said once he found a tomtit on the shelf pecking at the food they left there, just like a tomtit's impudence!

"Rashers are very good," said Bevis, "if you haven't got to cook them." It was his turn, and he was broiling himself as well as the bacon.

"Macaroni eats his raw," said Mark. They had often seen John Young eating thick slices of raw bacon in the shed as he sat at luncheon. "Horrible cannibal—he's worse than Pan, who won't touch it cooked."

He looked outside the gate—there was the slice of the cooked bacon Bevis had cut for the spaniel lying on the ground. Pan had not even taken the trouble to put it in his larder. But something else had gnawed at it.

"A rat's been here," said Mark. "Don't you remember the jack's head?"

"And mice in the cave," said Bevis.

"And a tomtit on the shelf."

"And a robin on the table."

"And a wagtail was in the court yesterday."

"A wren comes on the stockade."

"Spiders up there," said Mark, pointing to the corner of the hut where there was a web.

"Tarantulas," said Bevis, "and mosquitoes in the evening."

"Everything comes to try and eat us up," said Mark.

The moment man takes up his residence all the creatures of the wood throng round him, attracted by the crumbs from his hand, or the spoil that his labour affords. Hawks dart down on his poultry, weasels creep in to the hen's eggs, mice traverse the house, rats hasten round the sty, snakes come in for the milk, spiders for the flies, flies for the sugar, toads crawl into the cellar, snails trail up the wall, gnats arrive in the evening, robins, wrens, tomtits, wagtails enter the courtyard, starlings and sparrows nest in the roof, swallows in the chimney, martins under the eaves, rabbits in the garden among the potatoes—a favourite cover with all game—blackbirds to the cherry-trees, bullfinches to the fruit-buds, tomtits take the very bees even, cats and dogs are a matter of course, still they live on man's labour.

The sandy spot by the cliff had not been frequented by anything till the cave was made and the hut built, and already the mice were with them, and while Mark was saying that everything came to eat them up a wasp flew under the awning and settled on the table.

"Frances ought to do this," said Bevis, hot and cross, as amateur cooks always are. "Here, give me some mushrooms, they'll be nice. Don't you wish she was here?"

"Frances!" said Mark in a tone of horror. "No, that I don't!"

In the afternoon they did nothing but wait for Charlie's signal, which he faithfully gave, and then they idled about till tea. Pan did not come back till tea, and then he wagged his tail and looked very mysterious.

"What have you been doing, sir?" said Bevis. Pan wagged and wagged and gobbled up all the buttered damper they gave him.

"Now, just see," said Mark. He got up and cut a slice of the cold half-cooked bacon from the shelf. Pan took it, rolled his great brown eyes, showing the whites at the corners, wagged his tail very short like the pendulum of a small clock, and walked outside the gate with it. Then he came back and begged for more buttered damper.

After tea they worked again at the raft, putting in the bulwarks and carried the chest down to it for the locker. For a sail they meant to use the rug which was now hung up for an awning, and to put up a roof thatched with sedges in its place. The sun sank before they had finished, and they then got the matchlock—it was Mark's day—and went into ambush by the glade to see if they could shoot another rabbit. Pan had to be tied and hit once or twice, he wanted to race after the squirrels.

They sat quiet in ambush till they were weary, and the moon was shining brightly, but the rabbits did not venture out. The noise Pan had made barking after the squirrels had evidently alarmed them, and they could not forget it.

"Very likely he's been scratching at the burries too," whispered Bevis, as the little bats flew round the glade, passing scarcely a yard in front of them like large flies. "He shan't leave us again like he did this afternoon."

It was of no use to stay there any longer, so they went quietly round the shore of the island, and seeing something move at the edge of the weeds, though they could not distinguish what, for the willow boughs hung over, Mark aimed and fired. At the report they heard water-fowl scuttling away, and running to the spot Pan brought out two moorhens, one quite dead and the other wounded.

"There," said Bevis, "you've shot every single thing."

"Well, why don't you use shot?—you'll never kill anything with bullets."

"But I will," said Bevis; "I will hit something with bullets. The people in India can hit a sparrow, why can't I? It's my turn to-morrow."

But after supper, bringing out his journal, he found to-morrow was Sunday.

"No, I can't shoot till Monday. Mamma would not like shooting on Sunday."

"No—nor chopping."

"No," said Bevis, "we mustn't do any work."

All the while they were on the island they were, in principle, disobedient, and crossing the wishes of the home authorities. Yet they resolved not to shoot on the Sunday, because the people at home would not like it. When Bevis had entered the launching of the raft and the voyage to Serendib in the journal, they skinned the moorhens and prepared them for cooking.

"This cooking is horrible," said Mark.

"Hateful," said Bevis; "I told you we ought to have Frances."

"O! no; she would want her own way. She wants everything just as she likes, and if she can't have it, she won't do anything."

"There, it's done," said Bevis. "What we want is a slave."

"Of course—two or three slaves, to work and chop wood, and fetch the water."

"Hit them if they don't," said Bevis.

"Like we hit Pan."

"Tie them to a tree and lash them."

"Hard."

"Harder."

"Great marks on their backs."

"Howling!"

"Jolly!"

They played two games at bezique under the awning, and drank the last drop of sherry mixed with water.

"Everything's going," said Bevis. "There's no more sherry, and more than half the flour's gone, and Pan had the last bit of butter on the damper at tea—"

"There ought to be roots on the island," said Mark. "People eat roots on islands."

"Don't think there are any here," said Bevis. "This island is too old for any to grow; it's like Australia, a kind of grey-bearded place with nothing but kangaroos."

Soon afterwards they drew down the curtain and went to sleep. As usual, Pan waited till they were firm asleep, and then slipped out into the moonlight. He was lounging in the courtyard when they got up. By the sun-dial it was eight, and having had breakfast, and left the fire banked up under ashes—wood embers keep alight a long time like that—they went down to bathe.

"How quiet it is!" said Mark. "I believe it's quieter."

"It does seem so," said Bevis.

The still water glittered under the sun as the light south-east air drew over it, and they could hear a single lark singing on the mainland, somewhere out of sight.

"Somehow we can swim ever so much better here than we used to at home," said Mark, as they were dressing again.

"Ever so much," said Bevis; "twice as far." This was a fact, whether from the continuous outdoor life, or from greater confidence now they were entirely alone.

"How I should like to punch somebody!" said Mark, hitting out his fist.

"My muscles are like iron," said Bevis, holding out his arm.

"Well, they are hard," said Mark, feeling Bevis's arm. So were his own.

"It's living on an island," said Bevis. "There's no bother, and nobody says you're not to do anything."

"Only there's the potatoes to clean. What a nuisance they are!"

They began to dimly perceive that, perhaps, after all, women might be of some use on the earth. They had to go back to the hut to get the dinner ready.

"The rats have been at the potatoes," said Bevis. "Just look!"

Mark came, and saw where something had gnawed the potatoes.

"And lots are gone," he said. "I'm sure there's a lot gone since yesterday."

"Pan, why don't you kill the rats?" cried Bevis. Pan looked up, as much as to say, "Teach me my business, indeed."

"Bother!" said Mark.

"Bother!" said Bevis.

"Hateful!"

"Yah!" They flung down knives and potatoes.

"Would the raft be wrong on Sunday?"

"Not if it was only a little bit," said Bevis.

"Just to Pearl Island?"

"No—that wouldn't hurt."

"Let the cooking stop."

"Come on."

Away they ran to the raft, and pushed off, making Pan come with them, that he should not disturb the rabbits again. The spaniel was so lazy, he would not even follow them till he was compelled. He sat gravely on the raft by the chest, or locker, while they poled along the shore, for it was too deep to pole in the middle of the channel. But at the southern end of New Formosa the water shoaled, and they could leave the shore. One standing one side, and one the other, they thrust the raft along out among the islets, till they reached Pearl Island, easily distinguished by the glittering mussel shells.

A summer snipe left the islet as they came near, circled round, and approached again, but finding they were still there, sought another strand. Pan ran round the islet, sniffing at the water's edge, and then, finding nothing, returned to the raft and sat down on his haunches. The water on one side of Pearl Island was not more than four or five inches deep a long way out, and it was from this shelving sand that the crows got the mussels. They carried them up on the bank and left the shells, which fell over open, and the wind blew the sand into them. They found one very large shell, a span long, and took it as spoil.

There was nothing else but a few small fossils like coiled snakes turned to stone. Next they poled across to the islet off the extremity of Serendib, where Pan had made such a noise. To get there they had to go some distance round, as it was so shallow. They poled the raft in among the reed-mace or bamboos, which rose above their heads out of the water besides that part of the stalk under the surface. The reed-mace is like a bulrush, but three times as tall, and larger. They cut a number of these as spoils, and then landed. Pan showed a little more activity here, but not much. He sniffed round the water's edge, but soon returned and stretched himself on the raft.

"He can't smell anything here to-day," said Bevis. "There's a halcyon."

A kingfisher went by, straight for New Formosa. The marks of moorhens' feet were numerous on the shore and just under water, showing how calm it had been lately, for waves would have washed up the bottom and covered them. The islet was very small, merely the ridge of a bank, so they pushed off again. Passing the bamboos, they paused and looked at them—the tall stalks rose up around as if they were really in a thicket of bamboo.

"Hark!"

They spoke together. It was the stern and solemn note of a bell tolling. It startled them in the silence of the New Sea. The sound came from the hills, and they knew at once it was the bell at the church big Jack went to. The chimes, thin perhaps and weak, had been lost in the hills, but the continuous toll of the five minutes bell penetrated through miles of air. So in the bush men call each other by constantly repeating the same hollow note, "Cooing," and in that way the human voice can be heard at an extraordinary distance. Each wave of sound drives on its predecessor, and is driven by the wave that follows, till the widening circle strikes the shore of the distant ear.

"Ship's bell," said Bevis presently, as they listened. "In these latitudes the air is so clear you hear ships' bells a hundred miles."

"Pirates?"

"No; pirates would not make a noise."

"Frigate?"

"Most likely."

"Any chance of our being taken off and rescued?"

"Not the least," said Bevis. "These islands are not down on any chart. She'll be two hundred miles away by tea-time. Bound for Kerguelen, perhaps."

"We shall never be found," said Mark. "No hope for us."

"No hope at all," said Bevis. They poled towards Serendib, intending to circumnavigate that island. By the time they had gone half-way, the bell ceased.

"Now listen," said Mark. "Isn't it still?"

They had lifted their poles from the water, and there was not a sound (the lark had long finished), nothing but the drip, drip of the drops from the poles, and the slight rustle as the heavy raft dragged over a weed. They could almost hear the silence, as in the quiet night sometimes, if listening intently, you may hear a faint rushing, the sound of your own blood reverberating in the hollow of the ear; in the day it needs a shell to collect it.

"It is very curious," said Bevis. "But we have not heard a sound of anybody till that bell."

"No more we have."

There had been sounds quite audible, but absorbed in their island life they had not heard them. To-day they were not busy. The recognition of the silence which the bell had caused seemed to widen the distance between them and home.

"We are a long way from home—really," said Bevis.

"Awful long way."

"But really?"

"Of course—really. It feels farther to-day."

They could touch the bottom with their poles all the way round Serendib, but as before, in crossing to New Formosa, had to give a stronger push on the edge of the deep channel, to carry them over to the shallower water. It was too late now to cook the moorhens, and they resolved to be contented with rashers, and see if they could not get some more mushrooms. Directly they got near the hut, Pan rushed inside the fence and began barking. When they reached the place he was sniffing round, and every now and then giving a sharp short bark, as if he knew there was something, but could not make it out.

"Rats," said Mark, "and they've taken the bacon bits Pan left outside the gate."

Pan did not trouble any more when they came in. After preparing the rashers, and looking at the sun-dial, by which it was noon, Bevis went to look for mushrooms on the knoll, while Mark managed the dinner. Bevis had to go round to get to the knoll, and not wishing to disturb the rabbits more than necessary, made Pan keep close to his heels.

But when he reached the open glade, Pan broke away, and rushing towards the ivy-clad oak, set up a barking. Bevis angrily called him, but Pan would not come, so he picked up a stick, but instead of returning to heel, Pan dashed into the underwood, and Bevis could hear him barking a long way across the island. He thought it was the squirrels, and looked about for mushrooms. There were plenty, and he soon filled his handkerchief. As he approached the hut, Mark came to meet him, and said that happening to look on the shelf he had missed the piece of cooked bacon left there,—had Bevis moved it?

Chapter Four
New Formosa—Something has been to the Hut

"No," said Bevis. "I left it there last night; don't you remember I cut a piece for Pan, and he would not eat it?"

"Yes; well, it's gone. Come and see." They went to the shelf—the cooked bacon was certainly gone; nor was it on the ground or in any other part of the hut or cave.

"Pan must have dragged it down," said Bevis; "and yet it's too high, and besides, he didn't care for it."

"He could not jump so high," said Mark. "Besides, he has been with us all the time."

"So he has." They had kept Pan close by them, ever since he disturbed the kangaroos so much. "Then, it could not have been Pan."

"And I don't see how rats could climb up, either," said Mark. "The posts," (to which the shelf was fixed) "are upright—"

"Mice can run up the leg of a chair," said Bevis.

"That's only a short way; this is—let me see—why it's higher than your shoulder."

"If it was not Pan, nor rats, what could it be?" said Bevis.

"Something's been here," said Mark; "Pan could smell it when he came in."

"Something was up in the oak," said Bevis, "and now he's gone racing light to the other end of the island."

"Something took the bit of bacon on the ground."

"And gnawed the jack's head."

"And had the piece of damper."

"And took the potatoes."

"Took the potatoes twice—the cooked ones and the raw ones."

"It's very curious."

"I don't believe Pan could have jumped up—he would have shaken the other things off the shelf, too, if he had got his great paws on."

"It must have been something," said Bevis; "things could not go off by themselves."

"There's something in the island we don't know," said Mark, nodding his head up and down, as was his way at times when upset or full of an idea.

"Lions!" said Bevis. "Lions could get up."

"We should have heard them roar."

"Tigers?"

"They would have killed Pan."

"But you think there's one in the reeds."

"Yes, but he did not come here."

"Boas?"

"No."

"Panthers?"

"No."

"Something out of the curious wave you saw?"

"Perhaps. Well, it *is* curious now, isn't it?" said Mark. "Just think; first, Pan could not have had it, and then rats could not have had it, but it's gone."

"Pan, Pan," shouted Bevis sternly, as the spaniel came in at the gateway hesitatingly; "come here." The spaniel crouched, knowing that he should have a thrashing.

"See if anything's bitten him," said Mark. "What have you been after, sir?"

He examined Pan carefully; there were no signs of a fight on him—nothing but cleavers or the seeds of goose-grass clinging to his coat. Bang—thump—thump! yow! Pan had his thrashing, and crept after them to and fro, not even daring to curl himself up in a corner, but dragging himself along on the ground behind them.

"Think," said Mark, as he turned the mushrooms on the gridiron; "now, what was it?"

"Not a fox?" said Bevis.

"No; foxes would not swim out here; there are plenty of rabbits for them in the jungle on the mainland."

"Nor eagles?"

"No."

"Might be a cat."

"But there are no cats on the island, and, besides, cats would not take bacon when there were the two moorhens on the shelf."

"No; Pan would have had the moorhens too, if it had been him."

"So would anything, and that's why it's so curious."

"Nobody could have come here, could they?" said Bevis. "The punt's at the bottom, and the Pinta's chained up—"

"And we must have seen them if they swam off."

"Nobody can swim," said Bevis, "except you and me and the governor."

"No," said Mark, "no more they can—not even Big Jack."

"Nobody in all the place but us. It could not have been the governor, because if he found the hut he would have stopped to see who lived in it."

"Of course he would. And besides, he could not have come without our knowing it; we are always about."

"Always about," said Bevis, "and we should have seen footsteps."

"Or heard a splashing."

"And Pan would not bark at him," said Bevis. "No, it could not have been any one; it must have been something."

"Something," repeated Mark.

"And very likely out of your magic wave."

"But what *could* it be out of the wave?"

"I can't think; something magic. It doesn't matter."

They had dinner, and then, as usual, went up on the cliff to wait for Charlie's signal.

"I shall try and catch some perch to-morrow," said Mark, "if there's any wind. We're always eating the same thing."

"Every day," said Bevis, "and the cooking is the greatest hatefulness ever known."

"Takes up so much time."

"Makes you hot and horrid."

"Vile."

"It wants Frances, as I said."

"No, thank you; I wish Jack would have her."

Mark looked through the telescope for Charlie, and then swept the shores of the New Sea.

"How could anything get to our island?" he said. "Nothing could get to it."

From the elevation of the cliff they saw and felt the isolation of their New Formosa.

"It was out of your magic wave," said Bevis; "something magic."

"But you put the wizard's foot on the gate?"

"So I did, but perhaps I did not draw it quite right; I'll do it again. But rats are made to gnaw the lines off sometimes, and let magic things in."

"Draw another in ink."

"So I will. There's a sea-swallow."

"There's two."

"There's four or five."

The white sea-swallows passed them, going down the water, coming from the south. They flew a few yards above the surface, in an irregular line—an easy flight, so easy they scarcely seemed to know where each flap of the wing would carry them.

"There will be a storm."

"A tornado."

"Not yet—the sky's clear."

"But we must keep a watch, and be careful how we sail on the raft."

The appearance of the sea-swallow or tern in inland waters is believed, like that of the gull, to indicate tempest, though the sea-swallows usually come in the finest of weather.

"There's Charlie. There are two—three," said Mark, snatching up the telescope. "It's Val and Cecil. Charlie's waving his handkerchief."

"There, it's all right," said Bevis.

"They are pointing this way," said Mark. "They're talking about us. Can they see us?"

"No, the brambles would not let them."

"I dare say they're as cross as cross," said Mark.

"They want to come. I don't know," said Bevis, as if considering.

"Know what?" said Mark sharply.

"That it's altogether nice of us."

"Rubbish—as if they would have let *us* come."

"Still, we are not them, and we might if they would not."

"Now, don't you be stupid," said Mark appealingly. "Don't *you* go stupid."

"No," said Bevis, laughing; "but they must come after we have done."

"O! yes, of course. See, they're going towards the firs: there, they're going to cross the Nile. I know, don't you see, they're going round the New Sea, like we did, to try and find us—"

"Are they?" said Bevis. "They shan't find us," resentfully. The moment he thought the rest were going to try and force themselves on his plans, his mind changed. "We won't go on the raft this afternoon."

"No," said Mark; "nor too near the edge of the island."

"We'll keep out of sight. Is there anything they could see?"

"The raft."

"Ah! No; you think, when they get opposite so as to be where they could see the raft, then Serendib is between."

"So it is. No, there's nothing they can see; only we will not go too near the shore."

"No."

"What shall we do this afternoon?" said Mark, as they went down to the hut. Pan was idly lying in the narrow shade of the fence.

"We mustn't shoot," said Bevis, "and we can't go on the raft, because the savages are prowling round, and we mustn't play cards, nor do some chopping; let's go round the island and explore the interior."

"First-rate," said Mark; "just the very thing; you take your bow and arrows—you need not shoot, but just in case of savages—and I'll take my spear in case of the tiger in the reeds, or the something that comes out of the wave."

"And a hatchet," said Bevis, "to blaze our way. That would not be chopping."

"No, not proper chopping. Make Pan keep close. Perhaps we shall find some footmarks of the Something—spoor, you know."

"Come on. Down, sir." Pan accordingly walked behind.

First they went and looked at the raft, which was moored to an alder, taking care not to expose themselves on the shore, but looking at it from behind the boughs. They said they would finish fitting it up to-morrow morning, and then tried to think of a name for it. Bevis said there was no name in the Odyssey for Ulysses' raft, but as Calypso gave him the tools to make it, and wove the sail for him with her loom, they agreed to call the raft the Calypso. Then they tried to find a shorter way in to the knoll, which they called Kangaroo Hill, but were stopped by the impenetrable blackthorns.

As these were "wait-a-bit" thorns, Mark thought the island could not be far from Africa. Skirting the "wait-a-bits," they found some more hazel bushes, and discovered that the nuts were ripe, and stopped and filled their pockets. After all their trouble they had to go round the old way to get to Kangaroo Hill, and as they went between the trees Bevis cut off a slice of bark from every other trunk, so that in future they could walk quickly guided by the blaze, which would show too in the dusk.

From the knoll they walked across to the ivy-grown oak, and Bevis gave Mark a "bunt" up into it. Mark found a wood-pigeon's nest (empty, of course), but nothing else. The oak was large and old, not very tall, and seemed decaying; indeed, there was a hollow into which he thrust his spear, but did not rouse any creature from its lair. There was nothing in the oak. Bevis looked at the bark of the trunk, to see if any wild beast had left the marks of its claws in climbing up, just as cats do, but there was no trace.

They then went farther into the wood in the direction Pan had run away from Bevis, and found it sometimes open and sometimes much encumbered with undergrowth. Nothing appeared to them to be trampled, nor did they find any spoor. Pan showed no excitement, simply following, from which they supposed that whatever it had been it had gone.

After awhile they found the trees thinner and the ground declined, and here in a hollow ash, short and very much decayed within, there was a hive, or rather a nest of bees. There was a shrill hum round it as the bees continually went in and out, returning in straight lines, radiating to all parts of the compass, so that they did not care to venture too near. They appeared to be the hive-bees, not wild bees, but a swarm that had wandered from the mainland.

How to take the honey was not so easily settled, till they thought of making a powder-monkey, and so smoking them out, or rather stupefying them in the same way as the hives were taken at home with the brimstone match. By damping gunpowder and forming it into a cake it would burn slowly and send up dense fumes, which would answer the same as sulphur.

Then they could chop a way into the honeycomb. Seeing a tomtit on a bough watching for a chance to take a bee if one alighted before he went in, they considered it a sign they were off the mainland of Africa, as this was the honey-bird.

Several tall spruce firs grew lower down, and under these they could see over the New Sea to the south-east towards the unknown river. Here they sat down in the shade and cracked their nuts. One or two bees came to a burdock which flowered not far from their feet, but besides the hum as they passed there was no sound, for the light south-east air, playing in the tops of the firs, was too idle to sing. Yet the motion of the air, coming off the water, was just sufficient to cool them in the shade. Far away between the trunks they could see the jungle on the mainland.

Just below, on the shore of the island, a large willow-tree had been overthrown by the tempest on the day of the battle, and lay prone in the water, but still attached to the land by its roots. The nuts were juicy and sweet, but the day was so pleasant that Bevis presently put the nuts down and extended himself on his back. High above hung the long brown cones of the fir, and the dark green of its branches seemed to deepen the blue of the sky. With half-closed eyes he gazed up into the azure, till Mark feared he would go to sleep.

"Tell me a story," he said. "I'll tickle you, and you tell me a story. Here's a parrot's feather."

It was a wood-pigeon's, knocked out as the bird struck a branch in his rude haste. Mark tickled Bevis's face and neck. "Tell me a story," he said.

"My grandpa is the man for stories," said Bevis. "If you ask him to tell you the story of his walking-stick, he'll tell you all about it, and then two or three more; only you must be careful to ask him for the walking-stick one first, and then he'll give you five shillings."

"Regular moke," said Mark. "He stumped into London with the stick and a bundle, didn't he, and made five millions of money?"

"Heaps more than that."

"Now tell me a story."

"Tickle me then—very nicely."

"Now go on."

Chapter Five
New Formosa—The Story of the Other Side

"Once upon a time," said Bevis, closing his eyes now, "there was a great traveller who went sailing all round every sea—"

"Except the New Sea," said Mark. "Yes, except the New Sea which we found, and went riding over all the lands and countries, and climbing up all the mountains, and tramping through all the forests, and shooting the elephants and Indians and sticking pigs, and skinning boa-constrictors, and finding magicians—"

"What did the magicians do?"

"O! they did nothing very particular, one turned himself into a tree and was chopped up and burned in a bonfire and walked out of the smoke, and little things like that; and he went spying everywhere, and learned everything, and—"

"Go on—what next?"

"He went on till he said it was all no good, because if you went into the biggest forest that ever was you walked through it in about three years—"

"Like they did through Africa?"

"Just like it; and if you climbed up a mountain, after a day or two you got to the top; and if you sailed across the sea, if it was the greatest sea there ever was, you came to the other side in six months or so; so that it did not matter what you did, there was always an end to it."

"Very stupid."

"Very stupid, very; and he got tired of it always coming to the other side. He did so hate the other side, and he used to dawdle through the forests and lose his way, and he used to pull down the sails and let the ship go anyhow, and never touch the helm. But it was no use he always dawdled through the forest after awhile, and—"

"The wind always took the ship somewhere."

"Yes, to the hateful other side, and he got so miserable and what to do he did not know, and he could not stop still very well—nobody can stop still—and that's why people have got a way of spinning on their heels in some countries, I forget their names—"

"Dervishes?"

"Dervishes of course; well, he became a Dervish, and used to spin round and round furiously, but you know a top always runs down, and so he got to the other side again."

"Stupid."

"Awful stupid. Now tell me what else he did and could not help coming to the other side?" said Bevis.

"But it's you who are telling the story."

"O! but you can put some of that in."

"Well," said Mark, "if you walk across this island, you come to the other side, or sail down the New Sea in the Pinta, or if you swim out to Serendib, or if you climb up the fir-tree to the cones—"

"Always the other side," continued Bevis, "and so he said that this was such a little world he hated it, you could go all round the earth and come back to yourself and meet yourself in your own house at home in no time."

"It's not very big, is it?" said Mark. "Nothing is very big that you could go round like that."

"No, and the quicker you get round the smaller it is, though it's thousands and thousands of miles, so he said; and so he set out again to find a place where he could wander and never get to the other side, and after he had walked across Persia and Khorasan and Beloochistan—"

"And Afghanistan?"

"Yes, and crossed the Indus and Ganges, and been over the Himalayas, and inquired at every temple and of all the wise men who live in caves and hang themselves up with hooks stuck through their backs—"

"Fakirs."

"At last a very old man took pity on him, seeing how miserable he was, and whispered to him where to go, and so he went on—"

"Where?"

"To Thibet."

"But nobody is allowed to enter Thibet."

"No; but he had the pass-word, which the aged man whispered to him, and so they let him come in, and then he wandered about again for a long while, and by this time he was getting very old himself and could not walk so fast, so that it took longer and longer to get to the other side each time. Till at last, inquiring at all the temples as he went, they promised to show him a forest to which there was no other side. But he had to bathe and be purified first, and they burned incense and did a lot of magical things—"

"In circles?"

"I suppose so. And then one night in the darkness, so that he should not see which way they went, they led him along, and in the morning he was in a very narrow valley with a wall across so that you could not go any farther down the valley, nor could you climb up, because the rocks were so steep. Now, when they came to the wall he saw a little narrow bronze door in it— very low and very narrow—and the door was all covered with carvings and curious inscriptions—"

"Magic?"

"Yes, very magic. And the man who showed it to him, and who wore a crimson robe, over which his white beard flowed nearly down to the ground—I am sure that is right, flowed nearly down to the ground, that is just what my grandpa said—the old man went to the door and spoke to it in some language he did not understand and a voice answered, and then he saw the door open a little way, just a chink. Then he had to go on his hands and knees, and press his head and neck through the chink between the bronze door and the wall, and he could see over the country which has no other side to it. Though you may wander straight on for a thousand years, or ten thousand years, you can never get to the other side, but you always go on, and go on, and go on—"

"And what was it like?"

"Well, the air was so clear that he was certain he could see over at least a hundred miles of the plain, just as you can see over twenty miles of sea from the top of a cliff. But this was not a cliff, it was a level plain, and he could see at least a hundred miles. Now, behind him he had left the sun shining brightly, and he could feel the hot sunshine on his back—"

"Just as I did on my foot while I was fishing in the shadow?"

"Very likely—he could feel the hot sunshine on his back. But inside the wall there was no sun—"

"No sun?"

"No. Ever so far away, hung up as our sun looks hung up like a lamp when you are on the hill by Jack's house—ever so far away and not so very high up, there was an opal star. It was a very large star and so bright that you could see the beams of light shooting out from it, but so soft and gentle and pleasant that you could look straight at it without hurting your eyes, and see the flashes change exactly like an opal—a beautiful great opal star. All the air seemed full of the soft light from the star, so that the trees and plants and the ground even seemed to float in it, just like an island seems to float in the water when it is very still, and there was no shadow—"

"*No* shadow?"

"No. Nothing cast any shadow, because the light came all round everything, and he put his hand out into it and it did not cast any shadow, but instead his hand looked transparent, and as if there was a light underneath it—"

"Go on."

"And among the trees," said Bevis, pouring out the story from his memory word for word, exactly as he had heard it, like water from a pitcher filled at the spring, "among the trees the blue sky came down and they stood in it, just close by you could not see it, but farther off it was blue like a mist in the forest, only you could see through it and it shimmered blue like the blue-bells in the copse.

"He could see thousands of flowers, but he forgot what they were like except one which was like a dome of gold and larger than any temple he had ever seen. The grass grew up round it so tall he could not see the stalk, so that it looked as if it hung from the sky, and though it was gold he could see through it and see the blue the other side which looked purple through the gold, and the opal star was reflected on the dome. Nor could he remember all about the trees, having so much to look at, except one with a jointed stem like a bamboo which grew not far from the bronze door. This one rose up, up, till he could not strain his neck back to see to the top, and it was as large round as our round summer-house at home, but transparent, so that you could see the sap bubbling and rushing up inside in a running stream, and a sweet odour came down like rain from the boughs above.

"Now, while he was straining his neck to try and see the top of this tree, as his eyes were turned away from the opal sun, he could see the stars of heaven, and immediately heard the flute of an organ. For these stars—which were like our stars—were not scattered about, but built up in golden pipes or tubes; there were twelve tubes, all of stars, one larger than the other, and behind these other pipes, and behind these others tier on tier. Only there were twelve in front, the rest he could not count, and it was from these that the flute sound came and filled him with such transport that he quite forgot himself, and only lived in the music. At last his neck wearied of looking up, and he looked down again, and instantly he did not hear the starry organ, but saw instead the opal sun, and the shimmering sky among the trees.

"From the bronze door there was a footpath leading out, out, winding a little, but always out and out, and so clear was the air, that though it was only a footpath, he could trace it for nearly half the hundred miles he could see. The footpath was strewn with leaves fallen from the trees, oval-pointed leaves, some were crimson, and some were gold, and some were black, and all had marks on them.

"One of these was lying close to the bronze door, and as he had put his hand through, as you know, he stretched himself and reached it, and when he held it up the light of the opal sun came through it—it was transparent— and he could see words written on it which he read, and they told him the secret of the tree from which it had fallen.

"Now, all these leaves that were strewn on the footpath each of them had a secret written on it—a magic secret about the trees, and the plants, and the birds, and the stars, and the opal sun—every one had a magic secret on it, and you might go on first picking up one and then another, till you had travelled a hundred miles, and then another hundred miles, a thousand years, or ten thousand years, and there was always a fresh secret and a fresh leaf.

"Or you might sit down under one of the trees whose branches came to the ground like the weeping ash at home, or you might climb up into another—but no matter how, if you took hold of the leaves and turned them aside, so that the light of the opal sun came through, you could read a magic secret on every one, and it would take you fifty years to read one tree. Some of the leaves strewed the footpath, and some lay on the grass, and some floated on the water, but they did not decay, and the one he held in his hand went throb, throb, like the pulse in your wrist.

"And from secret to secret you might wander, always a new secret, till you went beyond the horizon, and then there was another horizon, and after that another, and you could go on and on, and on, and though you could walk for ever without weariness, because the air was so pure and delicious, still you could never, never, never get to the other side.

"Some have been walking there these millions of years, and some have been sitting up in the trees, and some have been lying under the golden dome flowers all that time, and never found and never will find the other side, which is why they are so happy. They do not sleep, because they never feel sleepy; they just turn over from the opal sun and look up at the stars and then the music begins, and as it plays they become strong, and then they go on again gathering more of the leaves, and travelling towards the opal sun, and the nearer they get the happier they are, and yet they can never get to it.

"While he looked he felt as if he must get through and go on too, and he struggled and struggled, but the bronze door was hard and the wall hard, so that it was no use. His mind though and soul had gone through; and he saw a white shoulder, like alabaster, pure, white, and transparent among the grass by the golden dome flower, and a white arm stretched out towards him, so white it gleamed polished, and a white hand, soft, warm-looking, delicious, transparent white, beckoning to him. So he struggled and struggled till it seemed as if he would get through to his soul, which had gone on down the footpath, when the aged man behind dragged him back, and the bronze door shut with an awful resonance—"

"What was that?"

"Hark!"

"Hark!"

Mark seized his spear; Bevis his bow.

"Is it something coming from the wave?"

"No, it's in the sky."

"Listen!"

There was a whirr above like wheels in the air, and a creaking sound with it. They stood up, but could not see what it was, though it grew louder and came nearer with a rushing noise. Suddenly something white appeared above the trees which had concealed its approach, and a swan passed over descending. It was the noise of its wings and their creaking which sounded like wheels. The great bird descended aslant quite a quarter of a mile into the water to the south in front of them, and there floated among the glittering ripples.

"I thought it was the roc," said Mark, sitting down again.

"Or a genie," said Bevis. "What a creaking and whirring it made!" Rooks' wings often creak as they go over like stiff leather, but the noise of a swan's flight is audible a mile or more.

"Go on with the story," said Mark.

"It's finished."

"But what did he do when they pulled him back? Didn't he burst the door open?"

"He couldn't. When he was pulled back it was night on that side of the wall, and the sudden change made him so bewildered that they led him away as if he was walking in his sleep down to the temple."

"What did he do with the magic leaf he had in his hand?"

"O! the wind of the bronze door as it slammed up blew it out of his hand. But when he came to himself and began to reproach them for pulling him away before he had had time even to look, they told him he had been looking three days and that it was the third night when the door was shut—"

"I see—it went so quick."

"It went so quick, like when you go to sleep and wake up next minute, and it's morning. But when he came to himself he found that his right hand which he had put through and which had cast no shadow was changed, it was white and smooth and soft, while the other hand and his face (as he was so old) was wrinkled and hard, so he was quite sure that what he had seen was real and true."

"Didn't he try to go back and find the door."

"Of course he did. But there was nothing but jungle, and he could not find the narrow valley; nor would they show him the way there again. They told him that only one was let through about every thousand years, and the reason they are so careful people shall not enter Thibet is that they may not stumble on the bronze door."

"And what became of him?"

"O! he lived to be the oldest man there ever was, which was because he had breathed the delicious air, and his hand was always white and soft like Frances's. Every night when he went to sleep, he could hear some of the star flute music of the organ, and dreamed he could see it; but he could hear it plainly. At last he died and went to join his soul, which had travelled on down the footpath, you know, towards the opal sun."

"How stupid to keep the door shut, and never let any one find it!"

"Ah, but don't you see the reason is because if it was open and people could find it, they would all run there and squeeze through, one after the other, like sheep through a gap, till the world was left empty without anybody in it, and they told him that was the reason. Grandpa says it is a pleasant thought that at least one goes through in a thousand years; if only one, that is something. My grandpa told me the story, and the son of the man told him—I mean the man who just looked through, or else it was his grandson or his great-great-grandson, for I know it was a long time ago. And there is no other side to that place."

"Let's go there," said Mark, after a pause, "you and me, and take some powder and blow the door open."

"If we could find it."

"O! we could find it; let's go to Thibet."

"So we will."

"And blow the bronze door open."

"And read the magic leaves."

"And go on down the footpath."

"And talk to the people under the golden dome flowers."

"I'm sure *we* could find the door."

"We *will* find it."

"Very soon."

"Some day."

Watching the swan among the glittering ripples, they cracked the rest of the nuts, and did not get up to go till the sun was getting low. It was not a wild swan, but one whose feathers had not been clipped. The wind rose a little, and sighed dreamily through the tops of the tall firs as they walked under them. They returned along the shore where the weeds came to the island, and had gone some way, when Mark suddenly caught hold of Bevis and drew him behind a bush.

Chapter Six
New Formosa—The Matchlock

"What is it?" said Bevis.

"I saw a savage."

"Where?"

"In the sedges on the shore there," pointing across the weeds. "I saw his head—he had no hat on."

"Quite sure?" Bevis looked, but could not see anything.

"Almost very nearly quite sure."

They watched the sedges a long time, but saw nothing.

"Was it Charlie, or Val, or Cecil?"

"No, I don't think so," said Mark.

"They could not get round either," said Bevis. "If they crossed the Nile like we did, they could not get round."

"No."

"It could not have been anybody."

"I thought it was; but perhaps it was a crow flew up—it looked black."

"Sure to have been a crow. The sedges do not move."

"No, it was a mistake—they couldn't get here."

They went on again and found a wild bullace.

"This is the most wonderful island there ever was," said Bevis; "there's always something new on or about it. The swan—I shall shoot the swan. No, most likely it's sacred, and the king of the country would have us hunted down if we killed it."

"And tied to a stake and tortured."

"Melted lead poured into our mouths, because we shot the sacred swan with leaden bullets."

"Awful. No, don't shoot it. There are currant-trees on the island too—I've seen them, and there's a gooseberry bush up in the top of an old willow that I saw," said Mark. "Of course there are bananas; are there any breadfruit-trees here?"

"Certain to be some somewhere."

"Melons and oranges."

"Of course, and grapes—those are grapes," pointing to bryony-berries, "and pomegranates and olives."

"Yams and everything."

"Everything. I wonder if Pan will bark this time—I wonder if anything is gone," said Bevis as they reached the stockade. Pan did not bark, and there was nothing missing.

They set to work now to make some tea and roast the moorhens, having determined to have tea and supper together. The tea was ready long before the moorhens, and by the time they had finished the moon was shining brightly, though there were some flecks of cloud. They could not of course play cards, so Bevis got out his journal; and having put down about the honey-bird, and the swan, and the discoveries they had made, went on to make a list of the trees and plants on the island, and the birds that came to it. They had seen a small flock of seven or eight missel-thrushes pass in the afternoon, and Mark said that all the birds came from the unknown river, and flew on towards the north-north-west. This was the direction of the waste, or wild pasture.

"Then there must be mainland that way," said Bevis; "and I expect it is inhabited and ploughed, and sown with corn, for that's what the birds like at this time of the year."

"And the other way—where they come from—must be a pathless jungle," said Mark. "And they rest here a moment as they cross the ocean. It is too far for one fly."

"My journal ought to be written on palm leaves," said Bevis, "a book like this is not proper: let's get some leaves to-morrow and see if we can write on them."

"Don't shipwrecked people write on their shirts," said Mark, "and people who are put in prison?"

"So they do—of course: but our shirts are flannel, how stupid!"

"I know," said Mark, "there's the collars." He went into the hut and brought out their linen collars, which they had ceased to wear. Bevis tried to write on these, but the ink ran and sank in, and it did not do at all.

"Wrong ink," he said, "we must make some of charcoal—lampblack— and oil. You use it just like paint, and you can't blot it, you must wait till it dries on."

"No oil," said Mark. "I wanted to rub the gun with some and looked, but there is none—we forgot it."

"Yellow-hammers," said Bevis, turning to his journal again; "what are yellow-hammers?"

"Unknown birds," said Mark. "We don't know half the birds—nobody has ever put any name to them, nobody has ever seen them: call them, let's see—gold-dust birds—"

"And greenfinches?"

"Ky-wee—Ky-wee," said Mark, imitating the greenfinches' call.

"That will do capital—Ky-wees," said Bevis.

"There's a horse-matcher here," said Mark. The horse-matcher is the bold hedge-hawk or butcher bird. "The one that sticks the humble-bees on the thorns."

"Bee-stickers—no, bee-killers: that's down," said Bevis. Besides which he wrote down nettle-creepers (white-throats), goldfinch, magpie, chaffinch, tree-climber, kestrel-hawk, linnets, starlings, parrots, and parrakeets. "I shall get up early to-morrow morning," he said. "I'll load the matchlock to-night, I want to shoot a heron."

He loaded the matchlock with ball, and soon afterwards they let the curtain down at the door, and went to bed, Bevis repeating "Three o'clock, three o'clock, three o'clock," at first aloud and then to himself, so as to set the clock of his mind to wake him at that hour. Not long after they were asleep, Pan as usual went out for his ramble.

Bevis's clock duly woke him about three, and lifting his head he could see the light through the chinks of the curtain, but he was half inclined to go to sleep again, and stayed another quarter of an hour. Then he resolutely bent himself to conquer sleep, slipped off the bed, and put on his boots quietly, not to wake Mark. Taking the matchlock, he went out and found that it was light, the light of the moon mingling with the dawn, but it was misty. A dry vapour, which left no dew, filled the wood so that at a short distance the path seemed to go into and lose itself in the mist.

Bevis went all round the island, following the path they had made. On the Serendib side he neither saw nor heard anything, but as he came back up the other shore, a lark began to sing far away on the mainland, and afterwards he heard the querulous cry of a peewit. He walked very cautiously, for this was the most likely side to find a heron, but whether they heard his approach or saw him, for they can see almost as far as a man when standing, by lifting their long necks, he did not find any. When he reached the spot where the "blaze" began that led to Kangaroo Hill, he fancied he saw something move in the water a long way off through the mist.

He stopped behind a bush and watched, and in a minute he was sure it was something, perhaps a cluck. He set up the rest, blew the match, opened the lid of the pan, knelt down and looked along the barrel till he had got it in a line with the object. If the gun had been loaded with shot he would have fired at once, for though indistinct through the vapour he thought it was within range, but as he had ball, he wanted to see if it would come nearer, as he knew he could not depend on a bullet over thirty yards. Intent on the object, which seemed to be swimming, he began to be curious to know what it was, for it had now come a little closer, and he could see it was not a duck, for it had no neck; it was too big for a rat: it must be the creature that visited the island and took their food—the idea of shooting this animal and surprising Mark with it delighted him.

He aimed along the barrel, and got the sight exactly on the creature, then he thought he would let it get a few yards closer, then he depressed the muzzle just a trifle, remembering that it was coming towards him, and if he did not aim somewhat in front the ball would go over.

Now it was near enough he was sure—he aimed steadily, and his finger began to draw the match down when he caught sight of the creature's eye. It was Pan.

"Pan!" said Bevis. He got up, and the spaniel swam steadily towards him.

"Where have you been, sir?" he said sternly. Pan crouched at his feet, not even shaking himself first. "You rascal—where have you been?"

Bevis was inclined to thrash him, he was so angry at the mistake he had almost made, angry with the dog because he had almost shot him. But Pan crouched so close to the ground under his very feet that he did not strike him.

"It was you who frightened the herons," he said. Pan instantly recognised the change in the tone of his voice, and sprang up, jumped round, barked, and then shook the water from his shaggy coat. It was no use evidently now to think of shooting a heron, the spaniel had alarmed them and Bevis returned to the hut. He woke Mark, and told him.

"That's why he's so lazy in the morning," said Mark. "Don't you recollect? He sleeps all the morning."

"And won't eat anything."

"I believe he's been home," said Mark. "Very likely Polly throws the bones out still by his house."

"That's it: you old glutton!" said Bevis.

Pan jumped on the bed, licked Mark, then jumped on Bevis's knees, leaving the marks of his wet paws, to which the sand had adhered, then he barked and wagged his tail as much as to say, "Am I not clever?"

"O! yes," said Mark, "you're very knowing, but you won't do that again."

"No, that you won't, sir," said Bevis. "You'll be tied up to-night."

"Tight as tight," said Mark. "Just think," said Bevis. "He must have swum all down the channel we came up on the catamaran. Why it's a hundred and fifty yards—"

"Or two hundred—only some of it is shallow. Perhaps he could bottom some part—"

"But not very far—and then run all the way home, and then all the way back, and then swim off again."

"A regular voyage—and every night too."

"You false old greedy Pan!"

"To leave us when we thought you were watching while we slept."

"To desert your post, you faithless sentinel." Pan looked from one to the other, as if he understood every word; he rolled up the whites of his eyes and looked so pious, they burst into fits of laughter. Pan wagged his tail and barked doubtfully; he had a shrewd suspicion they were laughing at him, and he did not like it. In fact, it was not only the flesh-pots that had attracted Pan from his post and led him to traverse the sea and land, and undergo such immense exertion, it was to speak to a friend of his.

They thought it of no use to go to sleep again now, so they lit the fire, and prepared the breakfast. By the time it was ready the mist had begun to clear; the sky became blue overhead, and while they were sitting at table under the awning, the first beams shot along over Serendib to their knees. Bevis said after breakfast he should practise with the matchlock, till he could hit something with the bullets. Mark wanted to explore the unknown river, and this they agreed to do, but the difficulty, as usual, was the dinner, there was nothing in their larder but bacon for rashers, and that was almost gone. Rashers become wearisome, ten times more wearisome when you have to cook them too.

Bevis said he must write his letter home—he was afraid he might have delayed too long—and take it to Loo to post that night, then he would write out a list of things, and Loo could buy them in the town, potted meats, and tongues, and soups, that would save cooking, only it was not quite proper. But Mark got over that difficulty by supposing that they fetched them from the wreck before it went to pieces.

So having had their swim, Bevis set up his target—a small piece of paper with a black spot, an inch in diameter, inked in the centre—on the teak, and fired his first shot at forty yards. The ball missed the teak-tree altogether, they heard it crash into a bramble bush some way beyond. Bevis went five yards nearer next time, and the bullet hit the tree low down, two feet beneath the bull's-eye. Then he tried at thirty yards, and as before, when he practised, the ball hit the tree five or six inches lower than the mark. He tried four times at this distance, and every time the bullet struck beneath, so that it seemed as if the gun threw the ball low.

Some guns throw shot high, and some low, and he supposed the matchlock threw low. So he aimed the fifth time above the centre, and the ball grazed the bark of the tree on the right-hand side very much as Mark's had done. Bevis stepped five yards nearer, if he could not hit it at twenty-five yards, he did not think it would be his fault. He aimed direct at the piece of paper, which was about five inches square, but the bullet struck three inches beneath, though nearly in a line, that is, a line drawn down through the middle of the paper would have passed a little to the left of the bullet hole.

This was better, so now he tried five yards closer, as it appeared to improve at every advance, and the ball now hit the paper at its lower right-hand edge. Examining the bullet holes in the bark of the tree, and noticing they were all low and all on the right-hand side, Bevis tried to think how that could be. He was quite certain that he had aimed perfectly straight, and as he was now so accustomed to the puff from the priming, that did not disconcert him. He kept his gaze steadily along the barrel till the actual explosion occurred, and the smoke from the muzzle obscured the view. It must be something in the gun itself.

Bevis put it on the rest unloaded, aimed along, and pulled the trigger, just as he would have done had he been really about to shoot. Nothing seemed wrong. As the heavy barrel was supported by the rest, and the stock pressed firm to his shoulder, pulling the trigger did not depress the muzzle as it often does with rifles.

He aimed again, and all at once he saw that the top sight must be the cause. The twisted wire was elevated about an eighth of an inch, and when he aimed he got the tip of the sight to bear on the paper, so that, instead of his glance passing level along the barrel, it rose slightly, from the breech to the top of the sight. The barrel was more than a yard long, so that when the top of the sight was in a line with the object, the muzzle was depressed exactly an eighth of an inch. An eighth of an inch at one yard, was a quarter at two yards, three eighths at three yards, at four half an inch, at eight it was an inch, at sixteen two inches, and at twenty-four three inches. This was very nearly enough of itself to account for the continual misses. In a gun properly made, the breech is thicker than the muzzle, and this greater thickness, like a slight elevation, corrects the sight; the gun, too, is adjusted. But the matchlock was the same thickness from end to end, and till now, had not been tried to determine the accuracy of the shooting.

Bevis got a file and filed down the sight, till it was only a sixteenth of an inch high, and then loading again, he aimed in such a way that the sight should cover the spot he wished to strike. He could see both sides of the sight, but the exact spot he wanted to hit was hidden by it. He fired, and the ball struck the paper about an inch below and two inches to the right of the centre. Next time the bullet hit very nearly on a level with the centre, but still on the right side.

This deflection he could not account for, the sight was in the proper position, and he was certain he aimed correctly. But at last he was compelled to acknowledge that there was a deflection, and persuaded himself to allow for it. He aimed the least degree to the left of the bull's-eye—just the apparent width of the sight—and so that he could see the bull's-eye on its right, the sight well up. He covered the bull's-eye first with the sight, then slightly moved the barrel till the bull's-eye appeared on the right side, just visible. The ball struck within half an inch of the bull's-eye. Bevis was delighted.

He fired again, and the ball almost hit the very centre. Next time the bullet hit the preceding bullet, and was flattened on it. Then Mark tried, and the ball again went within a mere trifle of the bull's-eye. Bevis had found out the individual ways of his gun. He did not like allowing for the deflection, but it was of no use, it had to be done, and he soon became reconciled to the concession. The matchlock had to be coaxed like the sailing-boat and our ironclads, like fortune and Frances.

Bevis was so delighted with the discovery, that he fired bullet after bullet, Mark trying every now and then, till the paper was riddled with bullet holes, and the teak-tree coated with lead. He thought he would try at a longer range, and so went back to thirty-five yards, but though he allowed a little more, and tried several ways, it was of no use, the bullet could not be relied on. At twenty yards they could hit the bull's-eye, so that a sparrow, or even a wren, would not be safe; beyond that, errors crept in which Bevis could not correct.

These were probably caused by irregularities in the rough bore of the barrel, which was only an iron tube. When the powder exploded, the power of the explosion drove the ball, by sheer force, almost perfectly straight—point-blank—for twenty or twenty-five yards. Then the twist given by the inequalities of the bore, and gained by the ball by rubbing against them, began to tell; sometimes one way, sometimes another, and the ball became deflected and hardly twice the same way.

Bevis was obliged to be content with accuracy up to twenty, or at most twenty-five yards. At twenty he could hit an object the size of a sparrow; at twenty-five of a blackbird, after twenty-five he might miss his straw hat. Still it was a great triumph to have found out the secret, and to be certain of hitting even at that short range.

"Why, that's how it was with Jack's rifle!" he said. "It's only a dodge you have to find out."

"Of course it is; if he would lend it to us, we should soon master it," said Mark. "And now let's go to the unknown river."

Chapter Seven
New Formosa—Sweet River Falls

The matchlock was slung up in the hut, and away they went to the raft; Pan did not want to come, he was tired after his journey in the night, but they made him. Knowing the position of the shoals, and where they could touch the bottom with the poles, and where not, they got along much quicker, and entered the channel in the weeds, which they had discovered beyond Pearl Island in the Pinta.

The channel was often very narrow, and turned several ways, but by degrees trended to the south-eastwards, and the farther they penetrated it, the more numerous became the banks, covered with a dense growth of sedges and flags. Some higher out of the water than others, had bushes and willows, so that, after awhile, their view of the open sea behind was cut off. They did not see any wild-fowl, for as these heard the splash of the poles, they swam away and hid. Winding round the sedge-grown banks, they presently heard the sound of falling water.

"Niagara!" said Mark.

"No, Zambesi. There are houses by Niagara, so it's not so good."

"No. Look!"

The raft glided out of the channel into a small open bay, free from weeds, and with woods each side. Where it narrowed a little stream fell down in two short leaps, having worn its way through the sandstone. The water was not so much as ran over the hatch of the brook near home, but this, coming over stone or rock, instead of dropping nearly straight, leaped forward and broke into spray. The sides of the worn channel were green with moss, and beneath, but just above the surface of the water, long cool hart's-tongue ferns grew, and were sprinkled every moment.

The boughs of beech-trees met over the fall, and shaded the water below. They poled up so near that the spray reached the raft; Mark caught hold of a drooping beech bough, and so moored their vessel. They could not see up the stream farther than a few yards, for it was then overhung with dark fir boughs. On the firs there were grey flecks of lichen.

"How sweet and clear it looks!" said Bevis. "Shall we call it Sweet River?"

"And Sweet River Falls?"

"Yes. It comes out of the jungle," Bevis looked over the edge of the raft, and saw the arch of water dive down unbroken beneath the surface of the pool, and then rise in innumerable bubbles under him. The hart's-tongue ferns vibrated, swinging slightly, as the weight of the drops on them now bore them down and now slipped off, and let them up.

By the shore of the pool the turquoise studs of forget-me-nots, with golden centres, were the brighter for the darkness of the shade. So thick were the boughs, that the sky could not be seen through them; there was a rustle above as the light south-east wind blew, but underneath the leaves did not move.

"I like this," said Mark. He sat on the chest, or locker, holding the beech bough. "But the birds do not sing."

The cuckoo was gone, the nightingale silent, the finches were in the stubble, there might be a chiff-chaff "chip-chipping," perhaps deep in the jungle, one pair of doves had not quite finished nesting on New Formosa, now and then parties of greenfinches called "ky-wee, ky-wee," and a single lark sang in the early dawn. But the jungle here was silent. There was no song but that of the waterfall.

Though there was not a breath of wind under the boughs, yet the sound of the fall now rose, and now declined, as the water ran swifter or with less speed. Sometimes it was like a tinkling; sometimes it laughed; sometimes it was like voices far away. It ran out from the woods with a message, and hastening to tell it, became confused.

Bevis sat on the raft, leaning against the willow bulwark; Pan crept to his knee.

The forget-me-nots and the hart's-tongue, the beeches and the firs, listened to the singing. Something that had gone by, and something that was to come, came out of the music and made this moment sweeter. This moment of the singing held a thousand years that had gone by, and the thousand years that are to come. For the woods and the waters are very old, that is the past; if you look up into the sky you know that a thousand years hence will be nothing to it, that is the future. But the forget-me-nots, the hart's-tongue, and the beeches, did not think of the ages gone, or the azure to come. They were there *now*, the sunshine and the wind above, the shadow and the water and the spray beneath, that was all in all. Bevis and Mark were there now, listening to the singing, that was all in all.

Presently there was a sound—a "swish"—and looking up, they saw a pheasant with his tail behind like a comet, flying straight out to sea. This awoke them.

Bevis held out the palm of his hand, and Pan came nearer and put his chin in the hollow of it, as he had done these hundreds of times. Pan looked up, and wagged his tail, thump, thump, on the deck of the raft. If we could put the intelligence of the dog in the body of the horse, size, speed, and grace, what an animal that would be!

"Lots of perch here," said Mark; "I shall come and fish. Suppose we land and go up the Sweet River?"

"It belongs to the king of this country, I expect," said Bevis. "He sits on a throne of ebony with a golden footstool, and they wave fans of peacocks' feathers, and the room is lit up by a single great diamond just in the very top of the dome of the ceiling, which flashes the sunshine through, down from outside. The swan belongs to him."

"And he keeps the Sweet River just for himself to drink from, and executes everybody who dares drink of it," said Mark.

Just then a bird flew noiselessly up into the beech over them, they saw it was a jay, and kept quite still. The next instant he was off, and they heard him and his friends, for a jay is never alone, screeching in the jungle. Looking back towards the quiet bay, it appeared as if it was raining fast, but without a sound, for the surface was dimpled with innumerable tiny circlets like those caused by raindrops. These were left by the midges as they danced over the water, touching it now and then.

"Did you hear that?" It was the sound of a distant gun shorn of the smartness of the report by the trees.

"The savages have matchlocks," said Bevis. "They must be ever so much more dangerous than we thought."

"Perhaps we'd better go," said Mark, casting off the beech bough.

The current slowly drifted the raft out into the bay, and then they took their poles, and returned along the channel between the reeds and sedge banks. It took some time to reach New Formosa.

"I wonder if the creature out of the wave has been," said Mark. "Suppose we go very quietly and see what it is."

"So we will."

Keeping Pan close at their heels, they stole along the path to the stockade, then crept up behind it to the gateway, and suddenly burst in. "Ah!"

"Here he is."

"Yow-wow!"

"O! it's the pheasant!"

"Only the pheasant!"

The pheasant, flying straight out to sea for the cornfields, halted on New Formosa, attracted by the glimpse he caught of the fence and hut. The enclosure seemed so much like that in which he had been bred, and in which he had enjoyed so much food, that he came down and rambled about inside, visiting even the cave, and stepping on the table.

When they came in so unexpectedly on him, he rose up rocket-like, and at first made towards the jungle, but in a minute, recovering himself, he swept round and went to the mainland by the Waste. He did not want to return to the preserves—anywhere else in preference.

While the dinner was preparing, Mark got out his fishing-rod, and fitted up the spinning tackle for pike, for he meant to angle round the island, and also some hooks for trimmers, if he could catch any bait, and hooks for nightlines, in case there should be eels. These trimmers and nightlines put them in mind of traps for kangaroos, they had no traps, but determined to set up some wires at a good distance from the knoll, so as not, in any case, to interfere with their shooting.

After dinner, as Mark wanted to go fishing, Bevis watched for Charlie, and looking through the telescope, saw the herd of buffaloes on the green hill under the sycamore-trees. One cow held her head low, and a friend licked her poll. A flock of rooks were on the slope, and had he not known, he could have told which way the wind blew, as they all faced in one direction, and always walk to meet the breeze. When they flew up he knew Charlie was approaching. Charlie did not stay after making the signal, so Bevis went down and walked round the island till he found Mark.

As yet, Mark had had no success, but he had fixed on a spot to set the nightlines. Returning along the other shore, fishing as he went, Bevis with him, they remembered that that night the letter must be taken to Loo to post, and thought they had better have a look at the channel through the weeds, or else by moonlight they might not get to the mainland so easily.

The best tree to climb was a larch which grew apart from the wood, and rose up to a great height, balanced each side with its long slender branches. The larch, when growing alone, is a beautiful tree. It is too often crowded into plantations which to it are like the 'Black Hole' of Calcutta to human beings. Up they went, Mark first, as quickly as sailors up the ratlins, for the branches, at regular intervals, had grown on purpose for climbing, only they had to jam their hats on, and not look higher than the bough they were on, because of the dust of the bark they shook down.

"There's the reapers," said Mark; "what a lot they have cut."

They could see the sheaves stacked, and the stubble, which was of a lighter hue than the standing wheat. Every now and then dark dots came to the golden surface of the wheat like seals to breathe. These dots were the reapers' heads.

"There's the pheasant," said Bevis, pointing to the Waste. The bird was making his way zigzag round the green ant-hills, towards the stubble. Sometimes he walked, sometimes he ran, now and then he gave a jump in his run. They lost sight of him behind a great grey boulder-stone, whose top was visible above the brambles and rush-bunches which surrounded its base.

"Jack's busy now up in the hills," said Mark, looking the other way towards the Downs. "He might just as well let us have the rifle while he's busy with the harvest."

"Just as well. I say, let's explore the Waste to-morrow. It is a wilderness — you don't know what you may not find in a wilderness."

"Grey stones," said Mark. "They're tombs — genii live in them."

"Serpents guarding treasures, and lamps burning; they have been burning these ages and ages —"

"Awful claps of thunder underground."

"We will go and see to-morrow — I believe there are heaps of kangaroos out there."

"There's the channel."

They could trace its windings from the tree, and marked it in their minds. At that height the breeze came cool and delicious; they sat there a long while silent, soothed by the rustle and the gentle sway of the branches. They could feel the mast-like stem vibrate — it did not move sufficiently to be said to bend, or even sway — so slight was the motion the eye could not trace it. But it did move as they could feel with their hands as the wind came now with more and now with less force.

When they descended, Mark continued fishing till they came to the raft. They embarked and poled it round the island to the other side ready to start in the evening. Then Bevis wrote the letter dating it from Jack's house up in the hills. It was very short. He said they were very well, and jolly, and should not come back for a little while yet, but would not be very long—this was in case any one should go up to see them. But when he came to read it through for mistakes, the deceit he was practising on dear mamma stood out before him like the black ink on the page.

"I don't like it," he said. "It's not nice."

"No; it's not nice," said Mark, who was sitting by him. "But still—"

"But still," repeated Bevis, and so the letter was put in an envelope and addressed. In the evening as the sun sank Mark tried for bait and succeeded in catching some, these were for the trimmers. Then they laid out the night-line for eels far down the island where the edge looked more muddy. To fill up the time till it was quite moonlight, they worked at a mast for the raft, and also cut some sedges and flags for the roof of the open shed, which was to be put up in place of the awning.

They supposed it to be about half-past nine when they pushed off on the raft, taking with them the letter, a list of things to be got from the town to save the labour of cooking, and the flag-basket. The trimmers were dropped in as they went. Mark was going to wait by the raft till Bevis returned under the original plan, but they agreed that it would be much more pleasant to go together, the raft would be perfectly safe. They found the channel without difficulty, the raft grounded among the sedges, and they stepped out, the first time they had landed on the mainland.

As they walked they saw a fern owl floating along the hedge by the stubble. The beetles hummed by and came so heedlessly over the hedge as to become entangled in the leaves. They walked close to the hedge because they knew that the very brightest moonlight is not like the day. By moonlight an object standing apart can be seen a long distance, but anything with a background of hedge cannot be distinguished for certain across one wide field. That something is moving there may be ascertained, but its exact character cannot be determined.

As they had to travel beside the hedges and so to make frequent détours, it occupied some time to reach the cottage, which they approached over the field at the back. When they were near enough, Bevis whistled—the same notes with which he and Mark called and signalled to each other. In an instant they saw Loo come through the window, so quickly that she must have been sleeping with her dress on; she slipped down a lean-to or little shed under it, scrambled through a gap in the thin hedge, and ran to them.

She had sat and watched and listened for that whistle night after night in vain. At last she drew her cot (in which her little brother also slept) across under the window, and left the window open. Her mind so long expecting the whistle responded in a moment to the sound when it reached her dreaming ear. She took the letter (with a penny for the stamp) and the list and basket, and promised to have the things ready for them on the following evening.

"And remember," said Bevis, "remember you don't say anything. There will be a shilling for you if you don't tell—"

"I shouldn't tell if there wurdn't no shilling," said Loo.

"You mind you do not say a word," added Mark. "Nobody is to know that you have seen us."

"Good-night," said Bevis, and away they went. Loo watched them till they were lost against the dark background of the hedge, and then returned to her cot, scrambling up the roof of the shed and in at the window.

They got back to the island without any difficulty, and felt quite certain that no one had seen them. Stirring up the embers of the fire, they made some tea, but only had half a cold damper to eat with it. This day they had fared worse than any day since they arrived on New Formosa. They were too tired to make a fresh damper (besides the time it would take) having got up so early that morning, and Bevis only entered two words in his journal— "Monday—Loo."

Then they fastened Pan to the door-post, allowing him enough cord to move a few yards, but taking care to make his collar too tight for him to slip his head. Pan submitted with a mournful countenance, well he understood why he was served in this way.

Chapter Eight
New Formosa—The Mainland

In the morning, after the bath, Mark examined the night-line, but it was untouched; nor was there a kangaroo in the wires they had set up in their runs. Poling the raft out to the trimmers they found a jack of about two pounds on one, and the bait on another had been carried off, the third had not been visited. Bevis wanted to explore the Waste, and especially to look at the great grey boulder, and so they went on and landed among the sedges.

Making Pan keep close at their heels, they cautiously crept through the bramble thickets—Pan tried two or three times to break away, for the scent of game was strong in these thickets—and entered the wild pasture, across which they could not see. The ground undulated, and besides the large ant-hills, the scattered hawthorn bushes and the thickets round the boulders intercepted the view. If any savages appeared they intended to stoop, and so would be invisible; they could even creep on hands and knees half across the common without being seen. Pan was restless—not weary this morning—the scent he crossed was almost too much for his obedience.

They reached the boulder unseen—indeed there was no one to see them—pushed through the bushes, and stood by it. The ponderous stone was smooth, as if it had been ground with emery, and there were little circular basins or cups drilled in it. With a stick Bevis felt all round and came to a place where the stick could be pushed in two or three feet under the stone, between it and the grass.

"It's hollow here," he said; "you try."

"So it is," said Mark. "This is where the treasure is."

"And the serpent, and the magic lamp that has been burning ages and ages."

"If we could lift the stone up."

"There's a spell on it; you couldn't lift it up, not with levers or anything."

Pan sniffed at the narrow crevice between the edge of the boulder and the ground—concealed by the grass till Bevis found it—but showed no interest. There was no rabbit there. Such great boulders often have crevices beneath, whether this was a natural hollow, or whether the boulder was the capstone of a dolmen was not known. Whirr-rr!

A covey of partridges flew over only just above the stone, and within a few inches of their heads which were concealed by it. They counted fourteen—the covey went straight out across the New Sea, eastwards towards the Nile. From the boulder they wandered on among the ant-hills and tall thistles, disturbing a hare, which went off at a tremendous pace, bringing his hind legs right under his body up to his shoulder in his eagerness to take kangaroo bounds.

Presently they came to the thick hedge which divided the Waste from the cornfields. Gathering a few blackberries along this, they came to a gate, which alarmed them, thinking some one might see, but a careful reconnaissance showed that the reapers had finished and left that field. The top bar of the gate was pecked, little chips out of the wood, where the crows had been.

"It's very nice here," said Mark. "You can go on without coming to the Other Side so soon."

After their life on the island, where they could never walk far without coming in sight of the water, they appreciated the liberty of the mainland. Pan had to have several kicks and bangs with the stick, he was so tempted to rush into the hedge, but they did not want him to bark, in case any one should hear.

"Lots of kangaroos here," said Bevis, "and big kangaroos too—hares you know; I say, I shall come here with the matchlock some night."

"So we will."

There was a gap in the corner, and as they came idling along they got up into the double mound, when Bevis, who was first, suddenly dropped on his knees and seized Pan's shaggy neck. Mark crouched instantly behind him.

"What is it?" he whispered.

"Some one's been here."

"How do you know?"

"Sniff."

Mark sniffed. There was the strong pungent smell of crushed nettles. He understood in a moment—some one had recently gone through and trampled on them. They remained in this position for five minutes, hardly breathing, and afraid to move.

"I can't hear any one," whispered Mark.

"No."

"Must have gone on."

Bevis crept forward, still holding Pan with one hand; Mark followed, and they crossed the mound, when the signs of some one having recently been there became visible in the trampled nettles, and in one spot there was the imprint of a heel-plate.

"Savages," said Bevis. "Ah! Look."

Mark looked through the branches and a long way out in the stubble, moving among the shocks of wheat, he saw Bevis's governor. They watched him silently. The governor walked straight away; they scarcely breathed till he had disappeared in the next field. Then they drew back into the Waste, and looked at one another.

"Very nearly done," said Mark.

"We won't land again in daylight," said Bevis.

"No—it's not safe; he must have been close."

"He must have got up into the mound and looked through," said Bevis. "Perhaps while we were by the gate."

"Most likely. He came across the stubble, why he was that side while we were this."

"Awfully nearly done; why it must have been the governor who startled the partridges!"

"Stupes we were not to know some one was about."

"Awful stupes."

They walked back to the raft, keeping close to the hedge, and crept on all fours among the ant-hills so as to pass the gateway without the possibility of being seen, though they knew the governor was now too far to observe them.

The governor had been to look at the progress made by the reapers, and then strolled across the stubble, thinking to see what birds were about, as it was not such a great while till the season opened. Coming to the mound, he got up and looked through into the Waste, over which (as over the New Sea) he held manorial rights. At the moment he was looking out into the pasture they were idly approaching him along the hedge, and had he stopped there they would have come on him. As it was, he went back into the stubble, and had gone some fifty yards with his back turned when they entered the gap.

"We might have been tortured," said Mark, as they stepped on the raft. "Tied up and gimlets bored into our heads."

"The king of this country is an awful tyrant," said Bevis. "Very likely he would have fixed us in a hollow tree and smeared us with honey and let the flies eat us."

"Unless we could save his daughter, who is ill, and all the magicians can't do her any good."

"Now they are hoping we shall soon come with a wonderful talisman. We must study magic—we keep on putting it off; I wonder if there really is a jewel in the toad's head."

"You have not inked the wizard's foot on the gateway," said Mark.

When they got home Bevis inked it on the boards of the gate; he could not do it on the rough bark of the gate-post. They then worked at the shed, and soon put it up in place of the awning, which was taken down and carried to the raft. Next the mast was erected, and sustained with stays; it was, however, taken down again, so as to be out of the way till required, and stowed at the side by the bulwarks.

The jack was cooked for dinner, and though not enough for such hungry people it was a pleasant change from the perpetual rashers and damper. After Charley had given the signal, they parted; Mark took his perch tackle and poled the raft out near Pearl Island, where he thought he might catch some perch. Bevis loaded the matchlock with ball, and went into ambush behind the ash-tree by Kangaroo Hill, to try and shoot a kangaroo.

Mark took Pan and worked the raft along till he was within forty or fifty yards of Pearl Island, and on the windward side. The wind had been changeable lately, showing that the weather was not so settled as it had been; it blew from the eastward that afternoon, just strong enough to cause a ripple. When he had got the raft into the position he wished, Mark put the pole down and took his rod.

The raft, as he had designed, floated slowly, and without the least disturbance of the water (such as his pole or oars would have caused) before the wind, till it grounded on a shoal ten yards from Pearl Island. Mark knew of the shoal, having noticed the place before when they were visiting the islets, and thought it would be a likely spot to find perch. The ripples breaking over the ridge of the shoal made a miniature surf there.

On the outer or windward side the perch would be on the watch for anything that might come along on the wavelets, and inside for whatever might be washed from the shoal. There were weeds at a short distance, but none just there, and such places with a clear sandy bottom are the favourite haunts of perch in waters like these. First he fished outside to windward, and his blue float went up and down on the ripples till presently down it went at a single dive, drawn under at once by an eager fish.

In a minute he had a perch on board about half a pound weight, and shortly afterwards another, and then a third, for when perch are on the feed they take the bait directly as fast as it can be put in to them. Now Mark, though excited with his luck, was cool enough to observe one little precaution, which was to use a fresh clean worm every time, and not to drop in one that had been in the least degree mauled. This required some self-control, for several times the bait was scarcely damaged, but it was a rule that he and Bevis had found out, and they always adhered to it.

For fish have likes and antipathies exactly the same as other creatures, and if one approaches a bait and turns disdainfully away it is quite probable that three or four more may check their advance, whether from imitation, or taking the opinion of the first as a guide to themselves. So Mark always had a fresh, untainted bait for them, and in a very short time he had six perch on the raft. He put them in the locker.

There was then a pause, he had exhausted that school. Next he tried fishing out towards the nearest weeds, a small bunch at the utmost limit of his throw, but as half an hour elapsed and he had no nibble he tried inside the shoal to leeward. In five minutes he landed a fine one, quite two pounds and a half, whose leaps went thump, thump on the deck like Pan's tail. Ten minutes more and he caught another, this time small, and that was his last. There were either no more fish, or they had no more credence.

He sat on the locker and watched his float till the sun grew low, but it was no use. He knew it was no use long before, but still he lingered. Gold-diggers linger though they know their claim is exhausted. The mind is loth to acknowledge that the game is up. Mark knew it was up; still he waited and let his float uselessly rise and fall, till he heard the report of the matchlock from the island, and then he poled homewards to see what Bevis had shot.

In ambush, under the ash-tree, and behind the fringe of fern—one frond was scorched where Mark had fired through it—Bevis watched with the gun ready on the rest. He had purposely gone a little too soon, that is, before the shadow stretched right out across the glade, because if you do not arrive till the last moment a kangaroo may be already out, and will be alarmed. Then it is necessary to wait till the others recover from their fear; for if one runs in, the sound of his hasty passage through the tunnels in the ground conveys the information to all in the bury.

Not far from him there was a bunch of beautiful meadow geraniums; some of their blue cups had already dropped, leaving the elongated seed-vessel or crane's bill, something like the pointed caps worn by mediaeval ladies. The leaves are much divided; perhaps the wind-anemone leaves (but these had withered long since) are most finely divided, and if you will hold one so that its shadow may be cast by the sun on a piece of white paper, you cannot choose but admire it. While he sat there, now and then changing the position of a limb with the utmost care and deliberation, not to rustle the grass or to attract attention by moving quickly (for kangaroos do not heed anything that moves very slowly), he saw a brown furze-chat come to a tall fern and perch sideways on the flattened yellow stalk.

Half an hour afterwards there came a sound like "top-top" from an oak on his left hand—not the ivy-grown one—and when he had by great exertion turned himself round, it is difficult to turn and still occupy the same space, he followed up all the branches of the oak cautiously till he found the bird. If you glance, as it were, broadcast up into a tree when it is in leaf, you see nothing, though the bird's note may fall from just overhead. Bevis first looked quickly up the larger leading branches, letting his glance run up them; then he caused it to travel out along the lesser boughs of one great branch, then of another, till he had exhausted all. Still he could not find it, though he heard the "top-top." But as he had now got a map of the tree in his eye, the moment the bird moved he saw it.

It ran up a partly dead branch, then stopped and struck it with its beak, and though the bird was no larger than a sparrow the sound of these vehement blows could have been heard across the glade. He saw some white and red colour, but the glimpse he had was too short to notice much. The spotted woodpecker is so hasty that it is not often he is in sight more than half a minute. Bevis saw him fly with a flight like a finch across to the ivy-grown oak, and heard his "top-top" from thence. One of the tits has a trick of tapping branches so much in the same manner that if he is not seen the sound may be mistaken.

There was now a little rabbit out, but not worth shooting. Restless as Bevis was, yet the moment he fixed his mind to do a thing his will magnetised the nerves and sinews. He became as still as a tree and scarcely heeded the lapse of time. Bees went by, which reminded him of the honey in the hollow ash, and he heard mice in the fern. The shadows had now deepened, and there were two thrushes and a blackbird out in the grass. Another little kangaroo appeared, and a third, and a long way off, too far to shoot, there was one about three parts grown, which he hoped would presently feed over within range.

After a while, as this did not happen, he began to think he would try and shoot two of the smaller ones at once. With shot this could have been easily done, for they were often close together. As he was watching the young rabbits, and asking himself whether the ball would strike both, a sense of something moving made him glance again up into the oak on his left hand. He did not actually see anything go up into it, but the corner of his eye—while he was consciously gazing straight forward—was aware that something had passed.

In a moment he saw it was a jay, which had come without a sound, for though the jay makes such a screech when he opens his bill, his wings are almost as noiseless as an owl's. A wood-pigeon makes a great clatter, hammering the air and the boughs; a jay slips into the tree without a sound. The bird's back was turned, and the white bar across it showed; in a moment he moved, and the blue wing was visible.

"Frances would like it," Bevis thought, "to put in her hat." The ferns hid him on that side, and careless of the rabbits, he gently moved himself round; the little kangaroos lifted their heads, the larger one ran to his bury, for to bring his gun to bear on the oak Bevis was obliged to expose himself towards the knoll. Now he was round there was this difficulty, the jay was high in the oak, and the rest was too low.

To aim up into the tree he must have extended himself at full length with his chest on the ground, that would be awkward, and most likely while he was doing it he should startle the bird. He gently lifted the heavy matchlock, sliding the barrel against the bark of the ash till he had it in position, holding it there by pressing it with his left hand against the tree. This gave some support while his wrist was fresh, but in a minute he knew it would feel the weight, and perhaps tremble. It was necessary to shoot quick for this reason, and because the jay never stays long in any one tree; yet he wanted to take a steady aim. He had not shot anything with the matchlock, though he had designed it.

Bevis brought the barrel to bear, covered the jay with the sight, then moved it the merest trifle to the left, so that he could just see the bird, and drew the match down into the priming. The bird was struck up into the air by the blow of the ball and fell dead. The wing towards him and part of the neck had been carried away by the bullet, which, coming upwards, had lifted the jay from the bough. On the side away from him the wing was uninjured; this was for Frances. There was no chance of getting a rabbit now, so he returned towards the hut, and had not been there many minutes before Mark came running.

When the jay and the perch had been talked about enough, they made some tea, and sat down to wait till it was moonlight. Bevis got out his journal and recorded these spoils, while the little bats flew to and fro inside the stockade, and even under the open shed and over the table just above their heads, having little more fear than flies.

Later on, having landed on the mainland, as they were going through the stubble to meet Loo, they saw something move, and keeping quite still by the hedge, it came towards them, when they knew it was a fox. He came down the furrow between the lands, and several times went nosing round the shocks of wheat, for he looks on a plump mouse as others do on a kidney for breakfast. He did not seem to scent them, for when they stepped out he was startled and raced away full speed. At the whistle Loo brought the flag-basket, heavy with the tinned tongues and potted meats they had ordered. She was frequently sent into the town on errands from the house, so that there was no difficulty at the shop. Bevis inquired how all were at home; all were well, and then wished her good-night after exacting another promise of secrecy. Loo watched them out of sight.

That evening they had a splendid supper on New Formosa, and sat up playing cards.

"How ought we to know that your governor and the Jolly Old Moke are all right," said Mark, "as we're on an island seven thousand miles away? Of course we do know, but how *ought* we to find out? There was no telegraph when we lived."

"Well, it's awkward," said Bevis—"it's very awkward; perhaps we had a magic ring and looked through it and saw what the people were doing, or, I know! there's the little looking-glass in the cave, don't you remember?"

"We brought it and forgot to hang it up."

"Yes; we saw them in a magic mirror, don't you see?"

"Of course—like a picture. First it comes as a mist in the mirror, as if you had breathed on it; then you see the people moving about, and very likely somebody going to be married that you want, and then you cry out, and the mist comes again."

"That's right: I'll put it down in the journal. 'Made magic and saw all the blokes at home.'"

They fastened Pan up as before at the door-post before going to bed, and gave him several slices of rolled tongue. They slept the instant they put their heads on the hard doubled-up great-coats which formed their pillows.

Chapter Nine
New Formosa—The Something Comes Again

About the middle of the night Pan moved, sat up, gave a low growl, then rushed outside to the full length of his cord, and set up a barking.

"Pan! Pan!" said Bevis, awakened.

"What is it?" said Mark.

Hearing their voices and feeling himself supported, Pan increased his uproar. Bevis ran outside with Mark and looked round the stockade. It was still night, but night was wending to the morn. The moon was low behind the trees. The stars shone white and without scintillating. They could distinctly see every corner of the courtyard; there was nothing in it.

"It's the something," said Mark. Together they ran across to the gateway in the stockade, though they had no boots on. They looked outside; there was nothing. Everything was perfectly still, as if the very trees slept.

"We left the gate open," said Bevis.

"I don't believe it's ever been locked but once," said Mark.

Neither had it. On the boards the wizard's foot was drawn to keep out the ethereal genii, but they had neglected to padlock the door to keep out the material. They locked it now, and returned to the hut. Pan wagged his tail, but continued to give short barks as much as to say, that *he* was not satisfied, though they had seen nothing.

"What can it be?" said Mark. "If Pan used to swim off every night, he could not have had all the things."

"No. We'll look in the morning and see if there are any marks on the ground."

They sat up a little while talking about it, and then reclined; in three minutes they were firm asleep again. Pan curled up, but outside the hut now; once or twice he growled inwardly.

In the morning they remembered the incident the moment they woke, and before letting Pan loose, carefully examined every foot of the ground inside the stockade. There was not the slightest spoor. Nor was there outside the gate; but it was possible that an animal might pass there without leaving much sign in the thin grass. When Pan was let free he ran eagerly to the gate, but then stopped, looked about him, and came back seeming: to take no further interest. The scent was gone.

"No cooking," said Mark, as they sat down to breakfast. "Glad I'm not a girl to have to do that sort of thing."

"I wish there was some wind," said Bevis, "so that we could have a sail."

There was a little air moving, but not sufficient to make sailing pleasant in so cumbrous a craft as the Calypso. They had their bath, but did not cross to Serendib, lest Pan should follow and disturb the water-fowl. So soon as they had dressed, the matchlock was loaded—it was Mark's day—and they brought the raft round.

Mark sat on the deck in front with the match lit, and the barrel balanced on a fixed rest they had put up for it, not the movable staff. Bevis poled the raft across to Serendib, and then very quietly round the northern end of that island, where the water was deep enough to let the raft pass close to the blue gum boughs. Coming round to the other side, Mark moved his left hand, which was the signal that they had agreed on, when Bevis kept his pole on the ground, dragging so as to almost anchor the Calypso.

In a quarter of a minute Mark fired, and Pan instantly jumped overboard. The force of his fall carried him under water, but he rose directly and brought the moorhen back to them. Bevis dragged him on board—the moorhen in his mouth—by the neck, for he could not climb over the bulwarks from the water. After the gun was loaded Bevis pushed on again slowly, but the report had frightened the others, and there were no more out feeding. They stayed therefore under the blue gum boughs and waited. Pan wanted to leap ashore and play havoc, but they would not let him, for it was impossible to shoot flying with their heavy gun.

Some time passed, and then Bevis caught sight of a neck and a head; there was nothing more visible, near the shore along which they had come. It was a dab-chick or lesser grebe. At that, the stern end of the raft, there was no rest, but Mark sat down and put the barrel on the bulwarks. Bevis whispered to him to wait till the dab-chick turned its head, for this bird, which swims almost flush with the water, goes under in an instant, having only to get his head down to disappear. He will dive at the faintest sound or movement that he does not recognise, but soon comes up again, and will often duck at the flash of a gun too quick for the shot to strike him. Mark waited his chance and instantly fired, and Pan brought them the grebe.

They waited what seemed a very long time, but nothing appeared, so Pan was thrown ashore by his neck crash in among the "gix" and meadowsweet. He did not care for that, he went to work in an instant. Mark got ready, for though he could not shoot flying he thought some of them would perhaps swim off. This happened, two moorhens came rushing out, one flew, the other swam as hastily as he could, and Mark shot the latter. But before he could load again Pan had disturbed the whole island, some went this way, some that, and all the fowl were scattered.

It was some time before they could get the excited spaniel on board; so soon as they could, Bevis poled the raft along to Bamboo Island, where several coots and moorhens had taken refuge. As they came near these being now on the alert began to move off. Mark aimed at one, but he was he thought not quite near enough: Bevis poled faster, when the moorhen at the splash began to rise, scuttling and dragging the long hanging legs along the surface.

Mark drew the match down into the priming, the shot widening as it went, struck up the water like a shower round the moorhen, which though only hit by one pellet, fell and dived: Pan following. The bird came up to breathe. Pan saw her, and yelped. He touched ground and ran plunging in the water, cantering, lifting his fore-paws and beating the water, for he could not run in the same way as ashore. He caught another glimpse of the bird, dashed to the spot, and thrust his nose and head right under, but missed her. By now the raft had come up, and they beat the weeds with their poles. The moorhen doubled into the bamboos and sedges, but they were so thick they hindered her progress, and Pan snapped her up in a moment.

From Bamboo Island, Bevis poled round to five or six banks covered with sedges, and Mark had another shot, but this time, perhaps a little too confident, he missed altogether. There did not seem any probability of their shooting any more, so they returned towards New Formosa, when Mark wanted to have one more look round the lower and more level end of that island. Bevis poled that way, and Mark, seeing something black with a white bill moving in the weeds, fired—a very long shot—and felt sure that he had wounded the bird, though for a minute it disappeared. Presently Pan brought them a young coot.

Mark had now shot three moorhens, a coot, and a dab-chick, but what pleased him most was the moorhen he had hit while flying, though but one shot had taken effect. He could not have shot so many with so cumbrous a gun had not the water-fowl been nearly all young, and had not some time gone by since the last raid had been made upon these sedgy covers; so that, as is the case on all uninhabited islands, the birds were easy to approach.

Finding that the sun-dial still only gave the time as half-past twelve, Mark wanted to try spinning again for jack if Bevis was not too tired of poling on the raft. Bevis was willing, so they started again, and he poled slowly along the edge of the broad bands of weeds, while Mark drew the bait through the water. He had one success, bringing a jack of about two pounds on deck, but no more.

Then, returning to New Formosa, they visited the wires set for kangaroos, which had been forgotten. One had been pushed down, but nothing was caught. The wires were moved and set up in other runs, with more caution not to touch the grass or the run—the kangaroo's footpath— with the hand, and the loops were made a little larger. If the loop is too small the rabbit pushes the wire aside; so that it had better be just a little too large, that the head may be certain to go through, when the shoulders will draw the noose tight. They did not sit down to dinner till past two o'clock, having had a long morning, no part of which had been lost in cooking.

Watching for Charlie in the afternoon, they reclined on the cliff under the oak, resting, and talking but little. The light of the sun was often intercepted, not entirely shut off, but intercepted by thin white clouds slowly drifting over, which like branches held back so much of the rays that the sun could occasionally be looked at. Then he came out again and lit up the waters in gleaming splendour. There was enough ripple to prevent them from seeing any basking fish, but the shifting, uncertain air was not enough to be called a breeze.

Lying at full length inside the shadow of the oak, Bevis gazed up at the clouds, which were at an immense height, and drifted so slowly as to scarcely seem to move, only he saw that they did because he had a fixed point in the edge of the oak boughs. So thin and delicate was the texture of the white sky-lace above him that the threads scarcely hid the blue which the eye knew was behind and above it. It was warm without the pressure of heat, soft, luxurious; the summer like them reclined, resting in the fulness of the time.

The summer rested before it went on to autumn. Already the tips of the reeds were brown, the leaves of the birch were specked, and some of the willows dropped yellow ovals on the water; the acorns were bulging in their cups, the haws showed among the hawthorn as their green turned red; there was a gloss on the blue sloes among the "wait-a-bit" blackthorns, red threads appeared in the moss of the canker-roses on the briars. A sense of rest, the rest not of weariness, but of full growth, was in the atmosphere; tree, plant, and grassy things had reached their fulness and strength.

The summer shadow lingered on the dial, the sun slowed his pace, pausing on his way, in the rich light the fruits filled. The earth had listened to the chorus of the birds, and as they ceased gave them their meed of berry, seed, and grain. There was no labour for them; their granaries were full. Ethereal gold floated about the hills, filling their hollows to the brim with haze. Like a grape the air was ripe and luscious, and to breathe it was a drowsy joy. For Circe had smoothed her garment and slumbered, and the very sun moved slow.

They remained idle under the oak for some time after Charlie had made the usual signal; but when the shadow of the wood came out over the brambles towards the fence Mark reloaded the matchlock, and they went into ambush by Kangaroo Hill among the hazel bushes this time on the opposite side. The hazel bushes seemed quite vacant, only one bird passed while they were there, and that was a robin, come to see what they were doing and if there was anything for him. In the butchery of the Wars of the Roses, that such flowers should be stained with such memories! it is certain as the murderers watched the robin perched hard by. He listened to the voice of fair Rosamond; he was at the tryst when Amy Robsart met her lover. Nothing happens in the fields and woods without a robin.

Mark had a shot at last at a kangaroo, but though Pan raced his hardest it escaped into the bury. It was of no use to wait any longer, so they walked very slowly round the island, waiting behind every bush, and looking out over the water. There was nothing till, as they returned the other side, they saw the parrots approach and descend into the ivy-grown oak. Bevis held Pan while Mark crept forward from tree-trunk to tree-trunk till he was near enough, when he put the heavy barrel against a tree, in the same way Bevis had done. His aim was true, and the parrot fell.

It had been agreed that Bevis should have the gun at night, for he wished to go on the mainland and see if he could shoot anything in the Waste, but still unsatisfied Mark wanted yet another shot. The thirst of the chase was on him; he could not desist. Since there was nothing else he fired at and killed a thrush they found perched on the top of the stockade. Mark put down the gun with a sigh that his shooting was over.

Bevis waited till it was full moonlight, putting down a few things in his journal, while Mark skinned three of his finest perch, which he meant to have for supper. To be obliged to cook was one thing, to cook just for the pleasure of the taste was a different thing. He skinned them because he knew the extreme difficulty of scraping the thickset hard scales. Presently Bevis loaded the gun; he was going to do so with ball, when Mark pointed out that he could not be certain of a perfectly accurate aim by moonlight.

This was true, so he reluctantly put shot. Mark's one desire was to fetch down his game; Bevis wished to kill with the precision of a single bullet.

They poled the raft ashore, and both landed, but Mark stayed among the bramble thickets holding Pan, while Bevis went out into the Waste. He did not mean to stay in ambush long anywhere, but to try and get a shot from behind the bushes. Crouching in the brambles, Mark soon lost sight of him, so soon that he seemed to have vanished; the ant-hills, the tall thistles, and the hawthorns concealed him.

Bevis stepped noiselessly round the green ant-hills, sometimes startling a lark, till, when he looked back, he scarcely knew which way he had come. In a meadow or a cornfield the smooth surface lets the glance travel at once to the opposite hedge, and the shape of the enclosure or one at least of its boundaries is seen, so that the position is understood. But here the ant-hills and the rush-bunches, the thickets of thistles and brambles gave the ground an uneven surface, and the hawthorn-trees hid the outline.

There was no outline; it was a dim uncertain expanse with shadows, and a grey mist rising here and there, and slight rustlings as pads pressed the sward, or wings rose from roost. Once he fancied he saw a light upon the ground not so far off; he moved that way, but the thistles or bushes hid it. A silent owl startled him as it slipped past; he stamped his foot with anger that he should have been startled. Twice he caught a glimpse of white tails, but he could not shoot running with the matchlock.

Incessantly winding round and round the ant-hills, he did not know which way he was going, except that he tried to keep the moon a little on his left hand, thinking he could shoot better with the light like that. After some time he reached a boulder, another one not so large as that they had examined together; this was about as high as his chest.

He leaned against it and looked over; there was a green waggon track the other side, which wound out from the bushes, and again disappeared among them. Though he knew that Mark could not be far, and that a whistle would bring him, he felt utterly alone. It was wilder than the island—the desolate thistles, the waste of rushes, the thorns, the untouched land which the ants possessed and not man, the cold grey boulder, the dots of mist here and there, and the pale light of the moon. Something of the mystery of the ancient days hovers at night over these untilled places. He leaned against the stone and looked for the flicker of light which he had seen, and supposed must be a will-o'-the-wisp, but he did not see it again.

Suddenly something came round the corner of the smooth green waggon track, and he knew in an instant by the peculiar amble that it was a hare. The long barrel of the matchlock was cautiously placed on the stone, and he aimed as well as he could, for when looked at along a barrel objects have a singular way of disappearing at night. Then he paused, for the hare still came on. Hares seem to see little in front; their eyes sweep each side, but straight ahead they are blind till the air brings them the scent they dread.

All at once the hare sat up—he had sniffed Bevis, and the same minute the flash rushed from the muzzle. Bevis ran directly and found the hare struggling; almost as soon as he had lifted him up Pan was there. Then Mark came leaping from ant-hill to ant-hill, and crushing through the thistles in his haste. As Mark had come direct from the shore he knew the general direction, and they hurried back to the raft, fearing some of the savages might come to see who was shooting on the mainland. Once on the island, as the perch were cooking, the game was spread out on the table—three moorhens, a coot, a dab-chick, a wood-pigeon, a hare, and the jack Mark had caught.

Of all the hare, or rather leveret, for it was a young one, was the finest. His black-tipped ears, his clean pads, his fur—every separate hair with three shades of colour—it was a pleasure to smooth his fur down with the hand.

"This is the jolliest day we've had," said Mark. "All shooting and killing and real hunting—real island—and no work and no cooking, except just what we like. It's splendid."

"If only Val and Cecil could see," said Bevis, handling the ears of his hare for the twentieth time. "Won't they go on when we tell them?"

"Don't talk about that," said Mark; "don't say anything about going home; that's the Other Side, you know."

"So it is. No, we won't say anything about it. Isn't he a beauty!"

"A real beauty," said Mark. "Now let's see how we can shoot a lot more to-morrow; it's your turn; will you let me shoot once?"

"Of course; twice."

"Hurrah! First let's get up very early and see if a kangaroo is out; then let's go round Serendib; and, I say, let's go nearly up to Sweet River Falls—not quite, not near enough for the savages—and, I say! there must be heaps of things in all those sedges we tried to walk through once!"

"We could pole across to them."

"Of course; and then get in ambush on the mainland in the evening, and shoot another parrot, and fish—no, fishing is slow, rather. Suppose we make a fish-spear and stick them! and stick it into the mud for eels. Could you think how to make a fish-spear, not my bone harpoon, an iron one—sharp?"

"I'll try."

"O! you can do it; and let's put up some more wires, and—I do declare, I forgot to put in some more trimmers; we might put twenty trimmers and nightlines—"

"And build a hut on Serendib to wait in in winter when the ducks come—don't you remember last winter—hundreds of them?"

"First-rate! But now to-morrow. How stupid we never brought any nets!"

"Well, that was stupid," said Bevis, still stroking his hare; he loved the creature he had slain. "I can't think how we forgot the nets."

"There's thousands of fish; we could haul out a boatful. Let's see, isn't there anything else we could do? Wish we had some ferrets! It's not the right time, but still it doesn't matter."

"Perhaps we could build a fence-net," said Bevis. "I forget the proper name; it's a stockade like a V, and you drive all the animals in with dogs."

"And a pit with strong spikes at the bottom in the corner. The perch are ready; move the things."

Bevis hung the hare up in the cave, but yet remained a moment to stroke the unconscious creature. The perch were very good indeed; as they were not in a hurry the fish had been cooked better. They played cards afterwards, discussing in the meantime various ways of killing the animals and birds about them.

Already in one day they had got more than enough to serve them for three or four, yet they were not satisfied. Like savages, they were hurried on by the thirst of the chase, like the thirst for wine; their tongues were parched with the dry sulphur fumes of powder; they hungered to repeat the wild excitement when the game was struck and hunted down. Had it been the buffaloes of the prairie, it would have been just the same; had it been the great elephants of inner Africa, they would have shot them down without even a thought of the ivory.

As they were fastening up Pan at the doorway before lying down they recollected the visit of the unknown creature on the previous night, and went out and padlocked the gate. The matchlock was loaded with shot, which did not require so accurate an aim, and was therefore best for shooting in a hurry, and instead of being hung up it was leaned against the wall as more accessible, and the priming seen to. A long candle was put in the lantern on the niche and left burning, so that if awakened they could see to get the gun at once. The creature went off so quickly that not a moment must be lost in shooting if it came again, and they said to each other (to set the clock of their minds) that they would not stop to listen, but jump up the second they awoke if Pan barked. This time they thought they should be sure to see the animal at least, if not shoot it.

Chapter Ten
New Formosa—The Tiger from the Reeds

Pan did bark. It seemed to them that they had scarcely closed their eyes; in reality they had slept hours; and the candle had burned short. The clock of their minds being set, they were off the bed in an instant. Bevis, before his eyes were hardly open, was lighting the match of the gun; Mark had darted to the curtain at the door.

There was a thick mist and he could see nothing: in a second he snatched out his pocket-knife (for they slept in their clothes), and cut the cord with which Pan was fastened up just as Bevis came with the gun. Pan raced for the aperture in the fence at the corner by the cliff—he perfectly howled with frantic rage as he ran and crushed himself through. They were now under the open shed outside the hut, and heard Pan scamper without; suddenly his howl of rage stopped, there was a second of silence, then the dog yelled with pain. The next moment he crept back through the fence and before he was through something hurled itself against the stockade behind him with such force that the fence shook.

"Shoot—shoot there," shouted Mark, as the dog crept whining towards them. Bevis lifted the gun, but paused.

"If the thing jumps over the fence," he said. He had but one shot, he could not load quickly: Mark understood.

"No—no, don't shoot. Here—here's the bow."

Bevis took it and sent an arrow at the fence in the corner with such force that it penetrated the willow-work up to the feather. Then they both ran to the gate and looked over. All this scarcely occupied a minute.

But there was nothing to see. The thick white mist concealed everything but the edge of the brambles near the stockade, and the tops of the trees farther away.

"Nothing," said Mark. "What was it?"

"Shall we go out?" said Bevis.

"No—not till we have seen it."

"It would be better not—we can't tell."

"You can shoot as it jumps the fence," said Mark, "if it comes: it will stop a minute on the top."

Unless they can clear a fence, animals pause a moment on the top before they leap down. They went back to the open shed with a feeling that it would be best to be some way inside the fence, and so have a view of the creature before it sprang. Mark picked up an axe, for he had no weapon but a second arrow which he had in his hand: the axe was the most effective weapon there was after the gun. They stood under the shed, watching the top of the stockade and waiting.

Till now they had looked upon the unknown as a stealthy thief only, but when Pan recoiled they knew it must be something more.

"It might jump down from the cliff," said Bevis.

While they watched the semi-circular fence in front the creature might steal round to the cliff and leap down on the roof of the hut. Mark stepped out and looked along the verge of the sand cliff. He could see up through the runners of the brambles which hung over the edge, and there was nothing there. Looking up like this he could see the pale stars above the mist. It was not a deep mist—it was like a layer on the ground, impenetrable to the eye longitudinally, but partially transparent vertically. Returning inside, Mark stooped and examined Pan, who had crept at their heels. There were no scratches on him.

"He's not hurt," said Mark. "No teeth or claws."

"But he had a pat, didn't he?"

"I thought so—how he yelled! But you look, there's no blood. Perhaps the thing hit him without putting its claws out."

"They slip out when they strike," said Bevis, meaning that as wild beasts strike their claws involuntarily extend from the sheaths. He looked, Pan was not hurt; Mark felt his ribs too, and said that none were broken. There were no fragments of fur or hair about his mouth, no remnants of a struggle.

"I don't believe he fought at all," said Bevis. "He stopped—he never went near."

"Very likely: now I remember—he stopped barking all at once; he was afraid!"

"That was it: but he yelled—"

"It must have been fright," said Mark. "Nothing touched him: Pan, what was it?"

Pan wagged his tail once, once only: he still crouched and kept close to them. Though patted and reassured, his spirit had been too much broken to recover rapidly. The spaniel was thoroughly cowed.

"It came very near," said Bevis. "It hit the fence while he was getting through."

"It must have missed him—perhaps it was a long jump. Did you hear anything rush off."

"No."

"No more did I."

"Soft pads," said Bevis, "they make no noise like hoofs."

"No, that was it: and it's sandy too." Sand "gives" a little and deadens the sound of footsteps.

"Let's go and look again."

"So we will."

They went to the gate—Pan, they noticed did not follow—and looked over again: this time longer and more searchingly. They could see the ground for a few yards, and then the mist obscured it like fleece among brambles.

"Pan's afraid to come," said Mark, as they went back to the shed.

"The fire ought to be lit," said Bevis. "They are afraid of fire."

"You watch," said Mark, "and I'll light it."

He drew on his boots, and put on his coat—for they ran out in waistcoat and trousers—then he held the gun, while Bevis did the same; then Bevis took it, and Mark hastily gathered some sticks together and lit them, often glancing over his shoulder at the fence behind, and with the axe always ready to his hand. When the flames began to rise they felt more at ease; they knew that wild beasts dislike fire, and somehow fire warms the spirit as well as the body. The morning was warm enough, they did not need a fire, but the sight of the twisted tongues as they curled spirally and broke away was restorative as the heat is to actual bodily chill. Bevis went near: even the spaniel felt it, he shook himself and seemed more cheerful.

"The thing was very near when we first went out," said Bevis. "I wish we had run to the gate directly without waiting for the gun."

"But we did not know what it was."

"No."

"And I cut Pan loose directly."

"It had only to run ten yards to be out of sight in the mist."

"And it seems so dark when you first run out."

"It's lighter now."

"There's no dew."

"Dry mist—it's clearing a little."

As they stood by the fire the verge of the cliff above the roof of the hut came out clear of vapour, then they saw the trees outside the stockade rise as it were higher as the vapour shrunk through them: the stars were very faint.

"Lu—lu!" said Mark, pointing to the crevice between the fence and the cliff, and urging Pan to go out again: the spaniel went a few yards towards it, then turned and came back. He could not be induced to venture alone.

"Lions *do* get loose sometimes," said Bevis thoughtfully. He had been running over every wild beast in his mind that could by any possibility approach them. Cases do occur every now and then of vans being overturned, and lions and tigers escaping.

"So they do, but we have not heard any roar."

"No, and we must have come on it if it stops on the island," said Bevis. "We have been all round so many times. Or does it go to and fro—do lions swim?"

"He would have no need to," said Mark. "I mean not after he had swum over here, he wouldn't go away for us—he could lie in the bushes."

"Perhaps we have gone close by it without knowing," said Bevis. "There's the 'wait-a-bit thorns.'"

They had never been through the thicket of blackthorn.

"Pan never barked though. He's been all round the island with us."

"Perhaps he was afraid—like he was just now."

"Ah, yes, very likely."

"And we hit him too to keep him quiet, not to startle the kangaroos."

"Or the water-fowl—so we did: we may have gone close by it without knowing." "In the 'wait-a-bits' or the hazel."

"Or the sedges, where it's drier."

"Foxes lie in withy beds—why should not this?"

"Of course: but I say—only think, we may have gone within reach of its paw ten times."

"While we were lying down too," said Bevis, "in ambush It might have been in the ferns close behind."

"All the times we walked about and never took the gun," said Mark; "or the bow and arrow, or the axe, or anything—and just think! Why we came back from the raft without even a stick in our hands."

"Yes—it was silly: and we came quietly too, to try and see it."

"Well, we just were stupid!" said Mark. "Only we never thought It could be anything big."

"But It must be."

"Of course It is: we won't go out again without the gun, and the axe—"

"And my bow to shoot again, because you can't load a matchlock quick."

"That's the worst of it: tigers get loose too sometimes, don't they? and panthers more often, because there are more of them."

"Yes, one is as dangerous as the other. Panthers are worse than lions."

"More creepy."

"Cattish. They slink on you; they don't roar first."

"Then perhaps it's a panther."

"Perhaps. This is a very likely place, if anything has got loose; there's the jungle on the mainland, and all the other woods, and the Chase up by Jack's."

"Yes—plenty of cover: almost like forest."

Besides the great wood in which they had wandered there were several others in the neighbourhood, and a Chase on the hills by Jack's, so that in case of a beast escaping from a caravan it would find extensive cover to hide in.

"Only think," said Bevis, "when we bathed!"

"Ah!" Mark shuddered. While they bathed naked and unarmed, had it darted from the reeds they would have fallen instant victims, without the possibility of a struggle even.

"It *is* horrible," said Bevis.

"There are reeds and sedges everywhere," said Mark. "It may be anywhere."

"It's not safe to move."

"Especially as Pan's afraid and won't warn us. *If* the thing had seen us bathing; It could not, or else—ah!"

"They tear so," said Bevis. "It's not the wound so much as the tearing."

"Like bramble hooks," said Mark. The curved hooks of brambles and briars inflict lacerated hurts worse than the spikes of thorns. Flesh that is torn cannot heal like that which is incised. "O! stop! panthers get in trees, don't they? It may have been up in that oak that day!"

"In the ivy: we looked!"

"But the ivy is thick and we might not have seen! It might have jumped down on us."

"So it might any minute in the wood."

"Then we can't go in the wood."

"Nor among the sedges round the shore."

"Nor the brambles, nor fern, nor hazel."

"Nowhere—except on the raft."

"Then we must take care how we come back."

"How shall we sleep!"

"Ah!—think, it might have come any night!"

"We left the gate open."

"O! how stupid we have been."

"It could kill Pan with one stroke."

"And Pan was not here: he used to swim off."

"Directly he was tied up, you recollect, the very first night, he barked—no, the second."

"It may have come *every* night before."

"Right inside the stockade—under the awning."

"Into the hut while we were away—the bacon was on the shelf."

"If It could jump up like that, it could jump the fence."

"Of course; and it shows it was a cat-like creature, because it could take one thing without disturbing another. Dogs knock things down, cats don't."

"No, panthers are a sort of big cat."

"That's what gnawed the jack's head."

"And why there was no mark on the ground—their pads are so soft, and don't cut holes like hoofs."

"The kangaroos too, you remember: very often they wouldn't come out. Something was about."

"Of course. How could we have been so stupid as not to see this before!"

"Why, we never suspected."

"But we ought to have suspected. You thought you saw something move in the sedges on Sunday."

"So I did—it was this thing: it must have been."

"Then it swims off and comes back."

"Then if we hunt all over the island and don't find It—we're no safer, because it may come off to us any time."

"Any time."

"What *shall* we do?"

"Can't go home," said Bevis.

"Can't go home," repeated Mark.

They could not desert their island: it would have been so like running away too, and they had so often talked of Africa and shooting big game. Then to run away when in its presence would have lowered them in their own estimation.

"Can't," said Bevis again.

"Can't," again repeated Mark. They *could* not go—they must face It, whatever it was.

"We shall have to look before every step," said Bevis. "Up in the trees—through the bushes—and the reeds."

"We must not go in the reeds much: you can't tell there—"

"No, not much. We must watch at night. First one, and then the other."

"And keep the fire burning. There ought to be a fence along the top of the cliff."

"Yes—that's very awkward: you can't put stakes in hard sand like that."

"We must drive in some—and cut them sharp at the top."

"What a pity the stockade is not sharp at the top!—Nails, that's it: we must drive in long nails and file the tops off!"

"And put some stakes with nails along the cliff—the thing could not get in quite so quick."

"The gate is not very strong: we must barricade it."

"Wish we could lock the door!"

"I should think so!"

Now they realised what is forgotten in the routine of civilised life—the security of doors and bolts. Their curtain was no defence.

"Barricade the door."

"Yes, but not too close, else we can't shoot—we should be trapped."

"I see! Put the barricade round a little way in front. Why not have two fires, one each side!"

"Capital. We will fortify the place! Loop-holes. The weak spot will be the edge of the cliff up there. If we put a fire there people may see it—savages—and find us."

"That won't do."

"No: we must fortify the edge somehow, stakes with nails for one thing. Perhaps a train of gunpowder!"

"Ah, yes. Lucky we've got plenty to eat. It won't be nice not to have the gun loaded. I mean while loading the thing might come."

"We've got plenty to eat."

"And I wanted a lot of shooting to-day," said Mark.

"All that's spoiled."

"Quite spoiled."

Yesterday they had become intoxicated with the savage joy of killing, the savage's cruel but wild and abandoned and unutterable joy: they had planned slaughter for to-day. To-day they were themselves environed with deadly peril. This is the opposite side of wild life: the forest takes its revenge by filling the mind with ceaseless anxiety.

"The sun!" said Bevis with pleasure as the rays fell aslant into the open shed. The sun had been above the horizon some little while but had been concealed by the clouds and thick vapour. Now that the full bright light of day was come there seemed no need of such intense watchfulness. It was hardly likely that they would be attacked in their stockade in broad daylight; the boldest beasts of prey would not do that unless driven very hard by hunger.

But when they began to prepare the breakfast, there was no water to fill the kettle: Mark generally went down to the shore for water every morning. Although they had no formal arrangement, in practice it had gradually come about that one did one thing and one another: Mark got the water, Bevis cut up wood for the fire. Mark had usually gone with the zinc bucket, whistling down to the strand merry enough. Now he took up the bucket, but hesitated.

"I'll come," said Bevis. "One can't go alone anywhere now."

"The other must always have the matchlock ready."

"Always," said Bevis, "and keep a sharp lookout all round while one does the things. Why the gun is only loaded with shot, now I remember!"

"No more it is: how lucky It did not jump over! Shot would have been of no use."

"I'll shoot it off," said Bevis—"our ramrod won't draw a charge—and load again."

"Yes, do."

Bevis fired the charge in the air, and they heard the pellets presently falling like hail among the trees outside. Then he loaded again with ball, blew the match, and looked to the priming; Mark took the axe in one hand and the bucket in the other, and they unlocked the gate.

"We ought to be able to lock it behind us," he said.

"We'll put in another staple presently," said Bevis. "Step carefully to see if there are any marks on the ground."

They examined the surface attentively, but could distinguish no footprints: then they went to the fence where the creature had sprung against it. The arrow projected, and near it, on close investigation, they saw that a piece of the bark of the interwoven willow had been torn off as if by a claw. But look as intently as they would they could not trace it further on such ground, the thin grass and sand would not take an imprint.

"Pads," said Bevis, "else there would have been spoor."

"Tiger, or panther then: we must take care," said Mark. "Pan's all right now, look."

Pan trotted on before them along the well-known path to the shore, swinging his tail and unconcerned. As they walked they kept a watch in every direction, up in the trees, behind the bushes, where the surface was hollow, and avoided the fern. When Mark had dipped, they returned in the same manner, walking slowly and constantly on the alert.

Chapter Eleven
New Formosa—The Fortification

Entering the stockade, they locked the gate behind them, a thing they had never done before in daylight, that they might not be surprised. After breakfast Bevis began to file off the heads of the nails, which was slow work, and when he had done five or six, he thought it would be handier to drive them into the posts first, and file them off afterwards, as they could both work then instead of only one. They had but one vice to hold the nail and only one could use it at a time. So the nails, the longest and largest they had, were driven into the stakes of the stockade about a foot apart—as near as the stakes stood to each other—and thus, not without much weariness of wrist, for filing is tedious, they cut off the heads and sharpened them.

Had these spikes been nearer together it would have been better, but that they could not manage; the willow-work split if a large nail was driven into it. Next they got together materials for barricading the door of the hut, or rather the open shed in front of it. To cut these they had to go outside, and Mark watched with the matchlock while Bevis chopped.

Poles were nailed across the open sides from upright to upright, not more than six inches asunder right up to the beam on two sides. This allowed plenty of space to shoot through, but nothing of any size could spring in. On the third, the poles were nailed across up to three feet high, and the rest prepared and left ready to be lashed in position with cords the last thing at night.

When these were put up there would be a complete cage from within which they could fire or shoot arrows, and be safe from the spring of the beast. Lastly, they went up on the cliff to see what could be done there. The sand was very hard, so that to drive in stakes the whole length of the cliff edge would have taken a day, if not two days.

They decided to put up some just above the hut so as to prevent the creature leaping on to the roof, and perhaps tearing a way through it. Bevis held the matchlock this time and watched while Mark hewed out the stakes, taking the labour and the watching in turn. With much trouble, these were driven home and sharpened nails put at the top, so that the beast approaching from behind would have to leap over these before descending the perpendicular cliff on to the hut. The fortification was now complete, and they sat down to think if there was anything else.

"One thing," said Mark, "we will take care and fill the kettle and the bucket with water this evening before we go to sleep. Suppose the thing came and stopped just outside and wouldn't go away?"

"Besieged us—yes, that would be awkward; we will fill all the pots and things with water, and get in plenty of wood for the fires. How uncomfortable it is without our bath!"

"I feel horrid."

"I *must* have a bath," said Bevis. "I *will* have a swim."

"We can watch in turn, but if the panther sees any one stripped it's more likely to try and seize him."

"Yes, that's true: I know! Suppose we go out on the raft!"

"Right away."

"Out to Pearl Island and swim there: there are no sedges there."

"Hurrah! If he comes we should see him a long way first."

"Of course, and keep the gun ready."

"Come on."

"First drive in the staple to lock the gate outside."

This was done, and then they went down to the raft, moving cautiously and examining every likely place for the beast to lie in ambush before passing. The raft was poled round and out to Pearl Island, on which no sedges grew, nor were there any within seventy or eighty yards. Nothing could approach without being seen.

Yet, when they stood on the brim ready to go into the water the sense of defencelessness was almost overpowering. The gun was at hand, and the match burning, the axe could be snatched up in a moment, the bow was strung and the sharp arrows by it.

But without their clothes they felt defenceless. The human skin offers no resistance to thorn or claw or tusk. There is nothing between us and the enemy, no armour of hide, his tusk can go straight to our lives at once. Standing on the brink they felt the heat of the sun on the skin: if it could not bear even the sunbeams, how could so sensitive and delicate a covering endure the tiger's claw?

"It won't do," said Mark. "No."

"Suppose you watch while I swim, and then you swim and I watch?"

"That will be better."

Bevis stopped on board the raft, threw his coat loosely round his shoulders, — for the sun, if he kept still, would otherwise redden and blister, and cause the skin to peel, — and then took up the matchlock. So soon as Mark saw he had the gun ready, he ran in, for it was too shallow to plunge, and then swam round the raft keeping close to it. When he had had his bath, he threw the towel round his shoulders to protect himself from the heat as Bevis had with his coat and took the gun. Bevis had his swim, and then they dressed.

Poling the raft back to the island, they observed the same precautions in going through the trees to the hut. Once Mark fancied there was something in the fern, but Pan innocently ran there before they could call to him, and as nothing moved they went to the spot, and found that two fronds had turned yellow and looked at a distance a little like the tawny coat of an animal. Except under excitement and not in a state of terrorism they would have recognised the yellow fern in an instant; but when intent on one subject the mind is ready to construe everything as relating to it, and disallows the plain evidence of the senses. Even "seeing" is hardly "believing."

They reached the hut without anything happening, and as they could not now wander about the island in the careless way they had hitherto done, and had nothing else to do, they cooked two of the moorhens. The gate in the stockade was locked, and the gun kept constantly at hand. A good deal of match was consumed, as it had to be always burning, else they could not shoot quickly. Soon the sense of confinement became irksome: they could not go outside without arming to the teeth, and to walk up and down so circumscribed a space was monotonous, indeed they could not do it after such freedom.

"Can't move," said Mark.

"Chained up like dogs."

"I hate it."

"Hate it! I should think so!"

"But we can't go out."

"No."

They had to endure it: they could not even go up to see the time by the dial without one accompanying the other with the gun as guard. It was late when they had finished dinner, and went up to watch for the signal. On the cliff they felt more secure, as nothing could approach in front, and behind the slope was partly open, still one had always to keep watch even there. Mark sat facing the slope with the gun: Bevis faced the New Sea with the telescope. The sky had clouded over and there was more wind, in puffs, from the south-east. Charlie soon came, waved the handkerchief, and went away.

"I wish he was here," said Bevis.

"So do I now," said Mark, "and Val and Cecil—"

"And Ted."

"Yes. But how could we know that there was a panther here?"

"But it serves us right for not asking them," said Bevis. "It was selfish of us."

"Suppose we go ashore and send Loo to tell Charlie and Val—"

"Last night," said Bevis, interrupting, "why—while I was out in the wilderness and you were in the thicket the thing might have had either of us."

"No one watching."

"If one was attacked, no one near to help."

"No."

"But we could both go together, and tell Loo, and get Charlie and Val and Cecil and Ted. If we all had guns now!"

"Five or six of us!"

"Perhaps if we told the people at home, the governor would let me have one of his: then we could load and shoot quick!"

"And the Jolly Old Moke would let me have his! and if Val could get another and Ted, we could hunt the island and shoot the creature."

Mark was as eager now for company as he had been before that no one should enjoy the island with them.

"We could bring them all off on the raft," said Bevis. "It would carry four, I think."

"Twice would do it then. Let's tell them! Let's see Loo, and send her! Wouldn't they come as quick as lightning!"

"They would be wild to help to shoot it."

"Just to have the chance."

"Yes; but I say! what stupes we should be!" said Bevis.

"Why? How?"

"After we have had all the danger and trouble, to let them come in and have the shooting and the hunt and the skin."

"Triumph and spoils!"

"Striped skin."

"Or spotted."

"Or tawny mane—we don't know which. Just think, to let them have it!"

"No," said Mark. "That we won't: we must have it."

"It's *our* tiger," said Bevis.

"All ours."

"Every bit."

"The claws make things, don't they?" said Mark: he meant the reverse, that things are made of tiger's claws as trophies.

"Yes, and the teeth."

"And the skin—beautiful!"

"Splendid!"

"Rugs."

"Hurrah!"

"We'll have him!"

"Kill him!"

"Yow—wow!"

Pan caught their altered mood and leaped on them, barking joyously. They went down into the stockade and considered if there was anything they could do to add to their defences, and at the same time increase the chances of shooting the tiger.

"Perhaps he won't spring over," said Mark; "suppose we leave the gate open? else we shan't get a shot at him."

"I want a shot at him while he's on the fence," said Bevis, "balanced on the top, you know, like Pan sometimes at home." In leaping a fence or gate too high for him they had often laughed at the spaniel swaying on the edge and not able to get his balance to leap down without falling headlong. "I know what we will do," he continued, "we'll put out some meat to tempt him."

"Bait."

"Hang up the other birds—and my hare—no—shall I? He's such a beauty. Yes, I will. I'll put the hare out too. Hares are game; he's sure to jump over for the hare."

"Drive in a stake half-way," said Mark, meaning half-way between the cage and the stockade. "Let's do it now."

There were several pieces of poles lying about, and the stake was soon up. The birds and the hare were to be strung to it to tempt the beast to leap into the enclosure. The next point was at what part should they aim? At the head, the shoulders, or where? as the most fatal.

The head was the best, but then in the hurry and excitement they might miss it, and he might not turn his shoulder, so they decided that whoever was on the watch at the moment should aim at the body of the creature so as to be certain to plant a bullet in it. If he was once hit, his rage and desire of revenge would prevent him from going away; he would attack the cage, and while he was venting his rage on the bars there would be time to load and fire again.

"And put the muzzle close to his head the second time," said Mark.

"Certain to kill then."

They sat down inside the cage and imagined the position the beast would be in when it approached them. Mark was to load the matchlock for the second shot in any case, while Bevis sent arrow after arrow into the creature. Pan was to be tied up with a short cord, else perhaps the tiger or panther would insert a paw and kill him with a single pat.

"But it's so long to wait," said Mark. "He won't come till the middle of the night."

"He's been in the day when we were out," said Bevis. "Suppose we go up on the cliff, leave the gate open, and if he comes shoot down at him?"

"Come on."

They went up on the cliff, just behind the spiked stakes, taking with them the gun, the axe, and bow and arrows. If the beast entered the enclosure they could get a capital shot down at him, nor could he leap up, he would have to go some distance round to get at them, and meantime the gun could be reloaded. They waited, nothing entered the stockade but a robin.

"This is very slow," said Mark.

"Very," said Bevis. "What's the use of waiting? Suppose we go and hunt him up."

"In the wood?"

"Everywhere—sedges and fern—everywhere."

"Hurrah!"

Up they jumped full of delight at the thought of freedom again. It was so great a relief to move about that they ignored the danger. Anything was better than being forced to stay still.

"If he's on the island we'll find him."

"Leave the gate open, that we may run in quick."

"Perhaps he'll go in while we're away, then we can just slip up on the cliff, and fire down—"

"Jolly!"

"Look very sharp."

"Blow the match."

They entered among the trees, following the path which led round the island. Bevis carried the matchlock, Mark the bow and arrows and axe, and it was arranged that the moment Bevis had fired he was to pass the gun to Mark, and take his bow. While he shot arrows, Mark was to load and shoot as quick as he could. The axe was to be thrown down on the ground, so that either could snatch it up if necessary. All they regretted was that they had not got proper hunting-knives.

First they went down to the raft moored to the alder bough as usual, then on to the projecting point where Mark once fished; on again to where the willow-tree lay overthrown in the water, and up to the firs under which they had reclined. Then they went to the shore at the uttermost southern extremity and sent Pan into the sedges. He drove out a moorhen, but they did not shoot at it now, not daring to do so lest the beast should attack them before they could load again.

Coming up the western side of the island, they once thought they saw something in the bushes, but found it to be the trunk of a fallen tree. In going inland to Kangaroo Hill they moved more slowly as the wood was thicker, and intent on the slightest indication, the sudden motion of a squirrel climbing a beech startled them. From the top of the green knoll they looked all round, and thus examined the glade. There was not the slightest sign. The feathers of a wood-pigeon were scattered on the grass in one place, where a hawk had struck it down. This had happened since they were last at the glade. It was probably one of the pigeons that roosted in the ivy-grown oak.

Crossing to the oak, they flung sticks up into the ivy; there was no roar in response. While here they remembered the wires, and looked at them, but there was nothing caught, which they considered a proof that the rabbits were afraid to venture far from their burries while the tiger, or whatever beast it was, was prowling about at night.

Returning to the shore, they recollected a large bed of sedges and reed-grass a little way back, and going there Bevis shot an arrow into it. The arrow slipped through the reed-grass with a slight rustle till it was lost. The spaniel ran in and they heard him plunging about. There was nothing in the reed-grass.

Lastly they went to the thicket of "wait-a-bit" blackthorn. Pan did go in, and that was as much, he soon came out, he did not like the blackthorn. But by throwing stones and fragments of dead branches up in the air so that they should descend into the midst of the thicket they satisfied themselves that there was nothing in it. It was necessary to cast the stones and sticks up into the air because they would not penetrate if thrown horizontally.

The circuit of the island was completed, and they now crept up quietly to the verge of the cliff behind the spiked stakes. The stockade was exactly as they had left it; Pan looked over the edge of the cliff into it, and did not even sniff. They went down and rested a few minutes.

There never was greater temerity than this searching the island for the tiger. Neither the bullet nor their arrows would have stayed the advance of that terrible beast for a moment. Inside their stockade and cage they might withstand him; in the open he would have swept them down just as a lady's sleeve might sweep down the chessmen on the board. Thus in his native haunts he overthrows a crowd of spear-armed savages.

"He can't be on the island," said Mark.

"It's curious we did not see any sign," said Bevis. "There are no marks or footprints anywhere."

"If there was some clay now—wet clay," said Mark, "but it's all sandy; his claws would show in clay like Pan's."

"Like a crab." Pan's footprint in moist clay was somewhat crab-shaped.

"Is there no place where he would leave a mark?"

"Just at the edge of the water the moorhens leave footprints."

"That would be the place, only we can't look very close to the edge everywhere."

"There's the raft; we could on the raft."

"Shall we go on the raft?"

"Suppose we go all round the island?" said Bevis, "on the raft."

"We never have been," said Mark. "Not close to the shore."

"No; let us pole round close to the shore—all round, and see if we can find any spoor in the shallows."

They went to the raft and embarked. As they started a crimson glow shot along under the clouds, the sun was sinking and the sky beamed. The wind had risen and the wavelets came splash, splash against the edge of the raft. Some of the yellow leaves of the willows floated along and fell on the deck. They poled slowly and constantly grounded or struck the shore, so that it occupied some time to get round, especially as at the southern extremity it was so shallow they were obliged to go a long way out.

In about an hour they reached the thick bed of reed-grass into which Bevis had shot his arrow, and as the raft slowly glided by Mark suddenly exclaimed, "There it is!"

There it was—a path through the reed-grass down to the water's edge—the trail of some creature. Bevis stuck his pole into the ground to check the onward movement of the raft. The impetus of the heavy vessel was so great though moving slowly that it required all his strength to stay it. Mark came with his pole, and together they pushed the raft back, and it ran right up into the reed-grass and grounded. Pan instantly leapt off into the path, and ran along it wagging his tail; he had the scent, though it seemed faint as he did not give tongue. They stood at the bulwark of the raft and looked at the trail.

Chapter Twelve
New Formosa—The Trail

At the water's edge some flags were bent, and then the tall grass, as high as their chests, was thrust aside, forming a path which had evidently been frequently trodden. There was now no longer the least doubt that the creature, whatever it was, was of large size, and as the trail was so distinct the thought occurred to them both at once that perhaps it had been used by more than one. From the raft they could see along it five or six yards, then it turned to avoid an alder. While they stood looking Pan came back, he had run right through and returned, so that there was nothing in the reed-bed at present.

Bevis stepped over the bulwark into the trail with the matchlock; Mark picked up the axe and followed. As they walked their elbows touched the grass each side, which showed that the creature was rather high than broad, lean like the whole feline tribe, long, lean, and stealthy. The reed-grass had flowered and would soon begin to stiffen and rustle dry under the winds. By the alder a bryony vine that had grown there was broken and had withered, it had been snapped long since by the creature pushing through.

The trail turned to the right, then to the left round a willow stole, and just there Pan, who trotted before Bevis, picked up a bone. He had picked it up before and dropped it; he took it again from habit, though he knew it was sapless and of no use to him. Bevis took it from his mouth, and they knew it at once as a duck's drumstick. It was polished and smooth, as if the creature had licked it, or what was more probable carried it some distance, and then left it as useless. They had no doubt it was a drumstick of the wild duck Mark shot.

The trail went straight through sedges next, these were trampled flat; then as the sedges grew wider apart they gradually lost it in the thin, short grass. This was why they had not seen it from the land, there the path began by degrees; at the water's edge, where the grasses were thick and high, it was seen at once. Try how they would, they could not follow the trail inland, they thought they knew how to read "sign," but found themselves at fault. On the dry, hard ground the creature's pads left no trail that they could trace. Mark cut off a stick with the axe and stuck it up in the ground so that they could find the spot where the path faded when walking on shore, and they then returned to the raft. On the way they caught sight of Bevis's arrow sticking in the trunk of the alder, and withdrew it.

At the water's edge they looked to see if there was any spoor. In passing through the reed-grass the creature had trampled it down, and so walked on a carpet of vegetation which prevented any footprints being left on the ground though it was moist there. At the water's edge perhaps they might have found some, but in pushing the raft up the beams had rubbed over the mud and obliterated everything. When they got on the raft they looked over the other bulwark, and a few yards from the shore noticed that the surface of the weeds growing there appeared disturbed.

The raft was moved out, and they found that the weeds had been trampled; the water was very shallow, so that the creature in approaching the shore had probably plunged up and down as the spaniel did in shallow water. Like the reed-grass the trampled weeds had prevented any footprints in the ooze. They traced the course the creature had come out for fully thirty yards, and the track pointed straight to the shore of the mainland so that it seemed as if it started at no great distance from where they used to land.

But when they had thrust the raft as far as this, not without great difficulty, for it dragged heavily on the weeds and sometimes on the ground, the marks changed and trended southwards. The water was a little deeper and the signs became less and less obvious, but still there they were, and they now pointed directly south. They lost them at the edge of the weeds, the water was still shallow, but the character of the bottom had changed from ooze to hard rock-like sand. Here they met the waves driven before the southerly wind, and coming from that part of the New Sea they had not yet explored. The wind was strong enough to make it hard work to pole the raft against it, and the spray dashed against the willow bulwark.

These waves prevented them from clearly distinguishing the bottom, though the water was very shallow, but then they thought if it had been calm the creature's pads would have left no marks on such hard sand. It was now more than an hour after sunset, and the louring clouds rendered it more dusky than usual so soon. The creature had evidently come from the jungle southwards, but it was not possible to go there that night in the face of the rising gale. The search must be suspended till morning.

Letting the raft drive before the wind, and assisting its progress by poling, they managed to get it by sheer force through the weeds into the clear deep water by the cliff, there they paddled it round, but unable to touch bottom, the waves drifted them over to Serendib. With continual labour they poled it along the shore of Serendib, nearly to the end of the island, and then half-way across, and paddling hard with the poles contrived to get over aslant. By the time they had moored it, it was quite dusk, and they were tired with the exertion of forcing the unwieldy craft in the face of the gale.

Hastening home they found the stockade just as it had been left, and lost not a moment in lighting the fires, one on each side of the hut, the wood for which had already been collected. The gate was padlocked, the kettle put on, and they sat down to rest. A good supper and strong tea restored their strength. They sat inside the cage at the table, and needed no lantern, for the light of the two fires lit up the interior of the stockade.

As it became later the hare and the birds were fastened to the stake for a bait, more wood was heaped on the fires, and last of all the remaining poles were lashed to the uprights of the shed, forming a complete cage with horizontal bars. The matchlock was placed handy, the bow and arrows laid ready, and both axes, so that if the beast inserted his paw they could strike it.

Cards were then drawn to see who should go to sleep first, and as Bevis cut highest, he went into the hut to lie down. But after he had been there about a quarter of an hour he jumped up, quite unable to go to sleep. Mark said he did not feel the least sleepy either, so they agreed that both should sit up. Till now they had been in the outer shed or cage, but Mark thought that perhaps the creature would not come if it saw them, so they went inside the hut, and made Pan come too. The curtain was partly let down and looped aside, so that they had a view of the stockade, and the lantern lit and set in the niche.

They could hear the wind rushing over the trees outside, and every now and then a puff entered and made the lantern flicker. The fires still burned brightly, and as nothing came the time passed slowly. Bevis did not care to write up his journal, so at last they fell back on their cards and played bezique on the bed. After a time this too wearied. The tea and supper had refreshed them; but both had worked very hard that day—a long day too, as they had been up so early—and their interest began to flag. The cards were put down and they stood up to recover their wakefulness, and then went out into the cage.

The fires still flickered, though the piles of wood were burnt through, and the sticks had fallen off, half one side half the other. The wind had risen and howled along, carrying with it a few leaves which blew against the bars. It was perfectly dark, for the thick clouds hid the moon, and drops of rain were borne on the gale. They would have liked to replenish the fires, but could not get out without unlashing several of the bars, and as Mark said the creature would be more likely to come as the fires burned low. Weary and yawning they went back into the hut and sat down once more.

"One thing," said Mark, "suppose he were to stay just outside the stockade—I mean if he comes and we shoot and hit him till he is savage, and don't kill him, well then if he can't get in to us, don't you see, when it is day he'll go outside the stockade and lie down."

"So that we can't go out."

"And there he'll stay, and wait, and wait."

"And stay till we are starved."

"We could not shoot him through the stockade."

"No. Or he could go up on the cliff and watch there and never let us out. Our provisions would not last for ever."

"The water would go first."

"Suppose he does that, what shall we do then?" said Mark.

"I don't know," said Bevis languidly.

"But, now you think."

"Bore a tunnel through the cliff to the sea," said Bevis, yawning. "I am so sleepy, and one get out and swim round and fetch the raft."

"Tunnel from the cave right through?"

"Straight right through."

"We shall beat him any way," said Mark.

"Of course we shall. Wish he'd come! O!"—yawning—"Let us go to sleep; Pan will bark."

"Not both," said Mark.

"Both."

"No."

Mark would not agree to this. In the end they cut cards again and Mark won. He stretched himself out on the bed and asked Bevis what he was going to do. Bevis took one of the great-coats (his pillow), placed it on the floor by the other wall of the hut, sat down and leaned back against the wall. In this position, with the curtain looped up, he could see straight out across to the gateway of the stockade, which was visible whenever the embers of the fires sent up a flash of light. Pan was close by curled up comfortably.

He put the matchlock by his side so that he could snatch it up in a moment. "Good-night," he said; Mark was already firm asleep.

Bevis put out his hand and stroked Pan; the spaniel recognised the touch in his sleep, and never moved. Now that it was so still, and there was no talking, Bevis could hear the sound of the wind much plainer, and once the cry of a heron rising harsh above the roar. Sometimes the interior of the stockade seemed calm, the wind blew over from the tops of the trees to the top of the cliff, and left the hollow below in perfect stillness. Suddenly, like a genie, the wind descended, and the flames leapt up on each side from the embers. In a moment the flames fell and the enclosure without was in darkness.

All was still again except the distant roar in the wood. A fly kept awake by the lantern crawled along under the roof, became entangled in a spider's web and buzzed. The buzz seemed quite loud in the silent hut. Pan sighed in his slumber. Bevis stretched his legs and fell asleep, but a gnat alighted on his face and tickled him. He awoke, shook himself, and reproached himself for neglecting his duty. The match of the matchlock had now burned almost away; he drew the last two inches up farther in the spiral of the hammer, and thought that he would get up in a minute and put some more match in. Ten seconds later and he was asleep; this time firmly.

The last two inches of the match smouldered away, leaving the gun useless till another was lit and inserted. Down came the genie of the wind, whirling up the grey ashes of the fires and waking a feebler response. The candle in the lantern guttered and went out. As the dawn drew on above them the clouds became visible, and they were now travelling from the north-north-west, the wind having veered during the night.

A grey light came into the hut. The strong gusts of the gale ceased, and instead a light steady breeze blew. The clouds broke and the sky showed. A crow came and perched on the stockade, then flew down and picked up several fragments; it was the crow that had pecked the jack's head. He meditated an attack on the hare and the birds strung to the stake, when Pan woke, yawned and stretched himself. Instantly the crow flew off.

Sunbeams fell aslant through the horizontal bars on to the table. Pan got up and went as far as the short cord allowed him; there was a crust under the table; he had disdained it last night at supper, when there was meat to be had, now he ate it. He gave a kind of yawning whine, as much as to say, "Do wake up;" but they were sleeping far too sound to hear him.

Mark woke first, and sat up. Bevis had slept a long time with his back to the wall, but had afterwards gently sunk down, and was now lying with his head on the bare ground of the floor. Mark laughed. Pan wagged his tail and looked at Bevis as if he understood it. Mark touched Bevis, and he instantly sat up, and felt for the gun as if it was dark.

"Why!"

"It's morning."

"He hasn't been?"

"No."

They unlashed the bars, let Pan loose, and went out into the courtyard. It was a beautiful fresh morning. There were no signs whatever of the creature having visited the place, neither outside nor in. They were much disappointed that it had not come, but supposed the wind and the roughness of the waves had deterred it from venturing across.

After breakfast, on looking at the sun-dial, they were surprised to find it ten o'clock. Then taking the matchlock, bow, and axe, as before, they started for the bed of reed-grass, thinking that the creature might possibly have come to the island without approaching the stockade. The danger had now grown familiar, and they did not care in the least; they walked straight to the place without delay or reconnoitring. The trail had not apparently been used during the night, a small branch of ash had been snapped off and blown on to it, and the waves and wind had smoothed away the disturbed appearance of the weeds.

As the wind was favourable and not rough, they at once resolved to sail to the south and examine the shore there, and if they could hit upon the trail to follow it up. But first they must have their bath at Pearl Island. They returned to the hut, put the hare and birds that had been hung on the stake inside the hut, and lashed up the bars, determined that the creature at all events should not have the game in their absence.

Then locking the gate of the stockade, they went to the raft, and bathed at Pearl Island. The mast was then stepped, the stays fastened, and the sail set. Bevis took the rudder and put it in the water over the starboard quarter, it was like a long, broad oar, the sail filled, and the heavy craft began to drive before the wind. Mark knelt in front to keep a sharp look-out for the shoals which they knew existed. As the Calypso drew so little water they passed over several without touching, where the Pinta, deep with ballast, had struck, and were soon past the farthest point they had reached in the boat.

Chapter Thirteen
New Formosa—Voyage in the Calypso

Surging along the Calypso sought the south, travelling but little faster than the waves, but smoothing a broad wake as she drove over them. Bevis held the oar-rudder under his right arm, with his hand on the handle, and felt the vibration of the million bubbles rising from the edge of the rudder to the surface. Piloting the vessel Mark sometimes directed him to steer to the right, and sometimes to the left.

There were four herons standing in a row on one sand-bank, they rose and made off at their approach; Bevis said he must have a heron's plume. They could just see the swan a long, long way behind in the broad open water off Fir-Tree Gulf. Not long after passing the heron's sand-bank, Mark said he was sure the water was deeper, as there were fewer weeds, but there was a long island in front of them which would soon bar their progress. It stretched from one mass of impenetrable weeds to another, and they began to think of lowering sail, when suddenly the raft stopped with a jerk, then swung round, and hung suspended.

"A snag," said Bevis, recovering himself.

Mark had been pitched forward, and had it not been for the willow-plaited bulwark would have gone overboard. They had the sail down in a moment, fearing that the mast would snap. As they moved on the deck the raft swung now this way now that like a platform on a pivot.

"If it had been the Pinta," said Mark, "there would have been a hole knocked in the bottom."

The thin planking of the boat would have been crushed like an eggshell; the thick beams at the bottom of the Calypso could not be damaged. The only difficulty was to get her off. They tried standing at one edge, and then the other, depressing it where they stood and lightening it at the other part, and at last by moving everything heavy on deck to one corner, she floated and bumped off. Looking over the bulwark they saw the snag, it was the top of a dead and submerged willow. Had they had a large sail, or had the wind been rough the mast would have snapped to a certainty; but the wind had been gradually sinking for some hours. They did not hoist sail again, being so near the long and willow-grown island, but let the raft drift to the shore.

The willows were so thick that it did not appear any use to carry the matchlock with them as the long barrel would constantly catch in the boughs. Bevis took his bow and arrows, Mark his axe, and they climbed ashore through the blue gums, compelling Pan by threats to keep close behind. The island they soon found was nothing but a narrow bank, and beyond it the water recommenced, but even could they have dragged the raft over and launched it afresh the part beyond would not have been navigable. It was plated with pond-weed, the brown leaves overlapping each other like scale-armour on the surface.

There seemed indeed more weed than water, great water-docks at the margin with leaves almost a yard long, branched water plantains with palm-like leaves and pale pink flowers; flags already a little brown, then sedges and huge tussocks; these last—small islets of tall grass—were close together in the shallow water like the ant-hills in the Waste. No course could be forced through or twisted in and out such a mass, and beyond it were beds of reed-grass, out of which rose the reddish and scaling poles of willow. At the distant margin they could see the tops of the trees of the jungle on the mainland. Where the water was visible it had a red tinge and did not look good to drink, very different from that at New Formosa. This was stagnant.

The current, slight as it was, from Sweet River Falls, passed between New Formosa and Serendib, hence the deep channel, and rendered the water there always fresh and pure. Over the pond-weed blue dragon-flies were hovering, and among the willows tits called to each other.

"It's South America," said Mark. "It's a swamp by the Amazon."

"I suppose it is," said Bevis. "We can't go any farther."

Without wading-boots it was impossible to penetrate the swamp, and even then they could not have gone among the black-jointed horse-tails, the stems of which were turning yellowish, for they would have sunk in ooze to the waist. It would have been the very haunt of the bearded-tit had not that curiously marked bird been extinct on the shores of the New Sea. They had never even heard of the bearded-tit, so completely had it died out there.

They moved a few yards along the bank, but found it was a ceaseless climb from stole to stole, and so went back to the raft, and poled close to the shore looking for traces of the creature. They poled from one end to the other, up to the banks of weeds and flags, but without seeing any sign. So far as they could tell the creature had not started from this place, but it might have swum out from any other part of the shore.

"He's not here," said Bevis. "We shall never hunt him out of all these sedges; I think we had better set a trap for him."

"In the reeds at home,"—New Formosa was home now.

"In his trail."

"Dig a pit," said Mark. "They dig pits for lions."

"Or set up a big beam to fall and crush him when he pushes a twig."

"Or a spring gun; would the matchlock do?"

"Only then we want another gun when we go to find him. He might sham dead."

"Wires are not strong enough."

"No; the pit's best," said Bevis. "Yes; we'll dig a pit and stick up a sharp spike in it, and put a trap-door at the top—just a slight frame, you know, to give way with his weight—"

"And strew it over with grass."

"And put the hare to tempt him."

"And shoot him in the pit!"

"Won't he glare!"

"Roar!"

"Gnash his grinders!"

"Won't his teeth gleam!"

"Red tongue and foam!"

"Hot breath—in such a rage!"

"Lash his tail!"

"Tear the sides of the pit!"

"Don't let's kill him quick. Let's make a spear and stick him a little!"

"Come on."

They seized the poles, all eagerness to return and dig the pit.

"Stupes we were not to do it before."

"Awful stupes."

"We never think of things till so long." Such has been the case with the world since history began. How many thousands of years was it after primeval man first boiled water to the steam-engine? How long from the first rubbing of electron or amber, and a leaping up of little particles to it, to the electric tramway?

They had sailed to the swamp quickly, but it occupied more than an hour to pole back to New Formosa, so that it was the afternoon when they moored the Calypso in the usual place. They were hungry and hastened to the hut, intending to begin the pit directly after dinner, when as they came near, Pan ran on first and barked by the gate. "Ah!"

"He's been!"

They ran, forgetting even to look at the match of the gun. There was nothing in the enclosure; but Pan sniffed outside, and gave two short "yaps" as much as to say, "I know."

"Reeds," said Bevis. "He's in the reeds."

"He heard us coming and slipped off—he's hiding."

"We shall have him! Now!"

"Now directly!"

"This minute!"

With incredible temerity they ran as fast as they could go to the bed of reed-grass in which they had discovered the trail. Pan barked at the edge; Bevis blew the match.

"Lu—lu—lu! go in!"

"Fetch him out."

"Hess—ess—go in!"

"Now! Have him!"

Pan stopped at the edge and yapped in the air, wagging his tail and hesitating.

"He's there!" said Bevis.

"As sure as sure," said Mark. Their faces were lit up with the wild joy of the combat; as if like hounds they could scent the quarry.

"Go in," shouted Bevis to the spaniel angrily. Pan crouched, but would not go. Mark kicked him, but he would not move.

"Hold it," said Bevis, handing the matchlock to Mark. He seized the spaniel by his shaggy neck, lifted and hurled him by main force a few yards crash among the sedges. Pan came out in an instant.

"Go in, I tell you!" shouted Bevis, beside himself with anger; the spaniel shivered at his feet. Again Bevis lifted him, swung him, and hurled him as far this time as the reed-grass. The next instant Pan was at his feet again. Encouragement, persuasion, threats, blows, all failed; it was like trying to make him climb a tree. The dog could not force his nature. Mark threw dead sticks into the reed-grass; Bevis flung some stones.

"You hateful wretch!" Bevis stamped his foot. "Get away." Pan ran back. "Give me the gun—I'll go in."

If the dog would not, he would hunt the creature from its lair himself.

"O! stop!" said Mark, catching hold of his arm, "don't—don't go in— you don't know!"

"Let me go."

"I won't."

"I will go."

They struggled with each other.

"Shoot first," said Mark, finding he could not hold him. "Shoot an arrow—two arrows. Here—here's the bow."

Bevis seized the bow and fitted the arrow.

"Shoot where the path is," said Mark. "There—it's there,"—pointing. Bevis raised the bow. "Now shoot!"

"O!" cried a voice in the reeds, "don't shoot!"

Bevis instantly lowered the bow.

"What?" he said.

"Who's there?" said Mark.

"It's me—don't shoot me!"

"Who are you?"

"Me."

They rushed in and found Loo crouching behind the alder in the reed-grass; in her hand was a thick stick which she dropped.

"How dare you!" said Bevis.

"How did you get here?" said Mark. "Don't you be angry!" said Loo. "But how dare you!"

"On our island!"

"Don't you—don't you!" repeated Loo. "You!"

"You!" One word but such intense wrath. "O!" cried Loo, beginning to sob. "You!"

"You!"

"O! Don't! He were so hungry." Sob, sob.

"Pooh!"

"Yah!"

"Yow—wow!" barked Pan. "He—he," sobbed Loo. "He—he—"

"He—what?"

"He were so hungry." Sob, sob. "Who?"

"Samson."

"Who's Samson?"

"My—y—lit—tle—brother."

"Then you took our things?" said Mark. "He—he—kept on crying."

"You had the damper—"

"And the potatoes—"

"And the bacon—"

"You didn't—didn't care for it," sobbed Loo. "Did you take the rabbit-skin?" said Mark. "Yes—es."

"But Samson didn't eat that; did he?"

"I—I—sold it."

"What for?"

"Ha'-penny of jumbles for Samson." Jumbles are sweets.

"How did you get here?"

"I come."

"How?"

"I come."

"It's disgusting," said Bevis, turning to Mark; "spoiling our island."

"Not a tiger," said Mark. "Only a girl."

"It's not proper," said Bevis in a towering rage. "Tigers are proper, girls are not proper."

"No; that they're not."

"Girls are—Foo!—"

"Very—foo!" Contemptuous puffing. "It's not the stealing."

"No; it's the coming—"

"Where you're not wanted—"

"Horrible!"

"Hateful!"

"What shall we do?"

"Can't kill her."

"Nor torture her."

"Nor scalp her."

"Thing!"

"Creature!"

"Yow—wow!"

"Tie her up."

"If we were savages we'd cook you!"

"Limb at a time."

"What *can* we do with her?"

"Let me stop," said Loo pleadingly. "Let *you* stop! You!"

"I can cook and make tea and wash things."

"Stop a minute," said Mark. "Perhaps she's a native."

"Ah!" This was more proper. "She looks brown."

"Copper coloured."

"Are you a savage?"

"If you says so," said Loo penitently. "Are you very sorry?"

"You're sure you're a savage?"

"Will she do?"

"You're our slave."

"Ar-right," (all-right), said Loo her brown eyes beginning to sparkle through her tears. "I'll be what you wants."

"Mind you're a slave."

"So I be."

"You'll be thrashed."

"Don't care. Let I bide here."

"I suppose we must have her."

"You're a great nuisance."

"Ar-right."

"Slave! Carry that." Mark gave her the axe. "And that." Bevis gave her the bow. Loo took them proudly.

"You're to keep behind—Pan's to go before you."

"Dogs first, slaves next."

"Make her fetch the water."

"Chop the wood."

"Turn the spit."

"Capital; we wanted a slave!"

"Just the thing."

"Hurrah!"

"But it's not so nice as a tiger."

"O! No!"

"Nothing like."

They marched out of the reed-grass, Pan and the slave behind.

"But how did you get here?" said Bevis, stopping suddenly.

"I come, I told you."

"Can you swim?"

"No."

"There's no boat."

"Did you have a catamaran?"

"What be that?"

"Why don't you tell us how you got here?"

"I come—a-foot."

"Waded? You couldn't."

"I walked drough't,"—i.e. through it.

They would not believe her at first, but she adhered to her story, and offered to wade back to the mainland to prove that it was possible. She pointed out to them the way she had come by the shoals and sedge-grown banks; the course she had taken curved like half a horse-shoe. First it went straight a little way, then the route or ford led to the south and gradually turned back to the west, reaching the mainland within sixty or seventy yards of the place where they always disembarked from the raft. It took some time for Loo to explain how she had done it, and how she came to know of it, but it was like this.

Once now and then in dry seasons the waters receded very much, and they were further lowered by the drawing of hatches that the cattle might get water to drink low down the valley, miles away. As the waters of the New Sea receded the shallower upper, or southern end, became partly dry. Then a broad low bank of sand appeared stretching out in the shape of half a horse-shoe the extremity of which being much higher was never submerged, but formed the island of New Formosa. At such times any one could walk from the mainland out to New Formosa dryshod for weeks together.

This was how the island became stocked with squirrels and kangaroos; and it was the existence of the rabbits in the burries at the knoll that had originally led to Loo's knowledge of the place. Her father went there once when the water was low to ferret them, and she was sent with his luncheon to and fro. That was some time since, but she had never forgotten, and often playing about the shore, had no difficulty in finding the shoal. The route or ford was, moreover, marked to any one who knew of its existence by the tops of sand-banks, and sedge-grown islets, which were in fact nothing but high parts of the same long, curved bank.

There was not more than a foot deep of water anywhere the whole distance, and often not six inches. This was in August, in winter there would be much more. Tucking up her dress she had waded through easily, feeling the bottom with a thick stick to guide her steps. The worst place was close to the island, by the reed-grass, where she sunk a little in the ooze, but it was only for a few yards.

At the hut the weapons were laid aside, and the slave put out the dinner for them. Bevis and Mark sat, one each side of the table, on their stools of solid blocks, Pan sat beside Bevis on his haunches expectant; the slave knelt at the table.

She was bare-headed. Her black hair having escaped, fell to her waist, and her neck was tawny from the harvest sunshine. The torn brown frock loosely clung about her. Her white teeth gleamed; her naked feet were sandy like Pan's paws. Her brown eyes watched their every movement; she was intent on them. They were full of their plans of the island; she was intent on them.

She ate ravenously, more eagerly than the spaniel. Seeing this, Bevis kept cutting the preserved tongue for her, and asked if Samson was so very hungry. Loo said they were all hungry, but Samson was most hungry. He cried almost all day and all night, and woke himself up crying in the morning. Very often she left him, and went a long way down the hedge because she did not like to hear him.

"But," objected Bevis, "my governor pays your father money, and I'm sure my mamma sends you things."

So she did, but Loo said they never got any of them; she twisted up her mouth very peculiarly to intimate that they were intercepted by the ale-barrel. Bevis became much agitated, he said he would tell the governor, he would tell dear mamma, Samson should not cry any more. Loo should take home one of the tins of preserved tongue, and the potatoes, and all the game there was—all except the hare.

Now Bevis had always been in contact almost with these folk, but yet he had never seen; you and I live in the midst of things, but never look beneath the surface. His face became quite white; he was thoroughly upset. It was his first glance at the hard roadside of life. He said he would do all sorts of things; Loo listened pleased but dimly doubtful, she could not have explained herself, but she, nevertheless, knew that it was beyond Bevis's power to alter these circumstances. Not that she hinted at a doubt; it was happiness enough to kneel there and listen.

Then they made her tell them how many times she had been to the island, and all about it, and as she proceeded recognised one by one, little trifles that had previously had no meaning till now they were connected and formed a continuous strand. In her rude language it occupied a long time, and was got at by cross-questioning from one and the other. Put into order it was like this.

Chapter Fourteen
New Formosa—The Captive

They arrived on Wednesday; Wednesday night Pan stayed in the hut with them, and nothing happened. Thursday night, Pan swam off to the mainland, and while he was away Loo made her first visit to the island, coming right to the hut door or curtain. Till she reached the permanent plank table under the awning and saw the remnants of the supper carelessly left on it, she had had no thought of taking anything.

The desire to share, if ever so secretly, in what they were doing alone led her there. So intense was that desire that it overcame her fear of offending them; she must at least see what they were doing. From the sedges she had watched them go to the island in the Pinta so many times that she was certain that was the place where they were. In wading off to the island by moonlight she caught a glimpse of the sinking fire inside the stockade, the glow thrown up on the cliff, and so easily found her way to the hut. Had Pan been there he would have barked, but he was away; so that she came under the awning and saw all their works—the stockade, the hut, and everything, increasing her eagerness.

After she had examined the place and wondered how they could build it, she saw the remnants of the supper on the table, and remembering Samson, took them for him. The rabbit's skin was hung on the fence, and she took it also, knowing that it would fetch a trifle; in winter it would have been worth more. She thought that these things were nothing to them, that they did not care about them, and threw them aside like refuse.

The second time she came was on Saturday morning, while they were exploring Serendib. When they were on Serendib she could cross to New Formosa in broad daylight unseen, because New Formosa lay between, and the woods on it concealed any one approaching from the western side. Her mother and elder sisters were reaping in the cornfields beyond the Waste, and she was supposed to be minding the younger children, instead of which she was in the sedges watching New Formosa, and directly she saw Bevis and Mark pole the raft across to Serendib she waded over.

She visited the hut, took a few potatoes from the store in the cave, and spent some time wondering at everything they had there. As she was leaving they landed from the raft, and Pan sniffing her in the wood ran barking after her. He knew her very well and made no attempt to bite, still he barked as if it was his duty to tell them some one was on the island. Thinking they would run to see what it was, she climbed up into the ivy-grown oak, and they actually came underneath and looked up and did not see her.

They soon went away fancying it must be a squirrel, but Pan stopped till she descended, and then made friends and followed her to the reed-grass, whence so soon as she thought it safe she waded across to the mainland. Busy at the hut they had no idea that anything of the kind was going on, for they could not see the water from the stockade. On Sunday morning she came again, for the third time, crossing over while they were at Bamboo Island, and after satiating her curiosity and indulging in the pleasure of handling their weapons and the things in the hut, she took the cold half-cooked bacon from the shelf, and the two slices that had been thrown to Pan and which he had left uneaten.

When they returned Pan knew she had been; he barked and first ran to the ivy-grown oak, but finding she was not there he went on and discovered her in the reed-grass. He was satisfied with having discovered her, and only licked her hand. So soon as everything was quiet she slipped across to the mainland, but in the afternoon, being so much interested and eager to see what they were doing, she tried to come over again, when Mark saw her head in the sedges. Loo crouched and kept still so long they concluded there was no one there.

It was the same afternoon that they looked at the oak for marks of claws, but her naked feet had left no trace. She would very probably have attempted it again on Monday night, but that evening they came with the letter and list of provisions, and having seen them and spoken to them, and having something to do for them, her restless eagerness was temporarily allayed. That night was the first Pan was tied up, but nothing disturbed him.

But Tuesday night, after they had been for the flag-basket, the inclination to follow them became too strong, and towards the middle of the night, when, as she supposed, Pan was on shore (for she had seen him swim off other nights), she approached the hut. To her surprise Pan, who was tied up, began to bark. Hastening away, in her hurry she crossed the spot where Pan hid his treasures and picked up the duck's drumstick, but finding it was so polished as to be useless dropped it among the reed-grass.

Wednesday night she ventured once more, but found the gate in the stockade locked; she tried to look over, when Pan set up his bark. She ran back a few yards to the bramble bushes and crouched there, trusting in the thick mist to hide her, as in fact it did. In half a minute, Mark having cut the cord, Pan rushed out in fury, as if he would fly at her throat, but coming near and seeing who it was, he dropped his howl of rage, and during the silence they supposed he was engaged in a deadly struggle.

Whether she really feared that he would spring at her, he came with such a bounce, or whether she thought Bevis and Mark would follow him and find her, she hit at Pan with the thick stick she carried. Now Pan was but just touched, for he swerved, but the big stick and the thump it made on the ground frightened him, and he yelped as if with pain and ran back. As he ran she threw a stone after him, the stone hit the fence and shook it, and knocked off the piece of bark from the willow which they afterwards supposed to have been torn by the claw of the tiger.

Hearing them talking and dreading every moment that they would come out, she remained crouched in the brambles for a long time, and at last crept away, but stayed in the reed-grass till the sun shone, and then crossed to the mainland. Thursday she did not come, nor Thursday night, thinking it best to wait awhile and let a day and night elapse. But on Friday morning, having seen them sail to the south in the Calypso, while they were exploring the swamp, she waded over, and once more looked at the wonderful hut and the curious cage they had constructed about the open shed.

She was so lost in admiring these things and trying to imagine what it could be for, that they had returned very near the island before she started to go. She got as far as the reed-grass and saw them come up poling the raft.

On the raft while facing the island they could not have helped seeing her, so she waited, intending to cross when they had entered the stockade and were busy there. But Pan recognised that she had been to the stockade; they ran at once to the reed-grass, as they now knew of the trail there, and discovered her. The reason Pan would not enter the reeds, even when hurled among them, was his fear of the thick stick.

"Stupes we were!" said Bevis.

"Most awful stupes!"

"Not half Indians!"

"Not a quarter!"

The whole thing was now so clear to them they could not understand why they had not rightly read the indications or "sign" that at last appeared so self-evident. But they were not the first who have wondered afterwards that they had not been wise *before* the event. It is so easy to read when the type is set up and the sentences printed in proper sequence; so difficult to decipher defaced inscriptions in an unknown language. When the path is made any one can walk along it and express disdainful surprise that there should ever have been any difficulty.

"But it's not proper," said Bevis. "I wish it had been a tiger."

"It would have been so capital. But *we've* got a slave."

"Where's she to sleep to-night?"

"Anywhere in the wood."

"Slave, you're to cook the hare for supper."

"And mind you don't make a noise when we're out hunting and frighten the kangaroos."

Loo said she would be as quiet as a mouse.

"We shall want some tea presently. I say!" said Mark, "we've forgotten Charlie!"

He ran up on the cliff, but it was too late; Charlie had been and waved his cap three times, in token that all was not quite right at home. Mark looked at the sun-dial; it was nearly five. They had not had dinner till later than usual, and then Loo's explanation and cross-examination had filled up the time. Still as Loo told them she was certain every one was quite well at home, they did not trouble about having missed Charlie. Mark wished to go shooting again round Serendib, and they started, leaving the slave in charge of the hut to cook their supper.

Mark had the matchlock, and Bevis poled the raft gently round Serendib, but the water-fowl seemed to have become more cautious, as they did not see any. Bevis poled along till they came to a little inlet, where they stopped, with blue gum branches concealing them on either hand. Mark knelt where he could see both ways along the shore; Bevis sat back under the willows with Pan beside him.

They were so quiet that presently a black-headed reed-bunting came and looked down at them from a willow bough. Moths fluttered among the tops of the branches, the wind was so light that they flew whither they listed, instead of being borne out over the water. The brown tips of a few tall reeds moved slightly as the air came softly; they did not bow nor bend; they did but just sway, yielding assent.

Every now and then there was a rush overhead as five or six starlings passed swiftly, straight as arrows, for the firs at the head of Fir-Tree Gulf. These parties succeeding each other were perhaps separate families gathering together into a tribe at the roosting-trees. Over the distant firs a thin cloud like a black bar in the sky spread itself out, and then descended funnel-shaped into the firs. The cloud was formed of starlings, thousands of them, rising up from the trees and settling again. One bird as a mere speck would have been invisible; these legions darkened the air there like smoke.

But just beyond the raft the swallows glided, dipping their breasts and sipping as they dipped; the touch and friction of the water perceptibly checked their flight. They wheeled round and several times approached the surface, till having at last the exact balance and the exact angle they skimmed the water, leaving no more mark than a midge.

Bevis watched them, and as he watched his senses gradually became more acute, till he could distinctly hear the faint far off sound of the waterfall at Sweet River. It rose and fell, faint and afar; the flutter of a moth's wings against the greyish willow leaves overbore and silenced it. As he listened and watched the swallows he thought, or rather felt—for he did not think from step to step upwards to a conclusion—he felt that all the power of a bird's wing is in its tip.

It was with the slender-pointed and elastic tip, the flexible and finely divided feather point that the bird flew. An artist has a cumbrous easel, a heavy framework, a solid palette which has a distinct weight, but he paints with a tiny point of camel's hair. With a camel's hair tip the swallow sweeps the sky.

That part of the wing near the body, which is thick, rigid, and contains the bones, is the easel and framework; it is the shaft through which the driving force flows, and in floating it forms a part of the plane or surface, but it does not influence the air. The touch of the wing is in its tip. There where the feathers fine down to extreme tenuity, so that if held up the light comes through the filaments, they seem to feel the air and to curl over on it as the end of a flag on a mast curls over on itself. So the tail of a fish—his one wing—curls over at the extreme edge of its upper and lower corners, and as it unfolds presses back the water. The swallow, pure artist of flight, feels the air with his wing-tips as with fingers, and lightly fanning glides.

Over the distant firs a heron came drifting like a cloud at his accustomed hour; from over the New Nile the call of a partridge, "caer-wit—caer-wit," sounded along the surface of the water. There was a slight movement and Bevis saw the match descending, an inverted cone of smoke darted up from the priming, and almost before the report Pan leaped overboard. Mark had watched till two moorhens were near enough together, one he shot outright and Pan caught the other.

At the report the heron staggered in the air as if a bullet had struck him, it was his sudden effort to check his course, and then recovering himself he wheeled and flew towards the woods on the mainland. Bevis said he must have a heron's plume. To please Mark he poled the raft to Bamboo Island, and then across to the sedgy banks at the southern extremity of New Formosa, but Mark did not get another shot. They then landed and crept quietly to Kangaroo Hill, the rabbits had grown suspicious, and they did not see one, but Pan suddenly raced across the glade—to their great annoyance—and stopped on the verge of the wood.

There he picked up a rabbit in his mouth, and they recollected the wires they had set. The rabbit had been in a wire since the morning. "It will do for Samson," said Bevis.

When they returned to the hut the full moon—full but low down—had begun to fill the courts of the sky with her light, which permitted no pause of dusk between it and the sunset. The slave's cheeks were red and scorched from the heat of the fire, which she had tended on her knees, and her chin and tawny neck were streaked with black marks. Handling the charred sticks with her fingers, the fingers had transferred the charcoal to her chin. The hare was well cooked considering the means, or rather the want of means at her command, perhaps it was not the first she had helped to prepare. Searching in the store-room she found a little butter with which she basted it after a manner; they had thought the butter was all gone, they were too hasty—impatient—to look thoroughly. There was no jelly, and it was dry, but they enjoyed it very much sitting at the plank table under the shed.

They had removed the poles on one side of the shed as there was nothing now to dread, but on the other two sides the bars remained, and the flames of the expiring fire every now and then cast black bars of shadow across the table. The slave would have been only too glad to have stayed on the island all night—if they had lent her a great-coat or rug to roll up in she would have slept anywhere in the courtyard—but she said Samson would be so wretched without her, he would be frightened and miserable. She must go; she would come back in the morning about ten.

They filled the flag-basket for her with the moorhens, the rabbit, the dab-chick and thrush, and a tin of preserved tongue. There were still some fragments of biscuit; she said Samson would like these best of all. Thus laden, she would have waded to the mainland, but they would not let her—they took the raft and ferried her over, and promised to fetch her in the morning if she would whistle, she could whistle like a boy. To Loo that voyage on the raft, short as it was, was something beyond compare. Loo had to pass the prickly stubble fields with her bare feet—stubble to the naked foot is as if the broad earth were a porcupine's back. But long practice had taught her how to wind round at the edge where there was a narrow and thistly band of grass, for thistles she did not care.

"Good-night, slave."

They poled back to the island, and having fastened Pan up, were going to bed, when Bevis said he wanted the matchlock loaded with ball as he meant to rise early to try for a heron. Mark fired it off, and in the stillness they heard the descending shot rattle among the trees. The matchlock was loaded with ball, and Bevis set the clock of his mind to wake at three. It was still early in the evening, but they had had little or no rest lately, and fell asleep in an instant; they were asleep long before the slave had crept in at her window and quieted Samson with broken biscuits.

The alarum of his mind awoke Bevis about the time he wished. He did not wake Mark, and wishing to go even more quietly than usual left Pan fastened up; the spaniel gave a half-whine, but crouched as Bevis spoke and he recognised the potential anger in the tones of his voice. From the stockade Bevis went along that side of the island where the weeds were, and passed the Calypso which they had left on that side the previous evening. He went by the "blazed" trees leading to Kangaroo Hill, then past the reed-grass where they had captured the slave, but saw nothing. Thence he moved noiselessly up through the wood to the more elevated spot under the spruce firs where he thought he could see over that end of the island without being seen or heard.

There was nothing, the overthrown willow trunk lay still in the water flush with the surface, and close to it there was a little ripple coming out from under a bush, which he supposed was caused by a water-rat moving there. Till now he had been absorbed in what he was doing, but just then, remembering the cones which hung at the tops of the tall firs, he looked up and became conscious of the beauty of the morning, for it was more open there, and he could see a breadth of the sky.

The sun had not yet stood out from the orient, but his precedent light shone through the translucent blue. Yet it was not blue, nor is there any word, nor is a word possible to convey the feeling unless one could be built up of signs and symbols like those in the book of the magician, which glowed and burned to and fro the page. For the blue of the precious sapphire is thick to it, the turquoise dull, these hard surfaces are no more to be compared to it than sand and gravel. They are but stones, hard, cold, pitiful, that which gives them their lustre is the light. Through delicate porcelain sometimes the light comes, and it is not the porcelain, it is the light that is lovely. But porcelain is clay, and the light is shorn, checked, and shrunken. Down through the beauteous azure came the Light itself, pure, unreflected Light, untouched, untarnished even by the dew-sweetened petal of a flower, descending, flowing like a wind, a wind of glory sweeping through the blue. A luminous purple glowing as Love glows in the cheek, so glowed the passion of the heavens.

Two things only reach the soul. By touch there is indeed emotion. But the light in the eye, the sound of the voice! the soul trembles and like a flame leaps to meet them. So to the luminous purple azure his heart ascended.

Bevis, the lover of the sky, gazed and forgot; forgot as we forget that our pulses beat, having no labour to make them. Nor did he hear the south wind singing in the fir tops.

I do not know how any can slumber with this over them; how any can look down at the clods. The greatest wonder on earth is that there are any not able to see the earth's surpassing beauty. Such moments are beyond the chronograph and any measure of wheels, the passing of one cog may be equal to a century, for the mind has no time. What an incredible marvel it is that there are human creatures that slumber threescore and ten years, and look down at the clods and then say, "We are old, we have lived seventy years." Seventy years! The passing of one cog is longer; seven hundred times seventy years would not equal the click of the tiniest cog while the mind was living its own life. Sleep and clods, with the glory of the earth, and the sun, and the sea, and the endless ether around us! Incredible marvel this sleep and clods and talk of years. But I suppose it was only a second or two, for some slight movement attracted him, and he looked, and instantly the vision above was forgotten.

Upon the willow trunk prone in the water, he saw a brown creature larger than any animal commonly seen, but chiefly in length, with sharp-pointed, triangular ears set close to its head. In his excitement he did not recognise it as he aimed. Behind the fir trunks he was hidden, and he was on high ground—animals seldom look up—the creature's head too was farthest from him. He steadied the long, heavy barrel against a fir trunk, heedless of a streak of viscous turpentine sap which his hand pressed.

The trigger was partly drawn—his arm shook, he sighed—he checked himself, held his breath tight, and fired. The ball plunged and the creature was jerked up rebounding and fell in the water. He dashed down, leaped in—as it happened the water was very shallow—and seized it as it splashed a little from mere muscular contraction. Aimed at the head, the ball had passed clean through between the shoulders and buried itself in the willow trunk. The animal was dead before he touched it. He tore home and threw it on the bed: "Mark!"

"O!" said Mark. "An otter!"

Their surprise was great, for they had never suspected an otter. No one had ever seen one there that they had heard of, no one had even supposed it possible. These waters were far from a river, they were fed by rivulets supporting nothing beyond a kingfisher. To get there the otter must have ascended the brook from the river, a bold and adventurous journey, passing hatches and farmhouses set like forts by the water's edge, passing mills astride the stream.

The hare had been admired, but it was nothing to the otter, which was as rare there as a black fox. They looked at its broad flat head—hold a cat's head up under the chin, that is a little like it—the sharp, triangular ears set close to the head, the webbed feet, the fur, the long tail decreasing to a blunt point. It must be preserved; they could skin it, but could not stuff it; still it must be done. The governor must see it, mamma, the Jolly Old Moke, Frances, Val, Cecil, Charlie, Ted, Big Jack—all. Must!

This was the cause then of the curious wave they had seen which moved without wind—no, Mark remembered that once being near the wave he had seen something white under the surface. The wave was not caused by the otter, but most likely it was the otter Pan had scented on Bamboo Island when he seemed so excited, and they could see no reason. The otter must be preserved—must!

While they breakfasted, while they bathed, this was the talk. Presently they heard the slave's whistle and fetched her on the raft. Now, Loo, cunning hussy, waited till she was safely landed on the island, and then told them that dear mamma and Frances were going that day up to Jack's to see them. Loo had been sent for to go to the town on an errand, and she had heard it mentioned. Instead of going on the errand she ran to play slave.

Charlie had had some knowledge of this yesterday, and waved his cap instead of the white handkerchief as a warning, but they did not see it. If mamma and Frances drove up to Jack's to see them, of course it would be at once discovered that they were not at Jack's, and then what a noise there would be.

"Hateful," said Mark. "It seems to me we're getting near the hateful 'Other Side.'"

Chapter Fifteen
New Formosa—The Black Sail

Now, at the Other Side, i.e. at home, things had gone smoothly for them till the day before, in a measure owing to the harvest, and for the rest to the slow ways of old-fashioned country people. When they had gone away to Jack's before in disgrace, Bevis's mother could not rest, the ticking of the clock in the silent house, the distant beat of the blacksmith's hammer, every little circumstance of the day jarred upon her. But on this occasion they had, she believed, gone for their own pleasure, and though she missed them, they were not apart and separated by a gulf of anger.

Busy with the harvest, there was no visiting, no one came down from Jack's, and so the two slipped for the moment out of the life of the hamlet. Presently Bevis's short but affectionate letter arrived, and prevented any suspicion arising, for no one noticed the postmark. Mamma wrote by return, and when her letter addressed to Bevis was delivered at Jack's you would have supposed the secret would have come out. So it would in town life—a letter would have been written saying that Bevis was not there, and asking where to forward it.

But not so at the old house in the hills. Jack's mother put it on the shelf, remarking that no doubt Bevis was coming, and would be there to-morrow or next day. As for Jack he was too busy to think about it, and if he had not been he would have taken little notice, knowing from former experience that Bevis might turn up at any moment. The letter remained on the shelf.

On the Saturday the carrier left a parcel for Bevis—at any other time a messenger would have been sent, and then their absence would have been discovered—but no one could be spared from the field. The parcel contained clean collars, cuffs, and similar things which they never thought of taking with them, but which mamma did not forget. Like the letter the parcel was put aside for Bevis when he did come; the parcel indeed was accepted as proof positive that he was coming. Jack's mother never touched a pen if she could by any means avoid it, old country people put off letter-writing till absolutely compelled.

On the Sunday afternoon while Bevis and Mark were lying under the fir-trees in New Formosa, dear mamma, always thinking of her boy and his friend, was up in her bedroom turning over the yellowish fly-leaves at the end of an old Book of Common Prayer, too large to go to and fro to church, and which was always in the room. Upon these fly-leaves she had written down from time to time the curious little things that Bevis had said. In the very early morning (before he could talk) he used to sit up in the bed while she still slept, and try to pick her eyelids open with finger and thumb. What else could a dumb creature do that wished to be looked at with loving eyes and fondled?

There it was entered, too, how when he was a "Bobby," all little boys are "Bobbies," he called himself Bobaysche, and said mejjible-bone for vegetable marrow. Desiring to speak of wheat, and unable to recall its proper term, he called it bread-seed; and one day stroking his favourite kitten asked "If God had a pussy?" It was difficult for him to express what time he meant, "When that yesterday that came yesterday went away," was his paraphrase for the day before yesterday.

One day in the sitting-room he fancied himself a hunter with a dart, and seizing the poker balanced it over his head. He became so excited he launched his dart at the flying quarry, and it went through the window-pane. In a day or two—workmen are not to be got in a hurry in the country—an old glazier trudged out to put in fresh glass, and while he cut out the dry putty and measured his glass, and drew the diamond point across, Bevis emptied his tool-basket and admired the chisels and hammers. By and by, tired of things which he was not permitted to use lest he should cut himself, he threw them in and handed the basket to the workman: "Here," he said, "Here—take your toys!"

Toys indeed. The old man had laboured fifty years with these toys till his mind had become with monotony as horny and unimpressionable as his hand. He smiled: he did not see the other meaning that those childish words convey.

Nothing then pleased Bevis so much as moving furniture, the noise and disturbance so distasteful to us was a treat to him. It was "thunder-boy" and "cuckoo-boy," as the thunder rolled or the cuckoo called; he could not conceive anything being caused unseen without human agency.

The Deity was human.

"Ah!" said he thoughtfully, "He got a high ladder and climbed up over the hedges to make the thunder."

"Has He got any little Bobbies?"

"No."

"I suppose He had when He was down here?"

"No."

"No," (with pity) "He didn't have no peoples." The pleasure of refusal was not to be resisted.

"Now do, Bobby, dear?"

"I san't: say it again."

"O! *do* do it."

"I san't: say it again."

"Now, *do*."

"I san't," shaking his head, as much as to say it's very dreadful of me, but I shan't. They could not explain to him that the glowing sunset was really so far away, he wanted to go to it. "It's only just over the blackberry hedge." Some one was teaching him that God loved little boys; "But does he love ladies too?"

As for papa he had to tell stories by the hour, day after day, and when he ceased and said he could not remember any more, Bevis frowned. "Rack your brains! rack your brains!" said he. A nightingale built in the hedge near the house, and all night long her voice echoed in the bed room. Listening one night as he was in bed he remarked, "The nightingale has two songs: first he sings 'Sir-rup—sir-rup,' and then he sings 'Tweet.'"

For his impudence he had a box on the ear: "Pooh! It went pop like a foxglove," he laughed.

At Brighton he was taken over the Pavilion, and it was some trouble to explain to him that this fine house had been built for a gentleman called a king. By-and-by, in the top stories, rather musty from old carpets and hangings: "Hum!" said he; "seems stuffy. I can smell that gentleman's dinner," i.e. George the Fourth's.

Visiting a trim suburban villa, while the ladies talked they sent him out on the close-mown lawn to play. When he came in, "Well, dear, did you enjoy yourself?"

"Don't think much of *your* garden," said Bevis; "no buttercups."

At prayers: "Make Bobby a good boy, and see that you do everything I tell you."

"You longered your promise," did not fulfil it for a long time. "Straight yourselves," when out walking he wished them to go straight on and not turn. "Round yourselves, round yourselves," when he wanted them to take a turning. When he grew up to be a big man he expressed his determination to "knock down the policeman and kill the hanging-man," then he could do as he liked. "Tiffeck" was the cat's cough.

Driving over Westminster Bridge the first time, and seeing the Houses of Parliament, which reminded him of his toy bricks, he inquired "If there was anything inside?" Older people have asked that of late years. As he did not get his wishes quickly, it appeared to him there were "too many perhapses in this place:" he wanted things done "punctually at now." A waterfall was the "tumbling water."

They told him there was one part of us that did not die. "Then," he said directly, "I suppose that is the thinking part." What more, O! Descartes, Plato, philosophers, is there in your tomes? The crucifixion hurt his feelings very much, the cruel nails, the unfeeling spear: he looked at the picture a long time, and then turned over the page, saying, "If God had been there He would not have let them do it."

"What are you going to be when you're a man?" asked grandpa. "An engineer, a lawyer?"

"Pooh! I'm going to be a king, and wear a gold crown!"

A glowing March sunset made the tops of the elms, red with flower before the leaf, show clear against the sky. "They look like red seaweed dipped in water," he said.

Such were some of the short and disconnected jottings in mamma's prayer-book: mere jottings, but well she could see the scene in her mind when the words were said. Latest of all, the second visit to the seaside, where, after rioting on the sands and hurling pebbles in the summer waves, suddenly he stopped, looked up at her and said, "O! wasn't it a good thing the sea was made!" It was indeed.

Every one being so much in the field, mamma was left alone, and wearying of it, asked Frances to come up frequently to her: Frances was willing enough to do so, especially as she could talk unreservedly of Big Jack, so that it was a pleasure to her to come. At last, on the Friday, as Bevis did not write again, his mother proposed that they should drive up to Jack's, and see how the boys were on the morrow. Frances was discreetly delighted: Jack could not come down to see her just now, and with Bevis's mother she could go up and see him with propriety. So it was agreed that the dog-cart should be ready early on Saturday afternoon. Charlie learned something of this—he played in and out the place, and waved his cap thrice as a warning.

Now, in the kitchen on Friday evening there was a curious talk of Bevis and Mark. Had it not been for the harvest something would have crept out about them among the cottagers. Such inveterate gossipers would have sniffed out something, some one would have supposed this, another would have said they were not at Big Jack's, a third might have caught a glimpse of them when on the mainland. But the harvest filled their hands with work, sealed their eyes, and shut their mouths. An earthquake would hardly disturb the reapers. So soon as they had completed the day's work they fell asleep. Pan's nocturnal rambles would have been noticed had it not been for this, though he might have come down from Jack's.

However, as it chanced, not a word was said till the Friday evening, when there came into the kitchen a labouring man, sent by his master to have some talk with the Bailiff respecting a proposed bargain. Every evening the Bailiff took his quart in the kitchen, and though it was summer always in the same corner by the hearth. He had no home, an old and much-crusted bachelor: he had a dim craving for company, and he liked to sit there and sip while Polly worked round briskly.

A deal of gossip was got through in that kitchen. Men came in and out, they lingered on the door-step with their fingers on the latch just to add one more remark. That evening when the bargain, a minor matter, had been discussed, this man, with much roundabout preliminary solemnly declared that as he had been working up in Rushland's field (about half a mile from the New Sea), he had distinctly heard Bevis and Mark talking to each other, and it seemed to him that the sound came over the water.

Sometimes he said he could hear folk talk at a great distance, four or five times as far off as most could, and had frequently told people what they had been conversing about when they had been a mile or more away. He could not hear like this always, but once now and then, and he was quite sure that he had heard Master Bevis and Master Mark talking something about shooting, and that the sound came from over the water. He did not believe they were at Jack's, there was "summat" (something) very curious about it.

The Bailiff and Polly and the visitor turned this over and over, and gossiped, and discussed it for some time, till the man had to go. They never for a moment doubted the perfect truth of what he had stated. Half-educated people are always ready to believe the marvellous, nor was there anything so unusual in this claim to a second sight of hearing, so to say. Once now and then, in the country, you meet with people who lay serious claim to possess the power, and most astonishing instances are related of it.

Whether being so much in the open air sharpens the senses, whether the sound actually did travel over the water, it is not possible to say, or whether some little suspicion of the real facts had got out, and this fellow cunningly devised his story knowing that sooner or later confirmation of his wonderful powers of hearing would be derived in the discovery of what Bevis had been doing. The only persons who could tell were John Young and Loo: the one was spell-bound by the bribe he knew he should obtain, Loo was much too eager to share the game to breathe a word. Poachers, however, get about at odd hours in odd places, and see things they are not meant to.

Still in the country the belief lingers that here and there a person does possess the power, and the story so worked upon the Bailiff and Polly, that at last Polly ventured in to tell her mistress. Her mistress at once dismissed it as ridiculous. She was too well educated to dream dreams. Yet when she retired, do you know! she sat a little while and thought about it, so contagious is superstition. In the morning she sent down to Frances to come an hour earlier—she wanted to see Bevis.

Frances came, and the dog-cart was at the door when Loo (who had been sent on an errand to the town—a common thing on Saturdays) rushed up to the door, thrust a letter into mamma's hand, and darted away.

"Why!" said she. "It's Bevis—why!" she read aloud, Frances looking over her shoulder:—"Dear Mamma, Please come up to the place where the boats are kept directly you get this and mind you come this very minute," (twice dashed). "We are coming home from New Formosa in our ship the Calypso, and want you to be there to see the things we have brought you, and to hear all about it. Mind and be sure and come this very minute, please."

Wondering and excited with curiosity, the two ladies ran as fast as they could up the meadow footpath, and along the bank of the New Sea, till they came to a clear place where the trees did not interfere with the view. Then, a long way up, they saw a singular-looking boat with a black sail.

"There they are!"

"They're coming!"

"What *can* they have been doing?"

"That is not the Pinta!"

"This has a black sail!"

The sail was black because it was the rug, an old-fashioned one, black one side and grey the other. After long discussion Bevis and Mark had decided that the time had come when they must return from the island, for if Bevis's mother went to Jack's and found they were not there, her anxiety would be terrible, and they could not think of it. So Bevis wrote a letter and sent Loo back with it at once, and she was to watch and see if his mother did as she was asked. If she started for the shore Loo was to raise a signal, a handkerchief they lent her for the purpose.

Some time after Loo went they embarked on the raft, and drifted slowly down before the south wind till they reached the Mozambique, where they stayed the raft's progress with their poles till Loo displayed the signal. The sail was then hoisted, and they bore down right before the wind.

With dark sail booming out the Calypso surged ahead, the mariners saw the two ladies on the shore, and waved their hands and shouted. Bevis steered her into port, and she grounded beside the Pinta. The first caress and astonishment over: "Where are your hats?" said Frances.

"Where are your collars?" said his mother. "And gracious, child! just look at his neck!"

As for hats and collars they had almost forgotten their existence, and having passed most of the time in shirt sleeves like gold-miners, with necks and chests exposed, they were as brown as if they had been in the tropics. Mark especially was tanned, completely tanned: Bevis was too fair to brown well. The sun and the wind had purified his skin almost to transparency with a rosy olive behind the whiteness. There was a gleam in his eye, the clear red of his lips—lips speak the state of the blood—the easy motion of the limbs, the ringing sound of the voice, the upright back, all showed primeval health. Both of them were often surprised at their own strength.

In those days of running, racing, leaping, exploring, swimming, the skin nude to the sun, and wind and water, they built themselves up of steel, steel that would bear the hardest wear of the world. Had they been put in an open boat and thrust forth to sea like the viking of old, it would not have hurt them.

Frances played with Bevis's golden ringlets, but did not kiss him as she had used to do. He looked too much a man. She placed her hand on her brother's shoulder, but did not speak to him as once she had done. Something told her that this was not the boy she ordered to and fro.

They could not believe that the two had really spent all the time on an island. This was the eleventh morn since they had left—it could not be: yet there was the raft in evidence.

"Let us row them up in the Pinta," said Mark.

"In a minute," said Bevis. "Get her ready; I'll be back in a minute—half a second." He ran along the bank to a spot whence he knew he could see the old house at home through the boughs. He wanted just to look at it—there is no house so beautiful as the one you were born in—and then he ran back.

There was a little water in the boat but not much, they hauled out some of the ballast, the ladies got in and were rowed direct to New Formosa. The stockade—so well defended, the cage before the door, the hut, the cave, their interest knew no bounds.

"But you did not really sleep on this," said Bevis's mother in a tone of horror, finding the bed was nothing but fir branches: she could not be reconciled to the idea.

The matchlock, the niche for the lantern, the marks where their fires had been, the sun-dial, there was no detail they did not examine: and lastly they went all round the island by the well-worn path. This occupied a considerable time, it was now too late to drive up to Jack's and the object was removed, but Bevis's mother, ever anxious for others' happiness, whispered to Frances that she would write and send a messenger, and ask Jack to come down to-morrow—surely he could spare Sunday—to bring back the parcel, and see the wonderful island.

When at last they landed the ladies, there was Charlie on the bank, and Cecil and Val, who had somehow got wind of it—they were wild with curiosity not unmingled with resentment. These had to be rowed to New Formosa and they stayed longer even than the ladies, and insisted on a shot each with the matchlock. So it was a most exciting afternoon for these returned shipwrecked folks. In the evening they had the dog-cart, and drove in to Latten with the otter to have it preserved.

They did not see much or think much of the governor till towards supper-time—Mark had snatched half an hour to visit his Jolly Old Moke and returned like the wind. The governor was calmly incredulous: he professed to disbelieve that they had done it all themselves, there must have been a man or two to help them. And if it was true, how did they suppose they were going to pay for all the damage they had done to the trees on the island?

This was a difficult question, they did not know that the governor could cut the trees if he chose, indeed they had never thought about it. But having faced so many dangers they were not going to tremble at this. They could not quite make the governor out, whether he was chaffing them, or whether he really disbelieved, or whether it was a cover to his anger. In truth, he hardly knew himself, but he could not help admiring the ingenuity with which they had effected all this.

He was a shrewd man, the governor, and he saw that Bevis and Mark had the ladies on their side; what is the use of saying anything when the ladies have made up their minds? Besides, there was this about it at any rate: they had gained the primeval health of the primeval forest-dwellers. Before gleaming eyes, red lips, sun-burned and yet clear skin, ringing voices and shouts of laughter, how could he help but waver and finally melt and become as curious as the rest.

In the end they actually promised, as a favour, to row him up to their island to-morrow.

Chapter Sixteen
Shooting with Double-Barrels

The governor having been rowed to the island, examined the fortifications, read the journal, and looked at the iron-pipe gun, and afterwards reflecting upon these things came to the conclusion that it would be safer and better in every way to let Bevis have the use of a good breech-loader. He evidently must shoot, and if so he had better shoot with a proper gun. When this decision was known, Mark's governor could do nothing less, and so they both had good guns put into their hands.

In truth, the prohibition had long been rather hollow, more traditional than effectual. Bevis had accompanied his governor several autumns in the field, and shot occasionally, and he had been frequently allowed to try his skill at the starlings flying to and fro the chimney. Besides which they shot with Jack and knew all about it perfectly well. They were fortunate in living in the era of the breech-loader which is so much safer than the old muzzle-loading gun. There was hardly a part of the muzzle-loader which in some way or other did not now and then contribute to accidents. With the breech-loader you can in a moment remove the very possibility of accident by pulling out the cartridges and putting them in your pocket.

Bevis and Mark knew very well how to shoot, both from actual if occasional practice, and from watching those who did shoot. The governor, however, desirous that they should excel, gave them a good drilling in this way.

Bevis had to study his position at the moment when he stopped and lifted the gun. His left foot was to be set a little in front of the other, and he was to turn very slightly aside, the left shoulder forwards. He was never to stand square to the game. He was to stand upright, perfectly upright like a bolt. The back must not stoop nor the shoulders be humped and set up till the collar of the coat was as high as the poll. Humping the shoulders at the same time contracts the chest, and causes the coat in front to crease, and these creases are apt to catch the butt of the gun as it comes to the shoulder and divert it from its proper place.

There is no time to correct this in the act of shooting, so that the habit of a good position should be acquired that it may be avoided. He had, too, to hold his head nearly upright and not to crane his neck forward till the cheek rested on the stock while the head was aside in the manner of the magpie peering into a letter. He was to stand upright, with his chest open and his shoulders thrown back, like Robin Hood with his six foot yew drawing the arrow to his ear.

Bevis was made to take his double-barrel upstairs, into the best bedroom—this is the advantage of the breech-loader, take the cartridges out and it is as harmless as a fire-iron—where there was a modern cheval-glass. The mirrors down stairs were old and small, and the glass not perfectly homogeneous so that unless the reflection of the face fell just in the centre a round chin became elongated. Before the cheval-glass he was ordered to stand sideways and throw up the gun quickly to the present, then holding it there, to glance at himself.

He saw his frame arched forward, his back bent, his shoulders drawn together, the collar of his coat up to his poll behind, the entire position cramped and awkward. Now he understood how unsightly it looked, and how difficult it is to shoot well in that way. Many good sportsmen by dint of twenty years' cramping educate their awkwardness to a successful pitch. It needs many years to do it: but you can stand upright at once.

He altered his posture in a moment, looked, and saw himself standing easily, upright but easily, and found that his heart beat without vibrating the barrel as it will if the chest be contracted, and that breathing did not throw the gun out of level. Instead of compressing himself to the gun, the gun fitted to him. The gun had been his master and controlled him, now he was the master of the gun.

Next he had to practise the bringing of the gun to the shoulder—the act of lifting it—and to choose the position from which he would usually lift it. He had his free choice, but was informed that when once he had selected it he must adhere to it. Some generally carry the gun on the hollow of the left arm with the muzzle nearly horizontal to the left. Some under the right arm with the left hand already on the stock. Some with the muzzle upwards aslant with both hands also. Now and then one waits with the butt on his hip: one swings his gun anyhow in one hand like an umbrella: a third tosses it over his shoulder with the hammers down and the trigger-guard up, and jerks the muzzle over when the game rises. Except in snap-shooting, when the gun must of necessity be held already half-way to the shoulder, it matters very little which the sportsman does, nor from what position he raises his gun.

But the governor insisted that it did matter everything that the position should be habitual. That in order to shoot with success, the gun must not be thrown up now one way and now another, but must almost invariably, certainly as a rule, be lifted from one recognised position. Else so many trifling circumstances interfere with the precision without which nothing can be done, a crease of the coat, a button, the sleeve, or you might, forgetting yourself, knock the barrel against a bough.

To avoid these you must take your mind from the game to guide your gun to the shoulder. If you took your mind from the game the continuity of the glance was broken, and the aim snapped in two, not to be united. Therefore, he insisted on Bevis choosing a position in which he would habitually carry his gun when in the presence of game.

Bevis at once selected that with the gun in the hollow of his left arm, the muzzle somewhat upwards; this was simply imitation, because the governor held it in that way. It is, however, a good position, easy for walking or waiting for ground game or for game that flies, for hare or snipe, for everything except thick cover or brushwood, or moving in a double mound, when you must perforce hold the gun almost perpendicular before you to escape the branches. This being settled, and the governor having promised him faithfully that if he saw him carry it any other way he would lock the gun up for a week each time, they proceeded to practise the bringing of the gun up to the shoulder, that is, to the present.

The left hand should always grasp the stock at the spot where the gun balances, where it can be poised on the palm like the beam of weights and scales. Instead of now taking it just in front of the trigger-guard, now on the trigger-guard, now six or seven inches in front, carelessly seizing it in different places as it happens, the left hand should always come to the same spot. It will do so undeviatingly with a very little practice and without thought or effort, as your right hand meets your friend's to shake hands.

If it comes always to the same spot the left hand does not require shifting after the butt touches the shoulder. The necessary movements are reduced to a minimum. Grasping it then at the balance lift it gently to the shoulder, neither hastily nor slowly, but with quiet ease. Bevis was particularly taught not to throw the butt against his shoulder with a jerk, he was to bring it up with the deliberate motion of "hefting."

"Hefting" is weighing in the hands—you are asked to "heft" a thing— to take it and feel by raising it what you think it weighs.

With this considerate ease Bevis was to "heft" his gun to the shoulder, and only to press it there sufficiently to feel that the butt touched him. He was not to hold it loosely, nor to pull it against his shoulder as if he were going to mortice it there. He was just to feel it. If you press the gun with a hard iron stiffness against the shoulder you cannot move it to follow the flying bird: you pull against and resist yourself. On the other hand, if loosely held the gun is apt to shift.

The butt must touch his shoulder at the same place every time. Those who have not had this pointed out to them frequently have the thick or upper part of the butt high above the shoulder, and really put nothing but the narrow and angular lower part against the body. At another time, throwing it too low, they have to bend and stoop over the gun to get an aim. Or it is pitched up to the chest, and not to the shoulder at all—to the edge of the chest, or again to the outside of the shoulder on the arm. They never bring it twice to the same place and must consequently change the inclination of the head at every shot. A fresh effort has, therefore, to be gone through each time to get the body and the gun to fit.

Bevis was compelled to bring the butt of his gun up every time to the same spot well on his shoulder, between his chest and his arm, with the hollow of the butt fitting, like a ball in its socket. One of the great objects of this mechanical training was that he should not have to pay the least attention to the breech of the gun in aiming. All that he had to do with was the sight. His gun, when he had thus practised, came up exactly level at once.

It required no shifting, no moving of the left hand further up or lower down the stock, no pushing of the butt higher up the shoulder, or to this side or that. His gun touched his shoulder at a perfect level, as straight as if he had thrust out his hand and pointed with the index finger at the bird. Not the least conscious effort was needed, there was nothing to correct, above all there was not a second's interruption of the continuity of glance—the look at the game. The breech was level with the sight instantly; all he had further to do with was the sight.

With both eyes open he never lost view of the bird for the tenth of a second. The governor taught him to keep his eyes, both open, on the bird as it flew, and his gun came up to his line of sight. The black dot at the end of the barrel—as the sight appears in the act of shooting—had then only to cover the bird, and the finger pressed the trigger. Up to the moment that the black dot was adjusted to the mark all was automatic.

The governor's plan was first to reduce the movements to a minimum; secondly, to obtain absolute uniformity of movement; thirdly, to secure by this absolute uniformity a perfect unconsciousness of effort of movement at all; in short, automatic movement; and all this in order that the continuity of glance, the look at the game, might not be interrupted for the merest fraction of a second. That glance was really the aim, the gun fitted itself to the gaze just as you thrust out your index finger and point, the body really did the work of aiming itself.

All the mind had to do was to effect the final adjustment of the black dot of the sight. Very often when the gun was thus brought up no such adjustment was necessary, it was already there, so that there was nothing to do but press the trigger. It then looked as if the gun touched the shoulder and was discharged instantaneously.

He was to look at the bird, to keep both eyes on it, to let his gun come to his eyes, still both open, adjust the dot and fire. There was no binocular trouble because he was never to stay to run his eyes up the barrels—that would necessitate removing his glance from the game, a thing strictly forbidden. Only the dot. He saw only the dot, and the dot gave no binocular trouble. The barrels were entirely ignored; the body had already adjusted them. Only the dot. The sight—this dot—is the secret of shooting.

The governor said if you shut the left eye you cannot retain your glance on the bird, the barrels invariably obscure it for a moment, and the mind has to catch itself again. He would not let Bevis take his eyes off it—he would rather he missed. Bevis was also to be careful not to let his right hand hang with all the weight of his arm on the stock, a thing which doubles the labour of the left arm as it has to uphold the weight of the gun and of the right arm too, and thus the muzzle is apt to be depressed.

He was not to blink, but to look through the explosion. Hundreds of sportsmen blink as they pull the trigger. He was to let his gun smoothly follow the bird, even in the act of the explosion, exactly as the astronomer's clockwork equatorial follows a star. There was to be continuity of glance; and thus at last he brought down his snipes right and left, as it seemed, with a sweep of the gun.

The astronomers discovered "personal equation." Three men are set to observe the occultation of a satellite by Jupiter, and to record the precise time by pressing a lever. One presses the lever the hundredth of a second too soon, the second the hundredth of a second too late, the third sometimes one and sometimes the other and sometimes is precisely accurate. The mean of these three gives the exact time. In shooting one man pulls the trigger a fraction too soon, another a fraction too late, a third is uncertain. If you have been doing your best to shoot well, and after some years still fail, endeavour to discover your "personal equation," and by correcting that you may succeed much better. It is a common error and unsuspected, so is blinking—you may shoot for years and never know that you blink.

Bevis's personal equation was a second too quick. In this, as in everything, he dashed at it. His snipes were cut down as if you had whipped them over: his hares were mangled; his partridges smashed. The dot was dead on them, and a volley of lead was poured in. The governor had a difficulty to get him to give "law" enough.

He acquired the mechanical precision so perfectly that he became careless and shot gracelessly. The governor lectured him and hung his gun up for a week as a check. By degrees he got into the easy quiet style of finished shooting.

The two learned the better and the quicker because there were two. The governor went through the same drill with Mark, motion for motion, word for word. Then when they were out in the field the one told the other, they compared their experiences, checked each other's faults, and commended success. They learned the better and the quicker because they had no keeper to find everything for them, and warn them when to expect a hare, and when a bird. They had to find it for themselves like Pan. Finally, they learned the better because at first they shot at anything that took their fancy, a blackbird or a wood-pigeon, and were not restricted to one class of bird with the same kind of motion every time it was flushed.

Long before trusted with guns they had gathered from the conversation they constantly heard around them to aim over a bird that flies straight away because it usually rises gradually for some distance, and between the ears of the running hare. If the hare came towards them they shot at the grass before his paws. A bird flying aslant away needs the sight to be put in front of it, the allowance increasing as the angle approaches a right angle; till when a bird crosses, straight across, you must allow a good piece, especially if he comes with the wind.

Two cautions the governor only gave them, one to be extremely careful in getting through hedges that the muzzles of their guns pointed away, for branches are most treacherous, and secondly never to put the forefinger inside the trigger-guard till in the act of lifting the gun to the shoulder.

For awhile their territory was limited as the governor, who shot with Mark's, did not want the sport spoiled by these beginners. But as September drew to a close, they could wander almost where they liked, and in October anywhere, on promise of not shooting pheasants should they come across any.

Chapter Seventeen
American Snap-Shooting

Meantime they taught Big Jack to swim. He came down to look at the cave on New Formosa, and Frances so taunted and tormented him because the boys could swim and he could not, that at last the giant, as it were, heaved himself up for the effort, and rode down every morning. Bevis and Mark gave him lessons, and in a fortnight he could swim four or five strokes to the railings. Directly he had the stroke he got on rapidly, for those vast lungs of his, formed by the air of the hills, floated him as buoyantly as a balloon. So soon as ever he could swim, Frances turned round and tormented him because the boys had taught him and not he the boys.

Bevis and Mark could not break off the habit of bathing every morning, and they continued to do so far into October, often walking with bare feet on the hoar-frost on the grass, and breaking the thin ice at the edge of the water by tapping it with their toes. The bath was now only a plunge and out again, but it gave them a pleasant glow all day, and hardened them as the smith hardens iron.

Up at Jack's they tried again with his little rifle, and applying what they had learnt from the matchlock while shooting with ball, soon found out the rifle's peculiarities. It only wanted to be understood and coaxed like everything else. Then they could hit anything with it up to sixty yards. Beyond that the bullet, being beaten out of shape when driven home by the ramrod, could not be depended upon. In October they could shoot where they pleased on condition of sparing the pheasants for their governors. There were no preserved covers, but a few pheasants wandered away and came there. October was a beautiful month.

One morning Tom, the ploughboy, and some time bird-keeper, came to the door and asked to see them. "There be a pussy in the mound," he said, with the sly leer peculiar to those who bring information about game. He "knowed" there was a hare in the mound, and yet he could not have given any positive reason for it. He had not actually seen the hare enter the mound, nor found the run, nor the form, neither had he Pan's intelligent nostrils, but he "knowed" it all the same.

Rude as he looked he had an instinctive perception—supersensuous perception—that there was a hare on that mound, which twenty people might have passed without the least suspicion. "Go into the kitchen," said Bevis, and Tom went with a broad smile of content on his features, for he well knew that to be sent into the kitchen was equivalent to a cheque drawn on the cellar and the pantry.

Bevis and Mark took their guns, Pan followed very happily, and they walked beside the hedges down towards the place, which was at some distance. The keenness of the morning air, from which the sun had not yet fully distilled the frost of the night, freshened their eagerness for sport. A cart laden with swedes crossed in front of them, and though the sun shone the load of roots indicated that winter was approaching. They passed an oak growing out in the field.

Under the tree there stood an aged man with one hand against the hoary trunk, and looking up into the tree as well as his bowed back, which had stiffened in its stoop, and his rounded shoulders would let him. His dress was old and sober tinted, his smock frock greyish, his old hat had lost all colour. He was hoary like the lichen-hung oak trunk. From his face the blood had dried away, leaving it a dull brown, the tan of seventy harvest fields burned into the skin, a sapless brown wrinkled face like a withered oak leaf.

Though he looked at them, and Bevis nodded, his eyes gave no sign of recognition; like a dead animal's, there was no light in them, the glaze was settling. In the evening it might occur to him that he had seen them in the morning. His years pressed heavy on him, very heavy like a huge bundle of sticks; he was lost under his age. All those years "Jumps" had never once been out of sight of the high Down yonder (not far from Jack's), the landmark of the place. Within sight of that hill he was born, within such radius he had laboured, and therein he was decaying, slowly, very slowly, like an oak branch. James was his real name, corrupted to "Jumps;" as "Jumps" he had been known for two generations, and he would have answered to no other.

One day it happened that "Jumps" searching for dead sticks came along under the sycamore-trees and saw Jack, and Bevis and Mark swimming. He watched them some time with his dull glazing eyes, and a day or two afterwards opened his mouth about it. "Never seed nobody do thuck afore," he said, repeating it a score of times as his class do, impressing an idea on others by reiteration, as it takes so much iteration to impress it on them. "Never saw any one do that before."

For seventy harvests he had laboured in that place, and never once gone out of sight of the high Down yonder, and in all that seventy years no one till Bevis and Mark, and now their pupil Jack, had learned to swim. Bevis's governor was out of the question, he had crossed the seas. But of the true country-folk, of all who dwelt round about those waters, not one had learned to swim. Very likely no one had learned since the Norman conquest. When the forests were enclosed and the commonalty forbidden to hunt, the spirit of enterprising exercise died out of them. Certainly it is a fact that until quite recently you might search a village from end to end and not find a swimmer, and most probably if you found one now he would be something of a traveller and not a home-staying man.

Tom, the ploughboy and bird-keeper, with his companions, the other plough-lads and young men, sometimes bathed in summer in the brook far down the meadows, splashing like blackbirds in the shallow water, running to and fro on the sward under the grey-leaved willows with the sunshine on their limbs. I delight to see them, they look Greek; I wish some one would paint them, with the brimming brook, the willows pondering over it, the pointed flags, the sward, and buttercups, the distant flesh-tints in the sunlight under the grey leaves. But this was not swimming. "Never saw any one do that before," said the man of seventy harvests.

Under the oak he stood as Bevis and Mark passed that October morning. His hand was like wood upon wood, and as he leaned against the oak, his knees were bent one way and his back the other, and thus stiff and crooked and standing with an effort supported by the tree, it seemed as if he had been going as a beast of the field upon all fours and had hoisted himself upright with difficulty. Something in the position, in the hoary tree, and the greyish hue of his dress gave the impression of an arboreal animal.

But against the tree there leaned also a long slender pole, "teeled up" as "Jumps" would have said, and at the end of the pole was a hook. The old man had permission to collect the dead wood, and the use of his crook was to tear down the decaying branches for which he was now looking. A crook is a very simple instrument—the mere branch of a tree will often serve as a crook—but no arboreal animal has ever used a crook. Ah! "Jumps," poor decaying "Jumps," with lengthened narrow experience like a long footpath, with glazing eyes, crooked knee, and stiffened back, there was a something in thee for all that, the unseen difference that is all in all, the wondrous mind, the soul.

Up in the sunshine a lark sung fluttering his wings; he arose from the earth, his heart was in the sky. Shall not the soul arise?

Past the oak Bevis and Mark walked beside the hedge upon their way. Frost, and sunshine after had reddened the hawthorn sprays, and already they could see through the upper branches—red with haws—for the grass was strewn with the leaves from the exposed tops of the bushes. On the orange maples there were bunches of rosy-winged keys. There was a gloss on the holly leaf, and catkins at the tips of the leafless birch. As the leaves fell from the horse-chestnut boughs the varnished sheaths of the buds for next year appeared; so there were green buds on the willows, black tips to the ash saplings, green buds on the sycamores. They waited asleep in their sheaths till Orion strode the southern sky and Arcturus rose in the East.

Slender larch boughs were coated with the yellow fluff of the decaying needles. Brown fern, shrivelled rush tip, grey rowen grass at the verge of the ditch showed that frost had wandered thither in the night. By the pond the brown bur-marigolds drooped, withering to seed, their dull disks like lesser sunflowers without the sunflower's colour. There was a beech which had been orange, but was now red from the topmost branch to the lowest, redder than the squirrels which came to it. Two or three last buttercups flowered in the grass, and on a furze bush there were a few pale yellow blossoms not golden as in spring, but pale.

Thin threads of gossamer gleamed, the light ran along their loops as they were lifted by the breeze, and the sky was blue over the buff oaks. Jays screeched in the oaks looking for acorns, and there came the muffled tinkle of a sheep-bell. A humble-bee buzzed across their path, warmed into aimless life by the sun from his frost-chill of the night—buzzed across and drifted against a hawthorn branch. There he clung and crept about the branch, his raft in the sunshine, as men chilled at sea cling and creep about their platform of beams in the waste of waves. His feeble force was almost spent.

The sun shone and his rays fell on red hawthorn spray, on yellow larch bough, on brown fern, rush tip, and grey grass, on red beech and yellow gorse, on broad buff oaks and orange maple, and on the gleaming pond. Wheresoever there was the least colour the sun's rays flew like a bee to a flower, and drew from it a beauty as they drew the song from the lark.

The wind came from the blue sky with drifting skeins of mist in it like those which curled in summer's dawn over the waters of the New Sea, the wind came and their blood glowed as they walked. King October reigned, and the wind of his mantle as he drew it about him puffed the leaves from the trees. June is the queen of the months, and October is king. "Busk ye and bowne ye my merry men all:" sharpen your arrows and string your bows; set ye in order and march, march to the woods away.

The wind came and rippled their blood into a glow, as it rippled the water. A lissom steely sense strung their sinews; their backs felt like oak-plants, upright, sturdy but not rigid; their frames charged with force. This fierce sense of life is like the glow in the furnace where the draught comes; there's a light in the eye like the first star through the evening blue.

Afar above a flock of rooks soared, winding round and round a geometrical staircase in the air, with outstretched wings like leaves upborne and slowly rotating edge first. The ploughshare was at work under them planing the stubble and filling the breeze with the scent of the earth. Over the ploughshare they soared and danced in joyous measure.

Upon the tops of the elms the redwings sat—high-flying thrushes with a speck of blood under each wing—and called "kuck—quck" as they approached. When they came to the mound Bevis went one side of the hedge and Mark the other. Then at a word Pan rushed into the mound like a javelin, splintering the dry hollow "gix" stalks, but a thorn pierced his shaggy coat and drew a "yap" from him.

At that the hare waited no longer, but lightly leaped from the mound thirty yards ahead. Bound! Bound! Bevis poised his gun, got the dot on the fleeting ears, and the hare rolled over and was still. So they passed October, sometimes seeing a snipe on a sandy shallow of the brook under a willow as they came round a bend. The wild-fowl began to come to the New Sea, but these were older and wilder, and not easy to shoot.

One day as they were out rowing in the Pinta they saw the magic wave, and followed it up, till Mark shot the creature that caused it, and found it to be a large diving bird. Several times Bevis fired at herons as they came over. Towards the evening as they were returning homewards now and then one would pass, and though he knew the height was too much he could not resist firing at such a broad mark as the wide wings offered. The heron, perhaps touched, but unharmed by the pellets whose sting had left them, almost tumbled with fright, but soon recovered his gravity and resumed his course.

Somewhat later the governor having business in London took Bevis and Mark with him. They stayed a week at Bevis's grandpa's, and while there, for Bevis's special pleasure, the governor went with them one evening to see a celebrated American sportsman shoot. This pale-face from the land of the Indians quite upset and revolutionised all their ideas of how to handle a gun.

The perfection of first-rate English weapons, their accuracy and almost absolute safety, has obtained for them pre-eminence over all other fire-arms. It was in England that the art of shooting was slowly brought to the delicate precision which enables the sportsman to kill right and left in instantaneous succession. But why then did this one thing escape discovery? Why have so many thousands shot season after season without hitting upon it? The governor did not like his philosophy of the gun upset in this way; his cherished traditions overthrown.

There the American stood on the stage as calm as a tenor singer, and every time the glass ball was thrown up, smash! a single rifle-bullet broke it. A single bullet, not shot, not a cartridge which opens out and makes a pattern a foot in diameter, but one single bullet. It was shooting flying with a rifle. It was not once, twice, thrice, but tens and hundreds. The man's accuracy of aim seemed inexhaustible.

Never was there any exhibition so entirely genuine: never anything so bewildering to the gunner bred in the traditionary system of shooting. A thousand rifle-bullets pattering in succession on glass balls jerked in the air would have been past credibility if it had not been witnessed by crowds. The word of a few spectators only would have been disbelieved.

"It is quite upside down, this," said the governor. "Really one would think the glass balls burst of themselves."

"He could shoot partridges flying with his rifle," said Mark.

Bevis said nothing but sat absorbed in the exhibition till the last shot was fired and they rose from their seats, then he said, "I know how he did it!"

"Nonsense."

"I'm sure I do: I saw it in a minute."

"Well, how then?"

"I'll tell you when we get home."

"Pooh!"

"Wait and see."

Nothing more was said till they reached home, when half scornfully they inquired in what the secret lay?

"The secret is in this," said Bevis, holding out his left arm. "That's the secret."

"How? I don't see."

"He puts his left arm out nearly as far as he can reach," said Bevis, "and holds the gun almost by the muzzle. That's how he does it. Here, see—like this."

He took up his grandfather's gun which was a muzzle-loader and had not been shot off these thirty years, and put it to his shoulder, stretching out his left arm and grasping the barrels high up beyond the stock. His long arm reached within a few inches of the muzzle.

"There!" he said.

"Well, it was like that," said Mark. "He certainly did hold the gun like that."

"But what is the difference?" said the governor. "I don't see how it's done now."

"But I do," said Bevis. "Just think: if you hold the gun out like this, and put your left arm high up as near the muzzle as you can, you put the muzzle on the mark directly instead of having to move it about to find it. And that's it, I'm sure. I saw that was how he held it directly, and then I thought it out."

"Let me," said Mark. He had the gun and tried, aiming quickly at an object on the mantelpiece. "So you can—you put the barrels right on it."

"Give it to me," said the governor. He tried, twice, thrice, throwing the gun up quickly.

"Keep your left hand in one place," said Bevis. "Not two places—don't move it."

"I do believe he's right," said the governor.

"Of course I am," said Bevis in high triumph. "I'm sure that's it."

"So am I," said Mark.

"Well, really now I come to try, I think it is," said the governor.

"It's like a rod on a pivot," said Bevis. "Don't you see the left hand is the pivot: if you hold it out as far as you can, then the Long part of the rod is your side of the pivot, and the short little piece is beyond it—then you've only got to move that little piece. If you shoot in our old way then the long piece is the other side of the pivot, and of course the least motion makes such a difference. Here, where's some paper—I can see it, if you can't."

With his pencil he drew a diagram, being always ready to draw maps and plans of all kinds. He drew it on the back of a card that chanced to lie on the table.

"There, that long straight stroke, that's the line of the gun—it's three inches long—now, see, put A at the top, and B at the bottom like they do in geometry. Now make a dot C on the line just an inch above B. Now suppose B is where the stock touches your shoulder, and this dot C is where your hand holds the gun in our old way at home. Then, don't you see, the very least mistake at C, ever so little, increases at A—ratio is the right word, increases in rapid ratio, and by the time the shot gets to the bird it's half a yard one side."

"I see," said Mark. "Now do the other."

"Rub out the dot at C," said Bevis. "I haven't got any indiarubber, you suppose it's rubbed out: now put the dot, two inches above B, and only one inch from the top of the gun at A. That's how he held it with his hand at this dot, say D."

"I think he did," said the governor.

"Now you think," said Bevis. "It takes quite a sweep, quite a movement to make the top A incline much out of the perpendicular. I mean if the pivot, that's your hand, is at D a little mistake does not increase anything like so rapidly. So its much more easy to shoot straight quick."

They considered this some while till they got to understand it. All the time Bevis's mind was working to try and find a better illustration, and at last he snatched up the governor's walking-stick. The knob or handle he held in his right hand, and that represented the butt of the gun which is pressed against the shoulder. His right hand he rested on the table, keeping it still as the shoulder would be still. Then he took the stick with the thumb and finger of his left hand about one third of the length of the stick up. That was about the place where a gun would be held in the ordinary way.

"Now look," he said, and keeping his right hand firm, he moved his left an inch or so aside. The inch at his hand increased to three or four at the point of the stick. This initial error in the aim would go on increasing till at forty yards the widest spread of shot would miss the mark.

"And now this way," said Bevis. He slipped his left hand up the stick to within seven or eight inches of the point. This represented the new position. A small error here—or lateral motion of the hand—only produced a small divergence. The muzzle, the top of the stick, only varied from the straight line the amount of the actual movement of the left hand. In the former case a slight error of the hand multiplied itself at the muzzle. This convinced them.

"How we shall shoot!" said Mark. "We shall beat Jack hollow!"

They returned home two days afterwards, and immediately tried the experiment with their double-barrels. It answered perfectly. As Bevis said, the secret was in the left arm.

When about to shoot grasp the gun at once with the left hand as high up the barrel as possible without inconveniently straining the muscles, and so bring it to the shoulder. Push the muzzle up against the mark, as if the muzzle were going to actually touch it. The left hand aims, positively putting the muzzle on the game. All is centred in the left hand. The left hand must at once with the very first movement take hold high up, and must not be slid there, it must take hold high up as near the muzzle as possible without straining. The left hand is thrust out, and as it were put on the game. Educate the left arm; teach it to correspond instantaneously with the direction of the glance; teach it to be absolutely stable for the three necessary seconds; let the mind act through the left wrist. The left hand aims.

This is with the double-barrel shot gun; with the rifle at short sporting ranges the only modification is that as there is but one pellet instead of two hundred, the sight must be used and the dot put on the mark, while with the shot gun in time you scarcely use the sight at all. With the rifle the sight must never be forgotten. The left hand puts the sight on the mark, and the quicker the trigger is pressed the better, exactly reversing tradition. A slow deliberative rifleman was always considered the most successful, but with the new system the fire cannot be delivered too quickly, the very instant the sight is on the mark, thus converting the rifleman into a snap-shooter. Of course it is always understood that this applies to short sporting ranges, the method is for sporting only, and does not apply to long range.

One caution is necessary in shooting like this with the double-barrel. Be certain that you use a first-class weapon, quite safe. The left hand being nearly at the top of the barrel, the left hand itself, and the whole length of the left arm are exposed in case of the gun bursting. I feel that some cheap guns are not quite safe. With a good gun by a known maker there is no danger.

The American has had many imitators, but no one has reached his degree of excellence in the new art which he invented. Perhaps it is fortunate that it is not every one who can achieve such marvellous dexterity, for such shooting would speedily empty every cover in this country.

Big Jack learned the trick from them in a very short time. His strong left arm was as steady as a rock. He tried it with his little rifle, and actually killed a hare, which he started from a furze bush, as it ran with a single bullet. But the governor though convinced would not adopt the new practice. He adhered to the old way, the way he had learned as a boy. What we learn in youth influences us through life.

But Bevis and Mark, and Big Jack used it with tremendous effect in snap-shooting in lanes where the game ran or flew across, in ferreting when the rabbits bolted from hole to hole, in snipe shooting, in hedge-hunting, one each side—the best of all sport, for you do not know what may turn out next, a hare, a rabbit, a partridge from the dry ditch, or a woodcock from the dead leaves.

Chapter Eighteen
The Antarctic Expedition—Conclusion

The winter remained mild till early in January when the first green leaves had appeared on the woodbine. One evening Polly announced that it was going to freeze, for the cat as he sat on the hearthrug had put his paw over his ear. If he sat with his back to the fire, that was a sign of rain. If he put his paw over his ear that indicated frost.

It did freeze and hard. The wind being still, the New Sea was soon frozen over except in two places. There was a breathing-hole in Fir-Tree Gulf about fifty or sixty yards from the mouth of the Nile. The channel between New Formosa and Serendib did not "catch," perhaps the current from Sweet River Falls was the cause, and though they could skate up within twenty yards, they could not land on the islands. Jack and Frances came to skate day after day; Bevis and Mark with Ted, Cecil, and the rest fought hockey battles for hours together.

One afternoon, being a little tired, Bevis sat on the ice, and presently lay down for a moment at full length, when looking along the ice—as he looked along his gun—he found he could see sticks or stones or anything that chanced to be on it a great distance off. Trying it again he could see the skates of some people very nearly half a mile distant, though his eyes were close to the surface, even if he placed the side of his head actually on the ice. The skates gleamed in the sun, and he could see them distinctly; sticks lying on the ice were not clearly seen so far as that, but a long way, so that the ice seemed perfectly level.

As the sun sank the ice became rosy, reflecting the light in the sky; the distant Downs too were tinted the same colour. After it was dark Bevis got a lantern which Mark took five or six hundred yards up the ice, and then set it down on the surface. Bevis put his face on the ice as he had done in the afternoon and looked along. His idea was to try and see for how far the lantern would be visible, as the sticks and skates had been visible a good way, he supposed the light would be apparent very much farther.

Instead of which, when he had got into position and looked along the ice with his face touching it, the lantern had quite disappeared, yet it was not so far off as he had seen the skates—skates are only an inch or so high, and the candle in the lantern was four or five. He skated two hundred yards nearer, and then tried. At this distance, with his eyes as close to the ice as he could get them, he could not see the light itself, but there was a glow diffused in the air where he knew it was.

This explained why the light disappeared. There was a faint and invisible mist above the ice—the iceblink—which at a long distance concealed the lantern. If he lifted his head about eighteen inches he could see the light so that the stratum of mist, or iceblink, appeared to be about eighteen inches in thickness. When he skated another hundred yards closer he could just see the light with his face on the ice as he had done the skates by day. So that after sunset it was evident this mist formed in the air just above the ice. Mark tried the same experiment with the same result, and they then skated slowly homewards, for as it was not moonlight they might get a fall by coming against a piece of twig half-sunk in and frozen firmly.

Suddenly there was a sound like the boom of a cannon, and a crack shot across the broad water from shore to shore. The "who-hoo-whoop" of the noise echoed back from the wood on the hill, and then they heard it again in the coombes and valleys, rolling along. As the ice was four or five inches thick it parted with a hollow roar: the crack sometimes forked, and a second running report followed the first. Sometimes the crack seemed to happen simultaneously all across the water. Occasionally they could hear it coming, and with a distinct interval of time before it reached them.

Up through these cracks or splits a little water oozed, and freezing on the surface formed barriers of rough ice from shore to shore, which jarred the skates as they passed over. These splits in no degree impaired the strength of the ice. Later on as they retired they opened the window and heard the boom again, weird and strange in the silence of the night.

One day a rabbit was started from a bunch of frozen rushes by the shore, and they chased it on the ice, overtaking it with ease. They could have knocked it down with their hockey sticks, but forebore to do so. From these rush-bunches they now and then flushed dab-chicks or lesser grebes which, when there is open water, cannot be got to fly.

Till now the air had been still, but presently the wind blew from the south almost a gale, this was straight down the water, so keeping their skates together and spreading out their coats for sails they drove before the wind at a tremendous pace, flying past the trees and accumulating such velocity that their ankles ached from the vibration of the skates. Nor could they stop by any other means than describing a wide circle, and so gradually facing the wind. Bevis began to make an ice-raft to slide on runners and go before the wind with a sail like the ice-yachts on the American lakes.

But by the time the frame was put together, and the blacksmith had finished the runners, a thaw set in. It is just the same with sleighs, directly the sleigh is got to work, the snow goes and leaves the heaviest and muddiest road of the year. The ice-yachts of America must give splendid sport; it is said that they sometimes glide at the rate of a mile a minute, actually outstripping the speed of the wind which drives them. This has been rather a puzzle why it should be so.

May it not be the same as it was with Bevis and Mark when they spread their coats like sails and flew before the gale with such speed that it needed some nerve to stand upright—till the vibration of the skates caused a peculiar numblike feeling in the ankles? They either did or seemed to go faster than the wind, and was not this the accumulation of velocity? As a bullet dropped from a window falls so many feet the first second, and a great many more the next second, increasing its pace, so as they were thrust forwards by the wind their bodies accumulated the impetus and shot beyond it. Possibly it is the same with the swift ice-yacht. The thaw was a great disappointment.

The immense waves of ocean rise before the wind, and so the wind rushing over the ice no longer firm and rigid quickly broke up the surface, and there was a tremendous grinding and splintering, and chafing of the fragments. For the first few days these were carried down the New Sea, but presently the wind changed. The black north swooped on the earth and swept across the waters. Fields, trees, woods, hills, the very houses looked dark and hard, the water grey, the sky cold and dusky. The broken ice drifted before it and was all swept up to the other end of the New Sea and jammed between and about the islands. They could now get at the Pinta, and resolved to have a sail. "An arctic expedition!"

"Antarctic—it is south!"

"All right."

"Let us go to New Formosa."

"So we will. But the ice is jammed there."

"Cut through it."

"Make an ice-bow."

"Be quick."

Up in the workshop they quickly nailed two short boards together like a V. This was lashed to the stem of the Pinta to protect her when they crashed into the ice. They took a reef in the mainsail, for though the wind does not seem to travel any swifter, yet in winter it somehow feels more hard and compact and has a greater power on what it presses against. Just before they cast loose, Frances appeared on the bank above, she had called at the house, and hearing what they were about, hastened up to join the expedition. So soon as she had got a comfortable seat, well wrapped up in sealskin and muff, they pushed off, and the Pinta began to run before the wind. It was very strong, much stronger than it had seemed ashore, pushing against the sail as if it were a solid thing. The waves followed, and the grey cold water lapped at the stern.

Beyond the battle-field as they entered the broadest and most open part the black north roared and rushed at them, as if the pressure of the sky descending forced a furious blast between it and the surface. Angry and repellent waves hissed as their crests blew off in cold foam and spray, stinging their cheeks. Ahead the red sun was sinking over New Formosa, they raced towards the disc, the sail straining as if it would split. As the boat drew near they saw the ice jammed in the channel between the two islands.

It was thin and all in fragments; some under water, some piled by the waves above the rest, some almost perpendicular, like a sheet of glass standing upright and reflecting the red sunset. Against the cliff the waves breaking threw fragments of ice smashed into pieces; ice and spray rushed up the steep sand and slid down again. But it was between the islands that the waves wreaked their fury. The edge of the ice was torn into jagged bits which dashed against each other, their white saw-like points now appearing, now forced under by a larger block.

Farther in the ice heaved as the waves rolled under: its surface was formed of plates placed like a row of books fallen aside. As the ice heaved these plates slid on each other, while others underneath striving to rise to the surface struck and cracked them. Down came the black north as a man might bring a sledge-hammer on the anvil, the waves hissed, and turned darker, a white sea-gull (which had come inland) rose to a higher level with easy strokes of its wings.

Splinter—splanter! Crash! grind, roar; a noise like thousands of gnashing teeth.

"O!" said Frances, dropping her muff, and putting her hands to her ears. "It is Dante!"

Bevis had his hand on the tiller; Mark his on the halyard of the mainsail; neither spoke, it looked doubtful. The next instant the Pinta struck the ice midway between the islands, and the impetus with which she came drove her six or seven feet clear into the splintering fragments. They were jerked forwards, and in an instant the following wave broke over the stern, and then another, flooding the bottom of the boat. Mark had the mainsail down, for it would have torn the mast out.

With a splintering, grinding, crashing, roaring, a horrible and inexpressible noise of chaos—an orderless, rhythmless noise of chaos—the mass gave way and swept slowly through the channel. The impact of the boat acted like a battering-ram and started the jam. Fortunate it was for them that it did so, or the boat might have been swamped by the following waves. Bevis got out a scull, so did Mark, and their exertions kept her straight; had she turned broadside it would have been awkward even as it was. They swept through the channel, the ice at its edges barking willow branches and planing the shore, large plates were forced up high and dry.

"Hurrah!" shouted Mark.

"Hurrah!"

At the noise of their shouting thousands of starlings rose from the osiers on Serendib with a loud rush of wings, blackening the air like a cloud. They were soon through the channel, the ice spread in the open water, and they worked the boat under shelter of New Formosa, and landed.

"You are wet," said Bevis as he helped Frances out.

"But it's jolly!" said Frances, laughing. "Only think what a fright *he* would have been in if he had known!"

Having made the boat safe—there was a lot of water in her—they walked along the old path, now covered with dead leaves damp from the thaw, to the stockade. The place was strewn with small branches whirled from the trees by the gales, and in the hut and further corner of the cave were heaps of brown oak leaves which had drifted in. Nothing else had changed; so well had they built it that the roof had neither broken down nor been destroyed by the winds.

During the frost a blackbird had roosted in a corner of the hut under the rafters, sparrows too had sought its shelter, and wrens and blue-tits had crept into the crevices of the eaves. Next they went up on the cliff, the sun-dial stood as they had left it, but the sun was now down.

From the height, where they could hardly stand against the wind, they saw a figure afar on the green hill by the sycamores, which they knew must be Big Jack waiting for them to return. Walking back to the Pinta they passed under the now leafless teak-tree marked and scored by the bullets they had fired at it.

Before embarking they baled out the water in the boat, and then inclined her, first one side and then the other, to see if she had sprung a leak, but she had not. The ice-bow was then hoisted on board, as it would no longer be required, and would impede their sailing. Frances stepped in, and Bevis and Mark settled themselves to row out of the channel. With such a wind it was impossible to tack in the narrow strait between the islands. They had to pull their very hardest to get through. So soon as they had got an offing the sculls were shipped, and the sails hoisted, but before they could get them to work they were blown back within thirty yards of the cliff. Then the sails drew, and they forged ahead.

It was the roughest voyage they had ever had. The wind was dead against them, and no matter on which tack every wave sent its spray, and sometimes the whole of its crest over the bows. The shock sometimes seemed to hold the Pinta in mid-career, and her timbers trembled. Then she leaped forward and cut through, showering the spray aside. Frances laughed and sang, though the words were inaudible in the hiss and roar and the rush of the gale through the rigging, and the sharp, whip-like cracks of the fluttering pennant.

The velocity of their course carried them to and fro the darkening waters in a few minutes, but the dusk fell quickly, and by the time they had reached Fir-Tree Gulf, where they could get a still longer "leg" or tack, the evening gloom had settled down. Big Jack stood on the shore, and beckoned them to come in: they could easily have landed Frances under the lee of the hill, but she said she should go all the way now. So they tacked through the Mozambique, past Thessaly and the bluff, the waves getting less in size as they approached the northern shore, till they glided into the harbour. Jack had walked round and met them. He held out his hand, and Frances sprang ashore. "How *could* you?" he said, in a tone of indignant relief. To him it had looked a terrible risk.

"Why it was splendid!" said Frances, and they went on together towards Longcot. Bevis and Mark stayed to furl sails, and leave the Pinta ship-shape. By the time they had finished it was already dark: the night had come.

On their way home they paused a moment under the great oak at the top of the Home Field, and looked back. The whole south burned with stars. There was a roar in the oak like the thunder of the sea. The sky was black, black as velvet, the black north had come down, and the stars shone and burned as if the wind reached and fanned them into flame.

Large Sirius flashed; vast Orion strode the sky, lording the heavens with his sword. A scintillation rushed across from the zenith to the southern horizon. The black north held down the buds, but there was a force in them already that must push out in leaf as Arcturus rose in the East. Listening to the loud roar of the oak as the strength of the north wind filled them,—

"I should like to go straight to the real great sea like the wind," said Mark.

"We *must* go to the great sea," said Bevis. "Look at Orion!"

The wind went seawards, and the stars are always over the ocean.